WHEREVER *You Go*

MONIQUE MULLIGAN

PILYARA PRESS

A catalogue record for this
book is available from the
National Library of Australia

Wherever You Go
Version 1.0
ISBN: 978-0-6483089-1-1
Cover art by Kellie Dennis at Book Cover By Design

Pilyara Press
Melbourne

Praise for *Wherever You Go*

'A deeply affecting, beautifully written and sensitively told story that tugs at the heartstrings. Readers will love the evocative descriptions of food peppered throughout.' – Vanessa Carnevale

'Unfolding with clear-eyed, soulful understanding and with deep respect for her characters, Mulligan's debut is a novel for those who crave stories about real people grappling with real life. A tender tale crafted with love and steeped in the healing togetherness that comes from sharing great food.' – Kim Kelly

'Monique Mulligan has such a beautiful way of putting words together. She never fails to give me shivers.' – Lily Malone

'Monique Mulligan takes us on an emotional rollercoaster in this deeply moving exploration of a marriage in distress. Have tissues ready!' – Lisa Ireland

For Blue Eyes. Thank you for listening to endless novel-writing updates and character dilemmas over our afternoon coffee

Wherever you go, there you are.

— JON KABAT-ZINN

PROLOGUE

GERMANY
MATT

I *can't do it.*
You must.

Matt wrestles duty and fear at the threshold of his wife's hospital room. Today marks two weeks since the accident. Two weeks since a phone call turned his blood to ice. Two weeks since life as they knew it was obliterated.

Just like that.

And today he has to tell Amy what happened. The enormity of responsibility almost propels him away. Out of the ward, the hospital, the town, the country. Anywhere but here, without a backwards look. His feet anchor to the floor, each forward step a battle.

He slumps into the chair at her bedside, then remembers he hasn't kissed her. When his lips meet her dry cheeks, the sweet staleness of her breath envelops him, and he rears back. She'd hate this, he thinks, sliding a stray hair away from her chapped lips. Slumping into his chair once more, he waits for her to wake.

'It could happen any moment,' a nurse said when he arrived at the ward earlier. He'd panicked and detoured to the cafeteria for a strong coffee.

Is it selfish that he wants his wife to wake and dreads it at the same time?

How am I supposed to tell her?

He knows *what* he has to tell Amy. Exactly what the doctor told him days earlier – words that ripped his heart to shreds, as they will hers. How did doctors share heartbreaking – no, life-shattering news – with such distant compassion? How did they do that, day after day? Maybe they got used to it.

Couldn't they tell her?

It's your job. You're her husband.

Fuck.

What is he supposed to say: 'You're lucky to be alive?'

A bitter laugh escapes him. *Lucky*. He doubts Amy will ever again believe in luck – or anything else – after hearing what he has to say. He has practised his speech for days, but the words still destroy him.

She stirs and mumbles, and Matt perches on the edge of his seat. Her eyelids flutter in her yellow-bruised face. When her eyes open, he'll be the first thing she sees. Will she know something's wrong? His pain is a neon light flashing to the world. How could she miss it?

He runs his fingers through his short, dark hair, wincing as knots tug at the roots. Grateful for the physical diversion from his heart-pain. He wants to tear it all out in angry handfuls. His grip tightens, but a nurse glances in as she walks past, and he takes Amy's hand instead.

Her cool hand is limp in his, her pulse slow and steady under his lips. There's so much to say. Should he start with the good news? 'Both your legs are broken and so is your pelvis. The doctors said you might struggle to have children in the future.'

He licks his lips. Maybe he should keep the second part to himself for now.

Because the bad news is so much worse.

CHAPTER ONE
WESTERN AUSTRALIA, THREE YEARS LATER

AMY

Fog swirls around pine branches, heavy and wet, as Amy and Matt Bennet drive down the valley and into their future. Amy shivers as a fluttery tightness grows in her chest, as if fog-tentacles are reaching into the car and wrapping around her heart. She breathes deeply – once, twice – trying to control her jumpiness. If Matt notices her unease, he doesn't react. His focus is on their destination – Blackwood, Western Australia, where their new home and new life await. New life. That's what Matt wants. All she wants is escape from the old one. Thinking beyond that scares the hell out of her.

Matt pats her knee. 'Not long now.'

Not long is too soon.

A log truck rumbles past. Matt lifts a hand in greeting, grinning when the driver returns the gesture. He adopted the habit four months ago when they decided to move to the country. The first time someone waved back, he fist-pumped the air. His enthusiasm has dimmed, but once out of the suburbs, he still waves at every tractor, truck or car they pass.

Amy wishes to be in that log truck, driving in the other direction.

Headlights loom on the wrong side of the road, shimmering beams bearing down. Amy snap-freezes and her mind shrieks a silent warning. She's dimly aware of Matt cursing, a horn blasting, of tyres meeting gravel and brakes straining in a painful cry. Sounds mix with memory.

Rain. Enormous headlights.

Shattering glass. Screeching, screaming, terrible sounds that never fade.

Ticking engine.

Silence in the back seat.

Darkness.

'Amy!'

She turns wild eyes on her husband. 'He could have killed us! That idiot nearly killed us!'

'Amy.' Matt cradles her face in his hands. When did he pull over? 'It's okay. We're okay.'

'It's not okay!' she yells, wrenching away. 'It's never okay for people like that to be on the road. He shouldn't have a licence. He was probably on the phone like—'

'Aims. He wasn't on the phone. It was a lapse of attention, but no one was hurt.'

'He shouldn't be driving if he can't keep his eyes on the road!'

'I know, I know.' Matt reaches for her and this time she doesn't pull away. He holds her till her heartbeat settles and she takes a deep, shuddering breath. It's been three years, but it feels like yesterday. 'Okay? Shall we go?'

She nods. But she can't help wondering if the near-miss is a warning. Fresh starts don't always come with smooth roads.

Blackwood looks different. Four months earlier they came down for a weekend when the town was vibrant with summer colour. It whispered a welcome hard to ignore. Now the leaves are crackle-brown and the town is cool shades of grey mottled with fuzzy light from the windows of waking homes.

Matt parks the car on the near-deserted main street. She turns to him, brow furrowed.

What? he mouths, hands spread out, all wide-eyed and innocent.

'Why are we stopping now? We're nearly there.'

'Thought we'd grab a coffee and something to eat. The removalists will be another hour or so,' he says, checking his watch. 'And I'm starving.'

'Okay. I'll wait here.'

His face falls. 'Don't want something? Coffee? Bacon and egg roll?'

'I'm not hungry. Wait – grab me a coffee. Double shot.'

His mouth twists the way it does when he's thinking. 'I thought we could stretch our legs a bit. We've been on the road for hours.'

'Fine.' Why does she get the feeling there's more to this than stretching their legs?

He gets out of the car, stretches and groans, then ducks his head back in. 'You'll need your coat. Bit nippy.'

Amy takes her time. Her neck is still knotted with tension from the near miss. Massaging her hip, she pulls her hair into a ponytail and reaches into the back seat for her jacket. At the last moment, she dives back into the car for her sunglasses. They're not in the centre console where she left them. Did they get dislodged when Matt swerved to avoid the idiot?

'Come on, Aims, it's freezing. What's taking you so long?' He's rubbing his hands together and shifting from side to side, his breath a white cloud.

She opens the back door. 'Can't find my sunnies. I can wait here if you're that keen to get moving.'

He exhales. 'Geez, Amy. It's bloody foggy and there's no one around. You don't need them.'

Faces, eyes full of curiosity, pity, blame: 'You're that woman from the newspaper.' Same words, different tone.

Ignoring him, she fumbles around until she locates the sunglasses wedged under the seat. 'Got them.'

Behind her there's another sigh. She ignores that too and walks stiffly towards Matt, sunglasses in place. They've been having this argument for a while now. And it's not the first row they've had today. Neither of them are morning people and they've been on the road since 4.30 a.m., but that's not what brought out the barbs. Moving to the country has brought out the worst in them, right when they need to be pulling together.

She read somewhere once that moving house was more stressful than divorce. Maybe she should have suggested that instead of moving. A blink later, she swipes the thought away like a pesky fly. Divorce is the last thing she wants. Her marriage is all she has left. It doesn't help that she still has no idea what she's going to do here. She's been searching online for part-time jobs, and the offerings have been slim to date. A bartender in the local pub. A cleaner at the school. Nothing she's suited for.

'Where are you going?' she says. He's heading in the opposite direction of the flickering 'Open' sign outside a bakery.

'Show you something,' he says. 'Remember that place we went to last time?'

Her eyes narrow. Something is definitely up. Pushing her arms into her coat, she follows him past dark shopfronts to the quaint café they visited months before. Amy remembers it well. It's where they decided to put the offer on their new house. Makes sense to go back now they've turned the idea into reality. Trite name – Tea 4 something. Vintage doilies on the table. Potpourri in bowls. But good, strong coffee. Plump scones with homemade jam. If they're open it'll be better than the bakery. Matt knows her well.

Her face falls when they reach the café. No steaming coffee in a vintage teacup today. It's closed. Boards cover the windows and a faded 'Business for sale' sign hangs from the door.

Matt motions to the sign. 'Thought you might be interested in this. It's fully kitted out, ready to go. Heard the owners wanted a sea-change.'

She stiffens. That's what he's up to. Another attempt to talk her into something he thinks she should do. 'I thought we were getting coffee.'

'Yeah, yeah, we will. But what do you think? You always wanted a café of your own and—'

'Years ago, Matt.' It's not entirely true. She's been wondering about it for a while but hasn't said anything. She wanted to bring it up in her own time. Now he's pre-empting her and it feels like she's sat on a stinging nettle. 'Are we getting coffee or not?'

'Why not now?' Grey eyes bore into her like nails.

'We've just got here, for God's sake. We haven't even moved in. I'll find something. In my own time. Don't push it.'

'It's a good idea. An opportunity. Something you might not have thought of.' He stabs at the sign. 'And it's right here in front of you. You could at least pretend you're interested. But no, you won't even give it a chance.'

'Stop. Trying. To. Fix. Me.' She turns away and counts to ten. When she turns back, his arms are crossed, lips thin.

Once upon a time she and Matt shook their heads at couples who argued in public. Now she doesn't care. 'You always do this. Force on me your ideas of who I should be. What I should do. You and everyone else. Go to therapy, Amy. Take your tablets, Amy. Get a job, Amy. Find a hobby, Amy. Have a—' she breaks off as an old man steps around them, averting his gaze while yanking his over-friendly dog away from Amy's legs.

For a moment, Amy and Matt face off like boxers in a ring, breathing heavily. Amy speaks first. 'I'm asking you to let me figure it out. One step at a time.'

Matt exhales sharply. 'Whatever,' he mutters and strides up the street to the bakery.

She wants to stomp that word into the ground.

By the time she catches up with him, the bakery door has clunked shut, leaking out the warm aroma of freshly baked bread. Amy debates waiting outside but it's cold and Matt has the car remote. When another car pulls up in front of the bakery, she sighs and pushes the heavy door. The coffee's probably substandard, but maybe a caffeine hit will help her get through the long day ahead without losing it.

Avoiding Matt, she gazes around, pleasantly surprised by the industrial-meets-hipster vibe, all black-and-white tiled floors and funky filament light globes. A shiny red espresso machine dominates the counter – maybe the coffee will be okay. Maybe she should stop making assumptions before she's given the place a chance.

Her stomach grumbles as the yeasty smell teases her fragile appetite awake. *Pain au chocolat*, fat croissants and Danish pastries mingle with fudgy brownies, passionfruit-iced vanilla slices and sugar-dusted apple pies. Artisan sourdough loaves, rolls and baguettes nestle in baskets among the more standard white-sliced fare.

Once upon a time Amy baked her own sourdough bread and served it thickly sliced and toasted, with buttery garlic mushrooms, smashed avocado and feta, poached eggs, or homemade jam and butter. Not margarine. That was before darkness wiped the light from her life, robbing her of the desire to do anything but sleep, stare and think. She gives Matt a sideways glance. He wants her to start baking again. He wants her to do a lot of things.

A thin woman in her sixties, with short grey curls peeking from under a white cap, places a tray of pastries on a glass-topped display cabinet.

'Can I help you?' she asks.

'Flat white for me. To go. Amy? Are you having one?'

'Yes.' She doesn't look at him, but directs a smile at the woman. Beside her, Matt sighs before ordering pre-made bacon and egg rolls to go.

'You're on the road early. Travelling down south then?' The woman is already turning away, reaching for disposable coffee cups, as if she knows the answer.

'Nope. We're moving to Blackwood today.' The woman turns back, her gaze curious. 'I'm Matt Bennet and this is my wife, Amy.'

The woman dips her head in understanding. 'Ah. I've seen you around,' she says to Matt. 'The old Thompson house? I'm June.' She squints out at the car and then her dark eyes flick back to Amy, down to her stomach, and up again. 'Just the two of you, then?'

'Yes. Just the two of us,' Matt says. His unspoken *for now* hovers between them.

Amy sighs. Half the town will know of their arrival by the end of the morning; the other half are bound to see the removal truck arrive. Small towns are hotbeds of gossip. June's not doing much to change that stereotype. Nor are the other two customers – mother and daughter without a doubt – listening with obvious interest. The hair on Amy's neck snaps to attention. She's learnt to heed that warning before.

'With you in a tick, Una, Sharon.' June tilts her head at Matt. 'Working at the mine, then?'

'How'd you know?'

'You don't look like a farmer. And you already told me you're not a tourist.'

He laughs. 'I'm an engineer.' He shifts from side to side. 'Sorry, is there a toilet here I can use?'

June points the way and Matt slopes off. Turning back to Amy, she asks, 'And you?' Her voice is flavoured with genuine interest. The older customer makes no secret she's interested too. Her spiky white hair seems to bristle with curiosity. Her daughter is outside, telling off a child in pyjamas who's halfway out of a car window.

'I ... I'm not sure yet.' Amy motions out the door. 'What happened to the other café down the road?' Why would Matt think she'd want to buy it? Doesn't he know how much work a café would be?

'Tea 4 2? Closed a while back. Owners went back to the city. Happens sometimes. People think a tree change will fix them, but—'

The unfinished sentence hangs between them as the spiky-haired woman pays for her bread and leaves, throwing Amy a final curious look. The coffee machine roars into life and Amy's mind whirls like the milk June is steaming. A café of her own? She wants to be anonymous. It's crazy to think of it. But if it's so crazy, why did she bring it up with a total stranger?

Matt joins her again and they wait in silence. Amy hopes the coffee tastes as good as it smells. Rich and dark. If she opens a café, she'll need a decent coffee supplier. *If.*

'Big house for two,' June comments, placing the cups in a cardboard carrier. Bacon and egg rolls are placed in a paper bag. 'Back in the day, it was always full of kids.' Amy flinches. 'I suppose you two—'

'How much do we owe you?' Matt breaks in.

Amy leaves him to it. As she steps out into the cold, she looks one way, then the other. Her gaze lingers on the near-empty road leading out of town. A loaded log truck rattles past, reminding her of the one they passed on the way in. How she wanted to be in it, driving in the other direction. She looks through the bakery window. Matt's still chatting with June. What if she walks down the road until she disappears into the fog?

CHAPTER TWO

AMY

As Matt drives slowly up a tree-lined street bordered both sides with houses from a bygone era, the fluttery tightness of anxiety returns.

This is it.

Make or break time.

Desperation brought them to Blackwood last summer. Their marriage was crumbling and they were helpless bystanders. When Matt suggested a long weekend getaway, Amy figured it couldn't hurt. Maybe zooming out from their life would refocus the blurry bits. What happened next surprised them both. Charmed by how pretty the town was, she'd blurted out two words: 'tree change'.

Matt seized them like a child grabbing candy. 'Tree change. Yes! It's just what our marriage needs.'

'A jump start,' she'd said, not expecting to find a 1950s character house open for inspection as they strolled up a leafy street. Not expecting the cosy feeling that covered her like a soft blanket as she and Matt walked from room to room, enticed by cleverly staged smells of warm bread and freshly brewed coffee. Not expecting the *yes* from deep in her gut. Their offer was accepted within the hour. After that, Amy wished she'd never said those two words. And then it was too late. They gave notice on their lease. Matt left his fly-in, fly-out job and secured an engineer position at the Timbertop lithium mine. Amy packed their life into boxes while he commuted between Blackwood and Perth to oversee much-needed renovations.

And now here they are at the gateway of their new start. Bringing old baggage along for the ride. They haven't said a word to each other since the bakery.

Matt parks in the driveway next to a small, silver hatchback. Couple of years old, if that. Generic make and model. The kind people hire at an airport.

Amy stiffens. 'What's that car doing here?' She knows the answer but asks anyway. She can't even look at it. It's the same colour as the other one. The colour of tears.

He turns off the engine. 'We talked about this, Amy.' He sounds strained. Like she's a scatterbrained teenager.

'No, we didn't. I'd remember that.'

'Yes, we did. Several times. I even showed you a picture.'

A vague memory stirs. 'Maybe I said *I'll think about it.* Something like that. It's not the same as *go ahead and buy it.*'

'You'll need something to get you around town when I'm at work.'

'I'll walk.' The last time she drove a car their four-year-old daughter died. One minute Pandora was sleeping in the back seat, the next she was gone. Forever sleeping in an apocalyptic world: screeching tyres, burning rubber, the iron tang of blood. Darkness, horror and wails.

'Fine.' His knuckles are white from gripping the steering wheel. 'It's there when you want it.'

How many times do I have to tell you I don't want to drive? The retort hangs on the tip of her tongue but they've already had a shaky start, so she reels it in. 'I won't.' Matt thinks she's being stubborn, but he doesn't get it. It's a lost cause, this car. 'You know I've tried. And every time, I've panicked. Nothing's worked.'

'Okay, fine.' There's none of the bite of the *whatever* earlier. It disturbs her. Indifference signals endings, not beginnings.

Neither one makes a move to go inside. The car windows fog up as they sit beside each other, but not together. The air fills with the greasy but tempting scent of bacon and eggs as Matt unwraps a roll and devours it in three quick bites. He treats eating like an Olympic sport. Amy chews on a hangnail. At this rate, their marriage will be lucky to survive the day.

A lump swells in her throat. Swallowing hard, she turns to Matt. This has to be nipped in the bud now. His grey eyes are searching behind his glasses. A trail of yolk dribbles from the side of his mouth. Without thinking, she wipes it off. He catches her hand, his touch warm, and breathes out, deeply, like he's been holding it in all morning. Smiles the way he used to, the way he did when she fell in love with him. It gives her strength.

'Let's start today over,' she says.

Before she goes inside, Amy pauses on the wraparound homestead verandah, hoping for a glimpse of the stunning valley views that sealed the deal. Instead, there's a monochrome landscape broken up by house lights; noise from the waking neighbourhood filters through the murky soup, mixing with the smell of wood smoke and damp ground. The house is bigger than she remembers, isolated by the fog that merges sky and earth into a crushing mass. The heavy gloom is infectious. The high-pitched, excited shout of a young girl-child carries over the side fence: 'Henry!' Matt didn't mention a little girl next door. Amy pushes open the door and follows the scents of fried food and coffee in search of her husband.

'Matt?' Her footsteps echo on the jarrah floorboards that line the hallway. She finds him on a picnic mat in the living room, finishing off his second bacon and egg roll.

'Come here,' he says, patting the mat like the day they first moved in together. An apartment near the beach. Full of hopes and dreams. They had an inside picnic that day too. Matt hands her the remaining roll and a coffee, before slugging his drink in one long gulp. She sips hers slowly. The room is chilly but the coffee's still warm. And it's good. Full-bodied and dark, the way she likes it, with crisp undertones of chocolate and smoke. As if it's been brewed to taste. Something about the phrase resonates: Brewed to Taste. Not a bad name for a café. Better than Tea 4 2. Whoever came up with that name lacked imagination.

'What do you think?'

'Of the roll?' She bites into it. It's cold but delicious: smoky bacon layered in a toasted ciabatta roll, topped with an egg and caramelised onion. She licks sauce from her finger, relishing the bite that tingles on her tongue. Homemade. 'It's good.'

'I meant the new paint, but that works too.' He waves his arm around the room. 'Different, huh?'

Once an insipid mustard colour, the lounge room is now a duck egg blue with white ceilings and skirting boards that highlight painstakingly polished floorboards. The built-in fireplace is also painted white, with a timber mantelpiece matching the floor. Amy chose the colour scheme, and is surprised by how well it works. Even without furniture to finish it off, the room resonates calm. She imagines retreating to this room with a book, curling up on the couch to lose herself in another world.

'It's great.' She hugs him, surprising herself. She's rarely generous anymore. There's an intake of breath before he pulls her close. Breathing in his Matt smell, she tells herself they've made the right choice.

He pushes aside her hair, whispers into her ear, 'Shall we christen the room before the removalists get here?' His tone holds a hint of jest, but his body dares her to take up the offer.

They did that in their first house. Christened every room, once, twice. But that was when they were everything to each other. When only the moment mattered. Now, she kisses his cheek lightly, and pulls him to his feet. 'Show me what else you've done before the guys get here.'

His answering laugh carries a breath of resignation, but he gives her the grand tour with pride. She says all the right things, and she means every word. He's gone above and beyond to make her feel comfortable, despite the lack of furniture and the mustiness the fresh paint can't quite disguise.

Matt pulls her close and lifts her face to his. 'This was the right move, hon. Just what we need.'

Amy can't help thinking that he's reassuring himself too. One day, they'll both believe it.

'Come on. I've saved the best for last.'

A cheap bottle of bubbly and a box of Lindt chocolates rest on the kitchen bench, courtesy of the estate agent, but that's not what makes Amy's hand clap to her mouth. The room is nothing like she remembers from their inspection in April. Then, the kitchen was a shabby throwback to the 1950s, complete with a red laminated benchtop barely big enough for a microwave oven, dusty floral curtains, and an old wood stove housed in a fireplace. It could have been her grandmother's kitchen. Now, it's a gleaming Hampton's-style showpiece: white cupboards, black-and-white tiles, modern stainless steel appliances, overhead pot racks with shining copper pots, and a red range cooker at its heart. An espresso machine is tucked away in a corner and a red whistling stovetop kettle rests on the cooker.

'Open the pantry,' Matt says. He's grinning like a kid at Christmas.

The walk-in pantry is meticulously ordered and stocked with everything a chef could want. Matt's gone all out. There's asafoetida, sumac, nigella seeds and harissa. Truffle salt, liquid smoke, tahini and chia seeds. Preserved lemons, peaches and apricots. 'OO' flour, Dutch cocoa, coffee beans and dark couverture chocolate buttons. He's even included a mind-boggling selection of teas: chai, organic rooibos, ginger, three cinnamon, sour apple and Moroccan mint.

'I love it,' she says. 'Thank you.'

Matt wraps his arms around her and pulls her to him. 'Been organising this since settlement. It's what you always dreamed of. Remember?'

A memory surfaces: *Pandora, wearing a child-sized chef's apron over her favourite purple leggings and* Frozen *T-shirt. Her face is dusted with flour. It's in her hair, up her arms, even on her toes. She's rolling out a lump of biscuit dough, and when she thinks her mother's not looking, she pokes a sweet morsel into her mouth. 'Mummy?' she asks, inspecting another dough ball before popping it into her mouth. 'Do we have to go on a holiday? I like it here with you.'*

After all this time, memories like these still hover at the edge of her thoughts. If only Amy could rewind to that day; she and Pandora devoured still-warm biscuits, sipped hot chocolate, and fell asleep on the sofa together. Amy's eyes close; she can almost smell the sugar-butter perfume of cooling shortbread mingled with the lingering scent of sweet apple in her daughter's hair. She inhales, deep and long, and smells fresh paint. Her eyes snap open. A week after that day they went overseas. Pandora never came back.

Pulling away from Matt, Amy traces her hands over the brand new wooden dining table designed to be the pulse of the house. Too big for two.

Her throat tightens. It wasn't supposed to be *only Matt and Amy*.

As if he's reading her mind, Matt's voice slices into her thoughts. 'I can't wait for the house to fill with the smell of your cooking again.' He pauses. 'And who knows, maybe you'll be cooking for more than two one day.'

His voice is light, but something in the tone tells Amy it's more than a hint. The last few months he's been testing the waters more often, but always stops short of saying outright he wants to try for another baby. But it's coming, and then she'll have to admit she doesn't want to do it again. Motherhood hadn't come naturally to her the first time. No graceful segue from pregnancy to parenting. She struggled to connect with Pandora, she struggled with postpartum depression. She didn't know who *Amy* was for months, until one day motherhood clicked. And look what happened. In her darkest moments, she believes she was punished. The rest of the time, she'd sell her soul to hear Pandora's voice one more time.

'Maybe we'll have a dinner party one day,' she says, feigning interest in the warming drawers on the range cooker. She was a chef when she and Matt met, passionate about all things food. Cooking, eating, sourcing the best products – she lived for it. That passion disappeared with a heartbeat one rainy afternoon. Will this kitchen bring it back? Blackwood's options for eating out look slim. A bistro and two pubs.

Unless you do something about it, a nagging voice says.

'You know what I mean.' Matt stands beside her. His voice is gentle. 'I don't want to push you, Aims. But when you're ready to think about trying again, let me know.'

His phone rings and he moves away to take the call, pinching her on the bum as he leaves. Amy watches him walk away, guilt nibbling at her mind's edge. He's right. This kitchen is everything chef Amy wanted. Matt's spared no expense to make her happy, to smooth her way into this new start.

But it won't bring back the woman he married. She's not even sure it will bring back his wife.

If only a new kitchen was all it took.

The removalists haven't turned up by the time the car is unpacked. Amy scribbles down a basic shopping list for Matt: milk, butter, cheese, barbecue chook. He's hungry and irritable; he wants the house in order before starting his new job midweek.

'Before I go, where do you want this?' he asks, pointing to a tightly taped carton near the door.

Amy doesn't need to look to know which box he means. She's pretended it doesn't exist since Matt pulled it, dust-covered, from the linen cupboard at the old house. In the car, its presence was like the fog still lingering outside.

'Take it to the op shop. Get rid of it. Whatever. We don't need that stuff anymore,' she says, avoiding his eyes and hoping like hell he ignores her like every other time. If he doesn't, then what?

'Amy.' His voice is low. 'It's not *stuff*.'

'We don't need it,' she repeats and turns her back, biting down on the lie. Ignores the frustration whooshing from his lips. The scrape of the carton as he lifts the box from the floor.

No!

'It's all we have left of our daughter. We're not getting rid of it.' The challenge hovers. 'I'm going to the shops. You find somewhere for Pandora's *stuff*. In this house.' The box thuds onto the table and Matt strides away, each heavy step a slap.

Trembling with relief, Amy turns her back on the box and starts wiping down the cupboards, glad she had the foresight to pack a cleaning cloth and disinfectant. Less than an hour into starting over, and their marriage is on a ledge again. With a sigh she tosses the rag into the sink and lifts the box, briefly closing her eyes as its heaviness leaches under her skin. She'll hide it on the highest shelf of the linen cupboard.

A knocking noise stops her in her tracks. She tilts her head. It comes again. One, two, three. Light, tentative, but definitely there. Not the knock of a man accustomed to moving furniture. Who else would it be? Still carrying the box, she pads down the hall, noticing for the first time how the cold seeps through her socks. They'll need a hall runner. And she needs her Ugg boots, which are in a truck some- where on the highway.

Balancing the box on one hip, she fumbles with the lock. Cold weather has swollen the wood and the door valiantly resists her pull. When she finally yanks it open, no one is there. The front yard is empty. There's no truck on the road. And then her eyes drop down to a small dark-haired child wearing purple sheepskin boots, a hot pink puffer jacket, and a rainbow-striped beanie. Amy's eyes shut and her arms clutch the box she wants but doesn't want. The cry of her heart spills out in a name.

'Pandora?'

Her arms open and Pandora's box falls to the ground.

CHAPTER THREE
MATT

Pandora's box is gone by the time Matt gets home from town. Dumping a grocery bag on the table, he decides against asking where it is. Knowing his wife, it'll be hidden away somewhere. Out of sight. Not out of mind. She would never get rid of it, no matter what she says. But the game, if that's what it is, tires him now. Pandora belongs wherever they go.

Amy runs her eyes over his purchases: local cheeses, fat green olives, cold chicken and a rosemary-infused sourdough loaf from the bakery. The way she avoids his eyes makes him wonder if she's still stewing over the box or him buying the car, but then he catches her wiping her eyes with the back of her hand.

'What's up, Aims?' He's at her side in an instant.

She shakes her head. 'It's okay.'

Matt waits.

Amy gives him a strained look. 'It's just … it's all a bit overwhelming, all this.' Her eyes are red and she swats a tear away.

'We haven't even started unpacking yet,' he jokes.

That earns him a short laugh. After a moment, she asks, 'Did you know there's a little girl next door? About … about *her* age?'

Matt swallows. He's seen the child from a distance once or twice when he's come down on weekends to paint and check in on the kitchen reno. And he's heard her playing outside, shouting at a kid called Henry.

Amy goes on without waiting for an answer. 'She turned up at the front door and wanted to come inside for a cup of Milo.'

Matt laughs. 'You serious? Did you give her one?'

'Do we have any?' She quirks an eyebrow. 'Of course I didn't. I'm a stranger. Besides, her mum came running up a second later, apologised and carried her home, kicking and screaming.'

'Sounds like a handful.' Pandora was like that. Full of spark. Knew exactly what she wanted.

'I'll say. Anyway, it freaked the hell out of me the way she appeared like that. I was thinking of her, of Pandora, and then there she was. Only it wasn't her at all, of course. But for a second ...' Amy trails off for a long moment and when she speaks again, her voice echoes with accusation. 'Same size, same tangled hair. Close up, she looks nothing like Pandora, but her eyes, Matt. Her eyes. The same grey-blue.'

Matt's spine tingles.

'You should have told me,' she sniffs.

'Would it have stopped you moving here?'

'Yes. No. I don't know.' She runs her hands through her hair. 'I wish I'd known, is all.'

The laboured sound of the removal truck ends the conversation. But as Amy gives her eyes a final wipe and moves away, Matt can't help wondering if he forgot to mention the little girl next door, or if he withheld that information on purpose. Either way, Amy can't expect everyone else's world to go on without children.

Daylight has faded by the time the truck rumbles away, leaving them alone amid an explosion of furniture and boxes. Bone-weary and ravenous, Matt removes boxes from a sofa and flops down, draping his legs over the edge of a coffee table. The fire's crackling and the muted, flickering light is a siren call for sleep. Amy joins him a moment later. She's dug out wineglasses from a box and fashioned a light supper. He digs in immediately, too tired to wait for wine to be poured and tasted. For a few moments, the only soundtrack he hears is chewing and the occasional sigh escaping from Amy – or is it him?

Leaning back, he surveys the lounge room. It's far from finished, but Amy's eclectic mix of antique cupboards, chairs and sideboards have married perfectly with the more contemporary neutral-coloured sofas. Boxes still rest on every available surface in the house, but he's too shattered to care. A few solid days of work will take care of it.

Amy shifts beside him, hand on one hip, rubbing. The injury flares up now and again when she's stressed and he has no doubt the hills around Blackwood will make it worse if she doesn't conquer her fear of driving. Another thing for them to work on.

'Are you okay?' he ventures. The firelight's too low to read the expression on her face.

'Tired.'

'That all?'

She shrugs. It's clear she doesn't want to elaborate and his chest tightens. Is she thinking of how much their little girl would have loved living here? Because the thought's barely left his mind all day. They were all set to sell up and raise Pandora in the country, in a small cottage on a big block, with chooks up the back. They'd been looking online at houses in a small south coast town. They were going to fill their house with kids. Three, maybe four, if he had his way. He always dreamed of having a big family. And then the accident tore his dream to shreds.

Tomorrow is never promised.

Someone said that after the memorial. Back then, his fists clenched in anger. Another in a long line of pithy comforts. These days he gets the meaning, but still cringes at the platitude.

'I'm impressed,' he says, changing the subject and reaching for the merlot he'd picked up in town. Amy gives him a questioning glance as he pours her a generous glassful. 'Not one argument about where to put furniture. Got to be a record. You don't see that on *The Block*.'

Her soft laugh eases his chest. Maybe she's thinking about that café for lease. She hasn't said anything, but when she nibbles her lip like she's been doing on and off all day it means something's snagged her interest. He has a feeling about the place. As soon as he'd seen the 'For Lease' sign, he'd known it was perfect for Amy; that it would give her something to do. Distract her.

He sniffs, then sips the wine. It's rich and velvety, with spiced fruit notes. Not bad. Once she's settled in they can talk about having another baby. He's waiting for the right moment to bring it up properly. Or waiting for her to say something first.

'To us,' he continues, raising his glass. Echoing him, she leans against his chest. The milk-and-honey scent of her shampoo tickles his nose, reminding him of his earlier desire to christen the room. He's tired but not that tired.

They sit in silence, sipping their wine, until the soft call of a boobook owl rouses him. It's the only outside noise he can make out. The cold evening has drawn the townsfolk inside early. Not even the dogs are barking.

'It's so quiet here,' she murmurs. 'Almost too quiet.'

'Mmm. Takes a bit of getting used to.' Matt drops to the floor and stretches his back, his hands a makeshift pillow. He rolls over to face her. Her hazel-green eyes search his, then close. Does she remember long-ago wine-flavoured kisses after languorous meals? He kneels, his lips brushing hers, tentatively, slowly. Her breath smells of wine and olives and when her lips open to his, he tastes her slowly, drinking her in.

'Shall we christen the room?' he asks, again. Her lips give him the answer he wants.

Afterwards, he lies awake in their new bedroom. Sleep hovers at the horizon of his mind, teasing him with the promise of relief, whirling away as tentacles of memory reach, poke and prod. Will this move to Blackwood save their marriage? Is it too late?

Despite what she's promised, he knows bumpy roads lie ahead. Words are only worth the weight of the action behind them. Beside him, Amy whimpers; a low keening from deep within.

'It will be okay,' he whispers, but who the words are for he cannot say.

CHAPTER FOUR

IRENE

I rene Knight stoops to retrieve half a shortbread biscuit from under a cushion. The biscuit crumbles onto the carpet she vacuumed earlier in the day, and she mutters under her breath. How many times has she asked Ashlee to eat over a bowl? Thousands? After disposing of the biscuit, Irene wipes milk droplets from the kitchen bench, and rinses the dregs from a plastic cup balancing on the edge of the table. The rest of the kitchen is tidy; dishes washed and stacked. In the bathroom, she wipes bathwater from the mirror and walls, hangs the sodden bathmat over the edge of the bath and two damp towels on the towel rack, shaking her head when her socked feet land in a puddle. Pulling off her socks, she tosses them into the laundry basket and heads back to the lounge room where her slippers should be next to her armchair.

She finds one under the chair and the other in Piglet's basket. The white terrier snuffles but barely moves as Irene slides the dog-smelling slipper from under the animal's belly. Piglet won't move until Irene sits in her chair and picks up the television remote, a signal for lap time. Putting the slippers on, Irene tries to remember when her days didn't revolve around picking up after others, but her head's foggy with exhaustion and she can't pinpoint a single example. At least Bonnie is getting the little one ready for bed – the muffled sounds of storytelling drift down the hall – and Irene can relax at last. All that's left to do is fold the washing and she'll do that with her granddaughter while they watch Netflix.

She's settling into her armchair, overflowing washing basket on the coffee table, when Bonnie joins her. Irene's granddaughter sets a tray next to the basket. On it are two cups of steaming chamomile tea and thick slices of baked lemon ricotta cheesecake Bonnie brought home from work.

Irene's eyebrows lift in surprise. Cake at this time of night? 'What's the occasion?'

'Nothing. Just thought you'd like some.' Bonnie passes her a plate and fork. She looks tired. 'Might want to wait for the tea to cool. I forgot to add cold water for you.'

They fold the washing in companionable silence while watching a fast-paced British thriller series. When the washing's done, Piglet snuggles onto Irene's lap and Ashlee's overfed cat, Flossie, leaps onto the coffee table and skulks towards Bonnie's uneaten cake.

'Oi!' The cat gives Irene a baleful stare and jumps down.

Bonnie doesn't react and Irene realises she's not watching the show, but is glued to her phone. Probably another fight with her boyfriend, Irene decides.

'Is something bothering you, love?' When Bonnie turns worried eyes on her, Irene presses the pause button on the remote. 'What is it? Come on, love, spit it out.'

'I've been offered a new job,' Bonnie blurts out.

'You have? Where?' Irene leans forward, confused, and Piglet jumps down with a grunt. 'I thought you liked working at Bistro Thyme.'

'I do. It's great. But … it doesn't pay enough money and the hours are all over the place. I need consistency. Reliable hours. More money.'

'More money? What on earth for?'

'To buy a house. With Jake.'

Irene stares at her. 'Already? You've only been together, what, four months? Isn't it a bit quick to be buying a house together? That's a big step, love.'

When she was twelve, Bonnie moved in with Irene and Sid after her mother – their only child – died. Fourteen years later, she still sleeps in the same bedroom, apart from the nights she stays at Jake's and the six months she spent backpacking in South-East Asia. When she came back she slotted into the house like she'd never left, and Ashlee was born eight months later. Their living situation didn't bother Irene then and doesn't now, even if the kerfuffle does her head in at times. Truth be told, she likes having company, especially now that Sid's passed. Irene babysits when needed; Bonnie shares the bills and house chores. A win-win all round. Sure, there's been the odd boyfriend here and there, but no one serious. No one that's made Bonnie inclined to move. Until now. Funny that she's brought it up the same day a young couple moved into Flo and Bill's old place next door.

'Oh, Reenie. Sometimes you just know, you know? Jake's the one,' Bonnie says. 'And I can't live with you forever. I have to make my own life.'

'I see.'

Irene understands Bonnie's desire to make her own life more than her granddaughter knows. When Ashlee turned four a few months earlier, Irene was all psyched up to plan a trip away. Somewhere overseas. Someplace new. Something for herself after years of putting others first. She wouldn't have to worry about the garden or house because Bonnie would be there, keeping things in order. Then the winds of change blew in. Jake Foster. Unease rippled through her the first time Bonnie brought him home. It still does.

She can see the attraction. He's a good-looker if you like the brooding type. Irene never has, but Bonnie's like her mum. A sucker for the Heathcliff type, completely swept away by the flattery and flowers Jake showers her with every day. But real love is about more than looks and flattery and flowers. And something about him doesn't ring true. He's got tickets on himself for a start. Thinks he's Mr Special. And Irene dislikes the way he ignores Ashlee, unless Bonnie's

25

watching. Then he puts on a good show, all fun and games. But it's Bonnie he wants, not her child, and it's clear as a summer's day to everyone but Bonnie.

But there's no point saying anything. And she wouldn't interfere anyway. People have to work things out for themselves.

Irene realises Bonnie's waiting for her to speak. She searches for words, something that isn't *I think you're rushing things*.

'Where's this job then? Bunbury?' More and more young people commute from Blackwood to Bunbury for work or uni these days. But Bonnie has always pooh-poohed that idea because she hates driving long distances. Then again, she's never wanted to move out of Irene's house until now.

'No.' Bonnie chews on her thumbnail, the way she always does when she's deeply worried. Irene's senses go on alert. 'It's up north.'

'Up north?' The next biggest town inland is forty minutes north-ish. A farming town, known for its apples. What on earth will Bonnie do there? Unless she's planning to leave Blackwood and move to Mandurah, or even worse, Perth. Irene shivers. She's never imagined not having Bonnie or Ashlee close by. It would change everything she knows about her life.

'It's a FIFO job. A hospitality one, with a big company. Great conditions, awesome pay. Same place Jake's working at, actually.'

Irene lurches forward. The remote falls to the floor but neither of them moves to pick it up. 'FIFO? As in, fly-in, fly-out?' She peers around the room. Sid used to love those candid camera shows. Is there a hidden camera in the room? 'You're not serious, love, are you? This is a joke, right?'

Bonnie shakes her head. 'No.'

'FIFO? But that means …' Irene pulls herself up from the chair and starts pacing. Her chest feels tight as questions squeeze her heart and head. 'That means you have to go away every couple of weeks, or whatever.'

'Two on, two off.'

Irene stares at her. Jake was trouble, but this. This takes the cake. 'Aren't you forgetting something, love? Or should I say, some*one*?' Her finger jabs the air. 'How will you look after your daughter if you're …' Irene stops. Shakes her head. 'No, love. You're not asking me to …'

Never in a million years has Irene imagined having sole responsibility for her granddaughter's child for two weeks a month. She's nearly seventy. It's time to spread her wings and spend the jam money she's been saving on the quiet. See the world a bit, like she always dreamed of. What with raising a troubled daughter, then her granddaughter because Erin wasn't able, and then Sid getting sick, there was never the opportunity. Always someone to take care of, something to do. One thing after another, a never-ending escalator. Now this.

'I wouldn't ask if it wasn't important,' Bonnie pleads. 'Please. Just for a year. That way Ashlee won't get uprooted and Jake and I can get the money together. It's the fastest way to get a deposit, Reenie. I'm never going to earn enough working as a waitress the rest of my life. And I've … I've given my notice.'

And I thought Bonnie and Ashlee moving a few hours away would change my life.

'No. No. There are other ways you can do this. Like renting. Why not rent a house in Blackwood together?' Irene says after a minute. No way is she offering for Jake to move in. 'Then you won't have to leave Ashlee. And you can keep working at Bistro Thyme.' She casts her eyes around the room, desperately; they land on a photo of her late husband. 'And you're going to get this place when I die anyway.'

'Don't say that. I don't want to think about it. And we can't live our lives waiting for you to …' Bonnie's face falls as her words trail off. She chews on her lip before going on. 'Jake wants us to live together and he's had enough of renting. And it's a buyer's market. Jake says we'll get something really nice if we time it right. It'll be worth it in the long run.'

Jake says, Jake says. Irene knows two things at that moment. One, this grand plan has Jake's name written all over it in sky-high capitals, and two, Bonnie's as blind as a bat when it comes to that man. Even when tears are sliding down her face, probably at the thought of leaving her daughter. Bonnie used to be independent and confident, but that man has turned her into an uncertain man-pleaser. But how can Irene say no when her twenty-six-year-old granddaughter wants to make a life for herself? Is it possible she resents Jake simply because he's taking Bonnie away from her? And Bonnie for seizing the opportunity to live the life she wants, not the one she was handed, like Irene?

'Twelve months,' Irene finds herself saying, ignoring the twinge in her chest. Picking up the remote, she hits the off switch. 'And no longer.'

CHAPTER FIVE
AMY

'Last one,' Matt says, slicing open a box with a Stanley knife. 'No idea what's in it. Just says *storage*.'

'Shouldn't we store it then?' Stretching her arms high above her head, Amy watches as he pulls out scrunched up newspaper and drops it onto the pile on the floor. They've been at this for days; unpacking and stacking, moving and removing. It's a relief to know this stage is at an end and they can move another step forward. Whatever that means. A new job for him. And, who knows, maybe a café for her? She's meeting the real estate agent tomorrow. Just looking, she reminds herself.

'Might as well check. Could be useful,' he says, pulling out a familiar rectangular object.

Amy's gut twists. She remembers packing that box a few years ago, eyes blurred, movements jerky. Before she can stop him, Matt turns over the frame.

'Look who's here,' he says, then turns the photo towards Amy.

Amy can't look. Her head shakes the tiniest fraction and she hears him sigh, then pull out another photo frame. Another. And another.

'We should put one in each room.' Matt places a close-up of their little girl – forever frozen in laughter – on the mantelpiece.

Amy's eyes squeeze tight. 'No! Not there. Or there. Take them away!'

His brow furrows. 'It's our daughter. I want to see her. I *need* to see her. And so do you.' His eyes are dark with determination and Pandora's smiling face stays where it is.

It's too much. Too soon. Eyes overflowing with tears, Amy backs away, arms hugging herself so tight she thinks she'll snap. 'I can't bear to look at them. It hurts too much. Don't make me.'

He hesitates and she thinks he'll come to her. Hold her. Instead, he gathers up the frames and the box and pushes past her. The study door slams.

When he comes out, she's tucked up in bed, trying to read. He says nothing about the photos. Says nothing at all. Goes through the motions of showering and brushing his teeth.

'Not yet,' Amy whispers when he finally slides into their bed, extra careful not to touch her.

After a long look, Matt nods and rolls away.

When his breathing becomes deep and regular, Amy reaches into her bedside drawer and pulls out a thin box. Inside, there's a small handprint, printed in primary colours onto a pink cardboard heart. Amy traces it with her index finger. *Goodnight, my little one.*

Switching off the light, she turns onto her side and waits for sleep to come, while gusts of wind shake the window in its old wooden frame.

Sometimes Amy feels like her marriage is like that pane of glass, rattling in the wind.

Weak light leaks through a gap in the heavy curtains. It's 7.30. Matt's side of the bed is empty and cold. Amy didn't hear his alarm or feel his lips brush her cheek. Unless he didn't bother.

Her head is fuzzy, her body heavy. Yawning, Amy regrets her spontaneous decision to view the café. But it kept stealing into her thoughts while the unpacking wore on, and then the call was made. Is she in a fit state of mind now to make any decisions?

Matt still doesn't know that buying the business is a possibility. No point getting his hopes up. His *told you so* face drives her nuts, and besides, she still hasn't decided whether or not to keep the appointment. There's one good reason to go ahead and about fifty not to, starting with the fact that she feels like crap.

Her muscles groan silently as she stretches her arms and legs from tip to toe. A quick Pilates workout to iron out the kinks and chinks? Or shower first? Opting for the shower, she swings her feet towards the floor, wincing as they meet cool wood. Matt hasn't set the timer for the ducted heating system, and she doesn't know how to work it. Shivering, she pads to the bathroom and turns on the shower; the old pipes creak in protest, mirroring her aching body. As steam clouds fill the bathroom, she recoils from her reflection: her too-pale face with its puffy eyes and a mop of sleep-kinked, honey brown hair peers back at her. Not exactly the face of a businesswoman.

Half an hour later – showered, stretched and dressed – she's nursing a coffee and watching the sun creep up the cloudless sky. Welcome relief after days of heavy rain. Casting off the patchwork blanket crocheted by Matt's mum for Pandora, she peeks outside to see if the ground has frosted. The window is blurred with condensation. She moves to wipe it, then decides to take a closer look at the garden. There's time. It's only a twenty-minute brisk walk into town.

Five if you drive. She can hear Matt saying it, see him jingling the keys with a meaningful look towards the expectant hatchback in the carport. Amy ignores imaginary Matt. Ignores the car that's the colour of tears and rain and pain. Ignores the sharp twinge in her hip when she steps down the stairs.

'I'll walk,' she says.

The still air carries an icy bite, but there's no frost. Zipping her fitted down jacket all the way up, she pulls her beanie over her ears. Her breath clouds, reminding her of the time Matt told Pandora you could tell who didn't brush their teeth in winter because their breath was purple. Pandora tested the theory every morning for a week, but her condensed breath remained white, teeth brushed or not. The memory is the icy freeze of sucking in air after eating a minty sweet.

The quarter acre property is three or four times bigger than the one they'd been renting in Perth. That one had a lap pool down one side, perfect for hydrotherapy. Tall potted plants with hard, angular leaves. Succulents pushing up between rust-coloured pea gravel. Not Amy's style – too modern and soulless – but it was only meant to be a roof over their heads and a place to recover. Not a home.

This garden reminds her of her grandmother's backyard: a combination of practicality and whimsy. Gran favoured the cottage garden look but didn't believe in gardens simply for flowers. The Thompsons must have had the same gardening approach. A good portion of the space has been devoted to growing food. Fruit trees, dormant and indistinguishable to her untrained eye. A loaded lemon tree and a mandarin with ripening fruit. A weeping plant she doesn't recognise. Rustic raised vegetable beds are neatly ordered in one corner, though the weeds have invaded, and two sturdy wine barrels hold medium-sized olive trees. The compost bays are both full of rich, earthy compost. And there are herbs: rosemary, lavender, thyme, oregano. Come spring, there'll be more. Amy pinches a rosemary tip between two fingers and breathes in the camphor-like scent.

It smells like her childhood.

Like the childhood Pandora never had.

A screen door bangs next door. Trampoline springs squeak: one-two, one-two. A high voice drifts over the fence. The little girl next door is bouncing and singing and laughing and thumping and she's so happy it makes Amy's heart squeeze. Pandora would have done that. She loved trampolines but there was no room in their courtyard. Begged for one that last Christmas. 'You can have one when we move to the country,' they'd promised. And they meant it. Amy wanted Pandora to have the best bits of her own childhood. And more. They'd already decided to relocate before school started. Not in the wheatbelt where Amy lived with her grandmother after her mother died. Somewhere cooler in the summer and wetter in the winter. Somewhere like Blackwood. And now they're here and Pandora's not. She'll never know the joy of snapping ruby-coloured berries off a mulberry tree, sweet juices popping on her tongue. Of biting into carrots, freshly pulled up and rinsed under the hose, still tasting of earth. Reaching into straw for warm eggs. Jumping on a trampoline and singing at the top of her voice.

Amy's phone alarm intrudes on her reluctant reverie. Quarter to nine. If she's going to cancel that appointment with the real estate agent, she needs to do it now. Near-numb fingers hover over the keypad before she buries the phone in her pocket. Suddenly she's anxious to get into town. To do more with her days than pottering aimlessly, watching Netflix, cleaning, cooking uninspiring meals and making lists she'll never use. Since Pandora died, days have melted into each other, and Amy's been suspended between old and new, unable to move on for fear of forgetting what was left behind. If she cancels the appointment, she'll remain in limbo.

And then her gaze falls on the hatchback. If she pretends it's not there, nothing will change. She has to try.

Marching inside, Amy discards her beanie and twists her hair into a topknot. Bag in hand, she jerks the car keys from the hook near the back door, yanks the door shut and stomps outside to the car. Her hand hesitates on the dew-covered door before she wrenches it open and slides in behind the wheel, breathing in. She grips the steering wheel with white-knuckled fingers. Turns the wheel back and forth a few times, like a child imitating a parent. And then her throat tightens and her forehead beads with sweat.

'I'll walk,' she whispers.

By the time Amy reaches Blackwood's main street, she's overheated and puffed, and her hip's killing her. Catching sight of herself in a shop window, she sighs at her flushed cheeks and the stray hairs escaping her topknot. Not the look she wanted for a business meeting, but what can she do? Her meeting's in ten minutes.

Blackwood is busier than she expected at this time of morning, but most people look like locals going about their chores, not tourists. Some offer up a curious or friendly 'hello' or nod, while others walk past as if she's invisible, which is fine by her.

She hobbles past the town's two watering holes, the bakery, pharmacy and a newsagency. Past a sweet-smelling gift shop, a touristy candy shop, and two supermarkets as different as apples and oranges; one is very much the nuts and bolts variety, while Blackwood Fresh is a foodie's delight, with a range of gourmet foods and products that would whet even a breatharian's appetite for eating. Surprisingly, Blackwood also boasts a wholefood store with bulk bins of dried fruit and nuts, coffee beans, herbs and spices, as well as local honey and fresh peanut butter. She walks inside and reaches for a scoop to fill paper bags with spices and dried foods to take home, until she remembers where she's supposed to be.

Five minutes later, she shifts from one foot to the other while the young real estate agent reels off his well-rehearsed sales pitch. Dust-covered tables and chairs are stacked haphazardly against one wall of the café, and menus are piled on a countertop between a till and a newish coffee machine and grinder. There's a French door-separated space that would work for large groups. The kitchen is closed in behind a wall, but the existing plant and equipment is modern and topnotch. That explains the inflated asking price.

'We've had a few bites. Get it? Café? Bite?'

Behind her, the agent giggles nervously at his joke, but Amy's too busy ticking items off her mental shopping list to respond. The business comes with all the relevant licenses, saving precious time, paperwork and money. But the furniture is not her style, the polished concrete floors and kitchen tiles need a deep clean, the colours and lighting are all wrong, and the kitchen needs opening up. There's staff, supplies, and security to consider. Marketing. Menus. The rocketing costs are enough to give her pause. It's not the amount. There's enough in the bank to cover her costs and then some.

But it's blood money.

'Someone else is very close to signing,' the agent says, clearing his throat.

She pictures her café: shiny concrete floors, rustic wood-framed chalkboards with ironic quotes, steampunk-inspired light fittings and fans, and a semi-open kitchen with tiled walls. Simple shelving lines one wall of the public space; gourmet items such as preserved lemons, olives, locally made curry pastes and spice mixtures share the space with fancy cookbooks, colourful platters and serving ware, and nifty cooking tools. It's laid-back and cosy, with a little free library and comfy chairs. Potted herbs on the tables. Good coffee, homemade cakes and scones, and a menu showcasing local, seasonal and sustainable products. No need to reinvent the wheel – just good food from ingredients close to home. Brewed to Taste: good food connecting community.

She pictures herself in the kitchen, sleeves rolled over her elbows and hair tucked under a cap, as she dishes up the *plat du jour*. It's where she belongs, doing what she does best: cooking and creating. Behind the scenes but still seen. Part of the community but blending into the background. No questions. No need for answers.

The easy way out.

'There's a chance the connecting shop will be up for lease soon. Opportunity for expansion!' the agent says in a flat voice that undermines his spiel. He's perfected the art of going through the motions while checking messages on his continually beeping phone.

Amy tunes him out. What should she do? She swore she'd never touch the compensation money from the accident. Refused to discuss it with Matt or anyone. To her, that money existed only as meaningless numbers on the unread bank statement emailed each quarter. But she can't buy the café without it. All the money she inherited from the sale of Gran's house went towards their new house. She gazes around the café, and into the kitchen, willing the space to tell her what to do. It doesn't.

Matt wouldn't have suggested buying the café if he didn't want her to use the money. But should she? Isn't it the same as a life for a new life? Kind of like her inheritance was, but worse?

Another memory pushes forward: *Pandora's face and hands are smeared with the rich chocolate cake batter Amy left on the bench when she ran out to bring in the washing. A pile of flour clouds the countertop and an egg has smashed on the tiles. Unaware that she's being watched, the little girl dips a wooden spoon in and out of Amy's prized Mason Cash mixing bowl.*

'Look, Mummy,' she says brightly when Amy moves into view. *'I'm a cooker like you.'* Her face falls. *'Mummy, why can't I come to work with you? I want to go wherever you go.'*

'Mrs Bennet? Do you need a few moments to think it over?' The bored-looking agent keeps his eyes on his screen. Probably checking Snapchat.

She contemplates knocking it from his hands accidentally-on-purpose, but then her eyes are caught by a flashing ad. He's not on social media, but checking out a popular jewellery website.

'Pandora,' she breathes out.

His head snaps up so fast he almost drops the phone. His cheeks flush red. 'Sorry about that, Mrs Bennet. Trying to buy my girlfriend a Pandora charm for our two-month anniversary. Thought I'd get her this gold heart. See?'

Amy stopped believing in signs after her mother drove into one when Amy was eight years old, leaving her to be raised by her grand-mother. Stopped believing in love until Gran's patient heart worked its magic. Stopped believing in life when Pandora died. But she can't ignore this, whatever it is.

'Buy the charm. Your girlfriend will love it,' she tells the agent, fumbling for her phone and walking outside. 'Matt?'

'Hey, what's up?'

'I want to buy the café.'

'Oh, okay. Good, that's good.' He sounds distant. Uninterested.

Amy wrinkles her brow. 'That's convincing. I thought you'd be more excited.'

'Sorry, Aims, it's not a good time. I've got to go. Talk later, okay?' He disconnects.

Amy stares at the blank screen. What's his problem?

An hour later, she waits in the pharmacy for a shop assistant to serve an elderly man whose list of complaints is as long as the day. Her hip's still throbbing and she used the last two anti-inflammatories last night. The pain's flared up again in the last few days, likely due to all the unpacking, and the up-and-down streets, but if it keeps up she'll need a stronger prescription from a doctor. She sighs. She's on the last repeat for her antidepressants too. And then it occurs to her: she doesn't need them anymore. With the café, she'll have plenty to distract her.

The old man shuffles past and she steps forward. Three people are still in front of her: a heavily pregnant teenager, and a middle-aged couple wearing matching mud-caked gumboots. The husband wants coffee and lunch, but the wife can't decide where to go.

'No, not the bakery. Did you see the line? Out the door. Ridiculous. No, no. Not the pub. Ugh. Their coffee tastes like dishwater. And the cups in the other one smell. You know? That smell? You know the one I'm talking about. I told you last time,' she says, unaware that her husband's rolling his eyes and the teenager's giggling.

Amy stifles a laugh. Next time they might have more choice. The paperwork is under way and she has a list of contacts for the renovations. If all goes to plan, she'll have the keys to the café next week, and Brewed to Taste will be born. A smile stretches across her face as the enormity of what she's done sinks in.

I've bought a café!

It feels surprisingly good. And then she remembers Matt's flat reaction and her smile fades. It's the first time she's taken an interest in doing anything since the accident and he's all *meh, whatever.* Strange.

She shifts her weight to her right hip when the teenager pushes past. Is Matt having second thoughts about using the money? Surely not. He's not the type to make a big deal of something and then back off. Matt thinks first, then acts. Thinks things to death sometimes. If he suggests something, he wants to make it happen. Her lips press together. *He could have bloody well shown some enthusiasm.*

'I can smell a foodie a mile off.'

Amy's heart sinks when she swings in the direction of the voice. It's that woman with chic, spiky hair who seems to pop up like a jack-in-the-box wherever she goes. At the bakery that first day. Coming out of a corner shop when Amy was going in. Even with her sunglasses on, Amy felt naked under the woman's burning stare.

She feels the same way now, but she can't pull the sunnies out in here. Matt keeps telling her not to worry about them, but she got into the habit of it soon after the accident. The media was a ravenous lion pouncing on helpless prey. Relentless. Calculating. One bite and everyone wanted a piece of her.

'Sorry?'

'You love food. I can tell. Saw you inside the wholefood store. The way you were looking at the spices and dried foods, as if you were imagining what you'd do with them, that was the first clue. And then you and that young man from the real estate agency went into the café with the silly name. Second clue. Shame it closed. We used to have book club there. Such a nice little café, although the coffee was a bit strong for my liking. And my spoon was dirty once or twice, but a quick word with the owner soon set that straight.' The woman's eyes drop to the envelope in Amy's hand. 'Am I right in guessing you're interested in buying it? I hope so. We need a new place for book club.'

There's a fine line between friendly curiosity and stickybeaking, and this woman's hurdled over it like a champion. Amy wants to nip the woman's twitchy nose, but stops short of snapping. She's a potential customer, after all. 'Sorry, do I know you?' she says, tucking the lease application into her handbag. 'Only, I don't discuss my personal business with strangers.'

The woman's lips purse briefly, then morph into a smile. 'No strangers in a town like this, dear, you'll soon find out. But I suppose you think I'm a nosy parker because I didn't introduce myself before asking questions. Funny, my daughter, Sharon, she works at the local paper; she always says I'd make a good reporter. Anyway,' she tilts her nose in the air and stands taller, 'I'm Una Mickle. President of the Blackwood Belles CWA. Winner of the Blackwood Regional Show chocolate cake competition ten years in a row. A foodie, like you.'

Amy stopped listening after the word 'reporter'. Part of the reason she came here was to get away from the media before someone suggested a *Where are they now?* story. It's about the right time for one of those too. Her chest tightens and unease spreads through her body. 'Nice to meet you,' she lies.

'Likewise. And you're Amy Bennet, correct?'

She sounds like a teacher and Amy instinctively stands up straighter. Her hip whimpers in protest. 'That's right.'

'And you've moved into the old Thompson house? Yes, yes, word gets around. You'll have to get used to that in a place like this. Just you and your husband, then, is that so? No little ones?'

'Yes. I mean, no, it's just the two of us.'

'Pity. Big house like that.' Una's gaze scalds like steam from a kettle before shifting to the shelf next to Amy. A knowing smile. 'I'm sure it won't be long before the pitter-patter of tiny feet.'

Amy raises her eyebrows in disbelief, then turns away, shaking her head slightly. *Some people.*

'Next, please,' the assistant calls.

Amy's forgotten what she came in to buy, but she can't leave empty-handed after queuing all this time. Her fingers stab for a box on the nearest shelf. 'Just this please. No bag, thanks.' The purchase completed, she turns to leave. 'See you,' she makes herself say to Una.

'You too. And,' Una inclines her head towards Amy's hand, the knowing smile still fixed in place, 'good luck.'

Amy thinks she means the café, but then she realises what Una's smiling at. She peers at the package to make sure. A sinking feeling pools in her gut.

What the—

No. Freaking. Way.

Straightening up, she pastes a smile on her face and slides past Una. 'Thanks. Bye.'

Outside, she shoves her purchase into the depths of her bag, caught between laughter and horror.

What were you thinking?

Not much, obviously.

Of all the things to randomly buy in front of the local busybody, she had to choose a pregnancy test.

CHAPTER SIX
MATT

M att's first day at Timbertop ends with a familiar bubbling in his gut. He's not sure when this started happening, but lately, whenever he drives home from anywhere, the same questions pop up. Is Amy walking on sunshine? Or will he be walking on eggshells? Her moods are like a summer storm. Unpredictable as hell.

Sometimes Matt plays a guessing game on the way home. He's usually way off. Amy can't be summed up with a smile or frown emoji, a thumbs up or down. If he described Amy's mood status on Facebook, he'd say 'It's complicated'. Kind of like their marriage. It never used to be like that. Amy would fling herself into his arms when he walked inside. Pepper his face with kisses. He used to call her Little Miss Sunshine. Couldn't wait to see her. But these days, he never knows whether to expect a smile or a *look*.

Knowing it's useless, he makes his guess as he walks through the carpark: eggshells. Last night's row over Pandora's photos makes it a near certainty. Resentment slithers in at the memory. It's been lurking all day, waiting for an opportunity to sink its fangs. Like now. And when Amy phoned in the middle of a meeting with his new boss.

Hand on the remote, he pauses, forehead wrinkling. Why did she call?

'You okay?' His boss, Carla, a tall brunette in her mid-thirties, stops mid-stride on her way to a late model four-wheel drive.

'Yeah, all good. Bit of a headache.'

'First days are always a killer, right? Information overload, and all that.'

Matt laughs. 'Pretty much.'

'Well, good to have you on board, Matt. Better let you get home. Unless,' Carla pauses, 'you want to join a few of us at the pub for a drink. Celebrate your first day.' She reels off names of people he can't put a face to and looks at him expectantly.

Matt's torn. A celebratory after-work drink would be nice. He wants to say yes. Knows he shouldn't. 'Thanks, but I've got to get home.'

'Another time, maybe.' Carla's phone beeps. 'That'll be the others, wanting to know where I am.' She waves and walks away, tapping into her phone.

Yawning, Matt gets into his car. No point putting off the drive any longer. And it's not like he doesn't want to see Amy. All he really wants to do is tell her about his first day at the mine over a coffee or a wine. He just doesn't have the energy for an Amy storm. He's still recovering from the last one. Last night it stole his sleep; he lay awake for hours, thinking about the shifting nature of their marriage. About Pandora's impact on its foundations. About grief. His and hers. When Amy lost it over the photos, he gave in and took them to his study, leaving her weeping. He still feels bad about that. But he's tired of the way Amy's grief, denial and self-absorption dictates everything in their life now. Tired of guessing games. Tired of putting *Matt* aside every freaking day. How's he supposed to cope with his own grief when he's always stepping around hers?

Something has to change.

'Coming to the pub?' a bear-like guy says through the window.

'Not today, mate. Cheers.' Matt puts on his seatbelt, but the keys stay gripped in his hand. They're making a new start, in a new town. Is he expecting too much, too soon?

'Give it time,' he says to the rear-view mirror, pushing the key into the barrel.

How much? his reflection wants to know. Matt has no answer. All he knows is that he can't go on living a grief-frozen life forever, no matter how much he loves his wife.

Inhaling deeply, he starts the engine: *Inhale the good shit, exhale the bullshit.* Repeat. His therapist calls it realistic relaxation. Works better than visualising rainforests and waterfalls. Another deep breath and Matt heads home, leaving the window down. Biting air rushes against his skin. Goosebumps rise under his shirt, but he doesn't care. The smell of dampness; musky wet timber from the jarrah and marri forests that line the road, dripping from a recent shower. The scent is strong and invigorating with soothing, earthy base notes. He wants to bottle the aroma. To stick his tongue out and taste the essence of the forest. To stay in this moment where he is simply a man called Matt.

Amping up the music, Matt sings along to 'Good Vibrations' as loud as he can, window still down. The psychedelic classic triggers a feel-good dopamine release that almost makes him believe he's ready for whatever mood awaits.

'But we're not done with the photos, Aims,' he says to the wind.

The heavenly smell of frying onions and garlic breaks through his head fog as he walks towards the house. Steeling himself, Matt heads inside.

'Aims? Where are you?'

'Kitchen.'

Relief washes through him when he finds Amy dicing carrots and celery with terrifying speed. Onions and garlic are sautéing in her beloved red cast-iron pot. A Bundt cake is cooling on a rack. Cake is a good sign.

Kissing her forehead, Matt indicates the pot. 'Smells good. What's for dinner? I'm starved. Barely had time for a lunch break today.'

'Lentil soup.' He wrinkles his nose and she tilts her head. Reminds him of his mother when she does that. 'Don't be like that. It's perfect for a winter's night. And it's the Middle Eastern one you love.'

'Nice.' Matt switches on the coffee machine. 'God, I need coffee. Can barely keep my eyes open.'

'Mmm.' Amy tips the diced vegetables into the pan, adds a bay leaf, and gives him a sideways look, as if she's expecting something. *What?*

He winces at her sudden cool tone. 'What's up?'

'Nothing.'

Matt looks for a clue, but she's intent on stirring the soup. His brow wrinkles and then he remembers.

'The café!' That's what she called about earlier, talking faster than the women on that *Gilmore Girls* show she loves, and wanted an answer about buying it then and there. That's what she's been waiting for him to mention.

'How could you forget?' she scolds, facing him. 'I've been dying to talk about it all afternoon. I thought we'd celebrate.'

Matt averts his gaze, remembering Carla's friendly invitation. 'Sorry, Aims, my head's all foggy from work.' Rubbing his temple, he scrambles for an appropriately enthusiastic response. 'So, you're finally a café owner, like you always wanted. How's it feel?'

'Almost an owner,' she corrects. 'They still have to do all the financials and you need to sign a few things … but pretty good, I think.' At the sink, she strains lentils. 'Are you sure it's okay to use the money?' The strainer wobbles in time with her voice. She's never seriously considered using the compo before. No wonder she's jumpy.

Matt goes to her and she sags against him briefly. 'Of course,' he says. 'Wouldn't have suggested it, would I?'

'I know. But … you know I always thought of it as blood money. Still do, a bit.'

Blood money. Whenever she uses those words, his insides scream. He forces himself not to cringe. 'It's not, though. You know it's not. I've been trying to tell you that for months. I'm glad you've finally decided to use it.'

'Yeah. I guess.' Pulling away, she tips the lentils into the pot and stirs in aromatic chicken stock and spices. The kitchen fills with the smoky sweet smell of cumin.

Matt steams the milk, rolling his shoulder muscles back and forth. There's more tension in his shoulders than the spy thriller on his bedside table, thanks to information overload from work. He opens his mouth to ask Amy if she'll rub his upper back later but she speaks first.

'You didn't seem overly interested when I called you earlier. I thought you'd be happy.'

'What? Of course I was.' Confused, he faces her. And then it comes to him. She was expecting a grand display of enthusiasm over the phone. Irritation flares. He bangs a cup onto the bench and swallows before speaking. 'Aims, I was in the middle of a meeting with my boss. And to be honest, it came completely out of left field. I didn't even know you were interested in the café, much less going in to view it.' He hadn't dared bring it up since she chewed his ear off and spat it onto the main street. And suddenly he's supposed to summon up the perfect level of excitement, just like that. Silence spans between them as he goes through the calming motions of making coffee. 'Actually, I thought we might have talked about it together first,' he says when he's done. 'Before you went and made a snap decision.'

'But it's what you wanted, isn't it? Me to buy that café. You could barely wait to show it to me.' She looks up from slicing cake, confusion wrinkling her brow.

'I did.' Why does he sound uncertain? It's exactly what he wanted. Amy to do something that brings her back to herself. Back to him. His mind clears. 'It's not that you've bought it. It's that … I'm used to us doing things together.'

'But … it would be my café. You have your own job. I already knew you wanted me to buy it, so I didn't need to talk to you. And, honestly, I didn't know for certain I wanted to do it until I saw it.' She gives him a quick look before deftly halving and juicing a lemon. 'You're not cranky, are you? Figured there was no point bringing it up before I checked it out. I might have hated it and then what would have been the point?'

'That's true,' he says. 'Caught me by surprise, that's all.'

Amy places a large slice of cake next to him. Her hand presses onto his for the briefest second. 'It's your favourite.'

Any residual irritation leaks away as he forks up a generous mouthful of the zesty orange yoghurt cake he loves. Cinnamon sugar is sprinkled on top, the way he likes it. Damn his fickle stomach. Sometimes he can't understand himself, let alone Amy. She's pissed at him, but makes his favourite cake. He's cranky back at her, but he wants that cake too much to stay cranky. 'I am happy,' he says, demolishing the treacherous dessert in four bites. 'But is it what you really want to do? You're not just doing it to get me off your back?'

'I'm not, don't worry. More cake?'

'Sure.' He polishes off the second slice faster than the first.

The soup simmers on the stove while they sip flat whites and Amy tells him about floor plans, colour schemes and furniture. Her eyes shine with enthusiasm and something he hasn't seen on her face in years: anticipation. He's surprised to find that she's already contacted tradesmen, and sourced the tables, chairs, and lights she wants to order. And completed the paperwork, drafted ads for staff, worked out open and close times, and arranged a quotation from a sign writer. All without a scrap of help from him.

'Geez, Aims, you haven't wasted time. And you're sure you can manage?' He means emotionally and by the way her lips thin, she knows it. It's starting to sink in how huge this decision is. His picture of their life in Blackwood changes the more she talks. 'It's a lot to juggle.'

'Not like I'll have anything else to do. And why are you being negative? You wanted me to do this, remember? I'll be fine. I *am* fine.' She sounds like she's convincing herself.

He wants to believe her, but recent history means the odds are high she won't be fine.

His phone pings with a message. It's his mum, asking about his day. He taps out a response while Amy tells him about some busybody who bailed her up in the pharmacy, and some people in gumboots, then it's back to the café.

'Are you going to keep the old name?'

'God, no.' She looks appalled.

'Thank God. It was pretty lame. What about calling it—'

'I'm calling it Brewed to Taste,' she tells him. 'I've already decided.'

'Oh.' So she doesn't need his help with that either. Although, it's a good name, he has to admit.

After half an hour of Brewed to Taste this and Brewed to Taste that, Matt tunes out. His bum's tired from sitting on the hard chair for so long. Amy's not interested in his input. Or in his day.

'So, the new job is going to be interesting,' he tries, giving her a significant look. She doesn't respond, too busy looking up something on the internet she wants to show him. Funny how men are expected to notice those looks and instantly understand the problem, but women ignore them.

'Oh, here it is,' she says, pushing the laptop around to face him. 'Look.'

He tries a couple more times, but the conversation always comes back to the café. Shifting restlessly, his mind drifts to his mental to-do list. Make lunch. Call Mum. Squeeze in a workout. He hasn't exercised in days.

'Matt? Are you listening?' Amy gives him a dirty look.

'What? Yes. Of course.' He stifles a yawn. When is it her turn to listen?

'I was *saying*,' she emphasises, getting up to stir the soup. Has she added preserved lemon? It won't be the same without that special Amy touch. 'This Una woman acts like she's only showing an interest in the newcomers, but ... I don't know. I've got a bad feeling about her. Her daughter's a *journalist*.'

His eyes widen. *Seriously?* The media didn't help them. Not at first. *What if—* With effort, he puts the brakes on the worry train. 'But, Aims, have you even seen the local rag? It's strung together with agricultural ads and the odd story about a giant pumpkin.' Before she can answer, he ploughs on. This is something he can help with. 'I know. Why don't you do the same to the busybody? Ask *her* questions. Find out about her. People love talking about themselves.' If Amy got the hint, she chose to ignore it.

'I don't want to get to know Una Mickle. She reminds me of this woman who used to visit Gran. Always looking for the juicy goss. Always giving advice people didn't want. Always telling people how great she was.' Between them Amy plonks a wooden platter with cheese, olives, flatbread and dip. 'Watch the pips in the olives.'

Matt smears feta on two triangles of bread and passes one to his wife. 'Think about it, Aims. If you ask the questions, you're directing her attention away from you. The art of deflection. It's your modus operandi, right?' Bracing for a tart response, he spoons Amy's smoky eggplant dip onto another piece of bread.

She yawns. 'God, I'm pooped. I haven't stopped since I got up.' Her chair scrapes across the floor. 'Going to have a shower before dinner.'

She pecks him on the head and walks out. Seconds later, the bedroom door thuds shut. Sighing, Matt picks up an olive. 'I'm pooped after my first day at work too, thanks for asking.'

CHAPTER SEVEN
AMY

'I hate being late,' Amy mutters as she yanks the back door. Like the front door, it's cold-swollen; it resists her tug like a petulant toddler. 'And I hate this stupid door.' She must have asked Matt to fix the doors half a dozen times. Another tug and it gives in. She strides down the stairs, annoyed she's left it so late to get into town. She's supposed to get a quote from a painter at nine, but got sucked down the rabbit hole of the internet.

At the carport, she pauses beside the neglected hatchback. If she's honest, she was lollygagging online because of her aching hip. The flare-up has worsened over the past few weeks, what with cold mornings and daily walks in and out of town to get the café sorted. Resting it would help, but she can't afford the time; there are tradies to meet, things to do.

'Driving will take some of the pressure off,' Matt reminds her when she's doing hip stretches at night.

He's right. But whenever she tries to drive, she freezes with fear.

Problem is, with early morning starts a given once Brewed to Taste opens, she's going to freeze if she walks. Blackwood winters are fridge-like compared to Perth. She can't win.

Which is why she's standing in front of the little car now,

wondering if today is the day. It stares back, unnervingly placid. *No rush. In your own time.*

Today it feels like the car is mocking her. Daring her. She fumbles for her keys, a metallic bundle of mixed emotions at the bottom of her bag, and unlocks the doors. All she needs to do is drive herself to town and back. It's not that hard. Is it?

'No! I'm not getting in that silly car,' the little girl yells from next door.

Hand on the door, Amy freezes. Pandora yelled the same thing the day she died. Even without seeing the other little girl, she can imagine the knitted brow, pouty lips, and stompy feet. Shivering, she shoves the keys in her coat pocket and walks into town.

The next day, pain shoots through her hip as Amy treads gingerly down the back stairs, determined to overcome her fear. She can't run a café if she can't walk. All the work she's done will be for nothing. She can't let that happen. Won't let it happen. Clutching the keys to her chest, she sucks in three deep breaths.

'Today's the day,' she says to the car.

It stares her down. *If you say so.*

Ignoring her racing heart, she unlocks the hatchback and climbs in. Her fingers tremble on the keys as she starts the engine. It idles for a moment. Nothing bad happens. She draws the seatbelt over her chest. Lowers the handbrake, pulls it into reverse, and presses the accelerator lightly. The car eases back, inch by inch.

She makes it all the way to the road, then straightens up and shifts into drive. Her foot is too heavy on the accelerator and the hatchback lurches. Amy's chest tightens and she slams on the brake so hard she jerks forward. Her chest tightens as a familiar horror movie plays out in her mind; she can't switch it off and she can't breathe.

Eventually, she becomes conscious of another vehicle waiting for her to move. Amy waves the dented four-wheel drive past, catching a glimpse of an older woman behind the wheel, and a little girl in the back seat with her face and chubby hands pressed up against the glass. Amy's hands go to her chest, as if to squash her heart back inside.

When her breathing slows, Amy leaves the hatchback parked on the street and goes back into the house, slamming the door on the told-you-so that follows her with every step. Except it doesn't slam because the stupid door is swollen; swearing, she shoves it with her backside. Tears of frustration and pain spill over, and she shuffles through her day under a cloud that refuses to lift.

CHAPTER EIGHT
MATT

When Matt gets home, Amy's hatchback is parked out the front. His forehead ripples with questions. What's it doing there? Did Amy drive somewhere? Inside, it's chilly and dark. At first he thinks the power's out, but then he finds Amy asleep on the couch, wrapped in the blanket his mum knitted. Her laptop is on the coffee table, next to a notepad filled with Amy's messy scrawl, a mug of cold tea, half a toasted sandwich, and an empty packet of anti-inflammatories. His heart pounds. He switches on the table lamp, grabs her wrist and peers closely at her face, holding his breath. She's breathing, slow and steady; he exhales. She hasn't done anything rash, but he can tell by her puffy, tear-stained cheeks that today is a thumbs down day.

Kneeling beside his wife, he kisses her cheek and pushes aside his disappointment and sadness. He's seen glimpses of the old Amy for the past month, the laughing girl-woman he first met in Greece. Now she's gone again. Helplessness almost unravels him. Amy's emotional roller-coaster isn't going to plateau any time soon, no matter what she tells herself. No matter what he wants. What goes up, must come down. Bandaids don't work for grief and depression.

She stirs. Pulls herself upright. 'Matt?' Her eyes are unfocused.

'Hey, darling.' He strokes stray hair back from her face. 'Did something happen today?'

'No, no. Just … one of those days. You know.'

He does know. If only she'd talk about it, talk to *him*. About her grief. About Pandora. It's like she's locked that part of their life in a safe and thrown away the key.

His eyes fall to the empty box of pain relievers. 'How's the hip?'

She shrugs. 'I've run out of tablets.'

'I'll go into town and get some.'

Amy gives a short laugh. 'I tried to get some myself. Didn't get me anywhere.'

'That why your car is out the front?'

Her gaze drifts to the window. 'Oh. I forgot I left it there.' She rubs her face. 'I tried to drive to town. Been trying to drive for days.'

'You have? Aims, that's great!'

'Is it?' She lies on her back and brings her left ankle to rest on her right knee. A groan escapes. 'Like I said, it didn't get me anywhere. I froze. As usual. Although,' she sighs, swapping her right ankle to her left knee, 'as you can see, I made it onto the road.'

'Baby steps.'

'Maybe. Anyway, how are you? How was your day?'

'Good. Busy.' He knows what she's doing. Turning the attention away from herself. 'Coffee?'

In the kitchen, Amy leans against the kitchen bench, as if she's holding herself up. His eyes narrow as recognition stirs. He knows sudden withdrawal when he sees it. 'You dizzy?'

'A bit. It's nothing. Probably stress from the café renovations.'

'Are you taking your antidepressants?' he asks.

Amy scratches her neck before answering. 'No.'

'What? Why not?'

'I was feeling better so I let them run out.'

'God.' He rubs his head. 'You don't … you don't do that. You're supposed to wean yourself off that medication slowly, with the help of a doctor. You *know* this.'

'I don't have a doctor here.' She avoids his gaze.

'Bullshit. Pick up the phone, make an appointment at the medical centre. It's simple. You can even do it with a phone app now.'

'It's my choice. I don't need them.'

He shakes his head in disbelief. 'Really? You're seriously telling me this after the way I found you earlier?' The stubborn set of her mouth reminds him so much of Pandora he has to look away. When he tries again, helplessness cracks his voice. 'Don't go making too many changes at once, hon. The café's a huge responsibility. And we've just moved.'

'I'm not. I've thought this through. My body is adjusting, that's all.'

'Yeah, because you're rushing things.'

'That's not true. Things are different here. I've got something to do now. That was the problem before. I had nothing to focus on.'

'Depression doesn't disappear in a puff of smoke,' he insists. 'You're *not* better.'

'Better? I'm never going to be *better* after—'

'You just said you were feeling—'

'You know what I meant!'

'Fuck!' The word slips out more harshly than he intended and the blinds come down over her eyes. He's doing this all wrong, but he can't stop and so he says what he's been wanting to say for weeks. Months. 'You're not the only one grieving. And you can't avoid talking about Pandora forever.'

With a strangled cry, she hobbles past him. 'Sometimes you make me want to run and never come back!' The bedroom door slams.

Cursing, Matt tips his coffee down the sink and goes outside to move Amy's car. The prickle of unease that started when she bought the café adds to the bubbling in his gut. Why does he feel like crap when he speaks his truth? Deep down, he knows his delivery was shit, but the way Amy wilfully ignores certain facts really gets to him. Patience has its limits. 'I'm off to the chemist,' he says, walking into their bedroom moments later. Amy is staring out the window in the direction of the carport, but she turns at the sound of his voice.

'I'll come with you,' she says.

CHAPTER NINE
AMY

The next day, dosed up on the strongest over-the-counter pain relief available, Amy averts her eyes from the hatchback and walks slowly into town to meet the cabinet-maker. When he messages to say he's running late, she detours into the bakery for a takeaway coffee.

'Hi, Amy. The usual?' June asks. 'How's the café coming along?'

Over the past few weeks, Amy's become a regular, and they've struck up a friendship of sorts. The older woman seems genuinely interested in how Brewed to Taste is taking shape. 'Good,' she says now, stuffing her sunnies into her bag. 'The shelves are going in today. Painting later this week. Then the lights. And I'm interviewing staff next week.'

'Much interest?'

'Yeah. A couple of guys stand out. Lots of experience. Apparently they used to work in that café before.'

'Nick and Devi?'

'You know them?'

'Sure do. Can't go wrong with them, Amy. Nick was head chef and Devi was sous chef. Perfect team.' She fits the lid onto Amy's reusable coffee cup with a cheeky wink. 'They got married last year. Here you go.'

Amy takes her cup. 'Well, if they work out, all I need is a barista, kitchenhand and waitstaff. Maybe an apprentice. We'll see.' After much thought, she'd decided to head up front of house, rather than work in the kitchen. Two head chefs were one too many, and great service was as important as the food on offer. Hiding in plain sight was a risky move, but how else could she manage Brewed to Taste and the customer experience? 'Thanks, June. Better run.'

Moments later, she's standing in the café, wishing there was a chair and contemplating her overwhelming to-do list. She downplayed it for June, but there's still so much to do. At night, her head throbs with everything that could go wrong with the café. She's overthinking, but at least when she worries about the café she spends less time in the past. And less time wondering why she and Matt are arguing more than ever.

Last night in bed she'd felt him willing her to reach out to touch him. She'd wanted to break the barrier that had formed between them, but she couldn't bring herself to do it. Couldn't make her hand move a few pathetic centimetres to the right to touch the man she'd been married to for ten years. Told herself that even if it temporarily smoothed things over, it wouldn't fix everything. Now she wishes he were here so she could breach that chasm in their bed, if only to restore an outer peace.

'We need to talk,' she says to the wall.

'Pardon?'

Startled, Amy swings around to see a burly intruder in his sixties, holding a toolbox in one hand and a ladder in the other. 'I didn't hear you come in. Are you—'

'Frank Taylor. Here to install your shelves. Sorry I'm late. Had to pick up the young bloke. How's your fancy kitchen going?' At her blank look, he continues. 'I did your reno a few months back. Top bloke, your husband. Get to know someone when you see them every day. Share a few stories.' His face shadows. 'Real sorry about your little girl. Your husband told me.'

'Oh. Thanks.' Amy swallows. What exactly did Matt say? How much did he tell this stranger?

'I haven't opened me mouth to anyone, don't worry. And he didn't tell me much.' After a gentle nod, Frank clumps to the door. 'Troy!' he bellows. 'Get your butt in here, mate. Teenagers,' he says, turning back to Amy. 'You know what they're like.'

Amy smiles, politely. 'So, do you need anything from me, or will I leave you to it? I've got a few things to sort out. What time do you want me back?'

'You're all good. About four should do it.' He pauses and gestures at the espresso machine on the bench. 'Actually, Mrs Bennet, wouldn't mind a cuppa while me and young Troy get sorted. Would you mind? Forgot me thermos.'

'Call me Amy. And, sorry, I don't have coffee beans yet.' His face falls. 'I can get you a coffee from the bakery if you like.'

'Won't say no. Cappuccino with two sugars and milk, thanks love.' As an afterthought, he calls out to his offsider, a gangly young man with a thatch of dark hair and thick black glasses. He's staring open-mouthed at the espresso machine. 'Troy? Want a coffee?' Frank shoots Amy a look of mock exasperation, as he fumbles for a ten dollar note. 'This lump here's me grandson. Helping me out while he looks for a real job, but faffs around in la-la land most of the time.'

Troy's fingers trace over the machine, then he turns slowly in a circle, a slight smile of wonder on his face. It's as if he's standing in a Paris cathedral for the first time. As she takes in the faded black Metallica T-shirt that probably belonged to his dad, the almond-shaped eyes, the jeans ripped at the knees, the dirt-caked boots, and the earbuds hanging over his shoulders, Amy senses an idea forming.

'What kind of work are you looking for?'

Troy strokes his chin. 'Dunno. Anything right now. Wouldn't mind being a barista. Reckon it'd be super cool.'

'It's tougher than you think. Pretty fast-paced at times. Ever used one of these?'

'Yeah. Like, smaller. Did a hospitality certificate in year eleven, had to make coffees for the teachers. Pretty good at latte art.' He grins.

'One time, at school, there was this mean as teacher who demanded a cappuccino, so I put a latte art di—'

'Troy! Remember who you're talking to, mate!' Amy stifles laughter at Frank's mortified expression. 'Get over here, ya peanut.'

'Sorry, miss.' Neck and face beetroot red, Troy slopes away.

'She might have given you a job, ya bloody numpty,' Frank mutters.

Fifteen minutes later, Amy offers Troy a cappuccino and a job.

'That's super amazing! Thanks!'

'You can work front of house with me to start, and we'll go from there.' Amy pauses. 'But if you *ever* make anatomical latte art, you're out. Got it?'

Frank thumps a spluttering Troy on his back. 'You're never going to live that down, ya peanut.'

'It was one time,' Troy protests. Stifling a laugh, Amy leaves them to it.

The rest of the day passes in a productive blur of planning and scheduling. Grey clouds have given way to solid rain that drums the tin roof, the perfect background music for a wintry day inside. Amy's washing dishes, a fall-apart pork ragú simmering on the range, when her phone pings with a message from Frank: *Will you be long? All done now.*

Swearing under her breath, she manages to tap out a response with shaking fingers: *On my way.*

Except she isn't on her way, not even close. Even if she jogs, she'll be at least fifteen minutes. If her dodgy hip doesn't collapse first. And she'll be soaked through by the time she gets there because no umbrella will stand up to the gusty wind that's blowing rain under the verandah. But if she stands here weighing up her limited options, she'll never get there.

Shit!

Amy ducks her head and runs. Her hands fumble with the remote, and the lock finally pops, and then she's sliding inside, hair plastered down her face. Wiping her face, she breathes deeply to calm her racing heart and starts the engine. Another breath and her foot lifts off the brake. The wipers chatter across the glass as she reverses down the driveway, out onto the road. Shifting into drive, she hesitates, right foot hovering over the accelerator before she yanks up the handbrake. Seatbelt! She fumbles with the belt until it clicks into place. Switches on the headlights. Releases the brake, breathing sharply when her foot connects with the accelerator. The car inches forward and then lurches to a halt. Until she clears the steamed up front windscreen, she's not going anywhere. Still shaking, she locates the defogger control. And that's when the memories force their way into the suddenly smothering space.

Rain pelts against the windshield, smearing the scenery as wipers flail from side to side. Humid breath coats the windows with a wet haze; the defogger is broken. One hand on the steering wheel, she reaches for a face flannel on the passenger seat. Rubs the windscreen. The car veers to the right as a puddle catches at the wheels. Hot fear pumps through her. It's as if the rain is driving, not her. Her grip tightens. She's driving on unfamiliar roads with her sleeping daughter in the back seat, and she can barely see.

Amy's mouth is dry, cheeks wet. Her breath comes in short, sharp gasps. She can't do it after all. It was stupid of her to try. Matt was right. She needs help. Amy pulls over, intent on calling Frank and making some excuse: her car's broken down and she can't make it. Which might work if she didn't need to get the café keys. Her mind spins like a chocolate wheel, clicking through her options. Ask Frank to lock up and drop the keys to her. Offer him a cuppa for his troubles. But then she can't sign off on his work.

Her phone beeps and Frank's name flashes on the screen. She doesn't need to read the message to know what it says.

Rain drums the roof, hard pellets of water nagging her to decide, decide, decide. The wipers chant relentlessly: *You. Can. Do. This.* Amy squeezes the steering wheel and cries out in frustration. The defogger has done its job; the way forward is clear. All she has to do is—

Amy's foot presses down and then the car is rolling forward and nothing's going wrong and it's still going forward and it's getting faster and so is her heart but bloody hell, she is driving. After three years, she is driving!

When the wheels catch on a puddle, she almost loses it right there. Panic rises from gut to throat, but she shoves it down by chanting with the wipers. *You. Can. Do. This.* And the wheels on the car go round and round, all the way to town.

After she parks – right out the front of Brewed to Taste, where Frank and Troy have no idea how momentous this moment is – Amy lets out a *whoop* of triumph. She's shivering from fear and excitement and sadness all at once, but she did it!

That night, Amy greets Matt with a deep kiss. He takes a breath and squints quizzically at her but comes back for more, groaning when she runs her hands under his shirt, his wall crumbling under her touch. She senses relief under his response; a sigh and a need fused into one.

'I'm sorry,' she whispers into his ear, flicking her tongue over his earlobe.

He tries to speak, but her mouth seals his words inside, seeking and finding all at once. His hands run under her shirt, tracing the skin she knows he's ached to touch for days.

'I've made a doctor's appointment for tomorrow.' Her lips whisper over his chest as she unbuttons his shirt. 'I'm going back on the anti-depressants, but I want a lower dosage. And stronger pain relief for my hip.'

His eyes are closed. 'Good.'

'The cabinet-maker was in today. Frank. Same guy who did our kitchen.'

'Mmm-hmm.'

'He's not a bad bloke, bit of a talker, but the shelves look great. I gave his grandson Troy a job. He's a barista in training. And I've got staff interviews scheduled for next week.' She kisses her way up to his neck. His hands reach for her breasts and she arches towards him. 'And I drove the car.'

He pulls back. 'What?'

'It's true! It's not that big a—'

'Aims?' He shucks his shirt aside.

'Yes?'

'Shut up and kiss me.'

Much later, they picnic on the living room floor, eating the ragù and sipping a peppery shiraz. Matt's wearing an unbuttoned shirt and cotton boxers, like he used to in their early days, when they'd get home from work and he would carry her off to bed, or the couch, or wherever took their fancy in the heat of the moment. Amy's thrown on tracksuit bottoms with one of Matt's old T-shirts and an oversized cardigan, and her feet are tucked up underneath her.

'I still can't believe you drove to town and didn't call me straight away,' Matt says, mouth full.

'Well, last time I did that you didn't like the interruption.'

'True.' He looks at his lap and nods. 'So … How did it feel?'

'Honestly? Scary as shit at first. I nearly couldn't do it. I had a flashback about … about the rain and all.' Tears well up, and she swipes them away. 'But as long as no one's in the car, I can do it.'

'Not even me?' She shrugs and Matt squeezes her hand. 'One step at a time. I'm so proud of you, Aims. That would have been tough.'

'It was.'

'I would have come with you if you wanted.'

'I know. But I think I had to do it myself.'

Nodding, Matt wipes his mouth on the back of his hand. 'I've been so worried, what with your hip playing up. This will make everything easier.'

Everything hovers between them, pregnant with meaning.

CHAPTER TEN

IRENE

Sliding out of a four-wheel drive that's seen better days, Irene sucks in frigid three-degree air. At 6.45 a.m., it's not quite sunrise, but the carpark facing the fog-veiled river is rapidly transforming into a lively marketplace, like it does every second Sunday of the month. All around, stallholders buzz like bees around a lavender bush. Irene waves at a few regulars and pulls on her heavy waterproof coat, dislodging her rainbow-striped beanie.

'Get a move on,' she mutters to herself, jamming the beanie back over her ears. The Blackwood Farmers Market is well known for its paddock-to-plate produce and it'll be swarming with people in two shakes of a lamb's tail. Flo's Kitchen, her jam and preserve stall, won't organise itself. She'll be lucky to get a coffee into her at this rate. A strong brew, none of that instant rubbish Bonnie guzzles.

'What?' Ashlee pipes up from the back seat. 'What'd you say, Reenie?'

'Nothing, love. Stay where you are for a tick.' Her great-granddaughter's practically fizzing with excitement, like a soft drink that's been given a good shake. To be honest, she could do with a few less bubbles today; running the market stall keeps her on her toes as it is. Looking after a lively four-year-old *and* a market stall will wipe her out for the rest of the day and tomorrow. Why did she agree to Bonnie's mad plan again?

'Reenie? Can I get out now? This seatbelt is squishing me.'

'You can undo it, but stay in the car, love. I have to set up the jams.' Irene passes Ashlee her favourite *Frozen* lunch bag. 'You can eat your brekky while I'm busy.'

'I want to help.'

'Brekky first.'

Ashlee tilts her head as if deciding whether or not to push the issue, and then lets out a dramatic sigh. 'Fi-i-i-ne.'

Irene swallows her own sigh and unloads boxes from the back of the four-wheel drive. Ashlee's the spit of her mother in more than looks. Easy to please most of the time, but she knows what she wants. And she can be a right drama queen at times, like Bonnie. But at least she's staying put in the car for now.

'Reenie? Why wouldn't you let Henry come to the markets?' Ashlee calls from the back seat. 'I wanted to play with Henry.'

'Because I said so, that's why.'

'It's not fair. Henry's my best friend. You're mean.'

Irene ignores her and stacks boxes on the trestle before moving around to unpack the jars, one by one. She's behind, but if she gets a rhythm going, she'll have time to grab that much-needed coffee from the coffee van. Might even reward herself with an almond croissant from the French patisserie stall. Her eyes close in anticipation of flaky butter pastry and sweet almond filling. She can practically taste it.

'Reenie? I have to wee.'

Irene nearly drops the A-frame chalkboard she's holding. Beside her, Ashlee hops from foot to foot, shivering and clutching between her legs. Her feet are bare of the red gumboots and thick green socks Irene wedged onto her feet before they left the house.

'Ashlee! Where are your boots?'

'In the car, silly. My feets were hot.' Ashlee rolls her eyes. 'I'm bustering, Reenie. Come on.'

'Boots on first, young lady.' Ignoring Ashlee's protruding bottom lip, she plonks the child onto a camping chair, and shoves the offending items where they belong. 'Now, let's go. Toot sweet.'

Bonnie left a few days earlier to start her new FIFO job. The preparations were frantic. She was teary-eyed one minute and excited the next, but away she went and now Irene's standing in a freezing toilet block, waiting for a four-year-old to wee.

'Ready, love?' she asks, after Ashlee's hands have been washed and dried. Ashlee grins. There are crumbs around her mouth and Irene's pity party turns into a rush of love. Poor little mite. It's not her fault. It'll be tough on her once she realises her mum's not coming home for two weeks. That's eternity for a four-year-old. 'Come on.'

'I'm hungry,' Ashlee says. 'I've eated all my food.'

Hand in hand, they pick their way across dew-soaked grass to the makeshift gate, where rugged up good Samaritans stand guard and collect gold coin donations for the Country Women's Association. Irene ducks her head when she spies Una Mickle. Bonnie calls her 'Yoo-hoo Una', which makes Irene snort and feel bad at the same time. She and Una have their differences, but they go back a long way. Head down, she propels Ashlee away from the volunteers. If Una bails her up, Flo's Kitchen might as well close for the day.

'Yoo-hoo! Irene!'

Irene forces her shoulders not to slump as she stops and turns. 'Hi, Una. Can't talk now. Running late.'

Una nods understandingly, as if Irene's always late, not because she has a child slowing her down. Then she looks down at Ashlee and her lips purse. 'I see Bonnie went up north, after all.'

'Yes.' Irene lowers her voice. 'Left a couple of days ago.'

Una tuts. 'Mothers didn't leave their children for a job in our day.'

'Men did. Still do.'

'That's different.'

'Is it?'

Una glares. 'I can see you're in a bit of a mood,' she sniffs. 'While I've got you, I wanted to ask about your new neighbours.'

Irene's gossip radar is well and truly tuned when it comes to Una Mickle and right now it's beeping frantically: *warning, gossip ahead!*

'Isn't that the mayor?' Irene asks, pointing and grinning when Una's head whips around. Works every time. Without wasting a second, she steers Ashlee away as fast as the little girl's legs will allow.

By the time the gates open, Irene's sweating. Flo's Kitchen is open for business, but only just. She's dying for a strong flat white, but she's stuck here for the next few hours. Tea from the thermos it is. Pouring a steaming mugful, she puts it aside to cool. Thank goodness Ashlee's happily occupied with her iPad. Forgot she was hungry as soon as Irene produced the darned thing. When Bonnie first came home with it, Irene was unimpressed. 'Children should be playing with toys, not looking at screens', she'd said. Now, she is grateful for small mercies.

Within minutes, the first customer appears and after that, it's a steady flow. Despite the cold weather, locals and brave visitors have turned out en masse to stock up on supplies from farmers around the region. Organic and free-range meats; cheeses and yoghurts; extra virgin olive oils; raw food treats; pastries and artisan breads; preserves, jam and honey; cordials and juices; and colourful tables of fruit and vegetables.

Irene was on the committee that established the market and not a week goes past that she doesn't feel proud of what Blackwood has to offer. People are everywhere, greeting acquaintances and friends, chatting with the vendors about the provenance of their products, and passing on tips and recipes. Watching them, Irene reaches out and ruffles Ashlee's hair. All those worries and grumbles for nothing. Between them, they'll figure it out.

She's making a sale when she recognises her new neighbour standing off to one side, sunglasses pushed on top of her head, scrutinising the label on a jar of apricot jam. Irene pulls her shoulders back. She's proud of her jam. She gets the fruit from her own trees and local farmers, and there's no artificial colours or flavourings. No additives or preservatives. It's a bit of a science getting the timing and quantities right, or magic, as her old friend Flo used to say on jam day.

Irene watches from the corner of her eye as the younger woman samples the jam. When the woman smiles, Irene feels a smile curve across her own face. *She likes it.* There's nothing like that first zing of fruity goodness eaten straight from a spoon, and that apricot jam is fragrant, bursting with summery flavour, not too sweet.

'I believe you're my next-door neighbour. Amy, isn't it? I'm Irene.' She grins. 'We meet at last. Was starting to think you were avoiding me.' Irene's joking, but the younger woman rears back. A fleeting look of alarm crosses her face. Something about her expression sparks a flicker of recognition so indistinct Irene wonders if she imagined it. 'Sorry, love, I startled you.'

'No, no, it's fine,' Amy says, pulling her sunglasses down. 'I wasn't avoiding … I've just been so busy …' She starts again, indicating the label on the jar she's holding. 'Irene? Not Flo?' She's smiling now, but Irene picks up a wary undercurrent, as if she's a soldier standing at attention while blending into the background. Why else the sunglasses this early on a winter's day?

'Flo? Me? Oh, no,' Irene laughs. 'No, Flo Thompson was my best friend. Your house used to be hers, you know. Many an hour I spent in Flo's kitchen, back in the day. The jam recipes,' she waves her arms at the display, 'were hers. Flo guarded them with her life, but when she got sick, she gave them to me. I keep Flo's kitchen alive by making these jams. Can't always fix the heart, but it keeps the hands busy.'

Amy gives her a curious look, as if she's heard something like that before. 'I like that way of putting it.' Wariness returns. 'Sorry, how do you know my name? The only neighbour I've met is … Bonnie. That's it. And her little girl. Ash …'

'Ashlee. My great-granddaughter. Bonnie's my granddaughter. They live with me. And to answer your question, apart from them mentioning you, I've heard your name around Blackwood a few times. You're opening a new café soon, aren't you?' Before Amy can answer, Ashlee scoots from under the table and tugs on their neighbour's coat. That child goes deaf at bedtime, but the second you say her name, she's all ears.

'You live next door to me,' Ashlee says to Amy. 'I came to your house and you dropped a box on your foot and said a rude word.'

Irene doesn't miss the sad expression that flits across Amy's face before she squats to Ashlee's eye level and lifts her sunglasses. 'Yes, you did. Sorry about the rude word.'

'That's okay. Jake says it all the time. I'm four.' Ashlee holds up three fingers and squints with searching eyes. 'Do you have any little girls like me?'

Amy's eyes squeeze tight before answering. 'No,' she says. 'I don't have a little girl.'

In that moment, Irene knows she and Amy Bennet have more in common than a dividing fence. Grief has engraved *not anymore* across her pale face. It's an expression Irene knows well. She was midway through a grief counselling course when Ashlee was born and although she didn't finish it, she can spot a woman who's lost a child a mile off. That's what she recognised earlier.

Ashlee's face falls briefly, then brightens as another question forms. 'Why not?'

Amy clears her throat. 'Um—'

'Look, Ash! Look at the worm! On your chair,' Irene breaks in, relieved when Ashlee dives under the table. One of these days that old chestnut won't work anymore. As Amy straightens, Irene reaches for the younger woman's hand. Their eyes meet in an exchange of understanding as brief as a breaking wave before Irene plucks a tissue from a box and passes it over. 'Here.'

'Thanks.' Amy dabs at her eyes, then draws her shades down, breaking their connection. Thrusting two jam jars and a debit card towards Irene, she says, quickly, 'I'll take these, thanks.' Her arms are crossed in front of her, fingers drumming, like she's desperate to get away but tethered by courtesy. 'Perhaps we can chat sometime about supplying Brewed to Taste, my café. It opens in a couple of weeks.'

'I'd love that.' Flo would be beside herself with pride. Fancy that!

'Reenie!' Ashlee pokes Irene in the side. Hard. 'There's no worm, Reenie,' she says. 'I looked and looked.' Her brows knit when Irene starts to laugh. 'It's not funny!'

When she looks up, her neighbour has gone.

Sharon Thompson and her feral trio pounce the second Amy leaves. They appear nearly every fortnight for free tastes, but Irene can't remember Sharon coughing up for a single jar. The kids aren't that bad, really, and the oldest two don't double dip anymore. One time she had to throw out three jars. All that waste and their mother didn't say a word. She hasn't bothered to rein her kids in since their dad moved to Bunbury and shacked up with someone else. Flo would have been mortified by her son's behaviour, even if she never did warm to Sharon. But still. Sharon needs to lift her game, for her kids' sakes.

As Sharon casually picks up jars, Irene tunes into gossip radio. Sharon's a chip off the old block, the spit of her mother Una at the same age, with the same nose for sniffing out people's dirty linen. Una tells everyone her daughter's a journalist, but that's stretching it. Sharon works as a part-time receptionist for the *Blackwood Gazette*, putting through calls and taking classifieds for what's politely called adult services. The editor only lets her take social pictures at the markets because he and the journo commute back to Bunbury on weekends. On cue, Sharon swings around and lifts her phone to snap a photo of something that's caught her eye.

When she turns back, wearing an expression she inherited from her mother, Irene cringes internally. *Of course. She's here for information.* Should have guessed by the way Sharon's faffing around. The kids are a cover, so it doesn't look bleeding obvious what she wants.

Irene plays dumb. 'How are you today, Sharon? Can I help you with something? That strawberry jam your young man's tucking into goes down a treat with pikelets. Oi! Sticks in the bin, young man.'

Ashlee stirs and Irene sends a prayer upwards. *Please God, let her stay still.* Irene hasn't been to church much since the markets started three years ago. It upset a few of her friends, but she reckons God's okay with it. If not, today's not the day to let her know.

'Just looking, thanks Irene,' Sharon says automatically.

'Leave you to it then.' Her eyes flit sideways. Ashlee hasn't moved and her eyes are glued to her screen, but the way her mouth twists to the side means she's on guard. She doesn't like Sharon's youngest, the worst double dip offender of the lot. 'Use a clean stick, darl,' Irene says firmly to the little boy.

'He's not *darl*,' Ashlee mutters behind her.

Irene's gaze drifts towards the coffee van, where a snaking line puts paid to her hopes of dashing over for a flat white. If Bonnie was here, Irene would be washing down a croissant with her second coffee right about now. And she wouldn't be dreading four little words from her great-granddaughter: *I have to wee*. Or worse. Her fingers tap the table. What she needs is an alternative action plan before the next market. Someone to help her out on market days for the next year. Maybe her friends could do a roster.

'Actually,' Sharon says, loudly, as if she's been trying to get Irene's attention. 'Couldn't help but notice you were talking to your new neighbour just now.'

'That's what neighbours do, Sharon. Talk to each other.' They used to, anyway. Up in the city, they reckon you're lucky to know your neighbour's name.

Sharon's lips purse. 'I've been wondering … her face is familiar. I've seen her before, I know it. Before she moved here, I mean. Just can't place her yet.' A sly smile. 'Any clue?'

'Nope. Sorry.' Irene remembers the faint flicker of recognition when she met Amy. Has she seen her face before? Or has Sharon put the idea in her head? Either way, Sharon can do her digging some-where else. Turning away, she addresses a woman who's squinting at the label on a jar of lemon butter. 'Hello! Would you like a taste?'

'No, thanks.' The woman walks away.

Irene thinks she might swipe the smirk off Sharon's face with one quick flick of the wrist. She raises her eyes to the sky and sends another message: *Make her go away*. Nothing happens. And then it does, and Irene's convinced someone's having a laugh up there.

'Yoo-hoo, Sharon. I've been looking for you everywhere. I've got those almond croissants you wanted. Lucky last. And a coffee. Watch out, it's hot.'

Irene muffles a groan as Una blows in like a cyclone and passes a takeaway cup to her daughter. The coffee smells good. She wants to snatch the cup from Sharon's hands. And the croissant Sharon's biting into.

Una carries on as if Irene's invisible. 'Kai, stop kicking your sister. Tyler, I'm sure you've had enough jam.' She spits on a tissue and wipes her grandson's face before turning to Sharon. 'I'll drop you off and then head to church unless you want to join me. No? Probably better to get the kids home, I think. They need a good clean up, don't they.'

Sharon rolls her eyes, but Una doesn't seem to notice. 'Have you got any raspberry jam, Irene? Oh, here it is. You can barely see it behind all these jumbled up jars. They need a bit of a tidy, don't they. No bag, that's fine. Goodness me, Irene, that child will get square eyes if she looks at the screen all morning, won't she.'

'Will not,' Ashlee mutters, indignantly, not looking up.

Una and Sharon drift away, still talking. Tidying the display Sharon's pesky kids messed up, Irene tries not to eavesdrop, but it's hard not to when they're barely two metres away and bellowing like foghorns.

'Mum? Can you take the kids this afternoon? I really need a break for a few hours.'

'Can't do, Sharon. I've got church,' Una says, directing a sideways glance at Irene, 'and then I've got a meeting about the Spring Festival this afternoon.'

Irene avoids Una's pointed gaze. She can't make the meeting because Ashlee's going to a birthday party at an alpaca farm.

'What about after that?' Sharon presses.

'Not today, Sharon. I'm busy. I've got my own life, you know.'

Finally, they move away. Irene slumps into her camp chair. Una might drive her spare, but Irene envies the woman's ability to set boundaries with her daughter. *I've got my own life, you know.* What would Bonnie have done if Irene had said that?

'Reenie? Can we go to the park?'

'Not yet, love.'

'But I've been waiting and waiting. I want to play.'

'Soon, love.'

'I'm hungry.'

'Eat your apple.'

'I'm not hungry for apple. I want chippies.'

'I'll get you some when we go home, okay, love?'

'Now!'

'No,' Irene snaps. 'Not yet. Soon. Later. When the market's finished.'

Ashlee starts to cry. 'I want to go home. I miss Mummy.' Snotty sobs rack her little body.

Gathering her great-granddaughter onto her lap, Irene makes a decision. She'll round up her friends to help at the markets. And she'll do her best to fill in the mother-gap for Ashlee. But after that, she's going to set some boundaries. Take a leaf out of Una's book and get her own life before it's too late. Bonnie will have to deal with it. If Sharon can, Bonnie can.

Irene holds a trembling child in her arms and ignores the sudden twinge of her bladder. Why does she feel like a selfish cow?

CHAPTER ELEVEN
AMY

'Come to the pub with us, Amy,' sous chef Devi pleads, eyes shiny and dark as coals.

'Not this time, guys. You go ahead. I've still got a few things to do.' After a jam-packed morning of team building and training, Amy wants a few minutes alone. Brewed to Taste opens in less than twenty-four hours, and her staff have no idea she's freaking out on the inside. She waves them off and slumps into one of the café chairs, massaging her temples with both hands. What if she's forgotten something? What if no one turns up?

'Amy? Got a minute?' Her head chef is standing in the café door-way, concern etched on his face.

'Nick! You scared me! I could have sworn you left with the others. Is something wrong?' She pushes her glasses up her nose, affecting a professionalism her jumping heart belies. Why does she assume the worst when someone wants to talk to her?

'No, no. Can I sit?' At her nod, he folds long legs under the table. 'I wanted to ask you something that's been playing on my mind.' He pauses so long her eyebrows lift in a gentle nudge. 'Are you sure you're okay with me being head chef?'

'Of course.' It's not entirely true. Not even Matt knows how much she's agonised over this. 'Why do you ask?'

'I know you used to be a chef. And when we were working on the menus, it was obvious how much you know about food. How much you love working with it. And yet,' he hesitates, 'I think by giving *me* the job, you're holding yourself back. And it makes me wonder why.'

Amy meets his gaze. His blue eyes pierce like lasers; she has this strange feeling that Nick can read her better than she can read him. Better than she wants him to. Disconcerted, she looks away. How can she explain her choice without revealing herself? They've been working side by side on the menu for two weeks but he's barely more than a stranger. He doesn't need to know that thinking too much about being out front makes her want to retch.

Her fingers drum her knee as she works out what to say. After seven weeks in Blackwood, no one recognises her from before. No one looks at her twice, apart from that woman in the pharmacy, and she's only seen her from a distance. Bonnie and Irene next door are curious in a friendly, get-to-know-you-over-the-fence kind of way. Nothing that makes her feel threatened. She's become so comfortable she rarely has the urge to hide behind dark glasses. It's the opposite in Perth. There, anonymity disappeared after the media got involved. But how long will her luck hold out? What if someone sees her for who she is?

Her eyes close. Nick's right. She's playing a game of smoke and mirrors and hoping no one will puff the smoke away. But it's necessary to make the café work. She's the owner, not an employee. That's what she told Matt and it's what she tells Nick now.

'Not at all. I need to be out front. How else can I keep an eye on everything?' She laughs. When he doesn't join in but keeps penetrating eyes trained on her, she adds, quickly, 'It's the right thing.'

Nick waits. Then, 'Why did you buy the café?'

'Why didn't you buy it?'

'Not enough money. Your turn. Was it because you can't imagine yourself not working with food? Or something else?'

She decides to lay her cards on the table. 'Truth is, Nick, I needed something to do. Something to wake—' she pauses mid-sentence, knowing she's close to revealing more cards than she wants, 'something to look forward to. And hospitality is what I do. What I used to do. It's a no-brainer.'

As if he can read her thoughts, Nick says: 'I get that. I do. I was in a bad way when I moved here. Devi and I, it wasn't easy being … being us. That's a whole other story. But sometimes you need something to help you see the light through the dark.'

She is silent and after a long moment, he fills the space. 'The people who owned this before, they were the same. Ran a string of successful cafés up in Perth. But because of what brought them here, they were missing something: passion. And I sense that in you too. You put up a good front, but I can see past it.'

She finds she can't look at him. Picks up a menu. Scans it like a proofreader on fast forward.

'I don't mean to pry. Or make you uncomfortable. All I'm wondering is if you can find your passion, the deep down one that makes you feel alive, if you're out front. Whether you need to be cooking to find it. Whether you can let go of whatever is holding you back. Or else Brewed to Taste will be flavoured by something that's missing rather than something that's vital. And I want to see this succeed. I have a feeling about this place.'

'As do I. But I have to do this my way,' she tells him, meeting his gaze. 'Whatever that means right now.'

Nick's eyes trace her face like a torch seeking in the dark. 'Okay. I've got your back. But, Amy? If you need to talk, I'm happy to listen.'

She nods, terrified to open her mouth. If she does, she won't be able to stop what comes out.

But his words burn long after he leaves.

Can you let go of what is holding you back?

Nick's words still ring of subtext, of something lying beneath the surface, of emotional coding, as if he understands her more than he should. Amy can't shake the feeling he was urging her to find a passion for more than cooking. As if he knows she's barely holding on from one day to the next. But how? How does he know this?

Does he know who she really is?

Does he know what she did?

The questions stalk her as she locks up. They shout at her, crowding her mind; she pushes them away, but they fight back, forcing the issue. Her head pounds as a scream wells from unfathomable depths. Her breathing quickens.

You've got this.

She repeats the mantra until her breathing slows. Scans the café, taking in the welcoming space. Breathes in the lingering scent of coffee and food. And then she reaches into her bag and retrieves a tattered drawing from her purse. Stares at it for a moment. Kisses it. Takes a deep breath.

We've got this.

'Yoo-hoo, Amy. Yoo-hoo.' Una Mickle waves from across the road, her brassy-haired daughter at her side.

Amy toys with pretending she didn't hear, but it's too late; they're crossing the road, and now they're in front of her, eyes roving over the signage on the window. It's as if they were lying in wait.

'I see your little café is opening tomorrow,' Una says. 'Brewed to Taste. Interesting name, isn't it, Sharon?'

Ignoring her mother, Sharon's small, sharp eyes move from Amy to the café façade. Amy fights the urge to don her sunglasses. 'I haven't seen anything on Facebook.'

Amy turned her back on Facebook after Pandora died. The social media backlash during the investigation left her a quivering mess every time she went online. Blame, speculation, hate – for every compassionate response there was a nasty one stirring things up.

'Don't read the comments,' Matt had urged. But like rubberneckers drawn to an accident, she couldn't *not* look, until one day she couldn't take anymore and deleted her account.

It wasn't just the trolls. Old school friends tracked her down and messaged her directly, hiding curiosity behind superficial sympathy for someone they no longer knew. Amy didn't want to be tracked down, didn't want to be Facebook friends with people she had nothing in common with but faded school memories. Why should they be privy to her life?

'I'm a bit behind with social media,' she says to Sharon now. 'Passing trade and word of mouth will be enough to start.'

'What, not even Instagram?' Sharon looks unconvinced. 'What about advertising? I work at the local paper. I can sort that for you.'

'Maybe down the track. See how it goes first.' Amy smiles at her potential customers, despite the gnawing in her gut. 'You'll have to stop in for a coffee and cake some time. See if my chocolate cake measures up to yours, Una.'

'Hmmm. I'll have to check my diary,' Una says, her voice cool. 'Goodness me, I'm so busy these days, what with the CWA, the Spring Garden Festival committee, church, and babysitting Sharon's lot.'

Whatever she says, Amy has the feeling Una has every intention of scoping out the café and cake as soon as she can.

Sharon rolls her eyes. 'Once a week after school, Mum.'

'Once a week bare minimum, more like. You'd leave them with me every afternoon if you could, Sharon. Always expecting me to—'

'As if! You always exag—'

Amy is inching backwards for a silent getaway when she hears her name.

'Now, now, Sharon. Amy doesn't want to hear our bickering, do you, Amy?'

'Oh, don't worry about it.' Her fingers twitch on her bag straps. 'But I really must get going. Still a lot to do before we open in the morning.' It's not true, but as an excuse, it's as good as any.

You don't need the sunnies. Smoke and mirrors.

Una tuts. 'Still? Dear me, that's leaving it a bit late, isn't it?'

'Not everyone is as anal as you, Mum.' Sharon trains her flinty gaze on Amy once more. 'You know, Mum and I have been saying, your face is so familiar. But we can't place you.'

Amy slips on her sunglasses. 'One of those unremarkable faces, I guess.'

'Yeah, it is, but I'm sure I know you from somewhere. It'll come to me.' Sharon pauses to twist up her bun, which has come loose in the wind. 'Can I interview you for the *New in Town* page of the paper? Find out what brought you here and so on? Our readers love getting to know newcomers.' A sly look passes between mother and daughter.

Una nods. 'Oh yes, Sharon. Great idea, don't you think, Amy? A nice bit of exposure?'

'No thanks, Sharon. I'm more of a behind-the-scenes person.' Suspecting she's only encouraged Sharon's curiosity, Amy regrets the words as soon as they're out.

Driving home, Amy recalls hearing that Sharon's ex-in-laws were the former owners of Amy's house. It disturbs her to think of Sharon in there, even if it was long before it was Amy's house. But knowing Sharon is a reporter at the local paper is worse.

Tension is a vice around her forehead, squeezing so hard she can barely think. What if Sharon works out who she is?

CHAPTER TWELVE
AMY

Before Pandora died, Amy relied on breadmaking for stress relief. The methodical kneading of dough by hand hypnotised her with the soft push-pull rocking motion. After Pandora died, kneading dough didn't have the same effect. How could she make bread when their daughter was dead? It was something the two of them liked to do together, connecting them in the same way it had Amy and her grandmother. Now, as she swallows two painkillers, she decides to try once more. Matt loves her rosemary and sea salt focaccia. It's the perfect accompaniment to the venison *osso bucco* she has planned.

An hour later, Amy places a plump ball of dough into the proving drawer and stretches her arms overhead. The methodical movements worked their magic; the tension of earlier has dissipated, or at least, faded. She's scrubbing her flour-crusted hands when there's a knock at the back door. She wants to ignore it, but the knocking is insistent. Sighing, Amy pads to the door and unlocks the latch. Matt says no one locks the back door here, but it's a city habit she can't seem to break.

'Hello!' Ashlee bellows.

'Hi, Ashlee.' Amy peers past her. 'Does your mum know you're here?'

'No. She's flying in a plane to work. It's a long, long way up there.' She points up.

'That's right.' Irene mentioned Bonnie's FIFO job during one of their quick chats out the front, like it was no big deal. Amy still thinks it's a strange set-up, and harder than Irene makes out. Surely at her age it's got to be tougher looking after a child than when you're in your twenties and thirties. Amy can't even imagine being responsible for a child again. She wasn't a good enough mother first time around. Who is she to judge someone else? 'Does Irene know you're here?'

'No, but Reenie does.' The little girl stares at Amy with hopeful eyes. 'Reenie said I was allowed to bring you some biscuits. I made them all by myself. Reenie said I could give you four but I already eated one.' She pushes a plastic bowl towards Amy that contains two lumpy choc-chip biscuits. A self-conscious smile flits across the little girl's crumb-freckled face.

That smile. That innocent face smeared with chocolate. The sticky fingers holding out a bowl. Amy's throat throbs with words she can't express. *Go home.*

Take the damn biscuits, Amy.

Amy squats. 'They look yummy.'

'They *are* yummy.' Ashlee pushes a biscuit between Amy's lips; it teases her with its sweet, chocolatey smell. 'Eat it.'

Amy has no choice. 'You were right,' she says through a mouthful. 'These bickies are very yummy.'

Ashlee beams. 'I know. I told you. Why have you got white stuff all over your face? You look like a ghost.'

Amy wipes her face. Flour. 'I've been making bread. It's messy work—'

'Mummy doesn't look dirty when she comes home from work. She's clean and she smells nice.'

Thanks. Amy resists the urge to sniff her armpits. Surely she's not *that* bad.

'I don't like it when Mummy goes to work. Why does Mummy have to go to work? Why can't she stay home with me?'

Pandora asked the same questions once. They're no easier to

answer now. How do you explain to a four-year-old that you *need* to work; not for the money, but because it's part of who you are? How do you explain the tearing feeling when you leave your child at day care? It was hard enough justifying her choice to Matt when she went back part-time, let alone her old-fashioned grandmother. Everyone had an opinion about working mothers then, and she suspects it's no different now. Didn't she have her own about Bonnie not five minutes earlier?

'That's a very good question,' she says, carefully. 'It's good to talk about these things, but you should probably ask your mum. Maybe you can go and ask her right—'

'I told you. She's gone to work on a plane. Can I have a hot Milo? I love Milo. It's my favourite.' She ducks around Amy's legs.

Amy's mouth drops open. 'I don't … I don't think I have any.'

'No Milo?' Ashlee turns a horrified gaze on her. 'Everyone has Milo. Why don't you have Milo?'

'I don't—' How does this child get Amy so tongue-tied?

'I know.' Ashlee tilts her head understandingly. 'It's because you haven't got any little girls like me. Or little boys. That's why you haven't got Milo.' She pats Amy's arm. 'Don't worry. I'll fix it. Wait here.'

Moments later, the little girl is back. Baffled more than irritated by the child's persistence, Amy opens the door. Ashlee bursts in as though she was leaning on it. Out of breath and red-cheeked, she thrusts a giant can of Milo towards Amy. 'I fixed you.'

Perched on a stool, Ashlee keeps up a constant stream of chatter about her 'very, very naughty' friend Henry, pausing only to instruct Amy. Amy can't help smiling to herself as she heats milk on the stove; it's not like she's never made the malty drink before.

Reaching for two mugs, her breath catches when she recognises a two-handled cup with Beatrix Potter kittens on it. How did that get in here? She sets it aside to pack away – out of sight, out of mind – but Ashlee spies it.

'I want my drink in the cat cup,' she says, eyes round.

Amy finds she can't say no. Biting her lip, she grates dark chocolate on top of the warm drink. 'Be careful, Ashlee, it's hot,' she says, placing the mug in front of her visitor.

'I like this cat cup. I've got a cat. He used to be a kitten, you know, but now he's a cat. Have you got a cat?'

'No.'

'You should have a cat.' Ashlee gives an emphatic nod. 'You look like a cat lady.'

Amy chokes on her drink. 'I look like a cat lady?'

'Yes. You look like someone who likes cats. Otherwise you wouldn't have a cat cup, would you?'

Ashlee polishes off her drink with a loud slurp, and jumps off the stool, wiping her mouth on the back of her hand. 'I'll come back later. Don't forget to write Milo on your shopping list.'

Back in the kitchen, Amy decides not to pack away Pandora's cat cup. Yet.

Later, *osso bucco* is in the oven, filling the kitchen with the smell of winter; a simmering mix of meat, tomatoes and vegetables. On the kitchen table a circle of dough rests on a baking sheet, awaiting the finishing touches before baking: fresh rosemary, olive oil, and sea salt flakes. Reaching for kitchen scissors, Amy heads outside for rosemary sprigs. The cooling air smells of damp earth. Magpies warble in the pale light, their afternoon melody rising on the air. Fairy wrens flit from branch to branch as Amy moves through the garden, mentally noting things to do. Weed. Trim. Pick lemons and oranges. Discard fallen fruit. Prepare the vegetable beds. And then there are the roses out the front, long overdue for their winter prune. She pictures Gran's horror at their wild state. When will she find the time to tend the garden the way it deserves?

In the distance, forestry log trucks rumble through town. Amy's used to them now – they roll up and down the main street, past Brewed to Taste, day after day. She no longer wishes she was aboard a semi, driving out of town, out of her sad life. Instead, she's planning a celebratory dinner with her husband, on the eve of her café's grand opening.

'Amy!' Ashlee roars from behind. She's holding a placid, extra-large cat around its stomach. It's wearing a pink collar and a frilly bonnet, and seems used to being carted around like a living teddy bear. 'This is Flossie. Flossie is my cat.'

'Wow! She's a nice big cat.' Amy snips three sprigs of rosemary. 'Are you supposed—'

'Flossie is not a *girl*. He's a *boy* cat,' Ashlee cuts in.

'Oh. Silly me.'

'You can't help it. I'm thirsty. I want some milk in the cat cup again, please.'

Oh, she's good, Amy thinks. This kid has figured out how to get what she wants, albeit in a frustratingly disarming manner. Pandora had Matt twisted around her little finger too. 'Come on then.'

'Flossie too. He likes milk.' She heaves Flossie up the steps and shoots Amy an expectant look.

'Fine. Flossie too.'

Inside, Amy half-fills the cat cup with milk, and swishes a few drops into a saucer for the cat. 'Does Irene – Reenie – know where you are?'

'I told her when she was on the toilet.' Ashley gulps her milk. When she speaks again, a milk moustache decorates her upper lip. 'Henry is very, very naughty. She's always chasing Flossie.'

'Does Henry chase Flossie much?' Amy asks, smiling at Ashlee's cute habit of mixing up he and she.

'Oh, all the time.' Ashlee dismisses the problem with a little wave. 'One time, Henry bit Flossie on the bum!' She giggles into her cup. 'Flossie was very, very mad. He hissed at Henry like this.' She makes a hissing noise, spraying milk over the bench.

Amy can't imagine anyone trying to bite a cat's bum. Who does Henry belong to? Sharon Thompson? It wouldn't surprise her if Sharon's kids were biters.

'But Henry's nice to you?' she asks.

'Oh, yes. Henry's my best friend. I have to take Flossie home now.

Next time I'm having my milk with lots and lots of Milo bits floating on the top so I can—'

'So you can eat them with a spoon,' Amy finishes, smiling at Ashlee.

They jump when Irene pokes her head through the back door, pink-cheeked and puffing. 'Ashlee Knight! I've been looking for you everywhere, you little rascal. I thought we were playing hide and seek.'

Ashlee giggles. 'I'm a good hider. I tricked you.'

Irene shakes her head in mock frustration. 'Sorry, Amy. Come on, miss, time to go.'

'Do you have time for a cuppa?' Amy offers, surprising herself.

'I do!' Ashlee shouts.

Half an hour later, Amy waves them goodbye and returns to her cooking, and reflects on the afternoon. Ashlee's a handful. So much like Pandora at that age, and yet completely her own person. The first time she saw Ashlee, it cut deep. Now, when she looks at Ashlee, she thinks *Pandora used to do that, Pandora would have loved a cat called Flossie and a friend called Henry*. The memories don't hurt like they used to. It's more like an ever-present ache, rather than a sharp soul-cut.

The dough is ready. Amy creates pockets in the dough with her fingertips. Olive oil, roughly chopped rosemary leaves, flaked sea salt crushed between her fingers, and yet more olive oil complete the topping. While the focaccia bakes, she finely chops flat-leaf parsley and grates lemon zest and garlic cloves for a gremolata. Only when Amy finally allows herself to relax with a cup of Earl Grey does worry nibble at the edges of her mind.

She's getting used to life in a small town. But she can't help feeling that something is not right. That something is aligning behind the scenes and her new life is about to come under fire.

CHAPTER THIRTEEN
MATT

M att has a secret. It eats at him slowly, constantly, creeping like mould. He'll burst if he holds it in much longer.

'Work wants me to go overseas,' he tells his mother in his lunch break. 'To a conference later this year. December.'

'Where?' Her tone is cautious, as if she suspects the worst.

'Germany.'

There's a small gasp, then silence. Matt imagines her clenching her mobile, mouth twitching. 'Have you told them what happened there?'

'No. They don't need to know. And it's not definite yet.'

'What will you do?' Helen says after a pause.

'I don't know, Mum. I don't know. I've known about the possibility for a week now, but I have no idea what to do.'

'Have you talked to Amy?'

'Not yet.'

'You need to tell her.'

'I will,' he promises. 'How's Dad?'

The burden of secrecy keeps him awake at night. His mind loops like a lasso, as he role-plays reactions, casting himself in the antagonistic roles of his employer and Amy. He imagines boarding the plane to the last place he saw his daughter alive, imagines how he'll cope with the rush of emotions attacking his body and soul. Truth is, he's guessing. Maybe he'll be fine. Maybe not.

How can you even consider it?

Amy vowed never to set foot in Germany again, despite her father living there. They were going to visit her father that day. Dom was going to meet his granddaughter for the first time. And Matt was supposed to join them a few days later, after a conference in Düsseldorf. Instead, they had a family reunion in a German hospital, clutching trembling hands around Amy's hospital bed.

She was comatose. Pandora was dead.

At home Matt escapes to the shower so Amy can't see the secret written on his face. He stands under the firm spray so long it takes the bathroom door opening to jolt him from his thoughts.

'Matt? You all right? You've been in there for ages. Twenty minutes at least.' There's a note of reproach in her voice, probably because he always complains about her long showers.

'Was waiting for you to join me.'

A short laugh tells him what she thinks of that. 'Thought you fell asleep in there. I made you coffee. Probably cold now.' The door shuts.

Matt watches the water drain away, until there's nothing left but a damp coating on the tiles. If only his worries would drain away as easily. He towels off, then digs in his drawer for loose pants and a long-sleeved T-shirt.

How can you even consider it?

The idea of going back to Germany scares the hell out of him. Yet part of him wants to go. To do something useful beyond turning up at work on time every day. So why does it feel like a betrayal? Is it so bad to want something for himself?

Freshly baked focaccia rests on a wire rack. A red Dutch oven sits on a trivet. A bold zinfandel from Pemberton is decanting on the table. Matt breathes in the intoxicating smells, fighting the urge to break off a piece of bread and shove it in his mouth, then wraps his arms around his wife. Yesterday Amy pushed him away. Not today.

'How are you feeling?' he says into her neck.

'Exhausted,' she says, leaning back into him. 'Excited. Freaked out. Can't believe we're opening tomorrow.'

'It's going to be fine. Blackwood will love Brewed to Taste.'

'Are you sure you can't be there?' Amy shifts in his arms. Not much, but enough to signal her disappointment.

'I would if I could.' He's leaving at the crack of dawn for a meeting in Perth and picking up Carla and two other team members on the way. Carla, who is definitely going to the conference in Germany, and has put his name forward to jointly represent the company. Abruptly, Matt pulls away from Amy, picks up the zinfandel and pours a smidge into an oversized wineglass. The wine is dark and brooding on the nose, like a brandy-soaked Christmas pudding. The palate is sweet and savoury: spice and candied fruits. The perfect pairing for Amy's *osso bucco*.

'How was work?' Amy asks, pulling two plates from a cupboard.

'Good.' He's not lying. Just holding back.

'Hungry?'

'Starving.'

Amy scoops buttery mash onto plates, then spoons the rich, meaty casserole on top. She brings them to the table as Matt half-fills two wine glasses. He hands one to her. 'To Brewed to Taste.'

'Cheers.' She sips slowly, swishing the wine around her mouth. He suddenly wants to kiss her. But is it out of guilt or desire? Oblivious, she says, 'Perfect. I was worried the *osso bucco* would overpower a zin, but this one holds its own.'

Over dinner, they talk about Ashlee, Una and Sharon. Mostly, they talk about Brewed to Taste. Matt keeps Amy talking by asking question after question. She's more than happy to indulge him. He tells her about one of the guys at work who fell asleep at his desk only to have his photo snapped and turned into an internet meme by someone in IT. Her throaty giggle sends a warm rush through him. God, he loves that laugh.

The only thing they don't talk about is Matt's secret. It divides them like the Great Wall of China. Eats at him while he polishes off a second serving of the stew. Gnaws at him while they finish the bottle of wine in front of the fire. But he can't tell her now, not when she's so excited and nervous about Brewed to Taste. He doesn't want to burden her with his problems, especially when nothing's definite.

But what if there is no battle? If she takes it in her stride, accepting that work is work, you do what you have to? It's possible. One good thing about Amy being distracted lately is that her up-and-down moods have flattened out. Sure, the antidepressants and the physio she's been seeing for her hip have helped, but she won't need either much longer at this rate. Having a purpose has worked wonders. But Matt knows he's kidding himself. Amy believes work is work, but not when it means revisiting where their daughter was killed.

How am I going to tell her?

Matt's eyes snap open but he can't see. His pulse is racing and he's breathing like he's run a marathon. It takes a moment to realise he's in bed. It's 4.30 and the room is pitch dark. He's woken from a dream, but all he can remember is a feeling of despair that's squeezed the air from him. He lies unmoving until his pulse slows. Then he fumbles in the dark for his clothes, slips out of the bedroom and into the bath-room, and stands under the shower until the despair lifts. After towelling off and dressing in a business shirt and trousers, he stares at his prematurely grey-streaked hair and bleary eyes. When will the dreams stop?

Moments later he's surprised to find Amy in the kitchen, rugged up in a fluffy dressing-gown and stirring milk in a small saucepan.

'What are you doing up?' he asks, filling a glass with water.

'I could ask you the same.' She turns tired eyes on him. 'Thought you were leaving at 5.30. You're ready early.'

'Couldn't sleep.'

'Me either. You okay?'

He shrugs. She used to be able to read him. Lately she's been consumed by her café. Does she see him at all? 'Best I can be on limited sleep. You?'

'Honestly? I'm freaking out about the opening. Worried about it all night. Want some hot milk and honey?'

'No, I'll get a coffee on the way.' He swallows a handful of vitamins and leans against the bench. Amy adds honey to her milk. He listens to the spoon clink on the sides of the cup. 'What are you worried for, Aims? It's going to be fine.' He wishes he could say the same for himself. There's a pit in his stomach that's getting deeper by the day. He's hopeless at keeping secrets.

'I don't know. Part of me can hardly believe it's really happening. I mean, I'm opening a café today. The other part of me feels sick to the stomach. Like, I'm actually going to vomit.' She drops the spoon and clutches her belly. 'God, maybe I am sick. Is my head hot?'

'You're not sick,' he says, kissing her forehead. It's cool, but not clammy. 'Don't set yourself up to fail, not now.'

Wind buffets the house and the windows rattle. A sudden burst of rain clatters on the tin roof. 'Shit,' he mutters. 'I hate driving in this weather.'

'Me too.' Her voice is small. Shaky.

'Crap. Sorry, Aims.'

How am I going to tell her?

She swallows. 'It's okay.' She takes her milk to the table and he joins her, trying to hide a yawn. 'Matt, do you think this weather will keep people away? Do you think I should have done more marketing? Was it a bad idea to open on a Wednesday?'

'Aims, it's going to be fine. Breathe.'

'What if someone recognises me?'

'They won't.' He mentally crosses his fingers.

'I just want Brewed to Taste to succeed.'

'It will.'

'It gives me a reason to get up every day. To keep going.' She blows on the milk and takes a tentative sip. 'You're right, I'm worrying too much. The café's fully stocked. The kitchen's prepped. Coffee's ready to grind. I've made a flourless chocolate cake, Persian love cake, and three types of muffins. All I have to do is make a ganache for the chocolate cake.' She ticks off each item on a different finger.

'See. You've got this.' His head spins and suddenly he can't wait to leave. To talk to someone else about anything but the café.

'You always say that. What if you're wrong?'

'I'm not.' He yawns, big and wide.

'It's a pity you have to go away.'

Matt gives her a sharp look. Has his mum said something to her?

'What?' she says. 'I'm not trying to make you feel guilty for not coming to the opening. I meant, since you're so tired, it's a pity you have to drive to Perth and back in a day. That job's got a lot more travel than you expected.'

You don't know the half of it. 'I'll be fine. I've done it before, remember.'

'True.' When Amy drains the last of her milk, Matt stares at the cup in shock. 'What?' she says, again.

'Since when did you start using Pandora's cup?'

She looks at the cup like she's seeing it for the first time. 'Didn't even realise I was. Found it in the cupboard yesterday when Ashlee came over.' She smiles. 'It feels kind of nice, using it.'

Matt looks away, unsure how to take that. How can Amy use their daughter's cup but refuse to display a single photo? Seemingly oblivious, she gets up to rinse the cup and saucepan. The stretching silence snaps as his chair scrapes against the floorboards. 'I've got to go.'

'Wish me luck,' she says.

'Good luck.' He kisses her cheek. 'I'll see you tonight.'

A gust of wind pounds the house. Amy turns worried eyes on him. 'Drive safe.'

Matt heads out to the car, shivering as cold rain stings his skin, shivering at the memories days like this never fail to awaken.

When am I going to tell her?

CHAPTER FOURTEEN
IRENE

I rene's mobile rings as she's buckling Ashlee into her booster seat. She knows it's Bonnie because of the ringtone. If Irene had her way, she wouldn't bother having a mobile, but Bonnie insisted it was for her safety and bought her a fancy touchscreen model that has her all thumbs. Most days she leaves it at home.

'Hi, Reenie. What are you up to today?'

Breathing heavily, Irene leans against the car. 'Ashlee and I are going to Brewed to Taste. Amy Bennet's café? It opens today.'

'That's right, wish her luck for me. Tell her I'll pop in on the week-end.' When she hesitates, Irene knows her granddaughter wants something. And she has a sinking feeling about what it is.

'I will.'

At that moment, Ashlee pops open her seatbelt and climbs out of the car. 'Mummy? I want to talk to Mummy!'

Sighing, Irene puts the phone on the car roof and grabs the hood of Ashlee's parka to stop the little girl running off. It took her ages to get Ashlee to the car. The little girl's been acting up since Bonnie started FIFO work. Fussing about going to kindy. Sucking her thumb again. Lately, she's been sneaking into Irene's room at night, wanting to sleep with her. Irene doesn't know what to make of it. It's not how things were done when she raised Erin. Kids slept in their own beds, where they belonged.

'In a minute, Ashlee. Get back in the car, there's a good girl.'

'Why do you always get to talk to Mummy first?'

'It's my phone, that's why. In you get.'

'I want a phone and I want to talk to—'

Irene shuts the door. 'I'm back. Been a bit hectic this morning. Thought it was a kindy day.'

'Tell Ashlee I'll FaceTime her tonight. I've got to be quick, Reenie. I'm on a break. Thing is, Jake wants me to stay in Perth tomorrow night when we fly in. You don't mind, do you?'

Irene does mind. She and June planned to go to a book launch tomorrow night. Now she'll have to cancel. Again. 'Well, I do have plans. Can you make it another night?'

'It's our six-month anniversary. Jake's planned it all. Dinner, a fancy hotel, you know.'

Irene would like to stay in a fancy hotel for once in her life, but she says nothing. If Jake's planned it all, it's a done deal. It wouldn't surprise her if Jake arranged it this way on purpose. Last time they were back he whisked Bonnie out for lunch and they were gone the whole day. The next day he took her bushwalking. Irene was supposed to have a break from babysitting, but when she reminded Bonnie, her granddaughter's eyes filled with tears. Is Bonnie scared to upset Jake?

'It's only one night, Reenie,' Bonnie pleads. 'One *more* night. Please?'

Ashlee's blowing raspberries against the car window and drawing pictures in her spit. Clenching the phone, Irene shuts her eyes. 'Ashlee misses you.'

Last night, Ashlee cried for half an hour at bedtime. 'Is Mummy going to die?' she'd asked between sobs. 'Are *you* going to die?' Irene lay beside her until sobs subsided into sleep. Had a sore neck for hours.

She doesn't tell Bonnie any of this, even though she should. It could be a phase.

'I miss her too.' Bonnie's voice is small. 'But, I'll take her to the indoor play centre in Bunbury on Saturday. We'll have the whole day together.'

Not if Jake has anything to do with it, Irene thinks. 'Okay, love. See you Friday afternoon.' Maybe if she let Jake move in, he wouldn't demand so much of Bonnie's time. Irene snorts. And maybe she'd rather run up and down the main street in her undies than have Jake live under her roof.

After Bonnie hangs up, Irene listens to the trees blowing in the wind, their leaves rustling with a thousand voices. Then she climbs into the car and faces her flushed great-granddaughter.

'Let's get a hot chocolate, shall we?' She starts the engine and reverses down the drive, stopping when she hears a little voice from the back seat.

'You forgot my seatbelt, silly.'

It's raining as Irene drives down the main street, but she finds a vacant spot right outside Brewed to Taste. The café door swings open and the smell of coffee registers around the same time she realises Una's coming out the door, umbrella poised for battle. Trust Una to get her nose in first.

'Morning, Irene. Ashlee.' Una gives Ashlee a disapproving look. 'I see the little one's tagging along today. Shouldn't she be at kindy?'

'I'm not little,' Ashlee says, indignantly. She tugs on Irene's arm. 'Why has Mrs Pickle got chocolate on her face?'

Una colours and wipes her face with a hanky. She's the only person Irene knows who carries a hanky instead of tissues.

'No kindy on Wednesdays,' Irene says. It comes out with a wheeze.

'Well, I hope you've got a babysitter for next Wednesday's book club. You chose this month's book, so it's your turn to lead, remember.' Una's pursed lips tell Irene what she thinks of *Gone Girl* by Gillian Flynn.

'Bonnie's back on the weekend. It'll be fine. So, what did you eat in there? Looks like you enjoyed it.' She can't resist the dig, but Una's too busy folding her hanky into a neat square to notice. Irene glimpses a cardboard box with a Brewed to Taste logo poking from Una's bag.

Una rolls her eyes. 'Some kind of flourless chocolate cake. All this gluten-free stuff, I don't know. It's like it's trendy or something. Anyway, it wasn't bad.' She gives Irene a meaningful look: *mine is better.* 'We might as well meet here, since the CWA hall is closed. It's a most inconvenient time for the council to do repairs, what with the fair coming up, but I suppose this place will do. Well, I must be off. Things to do, people to see.'

The clip-clop of her heels on the wet pathway makes Irene's head ring. Una riles her up like no other. Always has, since they first met at a CWA lunch. Both being new brides and new to Blackwood, they'd been seated together; Una all made up, hair expertly waved, while Irene was a makeup-free flower child, all maxi skirt and straight hair parted down the middle. 'I like your skirt,' Una had said, smoothing her perfectly ironed dress. 'The crinkled look suits you.' It was the first of many backhanded compliments.

'Reenie? You said I could have hot chocolate.' Ashlee glares from under a pink child-sized umbrella. 'You promised.'

'Yes, love, you can.'

'Well, why are you standing there, staring at Mrs Pickle? Come on!'

Inside, the café is busy. The blustery weather has enclosed the town in a damp embrace, drawing people indoors. Irene's pleased, for Amy's sake. Her neighbour seemed so nervous about it yesterday. The space undulates with voices that rise and fall above the intermittent grind and hiss of the coffee machine, the clink of cutlery and plates, and swing jazz music that makes Irene's feet tap. The air is cloaked with warming scents of freshly ground coffee, vanilla, apple, orange and cinnamon; Irene's nose twitches at the assault on her senses as she waves to people she knows: Nick, Devi and Troy. She didn't know Frank Taylor's grandson was working here. Fancy that.

Amy's face lights up when Irene greets her at the counter. 'Irene! You came. I'm so glad!'

'And me!'

'Especially you, Miss Ashlee.' Amy moves around the counter and bends forward to talk to Ashlee, hands on knees. 'Does a hot chocolate with extra marshmallows sound good?'

Ashlee beams. 'Can I help?'

'How about you sit at the special table today,' Amy points at a vacant corner table, 'and I bring you a treat?'

'You have a way with the little ones,' Irene observes as her great-granddaughter climbs onto a chair. 'Ashlee really responds to you.'

'Thanks.' Amy's face clouds briefly, then clears as fast as the compliment is dismissed. 'Now, what can I get you? A muffin? Something hot from the kitchen?'

What's her story? Irene wonders this as she orders, then joins Ashlee at their table. It's not the first time she's noticed how swiftly Amy directs the conversation away from herself. *How can I draw her out more?* Irene doesn't want to be a stickybeak, but something tells her Amy needs a friend.

The food arrives. Ashlee's eyes boggle at the hot chocolate loaded with marshmallows and sprinkled with grated chocolate, and crispy hot chips spilling from a paper cone. Irene's coffee is hot and robust, and the chocolate cake looks too good to eat. Drizzled with chocolate sauce and topped with shards of toffee, it's the sort of thing Bonnie would photograph and share with her friends on whatever it is she shares food pictures on. One bite in, Irene changes her mind; this cake is too good *not* to eat. Una's cake doesn't come close to this slice of heaven.

'I knew it,' Una hisses a week later, pulling out a chair opposite Irene and flicking a huffy look at the little girl glued to her iPad. 'Bonnie's taking advantage of you, Irene.' Shaking her head, she opens her handbag and uses her thumb and forefinger like pincers to lift out a pristine copy of *Gone Girl*.

Irene sighs. She'd known this would happen the moment Bonnie called to say she'd been held up at the dentist in Bunbury. But what else was she supposed to do? Host book club at her house, among the piles of washing she's too tired to fold and the toys that won't put themselves away? 'It was unavoidable,' she tells Una, rifling through her bulging handbag for her book. Water bottle. Hand sanitiser. Face wipes. *Ah, here it is. Dog eared and definitely read from cover to cover.* 'And Bonnie's picking up Ashlee on her way home, so it's not for long.'

Una huffs. 'All the same. You take on too much, Irene. Don't think I didn't see you puffing like a steam train earlier. You should see a doctor about that.'

Irene agrees, but keeps it to herself. She's been getting short of breath more often lately. At first she put it down to chasing around an active four-year-old, but sometimes walking around the house is enough to get her puffing. Lord knows how she'll get her garden in shape for the Spring Festival. Maybe she'll need to pay someone, although Sid would have a fit if he were alive, bless him. 'Oh, look, the others are here,' she says, waving four women through French doors separating their large communal table from the main dining area.

Moments later, Amy interrupts their unapologetically book-free chatter. 'Welcome to the Brewed to Taste event space,' she says, handing them menus. 'It's only open on weekends and by arrangement for groups like yours. And some special events I have cooking up here.' She taps her head before adding, 'It's counter service in the main café, but table service in here.'

'Special events ... sounds intriguing,' Irene says. Una's dying to know more, from the furrowed look on her face. Probably thinks Amy should get CWA presidential approval.

'Nothing settled yet.' Amy places jugs of water on the table. 'I'll tell you another time,' she whispers in Irene's ear. Straightening up, she introduces herself to the newcomers. As soon as they've given their orders, Una's CWA friends pepper Amy with questions. Only Una keeps her mouth shut, eyes on Amy the whole time. As if she's waiting for something. As if she's got her underlings to do her dirty work.

'You look familiar, dear,' Margaret Cooper says after a while. 'She does, doesn't she, Una? Where have I seen you before, dear?'

'You're probably mixing me up with a celebrity. People say I look like Emma Watson,' Amy says, with a short laugh that sounds forced.

Irene has no idea who Emma Whatsit is but recalls that Amy had a familiar look when they first met. That must be it.

'Who?' Margaret says. 'I don't know her, do you, Una? Harry Potter? Oh, yes, I've heard of that. The grandies are into it. Not very appropriate for children with all that witchcraft; that's what I tell my daughter, but does she listen?'

Una cuts in. 'Did my Sharon speak to you? About an article with the paper?'

'Not yet,' Amy says smoothly. 'But I'm already doing one with the quarterly paper – you know, the one for tourists. I'll take your orders up.' She heads back to the kitchen.

Una sniffs. 'Sharon would have done a better job than those ring-ins from Bunbury.'

'She's not a journalist though, is she?' Irene points out.

'She could have been, as well you know, Irene.' Sharon's job is a sore point for Una. Years ago, Sharon was supposed to study journalism at uni in Bunbury but fell pregnant with Shane Thompson's baby instead. Una didn't show her face at church for weeks. As for Shane and Sharon, well, Bob Mickle made sure they got married quick smart. Sharon never did get her degree after that.

Irene ignores her and raps on the table with a fork. All eyes are trained on her, even Ashlee's. 'Ladies, I've been dying to talk about *Gone Girl*. Who wants to start? What did you think?' The women reach for their books, all business. Irene searches her bag for her notes. Where did she put them? She sighs when she finds the sheet of paper, crumpled into a ball. When she opens it, fine sand spills onto her lap. How did that get there?

'The book's almost too clever,' June from the bakery says, fitting her reading glasses, 'and it's like the author is playing a game with readers.'

'Hmmph. I didn't think it was clever at all. They were awful people. Married people don't play games with each other,' Una says, with another sniff. Irene knows this to be untrue. And she knows Una doesn't believe it either. The rest of the table might think Una's marriage to Bob was healthy, but Irene saw the bruises. She gave Una a place for a night. They never spoke of it again.

'Don't they?' Irene wonders aloud.

'Course they do,' June puts in. 'They do it to manipulate. Because they want something.'

'They shouldn't,' Una says. 'Anyway, what would you know? You've never been married.'

June rolls her eyes at Irene before answering. 'Don't have to be married to know how relationships work.'

'Harold and I used to play games sometimes,' Margaret says suddenly. 'It was rather fun, all that dressing up.'

Una splutters into her drink, setting off a coughing fit that takes a good smack on the back from Margaret to ease, and Irene directs the conversation to safer pastures. But when Amy appears with their food and drinks, the women's attention is diverted once more.

'Oh, my Lord,' June says to Amy, after tasting the chocolate cake, 'this is to die for.'

'I'm thinking of entering it in the Blackwood show next year.' Amy directs a teasing smile in Una's direction before returning to the counter.

Everyone laughs, except Una, whose lips are pursed as she pushes her half-eaten chocolate cake away. 'Actually, I think it's a bit dry,' she stage whispers to Margaret.

'Someone had sour grapes for breakfast,' June mutters. Then, 'If you don't want that cake, I'll eat it.'

Irene turns her attention to Ashlee, who's curled up in an armchair near the window and tapping on her iPad. The little girl grins widely when Amy crouches down beside her and places a mini choc-chip muffin and a milkshake on the table.

'Mummy's got a sore tooth,' Ashlee informs Amy in a louder than necessary voice because her headphones are still on. Pulling her lips apart, she pokes a finger into her mouth. 'And I've got a wobbly one, but it's not sore unless I do this. Want to feel?'

'No, thanks,' Amy says.

Laughing, Irene turns back to the table. 'Where were we, June?'

'I was just asking what everyone thought of the sex scene between Amy Dunne and Desi Collings?' Irene stifles a grin as June adds, 'Una? What did you think?'

Una's face is as red as her thick, woollen scarf. 'Well, June … as you know, I'm not into sex.' The women dissolve into laughter.

'So your old man used to say,' June quips.

Irene splutters into her drink and shoots a look across to Ashlee. *Good, she's got her headphones on.* The last thing she needs is Ashlee asking her what sex is. No way she's taking on *that* talk for Bonnie.

Una glares, arms folded. 'In books, ladies. I meant, in books. So, I skipped *that* part. All the *inappropriate* parts.' Sotto voce, she adds to Margaret, 'I couldn't stomach the sex. I don't like too much of it.'

'Yep. Bob used to say that too.' June winks at Irene, who knows there's no way stuffed shirt Bob Mickle would have admitted that, but can't help smiling.

'In books! You're always twisting my words,' Una huffs but no one's listening, all too busy laughing. She'd explode if she knew June had proposed *Fifty Shades of Grey* next. Irene said no, but can't deny she's curious to know what all the fuss was about.

Taking pity on Una, she steers the conversation away from sex and death, which is tricky with a bunch of older women. Sometimes sex and death is all they go on about. They want one and fear the other. Or is it the other way around?

Glancing at the armchair, Irene gasps. Ashlee is gone; her iPad is face down on the floor, headphones discarded in a tangle.

'Where's Ashlee?' Her book falls to the table; her heart thumps as she scans the room.

'I'll look out the front.' June jumps up.

'I'll check the ladies.' Una bustles off.

Irene races to the counter. 'Have you seen Ashlee?' she calls out to Amy.

A look of confusion crosses Amy's face. 'She was over there a minute ago … I'll check out the back.'

She rushes off. A door slams somewhere and Amy's voice joins the harmony of calls.

Irene can't breathe. It feels as though the walls are pushing in on her.

And then she feels it. A tug on the arm.

'Here I am, Reenie.' Perched on Amy's hip, Ashlee burrows her face into Amy's neck. In a muffled voice, she adds, 'I was looking for Mummy.'

'I found her in the courtyard out back. I don't know how she got past us all without anyone noticing,' Amy says in a low voice, handing Ashlee over.

'Oh, love. I was so worried.' Nodding her thanks at Amy, Irene holds the little girl tight, struck by a desire to cry and not just because of all the drama. 'Let's go home.' She stands up too fast and grabs a table as a wave of dizziness washes over her. As soon as it passes, she marches over to message Bonnie and collect her things.

'I'm fine,' she tells her friends, ignoring their concerned looks.

'I'm fine,' she tells Amy, waving away the younger woman's offer to tear up the bill.

'I'm fine,' she tells Bonnie later, cursing the two little words that trap her in a life of pleasing everyone but herself.

But the countdown is on.

CHAPTER FIFTEEN
AMY

Amy closes her eyes and wills the disembodied voice on her meditation app to guide her into relaxation. Five weeks have passed in an exhilarating whirl since Brewed to Taste opened and she's exhausted. But happy. Aside from a few settling in glitches, Brewed to Taste has surpassed her expectations.

Her eyes flick open when Matt taps her on the shoulder. Fresh from a shower, he's dripping water onto the carpet. His mouth moves. She pulls her earbuds out. 'Sorry?'

'Have we got any spare electric toothbrush heads?'

'Try my side of the cupboard.' She tries not to sigh as he rustles and bangs around in the cupboard. When he stops, she pops in the earbuds and resumes her meditation. She's on her third deep breath when he's back.

'What's this?' Matt waves a box in front of Amy's face. His lips tremble, as if he wants to smile, but is forcing it back.

Shit! It's the pregnancy test she bought by mistake and meant to throw out. Unless she didn't mean to at all.

'Oh, that,' she says, playing for time, 'it's nothing.'

'Nothing? It's not nothing. It's ...' The hopeful look on his face saddens her and pisses her off at the same time. 'Aims, are you ... do you think you're—'

'No. I'm not.' The pill makes sure of that.

'Are you sure? Why would you have a—' With his hair spiked up from the shower, he looks like a younger version of himself. The Matt she couldn't keep her hands off.

'I bought it by mistake.' The story tumbles out. He nods like he understands, but there's no missing his disappointment. Amy swallows. Disappointment is worse than anger.

And then she makes everything worse. 'Look, chuck it in the bin. It's not like I'm going to need it any time soon.'

Matt's jaw works as if he wants to say something, then he turns on his heel and closes himself in the bathroom. Amy hears a thunk as the box meets the bin. The buzz of the electric toothbrush. The flush of the toilet.

When he comes out again, hair smoothed down and pyjamas on, his face is blank. Amy thinks he's been crying but before she can ask, he's gone. The study door clicks shut.

Unsettled, she gives up on meditating, turning over Matt's reaction in her mind. Why didn't she get rid of that test? And then her thoughts turn to the café. Lately, Matt's attitude towards Brewed to Taste has changed from supportive to resentful. It's crept in like a slow but debilitating sickness. Comments here and there about her long hours. Pressing her to take a day off. Arguments springing out of nowhere.

'I hardly ever see you,' he'd said, a few nights before. They were clearing up after a baked fish dinner. 'I feel like I have to make an appointment.'

'You've seen me all day today,' she'd pointed out. She was all set to go in on her day off – 'to make sure they're okay' – when Matt asked if she'd forgotten something. She had. Their wedding anniversary.

'Only because I insisted,' he said, 'and don't try to tell me again that you remembered our anniversary. I know it was the last thing on your mind.'

He'd kissed her, but his words stung.

They still sting now.

A branch, scuffling on the gutter, wakes Amy. As she rolls over to check the time – almost midnight – she realises Matt's side of the bed is cold, like he hasn't come to bed at all. Pulling on a dressing-gown, she pads down the hall to his study. He's bent over his leather top antique desk, writing in a notebook she doesn't recognise. The light from his banker's lamp casts a warm glow around him, though the air is cool. The only sound is the scratch of pen on paper and the tick-tick of Gran's antique mantel clock.

'Matt?'

He jumps. His left hand covers his writing. 'Amy. What are you doing up?' Closing the notebook, he pushes it to the side, laying down his pen at the same time. It's so smoothly done Amy wouldn't have noticed except it's out of character for Matt to be writing in what looks to be a journal.

'I woke up and you weren't there.' She stands behind him.

'Can't sleep.'

Peering over his shoulder, she asks, 'What are you writing?'

His shoulders tense under her hands. 'Notes for work. Got a big meeting with the head honchos from Perth tomorrow.'

'You didn't mention that before.' She moves next to him, searches his face. He's never written work stuff in a leather bound journal before. Pocket-size, spiral bound notebooks are more his style.

His raincloud-grey eyes flicker. 'Didn't I? I'm sure I did. Go back to bed. I'll be there in a minute.'

As she moves out of the room, she hears the distinctive sound of a key turning in a lock. He joins her a moment later. She lies next to him, wondering what he was writing and why he locked it away. Does it have anything to do with him being so distant lately? Disappearing off to the study, closing the door. He's been distracted for weeks. Is he worried about his job? There's been talk of cutbacks at the mine.

'Matt?'

'What?' His voice is a sleepy sigh.

'Are you sure? You're okay, I mean? You'd tell me if something was wrong?'

She thinks he's fallen asleep, but then he says, 'Of course I would.' He pats her side. 'Can I go to sleep now?'

Walking with Matt into Bistro Thyme for a belated anniversary dinner, Amy's eyebrows lift in approval. The elegant interior is a welcome surprise with its Arctic-white tablecloths, frosted glass candleholders and leather-backed carver chairs. Smooth jazz adds a relaxed ambience while robust flavours of wine and herbs create an enticing perfume. A bank of windows showcases the riverside park where fairy lights twinkle in the trees.

'This reminds me of bistros in France,' Matt says, pulling out a chair for her. 'Remember that one we went to on Île Saint-Louis?'

'God, yes, where no one spoke English.'

'And you asked for *soupe du maire* instead of *soupe de la mer?*'

She punches him lightly on the arm. 'Soup of the mayor! You couldn't stop laughing and I had no idea. I was so embarrassed.' It was their honeymoon, she remembers now. 'I'd forgotten about that.'

'We had some good times.' His words are tinged with sadness and she looks away so he can't see the tears that have come from nowhere. His hands squeeze hers across the table.

They share entrées of confit duck croquettes and charred prawns and seared scallops. For a main, Amy chooses seafood *bouillabaisse* and Matt has the *coq au vin*. As they eat, they reminisce about the first time they met in Greece. About the food they dared each other to eat while backpacking around Europe, from haggis in the Scottish Highlands to *andouillette* in Lyon. About the dodgy hotel in Spain that came with free bed bugs and a one-eyed cat in the shared bathroom.

It comes as a surprise to Amy that she can talk about travelling with fondness instead of pain. But it doesn't make her want to go overseas again and she says as much to Matt, as she wipes her plate clean with the last heel of bread. A funny look crosses his face as he finishes the last of his wine.

'What?'

'Nothing.'

'What was that look?' she presses, but he shakes his head. *Nothing.*

The waiter brings out dessert – *fondant au chocolat* for Matt and *crème brûlée* for Amy – and that's when the night goes south, like a melting ice cream on a boiling summer's day.

'Have you thought about what I said the other night?' Matt wants to know after he orders brandy.

'About what?'

'About cutting back your hours.'

The question chafes like it did the last time he brought it up. 'You know I can't do that yet. The café's only been open six weeks.'

'Surely you can get two days in a row.'

'I do. Sundays and Mondays.' The café closes on Mondays.

'And I work on Mondays, and most Sundays you end up going in for a few hours. And practically every night you're going over the books or nutting out some recipe with Nick.'

It's the same thing he said last week and Amy wants to shake him. 'Even if I did, it wouldn't be the same as a regular Saturday–Sunday weekend. Hospitality doesn't work that way. You know that.' He looks unconvinced, but he shouldn't. It's not like it's new to him. She was a trainee chef when they met.

Their drinks arrive and Matt waits before answering. His tone is reasonable, as if he's been rehearsing for a week. 'It's your café. You can do what you want. Why don't you hire another front-of-house person? Take weekends off.'

Amy throws the napkin down. 'We've been over this already. I can't. Not yet. Maybe next year.' She takes a deep breath. 'What did you expect when you suggested I open a café?'

He wipes his lips before answering slowly. 'I didn't expect … I didn't expect to never see you. I thought it would be different. It's hard going from seeing you all the time to not at all. I thought we were coming here to work on *us*.'

How is she supposed to answer that? *It was his idea.* Stalling, she sips her brandy. It tastes bitter and she pushes it away. 'Do you think I'm not trying? I mean, you wanted me to *do* something and I am doing something. What more do you want from me?'

'Time.' Matt reaches for her hands across the table. 'I want to see my wife. Hang out with you on weekends. Travel with you again. Talk about what our future looks like. I want you to think about how you can fit *us* in.'

Amy snatches back her hands. 'So you're saying this isn't enough. *I'm* not enough. You want me to be the happy little homemaker—'

'No! I'm saying—'

'I know what you're saying. You want more. Geez, Matt. First you push me to open a café, now you push me to work less. I'm scared to death every day that someone will recognise me, but I'm putting myself out there, even though Sharon and Una give me the creeps whenever they come in. I'm doing it because of you. I'm trying to move on, like you have. But no, that's not what you want now. Now you want me home, cooking in our kitchen. God, sometimes I wish I'd never bothered. With any of it. It's a waste of time. You never listen to a thing I say.'

'I've moved on? I don't listen? Seriously?' Now bitterness edges his voice. 'Every single day you talk about Brewed to Taste this and Brewed to Taste that. You have no idea what's going on at my work and in my head because it's all about what's going on with *you*.'

'What the hell?'

Matt shooshes her; she contemplates stuffing her napkin in his mouth, but lowers her voice instead. 'I ask you about work.'

'Really? *How was your day?* followed by *Gee, I'm tired because the café is sooo busy.* You have no idea what's going on at my work.'

In that moment, Amy hates him. She opens her mouth to defend herself and Matt lifts his hand. Shuts her down.

'Not now. Don't say anything more, Amy. Please.' His eyes are black and shiny. Raw pain shimmers from him as their eyes lock for a loaded moment. And something else. Sorrow. 'Not everything is about you. You are not the only one hurting. Not the only one trying to move on. But while I've been hoping moving here would do you – and *us* – some good, you're completely wrapped up in yourself. I'm sick of it.'

It sounds dangerously like an ultimatum. 'What are you saying?'

'I don't know.' He tosses his napkin on the table and stands, muttering something about paying the bill. He takes a step, then stops. 'All I know is that I want you to put *us* first.'

CHAPTER SIXTEEN
AMY

Driving home, tension is like a thick Blackwood fog, pressing, squeezing; the sounds of discontent vibrate in Amy's ears as they move to the car, into their house – stiff footsteps, slammed doors, economical words. They don't speak about the argument. In bed, Matt rolls away from her and turns out his light. Amy lies awake, his words preying on her mind; each time she moves, she's keenly aware of the invisible barrier between them. The next move is hers, Matt's made that clear. She has to let go of something, meet him halfway.

'Nick, I can't come in on Sundays anymore,' she blurts out the next day when they're locking up the café. 'Matt and I really need to spend some time together.'

Nick nods and she knows he gets it. He and Devi only have Mondays. 'You know you don't have to worry about a thing, right?'

'I know, but ...'

'No buts.'

Several weeks pass and now on Sundays the café barely crosses her mind. Sundays are for working in the garden or leisurely drives to nearby towns. For making love without haste. Meandering walks along the river or wildflower hunting in the bush. For rediscovering each other.

Which is why the message flashing on her phone a few weeks into *Mission: Couple Time* twists her stomach into a pulsing knot: *Jess and Troy called in sick. Suspect gastro. You free?*

She's about to type *no* when a second text pings: *Wouldn't ask if I didn't think we'd get smashed. That mothers group is in.*

Amy bites her lip. Matt thinks she's getting ready for a jazz festival. Nick needs an answer. She wants to hide under the bed. Whatever she does, someone will be unhappy. Then she snatches up the phone and taps out a response: *OK. See you in 30.*

What choice does she have? Brewed to Taste is her responsibility. Work is work.

Swallowing, Amy goes in search of her husband. He's serving up breakfast – garlicky buttered mushrooms on thick sourdough that she has no time to eat – and greets her with a bright smile. Within seconds, that smile thins into a hard line.

'We can still go out, just a bit later,' she promises.

'Fine.' He sits alone at the table and begins eating.

An hour later, Amy settles the Blackwood mothers group at the long table. Most of the faces are new, but she recognises Bonnie from next door and Sharon Thompson. She starts her usual welcome spiel, but can't get a word in. Everyone's trying to outdo each other with stories about their kids. It's enough to set her teeth on edge. She'd forgotten that mothers groups were the same everywhere, all talking over each other to compete for titles like Worst Supermarket Tantrum Ever, Most Gifted Baby, Biggest Public Poo, Projectile Vomit Champion, and Blackwood's Laziest Husband. Playing round-the-table games like I'm More Tired Than You and I Haven't Had Sex In [insert number] Weeks. Not one of them wanted to talk about other things that mattered, like climate change or politics. She went out with a similar group once. Never again.

The women go on, oblivious to Amy squeezing past to set water bottles on the table and hand out menus.

'What about the time Ava peed on stage at the dance recital?'

'Oh my god, that was *so* funny.'

'One time, when we were visiting Dave's mum – you know how she is about her house, yeah? – and Emma projectile vomits all over the new white carpet in the living room. And Dave's mum's screaming at me to get Em off the carpet and Dave's laughing – fat lot of help he is – and I'm thinking, why'd you buy white bloody carpet, you know?'

Everyone thinks it's hilarious, except Amy, who simply wants to take their orders and get out of there. The sooner they eat, the sooner they'll leave. She's told Nick she'll stay until they go. She has a date with Matt at a winery.

'You must be wondering what we're going on about,' Sharon says after ordering Apple Pie French Toast and a milkshake. 'You'll understand when you and your handsome hubby have kids.' She turns to her friends. 'Speaking of handsome, girls, have you *seen* Amy's hubby around town? Sizzling. I'll bet it's no problem practising baby-making with him, hey.' Sharon fans herself theatrically, waggling her eyebrows as she laps up her friends' attention.

Sharon Thompson has no idea what she's on about. No idea what Amy and Matt have lost. Amy thinks it's lucky she's not holding a water bottle. Otherwise she might tip its fridge-cold contents on Sharon's clueless head.

'Geez, Sharon,' Bonnie cuts in. 'That's a record. Five minutes before you mentioned sex.'

'Well, you know,' Sharon grins, licking her lips. 'We always end up talking about it sooner or later. Might as well make it sooner.'

'Those who aren't getting any talk about it, huh?' Bonnie shoots back. She's smiling, but the words hint at some unspoken warning.

Sharon flicks Bonnie a withering look. 'Whatever.'

Amy scoots back to the counter. Those women might be balancing kids, husbands and sex, but she has her own juggling act: customers, coffee, and a casual employee with no clue how to operate the coffee machine. Nick was right. Brewed to Taste is getting as smashed as avocado on toast today, with the mothers group as well as out of towners going to and from the jazz festival.

She's wiping down a table when Bonnie taps her arm.

'Ignore her,' Bonnie says, motioning to Sharon. 'She's been a bit of a bitch since her husband did a runner. Although she's always been a nosy Nellie, just like her mum.' She leans in conspiratorially. 'I call them Yoo-hoo Una and Sticky-nose Shaz when I'm really cheesed off with them. Which is most of the time, to be honest.'

Amy can't help laughing.

As if she knows they're talking about her, Sharon's eyes land on them. They burn like a hot summer day. Amy's stomach clenches again.

'If she's a journalist, I suppose it's her job,' Amy says, casually.

'What? Sharon? A journalist. As if.' Bonnie snorts. 'Wannabe journo, more like. She's a part-time receptionist at the paper. Is that what she told you? That she's a journo?'

Amy's stomach unknots as relief washes over her. All this time she's been worried about Sharon for nothing. 'No ... I assumed when she ... it doesn't matter.' She straightens up as the door opens and a group of six spills in. 'I've got to go. Another group's come in. I don't know what it is about today.' Matt's right. She needs to rethink staffing levels soon. Maybe even before the upcoming Spring Garden Festival.

'It's busy all right.' Bonnie hesitates. 'Can I do anything? Make coffees? Serve?'

Amy stares at her. 'Seriously? I mean, have you worked in a café before?'

'Hell, yeah. I used to waitress at Bistro Thyme before I started FIFO. And I'm a trained barista too, so ... '

'But ... it's your day off. And you're here with your friends.'

'Honestly, if one more person tells a poo story, I'll scream. Let me help. I've got two hours before I have to get Ash from a birthday party, and I'd rather make coffee than listen to that lot all morning.'

Without waiting for an answer, Bonnie marches to the counter and starts serving customers. Behind her, Nick and Devi give Amy a thumbs up. Stepping behind a counter in an unfamiliar café is daunting, but the young woman's a natural. Makes coffee like a champion, but priding quality over speed. Delivers the espresso experience with a smile. The customers love her.

'I could use someone like you here,' Amy says later, when they're getting ready to leave. She checks the time. With any luck she and Matt can still make the festival. She texted him earlier but hasn't heard back. 'Don't suppose you want casual work when you're in town?' It's a long shot, but worth a try.

'I would, but …' Bonnie trails off as she unties her apron. 'I'm already away from Ashlee so much. I feel guilty leaving her with Reenie all the time, as it is.'

'Do you like FIFO work?' Amy's genuinely curious. Bonnie looks miserable.

'Not really. It's exhausting. Like, you get back from a shift and spend days adjusting the body clock. And then you have to fit all your appointments and chores in, and next thing, it's time to go. The money's great, but I'm only doing it because Jake – my boyfriend – wants us to save a house deposit faster.' She swallows before adding, 'I hate leaving Ashlee behind. I miss her so much. And she totally plays up when I'm home. Like she's punishing me, you know?'

Amy does know. Pandora used to pay her back now and then. Little things like flicking cereal at the ceiling when they had to leave. Impossible to get off when it was dry. Big things like screaming her head off when Amy left her at day care. An idea blossoms. 'Why don't you give it up? You could work here.'

'I told Jake I want to. He said,' Bonnie's voice cracks, 'he said, if I didn't care about buying a house and being with him, that's fine.'

Bastard.

Amy sends Matt a message – *On my way. Picnic in park instead?* – while she thinks of something helpful to say.

'Sorry, you don't need to know all this. You barely know me. But I feel like I can talk to you.' Bonnie grabs her bag. Her eyes are glassy. 'What would you do?'

This time Amy doesn't hesitate. If Pandora were alive, she would never let her go. 'I can't tell you what to do,' she says, fishing her keys from her bag. 'But if it were me, I would make every moment with my daughter count.'

CHAPTER SEVENTEEN
AMY

M att's not home. A note on the kitchen table says: Gone to festival with friends from work. Disappointed, Amy potters about the house, plumping up pillows, wiping down the kitchen table, sweeping the floor, wishing she hadn't been called in. She'd been excited about the jazz festival. Even prepared a gourmet picnic. And now Matt's off doing his own thing.

She's peeling vegetables for dinner when her gaze drifts out the window. No word from Matt yet, but surely he'll be home soon. She's preparing a feast. Lemon and herb roast chicken. Asparagus and some broad beans Irene gave her. They'll talk over wine and cheese. Maybe they'll make love. And next Sunday will be back to normal. They'll go out somewhere. Buy picnic food from the markets. Drive to the beach.

Half an hour later, Matt's still not home. Amy wanders out to the garden to wait. Pulls up weeds close to emerging bulbs. Fills the bird-bath with water. Bites into a strawberry and spits it out. Not ripe yet. Pops peas from a pod. After fifteen minutes of aimless pottering, she's out of things to do, so when Irene calls her over for a cuppa, she finds herself agreeing.

Irene's house is a jumbled rainbow of toys, patchwork and books, and smells like freesias. She spies a vintage creamer filled with fresh blooms. Framed photos of family members at different ages congregate on every available surface. She picks up one of a woman in her twenties, the spit of Bonnie, but it can't be her because the clothes are nineties grunge.

'Make yourself at home,' Irene says, nudging Flossie off a chair and moving a washing basket filled with neatly folded clothes. 'Sorry about the mess. Coffee or tea?'

'Tea, please.' As soon as Amy settles into a cosy armchair, the cat jumps onto her lap and starts kneading. Patting the cat, she looks around the room and sees that it suits Irene perfectly. It's messier than Gran's house would have been but feels the same. Warm. Comfortable.

What does Irene think of her picture-perfect house with nothing out of place? No family photos proudly displayed. Nothing that hints at the past. For a split second, Amy wants to live like Irene. But every time she sees a photo of Pandora, she hates herself. It's her fault her daughter died.

'Here we go.' Irene lowers a tray to the coffee table.

Next to a teapot, Amy spies a plate of biscuits that look suspiciously like *amaretti*. Her favourite when she was a little girl. She takes a biscuit and bites. The crisp shell gives way to a chewy centre tasting of almonds and the faintest hint of lemon. They taste like Sardinia.

'Oh my god, they are *amaretti*!' Amy can't resist. She takes another. 'Did you make them?'

'Oh, no, love. I bought them at the markets last week.'

'They're divine. I can show you how to make them if you like. An old lady in Sardinia taught me how. They're so easy and they're gluten-free,' Amy says through a mouthful. 'Egg whites, ground almonds, caster sugar, and you're supposed to use bitter almonds, but I use a good splash of Amaretto liqueur. I must make some for the café.' She taps a note into her phone.

'You've been to Sardinia?'

'Lived there for a couple of months when I was twenty. Beautiful place.' At Irene's raised eyebrows, Amy continues. 'I travelled a lot when I was younger. Did the whole backpacking thing around

Europe, you know, the gap year experience? Worked for two years in a restaurant to save up. Do you mind?' At Irene's smile, she reaches for another *amaretto* and groans.

Irene breaks the biscuit-chewing silence. 'I've never travelled myself. Never had the money when I was young, and it wasn't really the done thing then, these gap years … and then, well, life got in the way. I've always wanted to see Italy though. Anywhere outside this state, actually.'

'What's stopping you now?'

'It's a bit hard at the minute, love. Maybe after Bonnie moves in with Jake and stops that FIFO nons— work. We'll see. Have you and Matt travelled much together?'

Amy swallows. The biscuit suddenly seems too big for her throat. She sips her tea. 'I … yes. But not for a long time.'

'Sometimes it's hard to come up with the money.'

'It's not the m—' Amy pauses. 'Yes. It is hard sometimes.'

'Do you miss it? Travel?'

'No.' Amy whips out the word too fast and Irene gives her a curious look. Quickly, Amy covers up. 'So, are you all ready for the Spring Garden Festival? Do many people come to it?'

To her credit, Irene doesn't push it. Instead, while Piglet snores on her lap, she tells Amy about how garden-loving tourists come from all over, even Perth, to the festival. Flossie stretches and yawns then snuggles into Amy once more. Maybe she should get a cat. Or a dog. A little lap one, like Piglet.

Darting a look at a clock on a side table, Amy decides to make a move. The chicken needs to go in the oven and Matt will be home soon. She shifts forward and Flossie squints suspiciously through one eye.

But Irene clearly has other ideas. She reaches for the silver-framed photo Amy picked up earlier. 'This is my daughter. Erin. Bonnie's mum.'

'Bonnie looks exactly like her.' Amy pauses. 'Where is she? Does she live near here?'

'Oh no, love. She died a long time ago. When Bonnie was twelve.' Amy can't hold back a gasp. 'Sid and I raised her.'

'I'm so sorry.' Amy shifts again. The chair feels like a rowboat being tossed on surging waves. 'I didn't know.'

'Well, why would you, love? Erin was a … a troubled girl. I'll tell you about her some day.' She pauses. 'And maybe one day you can tell me about your little one.'

It's as if the chair's been snatched out from under her. Amy's bottom lip quivers. 'How did …'

'I know what grief looks like. From the inside out. I saw it the first day I met you.'

Suddenly, Amy is suspicious. Is Irene in cahoots with Una and Sharon? When no one recognised her after the article in the tourist paper, she told herself to stop worrying. Now the worry is back. The armchair feels as if it will capsize if she doesn't move. Immediately.

'I thought I'd offer a friendly ear if you ever wanted to talk,' Irene continues.

Amy stands sharply, dislodging the cat, who gives her a disgruntled look before licking its paw. 'I don't mean to be rude, Irene, but it's none of your business.'

There's an intake of breath, but Irene says nothing. Instead, she sits and listens like some kind of counsellor while Amy spews an emotional mess. 'You think that because you're my neighbour you're entitled to pry? Why do people assume that because you're new in town you're fodder for gossip? Why do they have to know if you've got children or had children or even want children? Why do they have to know who we were before we got here? Why can't we just *be* who we are now?'

Amy knows she's gone too far, but she can't seem to stop. Right now, Irene is Una, Sharon and everyone in Blackwood fused into one overbearing, meddling stranger. Irene is Matt, who's not home, and Irene is *Amy*, who makes her angrier than anyone in the world.

'I'm so sorry, Amy.' Another breath. 'I'd like to be your friend, when and if you need one.' Irene's eyes shine with unshed tears as their eyes meet. 'I know it's hard. I know.'

'You know nothing about me. Nothing,' Amy whispers and pushes blindly past the older woman.

Why can't people leave me alone? And where the bloody hell is Matt? Back in her kitchen, Amy slams the chicken into the oven and leans against the bench, breathing hard. Her face is wet and she wipes it roughly with a towel. What was Irene thinking? As if Amy was going to talk about private things with someone she barely knows. Tossing aside the towel, she rummages in the fridge for asparagus, pushing Irene's broad beans to the back of the chiller. They'll have minted herb peas instead.

She's still stewing when Matt comes home.

'Nice of you to come home,' she snipes. 'Couldn't have waited before you took off with some workmates? Since when have you done that? You've never even mentioned these friends.'

'I had no idea how long you were going to be,' he says, reasonably, going to the fridge. 'Do you expect me to wait around and do nothing all day?'

'No. But I thought we were going together.' She realises she's about to cry again. 'I'm sorry. I had to go in.'

Matt pauses. Amy waits for him to contradict her but he doesn't. 'I know.' She sniffs again and he gives her a searching look. 'Is something else wrong?'

'Yeah. Irene started asking personal questions and I kind of lost it.' Amy fills him in, but the more she talks, the more unsettled she is. Why does it feel like he's not on her side? 'I was only setting boundaries.'

Matt arches his eyebrows. 'Sounds to me like she was reaching out but you shut her down. Like you do with anyone who tries to get close.'

His words bite. 'I do *not*. I'm just sick of people prying. That's what I wanted to get away from. You know that.'

'She wants to be your friend. Or did. It's not the same as prying.' Matt sounds weary. He gets up and takes her face in his hands. 'I'm sure you'll figure out what to do. I'm off to shower.'

In the dark of night, it occurs to her that Matt avoided her question about his friends. But the thought doesn't stick, and by morning, she's forgotten.

CHAPTER EIGHTEEN
IRENE

'Yoo-hoo!' Absorbed in weeding her garden the next day, Irene nearly puts her back out when Una creeps up behind her. 'Oh, there you are, Irene. I've been calling you. Off in dreamland, are you?'

Wincing, Irene squints up at the other woman. Not a hair out of place, lipstick perfectly applied. A little heavy on the powder. Piglet launches herself at Una's shoes, sniffing them with great interest. Una nudges the small dog away with one foot and makes a *tsk* sound as her gaze swims around the yard. 'Goodness me, you still have a fair bit to do, don't you?'

Irene rolls her eyes under her sunhat. Sometimes she wants to tell Una what she can do with her tuts and *tsks*. 'Anything in particular you wanted, or did you stop by to compliment my beautiful garden?'

'No need to be snarky, Irene. Since you weren't at church *again*,' – a tiny shake of the head – 'I popped around to remind you about the pre-festival afternoon tea on Thursday. At my house, of course. 1.30.'

It's the first Irene's heard of any such thing. But Thursday rings a bell. An appointment ... *doctor*. 'I can't make it. I have an appointment.' And she'll have to pick up Ashlee from kindy at half-two. Bonnie flies out again tomorrow.

Tsk. 'Well, if that's more pressing,' Una huffs, 'fine.' She turns to leave, but not before a parting remark that stings worse than her backhanders. 'Oh, I almost forgot. I'm going on a South Pacific cruise in the new year with a few ladies from church. New Caledonia and Vanuatu. I'm thrilled to bits, of course. You should come along. Think about it.'

Fat chance, Irene thinks. 'I will,' she lies, conscious of a sharp poke in the gut. Envy. She's jealous of Una. At her age. But she's pretty sure Una dropped in just to crow about the cruise. The afternoon tea reminder is a cover, for sure. But it won't be long now and she'll have news of her own. Once Bonnie and Jake have this deposit sorted there'll be no stopping her.

'Good, good. Now, I'll leave you to your gardening. Goodness knows, you'll need every spare minute, won't you, what with looking after the little one all the time.' *Tsk.*

She sweeps away importantly, missing Frank Taylor by a whisker. Thank God he was late. Una would have a field day if she knew Irene was paying for help.

Irene wanders around her garden, aching but pleased with the results of the day's work. Bursting with fragrant lavender, exuberant spring bulbs, colourful perennials, aromatic roses and romantic cottage plants, her garden is at its best this time of year. She pauses to smell her favourite rose, the Lady of Shalott, named after the Tennyson poem. Sid loved that poem and she'd sourced the variety after he died. She likes to think Sid enjoys the salmon pink, chalice-shaped flowers, wherever he is resting. After a final sniff of the flowers' spicy perfume she moves on.

A carpet of snowdrops rings the garden's statement piece, a stunning weeping peach dressed to impress with deep crimson blossoms. Sid insisted on buying a mature tree, even though it cost hundreds of dollars at the time. He never got to see it in its full glory. Missed it by weeks. For weeks after that, it was like a giant pink slap.

As she makes her way to the wisteria-covered gazebo, where she'll set up refreshments on the festival weekend, she breathes in the sensual jasmine, which embraces the fence in heady, wanton style, before sinking into the swing chair on the verandah to catch her breath. Bonnie and Ashlee will be home soon. She might as well grab a last few minutes of peace.

Leaning forward, she rubs her knees, then her back. She'll need a heat pack later, and Bonnie will tell her off for doing too much. Bonnie doesn't understand that Irene's got to get the garden into shape before the Spring Garden Festival. Her sensory garden walk always draws crowds and she doesn't want to disappoint anyone. No, a little pain is a small price to pay for the pleasure she sees when people visit her garden. Being short of breath worries her more. Sid had the same symptom. Turned out it was a blocked coronary artery and by then, it was too late. He had a heart attack in hospital and that was that. At the memory, she exhales a sharp sigh. Piglet looks up from her snoozing spot on Irene's lap, liquid eyes questioning. She misses Sid too.

'Shh,' Irene says, taking deep, grounding breaths while running her free hand over the little dog's back. She wills all her negative thoughts to float away before the girls come home.

A car pulls up next door. A door slams. She can just make out Amy's head over the fence. Yesterday she watched Amy run away with an ache in her gut. It's been in the back of her mind all day. She's not hurt by Amy's outburst. Heavens, she took out her anger and guilt on Sid often enough over the years. And one thing she knows by heart is that grief is as unpredictable as Melbourne weather. It stalks you like a shadow and jumps out when you least expect it. *Boo!* Sometimes it knocks you over. Other times, it's a warm trickle of tears. Staring at the house next door, she's overcome by the feeling that she handled it all wrong. Wrong timing, wrong place. If and when Amy wants to share her story, she will.

The young woman is such a paradox. At times she exudes confidence and warmth, especially when she's working. Other times her movements are more tentative, as if she's a dried leaf caught in a windy ballet. Over the past months, Amy appears to have emerged from the cocoon of sadness she wore when she first arrived in town. Now, Irene senses Amy's wings are starting to unfurl as she settles into Blackwood life and carves out a place for herself.

'I hope I haven't set her backwards,' she says out loud. 'I'll keep my distance for a few days, Piglet.' The little dog gives a small yip.

Her eyes drift to a wine barrel that's home to an Erin Farmer camellia, a pink and white hybrid she tracked down because of its name. Erin used to tuck camellias behind her ears and Sid would mock-growl at her to leave his camellias alone. And then Irene remembers something else she recognised in Amy earlier. Grief, yes, but something more. Something forceful and insidious, below the surface yet out there plain as day.

Guilt.

Irene has her own version. Everyone does. Hers popped up the day Erin took her first breath. Was she a good enough mother? Was she doing it right? And later, when Erin's mental health deteriorated, guilt was a constant but unwelcome companion, starting every jabbing sentence with 'You should have …' and 'If only you …'

It's been fourteen years and Irene still blames herself for her daughter's death. If only they'd sent her to a different school then she wouldn't have been introduced to the drugs and that bad-news group she fell in with. If only they'd gotten her help for her depression sooner. If only she'd been a better mother. She'd bet her entire garden that Amy thinks the same thing every day of her life. *If only I'd been a better mother.* She'd bet her house something happened to Amy and Matt's child overseas. And whatever it was, Amy can't forgive herself.

Irene gets up to feed the chickens, Piglet following at her heels. For a time she's lost in conversation with the girls who respond with low-pitched tuck-tuck noises, different to their usual cackling and cluck-ing. Chickens made at least twenty-four different sounds, she'd read once. She ruffles the friendliest hen's feathers, then picks up an egg and places it carefully into a basket.

Back on the verandah, the wind chimes tinkle and clunk in the afternoon breeze. Irene sits with her memories of Sid and Erin until Bonnie and Ashlee come home. As her great-granddaughter runs towards her, she levers herself up, ignoring her creaking knees and stiff back, and bids the holes in her heart goodnight.

CHAPTER NINETEEN
AMY

Blackwood heaves with tourists attending the Spring Garden Festival. Amy hasn't seen the town so busy, but all the locals act like it's nothing new. Brewed to Taste is jam-packed, with an electric energy and steady clink of cutlery against plates that keeps the staff smiling despite being run off their feet. As soon as one table empties, it's snapped up by someone else. But as long as the kitchen doesn't run out of food, Amy doesn't mind.

'Pick up, table four,' she calls out to Troy, as Nick slides two plates onto the pass.

Nick and Amy's spring menu is a hit; the baked buffalo mozzarella and prosciutto served with asparagus and almond crumb is the top-seller. Nick's plated at least twenty orders, with the asparagus, broad bean and mint bruschetta coming a close second.

'Pick up, table eight.' She drizzles lemon-infused extra virgin olive oil over the salads milliseconds before Troy arrives. Watching his confident stride, a pencil behind his ear, she reflects on how far he's come in such a short time. And if she's not mistaken, that buff young bloke with the *Star Wars* T-shirt is giving him the eye.

'Going on my break,' she calls out when the rush is over. Grabbing her water bottle, she heads to the staff courtyard behind the café, sinking into one of two wicker chairs propped up against an ivy-covered wall and rotating her ankles first one way, then the other. Tonight she will slip her tired feet into a warm footbath with a scoop of Epsom salts and a dash of peppermint. She wants them in good shape for tomorrow, when she and Matt experience the festival for themselves. They have a whole day planned; morning tea at the Blackwood House Garden Fair, followed by a walking tour of Blackwood's best spring gardens.

She frowns. Irene's garden is on the tour. Should they skip that one? Things have been cool between them for the last two weeks. They've waved politely if they've spotted each other outside, but that's about it. It's up to Amy to extend the olive branch, but her stubborn heart won't allow it. Amy's head tells her that Irene shouldn't have stuck her nose in, but her heart knows she can't face this woman who seems to look deep into Amy's soul, like Gran did.

Guard your heart, but don't make it a forbidden place. That's what Gran used to say.

Is that what she's done? Does she need to confide in someone like Irene? Or Bonnie? But what if they tell other people? Like Sharon Thompson or Una Mickle? Amy can't bear people looking at her, feeling sorry for her. Judging her. She's experienced enough of that already.

Amy shakes her head. Matt's right. She does push people away. All along she's been telling herself she has to stay detached for protection, but now that Irene's pulled away, she's surprised by what she feels.

I'm lonely.

It's not as if no one talks to her during the day; running a business means she's not a hermit. People say hello; she responds. She's not antisocial. Still, she's come to like Irene and Ashlee popping in when the mood takes them. Ashlee hasn't come over all week. Amy's heard her outside, playing with that Henry boy, yelling, 'Oh, Henry, stop that!'

Her alarm beeps. Break is over.

And as she walks through the kitchen, she resolves to mend what she's broken.

'Amy? Amy Bradford?'

Balancing three bruschetta orders on her arms, Amy freezes mid-step out the front of the café. She knows that voice, but hasn't heard it for a long time. Deftly depositing the plates on their assigned table, she pastes a smile on her face and turns to face a blast from the past.

Her old friend Kel from Perth is sitting at a table for four. Two small backpacks rest on chairs opposite Kel. Amy hasn't seen her for at least a year. They'd met while working in a restaurant and built a firm friendship based on fun, girls' nights and a mutual love of food. They'd been the best of friends until Amy's life was ripped apart and Kel, busy with twins, had no idea how to help fuse it back together. Lost in a void of uncertainty about what to say or do, their friendship faded like blooms on a tired rose.

What the hell is she doing here?

'Amy! Oh my God, it *is* you! What are you doing down here?'

Before her brain can compute what Kel being here means, Amy finds herself wrapped in her old friend's arms. It's a second before she hugs Kel back, Amy's movements stiff, awkward. 'I live here now. This is my café.'

'No way! I had *no* idea. I haven't heard from you for yonks,' Kel chides, bumping her hip into Amy's the way she used to do. Amy grins, despite the tightness in her chest. God, she's missed her.

'I haven't exactly heard from you either,' Amy returns, knowing full well she made it impossible. She'd changed her mobile number the same day she deleted her Facebook account. Didn't bother passing her new number on to anyone except Matt and his parents.

Kel goes quiet. 'You're right. And I'm right. Neither of us have … it was all so … I didn't know what to …' Trailing off, her eyes dart around like a bee high on nectar.

Don't say anymore! Amy lowers her voice. 'It's okay, Kel. Really. And we're doing okay. Moving on, you know.' She says it lightly, but cringes inside. It's such a cliché. And it's only half true. She's moved house and she's got something to do every day, but inside she's still stuck in that car on a German road, listening to a never-ending soundtrack of rain and pain. And no one knows it but her. Maybe Matt. Swallowing, she sneaks a look at the door. The others will be wondering where she is. 'Um, I have to—'

'Well, I'm glad to hear that, Amy. Although …' Kel hesitates, then ploughs on, 'I suppose you don't ever move on completely, right?'

Amy grips the menu she's holding, willing away the familiar burn of tears. Gathering her face into a mask, she meets her friend's eyes. She can't fall apart here. Not today. 'No. Not completely. I really have to—'

'Mummy! Who's that lady? Did you get chips? We're starving!'

A mixture of embarrassment and anxiety crosses Kel's face. No, not embarrassment, Amy thinks. Guilt.

Twins, a boy and a girl, move towards them, their words jumbling together in excitement. They were toddlers last time Amy saw them. George and Charlotte. Eighteen months younger than Pandora. Their father Drew stands behind them, mouth wide with shock.

Kel interrupts. 'Be a sec, kids. Drew, go inside and order, would you? I'll have the bruschetta and a kombucha.' Drew nods and, after giving Amy a hug, drags the twins inside.

'I could have taken your—' Amy starts, but Kel ignores her.

'I know you're busy, but before you go … I get why you disappeared off the radar. But I really want us to reconnect. Can we? On Facebook? Or …' her words trail off and she gives Amy a hopeful look.

'Sure,' Amy says, surprising herself. 'I'm not on Facebook, though.' Troy keeps telling her people expect it these days. She's still holding out on Facebook but gave in and let Troy start an Instagram account for the café. His food photos are mouth-watering. She takes out her phone. 'What's your number? I'll text you and then you'll have mine.' After pressing send, she pauses and gives Kel a hug. 'I didn't realise I missed you until now.'

The next day, Amy and Matt drive to Blackwood House, along the banks of the Ford River. The rambling gardens are jammed with tourists and townsfolk. Roses, camellias, lavenders and blossom-veiled deciduous trees fringe the market stalls on the lush emerald lawn. Families stroll along the riverbank, edged with lanky river gums. The atmosphere is cheerful; the sounds of laughter and chatter are as colourful as the flower petals holding court. Amy squeezes Matt's hand as they take in the stunning displays.

The panic attack comes from nowhere. One minute, Amy's enjoying the fair; the next, she's gasping for breath, as if her ribs are being crushed by the crowds, as if her ears will burst from the noise. Matt leads her to a gazebo; she closes her eyes and tries to listen to his voice, soothing and slow, forcing away fears that the structure is a cage and she is a curious, pacing attraction.

'You right?' Matt asks.

'I think so. Sorry.' She hasn't had a panic attack since that day he found her near-catatonic on the sofa. But she's been unsettled since bumping into Kel.

'Don't be. It happens.' He doesn't sound convinced. 'Want to go home?'

She nods weakly. Taking her hand, he leads her out of the gazebo.

'Amy!' She swings around. Kel gets up from a picnic blanket, says something to her family, and runs over, an expression of concern on her face. She greets Matt with a quick hug before plunging in. 'Do you guys know someone called Sharon? She came up to me before and acted like she knew me, but I'm certain I've never met her before. She asked about *you*, Amy.'

'Yeah, I know her,' Amy says, slowly, as ice runs through her veins. She and Matt exchange a look. 'What else did she say?'

'She was all, "You were talking to Amy Bennet yesterday. How do *you* know Amy?" And I said, without even thinking, "Bennet? You mean Bradford?" And she looked at me like a light bulb had switched on. And then, she starts tapping into her phone like she's forgotten I'm there, and her fake nails are going tap-tap-tap, and she goes,' Kel lowers her voice, 'she goes, "Holy hand grenades! I knew it," and bolted. It creeped me out, Amy. Is she a journalist or something?'

'No. Just someone from town being nosy.' Amy has a sudden urge to scream. 'Look, Kel, thanks for the heads up. Got to go.'

'Wait, Amy … did I do something wrong? I tried not to tell her anything, but she caught me off guard for a sec and that face she made …'

Amy forces herself to sound reassuring. 'No, it's fine. Really. We've been using my maiden name here so we can have some privacy, that's all. But, Kel, if anyone else asks about me, please, don't tell them anything, okay?' After a quick hug, Kel returns to her family, and Amy and Matt stride away, saying nothing until they get to the car.

'Fuck.' Matt's jaw clenches. He sits in the car but doesn't start the engine. She wants him to say something, anything, to reassure her. Tell her it's nothing to be worried about.

Even if it's not true.

'What should we do?' she asks. 'What does this mean? What's going to happen?' The questions tumble out as if a gate of fear has been unlocked.

'I don't know,' he squeezes out.

Amy stares at him. *That's all you've got?* It's not enough. She needs more. She tries to take his hand, but he moves it away. The movement is so slight it could be coincidence, but Amy knows it's no accident. She crosses her arms.

'Matt! I'm freaking out here. I can't go through all that again. I'll lose everything. Everything I've worked for. What do you think she'll do?'

'I *don't* know.' The words grind from gritted teeth. The heat of his fear and frustration sears like a fire she's too close to, and Amy looks out the window. His voice softens. 'Give me time to process this, okay? We'll talk about it later. Not here.'

Back at home, he pulls her close. 'It'll be fine, Aims. Whatever happens, we'll get through it.'

But the words sound hollow. Empty of belief.

For days, Amy's on tenterhooks, waiting for Sharon to make her move. Looking over her shoulder, expecting Sharon to materialise like a cackling ghoul. And when she doesn't, when Amy hears nothing, her fear eases. Maybe that's the end of it. Sharon and her mother have satisfied their curiosity, and now they've moved on to someone else, someone more interesting than Amy. And when a niggling voice insists Sharon is merely biding her time, she blocks her ears like Pandora used to do.

La-la-la, I can't hear you.

It's the waiting that's hardest. Waiting for someone to say something. To point the finger. To regard her with narrowed eyes or a sympathetic head tilt. It's hard to tell which is worse.

But when nothing happens, when she doesn't see Sharon or Una around town in the days that follow, she starts to believe it doesn't matter if people find out. What's the worst that could happen?

CHAPTER TWENTY

AMY

What will I do for the rest of the day?

The following Monday Amy is home alone, crossing items off her to-do list. Doctor appointment, check. Haircut, check. Online meeting with her bookkeeper, done. All she has left to do are her daily Pilates exercises. A free afternoon and nothing to do with it.

'Catch up with someone. Invite someone over for a cuppa,' Matt said when she asked him earlier.

'Like who?'

He had no answer.

'Who?' she says now. The word echoes in the empty room. It's a lonely sound; there's no one to hear it and nothing to soften it.

It's all right for him. Matt's never needed many friends. And when she moved to Blackwood, Amy would have said she needed none. After all, she cut ties with the ones who didn't desert her after Pandora died. They still had their kids. She told herself Matt was all she needed. Only he could hold her up when she was falling apart (which was eighty per cent of the time before moving here). But she needs more now. Catching up with Kel has reawakened her need to spend time in the company of women. Women who are easy to talk to, non-judgemental, safe. Like Gran.

Like Irene.

Amy's only friends – if she can call them that – are the people she works with. They laugh and chat together, but no matter what, she's still the boss. There's a line. Besides, they have better things to do on Mondays, the only day Brewed to Taste is closed, than hang out with the boss. Still. It's good to foster team spirit. She makes a note to arrange a team lunch or drinks once a month, if that suits them all. But if not them, who else is there?

Biting into a hummus-coated carrot stick, Amy ponders her dilemma. She barely has time to paint her toenails, let alone actively make friends. On one hand, she ticks off the Blackwood women she'd feel comfortable hanging out with: Irene, Bonnie, June. All three of them seemed to like her for *her*, not because they had to. Even though she keeps them at arm's length. Except June's working at the bakery, Bonnie's up north again, and Amy's managed to alienate Irene, the kindest person she's met in town.

It's time for that olive branch, she decides. She's lost so many people already. But how can she make things right with Irene? Amy chews on carrot and celery sticks until the solution comes to her in Gran's wise voice: *Do what you do best.*

Not only will she bake a peace offering, she'll invite Irene, Bonnie and Ashlee over on Sunday for an Italian feast. If you can't go to Italy, why not bring it to you? And it's the perfect way to test out an idea for the café event space that's been brewing for weeks: a monthly supper club with a travel theme. Feasts where people travel the world without leaving the kitchen. No one knows about it. Not even Matt.

Amy connects to Spotify and selects her favourite music mix. Pulling out her family recipe book – the dog-eared, stained one with recipes from Gran, Matt's mum Helen, and the ones she's developed over the years – she turns the pages without anything leaping out at her. She wants to make Matt something too; something to thank him for all that he is to her. He doesn't hear it enough from her. And then it comes to her. Lemon meringue pie. Matt's all-time favourite.

She'd made it for his birthday the first year they celebrated it together, and every year until … until the year Pandora died, she realises with a gasp. That year, he spent his birthday making funeral arrangements; she spent hers undergoing rehabilitation. The next year they were tied up with lawyers and police investigations. Birthdays seemed inconsequential then, and as for celebrating Pandora's life every year, she couldn't face it. Could she now?

Indecision and guilt toy with her, but she gives them a hard shove aside and starts collecting ingredients for the pastry.

One step at a time. A peace offering is a good place to start. After that, she can take the next step.

Outside, Amy heads for the lemon tree, a calico tote bag slung over her shoulder. Next door, Irene's chooks cackle and Ashlee's calling Henry again. That boy. He seems to visit a lot, and drives Ashlee crazy by the sound of it, but Irene's never complained about him. Must have the patience of an angel to put up with a little terror like that. Amy realises she's never seen the little boy, only heard him making loud, taunting sounds in response to Ashlee's bossiness.

She pokes her head over the fence. No sign of Ashlee. Or Henry. They must have gone inside. When she turns back a large white goose is eyeballing her. Its eyes are beady, its mouth open. What the hell is a goose doing in her backyard? Clutching the bag to her chest, Amy edges back. The goose follows, making an insistent braying sound.

'Go away,' she shouts, waving her bag in its face. 'Go back to wherever you came from.'

The goose doesn't flinch. Its eyes are more intent than before, its honking even more excited. Its beak stabs towards Amy and she does the only thing a woman can do when confronted by a mad goose in her backyard. Squeals and bolts. She spots the three-step ladder she left next to the lemon tree and darts towards it, chased by the crazy bird from hell. Scrambling to the top rung, she perches there, panting and holding a branch for balance.

'There,' she says, a note of triumph despite her precarious position. 'You can't get me now.'

The goose regards her with a look that seems to say, 'I've got all day,' and continues honking.

After five minutes of bag shaking and goose threatening, the face-off shows no sign of easing. If Amy didn't know better, she'd swear Irene's chickens were cheering, but whether for the goose or Amy, she wasn't willing to bet.

'Henry, where are you, you silly goose? I can hear you!'

Ashlee tears up the driveway. The goose turns at the sound of the little girl's voice and runs towards her, like a dog returning to its owner. 'There you are! I've been looking everywhere for you.' She folds the bird into a clumsy embrace.

Amy climbs down the ladder, grimacing at the ache from her cramped muscles. Ashlee looks at her in surprise. 'Why were you in the tree, Amy?'

'That goose chased me. It was trying to bite me.'

'Henry wouldn't bite anyone. She's friendly.' Ashlee looks over Amy critically. 'It's the bag. Henry thinks you have food in that bag.'

Amy fingers the bag on her shoulder. 'This one?' The goose honks and Amy steps back.

'Yes. It's same as our food bag.'

Amy looks from Ashlee to the goose and back again. 'And this goose, Henry, is a pet?'

'Yes.'

'Isn't Henry a people's name?'

'No. It's a goose name.'

Amy starts to laugh. 'I thought Henry was a boy.'

'She's not a *boy*. Henry is a *girl*.' Ashlee flings her arms heavenward.

'Ashlee?' Irene pokes her head over the hedge. 'Have you found Henry?'

'He's ... she's here, Irene,' Amy calls, removing the bag from her shoulder. Henry chooses that moment to dash forward, honking furiously, and without thinking, Amy runs, squealing as the goose chases her around the garden.

'Henry! Stop that, you naughty goose! Henry! Stop chasing my Amy!' Ashlee sounds furious. 'Reenie! Save her!'

'Drop the bag,' Irene cries out, jogging up the driveway with Piglet at her heels. 'Drop. The. Bag.'

Amy overbalances and slips on a muddy patch, landing bottom up. Henry pecks Amy's bum and stalks back to her owner.

'Amy? Are you okay?' Irene reaches out a hand. As she helps Amy up, Piglet faces off with Henry, yapping and skipping. The goose hisses and the dog shrinks back, whimpering.

'Thank you. I'll be fine.' Amy tries to sound dignified, but it's hard to do with leaves in her hair, mud all over her clothes, and a goose-pecked bum.

Irene's mouth twitches.

'I can't believe your goose bit my bum,' Amy says.

Irene's mouth twitches harder. A snort escapes her lips and she covers her mouth with her hands.

Amy's lips jiggle, despite her hurt pride.

'You're a very, very naughty goose, Henry.' Ashlee pushes Henry down the driveway. 'Stop it, Henry. Stop it!'

Amy's eruption of giggles turns into full-blown laughter verging on hysteria. Ashlee stamps her foot.

'Why are you laughing? It's not funny! Henry keeps pecking me!' Ashlee is shrill with injustice. 'Stop laughing at me!'

Mouth still twitching, Irene's by her side in an instant, mollifying her red-faced great-granddaughter.

As Amy watches them a familiar ache replaces the laughter of moments before. But this time, it doesn't hurt as much.

'Will you come inside for a hot drink?' she offers. The lemon meringue pies can wait.

Ashlee's face brightens. 'Milo?'

'You got it. Irene?'

Irene smiles. 'Sure. I'd love to. I've just got to put Henry back in her pen.'

'Yippee!' With a joyful grin, Ashlee squeezes between them and forces her hands into theirs.

'A goose pecked your bum? I wish I was there to see it,' Matt chortles through a mouthful of lemon meringue pie. He practically leapt on it when he got home. Like he was trying to make up for all the lost pies in one go.

'I'll show you the bruise later.'

'Promise?' His lips brush hers and his hands cup her bottom. He tastes of lemon and sugar and she lets her lips linger, before pulling back.

'Maybe. If you behave.'

'Oh, I promise I can be very good. Or bad, if you want.' He licks her ear. 'I'll even kiss it better. Your bum.'

Laughing, she pushes him away. 'Before you get too distracted—'

'I like distracted.' Another flick with his tongue.

'Matt! I'm trying to— ooh, that feels good. No, wait. I need to ask you something.'

Sighing theatrically, he helps himself to another wedge of pie. 'Mmm-hmm?'

'Would you mind if I invited Irene over for dinner Sunday night? I thought I'd cook an Italian feast. Bring Italy to her, since she's never been out of Australia.'

He keeps chewing, so she goes on. 'Also, I texted Bonnie about the idea and she said it's Irene's seventieth birthday on Sunday. So, I thought we could also invite Bonnie – she's flying back on Thursday – and Ashlee to make it a little surprise party.'

'We haven't had a themed dinner party in years.' Matt grins, nodding. 'Of course. Will you go the whole hog? Italian music? Italian wine?' He hesitates. 'What about her partner?'

'Jake? He's staying in Perth for the weekend. Apparently he reckons it's boring in Blackwood.'

Matt snorts. 'That's good. I mean, he's a bit of a tool.'

'That's putting it nicely.' Amy's met Jake twice and wasn't sold on him either time. Good looks sometimes mask an ugly character, that's what Gran always said. And going by the dismissive way Jake treated Ashlee and Irene when Bonnie turned her back, Amy thought Gran was onto something.

'So, that's settled, then?' Matt pushes away his plate and cocks his eyebrow cheekily. 'Can we talk about other things now? Like that bruise on your bum you promised to show me?'

Amy smudges meringue onto his nose and darts out of his reach. A sense of deja vu tingles her from head to toe. 'You'll have to catch me first.'

CHAPTER TWENTY-ONE
IRENE

The last glimmers of sun hover on the horizon as Irene treads carefully down her driveway. The silvereyes sing their night song – in a flash of whimsy she imagines they are singing a birthday song – and the light wind rustles through trees. The air is fresh; she pulls her shawl tightly around her, and draws a deep, invigorating breath. If she tries hard enough, she can nearly block out what Dr Ghorbani told her earlier.

Angina. That's what the doctor reckons she's got, even though she doesn't have any of the known risk factors. She's not overweight, she's never smoked a ciggy in her life (that joint she confiscated from Erin and shared with Sid doesn't count, does it?) and she exercises (chasing after a four-year-old definitely counts). Now she's got to have a blood test and an ECG to confirm the diagnosis, and do that without Bonnie knowing. It'll only worry her and Lord knows, with that Jake ruling her life she's got enough to worry about. The poor girl was devastated when she got home on Thursday. Reckons he broke up with her. Good riddance, Irene wanted to say, but didn't. Lucky, because it was a false alarm. Again.

'What if it *is* angina?' she'd asked Dr Ghorbani.

'Medication. Pace yourself. Reduce stress,' he said. 'I mean it, Irene.'

Irene can't do much about the stress in her life, but she'll worry about that if and when she has to. Tonight she wants to forget what the doctor said and share a meal with friends, even if they have no idea it's her birthday.

She glances at her front verandah. The light is on for Bonnie, who's gone out somewhere with Ashlee. An engagement party, or something. When Bonnie said she'd arranged a birthday lunch at Brewed to Taste in place of dinner, Irene swallowed her dismay. Birthday dinners were a tradition in their home. Amy's dinner invitation went some way to lifting her spirits, but despite her anticipation, disappointment lurks. Logically, she knows things will change when Bonnie moves out. But you only turn seventy once.

Matt opens the back door before she can knock. 'Welcome,' he says. 'Amy's in the kitchen. Follow your nose.'

She follows the scent trail of garlic, tomato, onion and basil to the hub of the house. Amy is stirring something in one of those heavy cast-iron pots Irene's always coveted. Over a red, fifties-style halter dress, Amy's wearing a floral retro-style apron. Irene feels dowdy next to her.

'Hi, Irene! Prosecco?'

Irene furrows her brow at the unfamiliar word. 'I don't speak Italian, dear.'

Amy laughs. 'Sorry. Prosecco is an Italian sparkling wine. Would you like a glass?' On cue, Matt passes Irene a crystal flute.

Irene sniffs the unfamiliar drink. The pamphlet Dr Ghorbani gave her said to watch alcohol consumption, but surely a glass or two won't hurt. She doesn't mind a tipple with friends now and then.

Amy tilts her glass. 'I believe it's your birthday, yes?'

Ashlee tumbles out of the pantry. 'Happy Birthday, Reenie!' she bellows, throwing herself at Irene.

'Surprise!' Bonnie squeals.

'Dear me,' Irene manages between hugs. 'You kept that a secret, girls. Fancy telling me you had other plans.'

'Come and see the party table,' Ashlee says, taking Irene by the hand. 'I helped make it pretty.'

The oversized kitchen table has a centrepiece of blush-pink roses – the Queen Elizabeth variety that used to be Flo Thompson's pride and joy – and has been set with blue and white plates, shiny silver-plated cutlery and sparkling wine glasses. Irene fingers the elegant lace tablecloth; delicately woven with an intricate pattern, it looks and feels expensive, like everything else on the table.

'Beautiful, isn't it?' Amy hands her a small present, waving off Irene's protests. 'The tablecloth is from Burano.' At Irene's blank look, she clarifies. 'An island off Venice. It's famous for lacemaking.'

'I'd be worried about spilling things on it.' Irene tips her head at Ashlee.

'It's meant to be used,' Amy says with a smile, returning to the stove.

Off to one side, a distressed wood-framed chalkboard is perched on a tall display easel, with the night's menu chalked on it in neat lettering. Irene squints at the unfamiliar Italian words: *antipasti*, *primi*, *secondi* and *dolci*. All that food! Amy wasn't exaggerating about a feast.

'Come here, Reenie,' Ashlee calls from a stool at the kitchen bench.

Irene sits beside her great-granddaughter as Matt places a long, wooden plank in front of them. It's piled with food. Toasted bread rounds spread with a variety of toppings; chargrilled and marinated eggplant, zucchini, capsicums and mushrooms; torn mozzarella balls; round, green olives; and cured meats – prosciutto, salami. It's like being in a fancy restaurant, Irene thinks, just as Ashlee spits an olive onto the bench, her face screwed up.

'The toasted bread is called crostini,' Matt explains, handing out small plates. 'These ones have tomato and olive, these have smashed broad beans and peas, and these have herbed cheese.'

Irene needs little encouragement. Her stomach's been grumbling since she walked in the door. Biting into a crostino topped with fine herbs and creamy cheese, she closes her eyes. It's the best thing she's tasted in her life.

She sits at the kitchen table and opens her gifts while they watch, self-conscious but enjoying the attention. She thumbs through the book about Italy from Amy and Matt, and strokes the handmade patchwork quilt featuring Ashlee's hand and footprints in rainbow colours from Bonnie. Ashlee saves her gift for last: a red, yellow and blue macaroni necklace on black wool.

'Wow!' Irene hangs the necklace around her neck and hugs her great-granddaughter, breathing in her little girl smell of bubble bath, shampoo and sweat.

'I made it at kindy,' Ashlee informs her. 'It's for you and it's for wearing, not eating.'

'We'll eat this instead.' Amy lowers a platter onto the table. 'Pumpkin arancini and fried zucchini flowers.'

'Yuck! I'm not eating flowers,' Ashlee tells her and turns to Bonnie. 'Can I have one of those ball things?'

Golden and crisp, the arancini ooze mozzarella cheese. Irene wants another, but reaches for a zucchini flower, holding it between two fingers before pushing it into her mouth. It's like spring bursting to life in her mouth.

'What's in this?' Wiping her face, Irene catches Amy watching her, biting her lip.

'It's a blend of prosciutto, herbs, ricotta and parmesan. Do you like it?'

'Ish good,' Irene manages. Amy grins. Irene swallows, then adds, 'Oh, before I forget, there's no book club this week. We've changed it to the next fortnight.'

Amy gives her an inquiring look.

'Margaret's gone up to Broome with her husband,' Irene tells her, 'and Una's at the Gold Coast with Sharon and the kids for the school holidays. Going to do all the theme parks, so she says.'

'Good. I mean, it's nice for her to see family, isn't it, Matt? When did they go?'

'Just after the garden festival.'

Amy and Matt exchange a long glance. 'Always good to have a holiday,' Matt agrees, reaching for a bottle of wine. 'Top up, Irene? Got a nice bottle of Swan Valley sangiovese.'

Irene has the strange feeling there's more to that exchange of looks, but it's none of her beeswax. 'Just a little.' She holds up her hand. 'That'll do.'

Beside her, Ashlee drinks lemonade from a wine glass with the delight of a small child playing grown-ups. Bonnie asks Amy how to make arancini – Amy tells her she makes a double batch of risotto the night before and saves half for the rice balls.

'I'll teach you,' she adds, to Bonnie's delight.

Their clear connection, despite an eight-year age difference, warms Irene's heart. They need each other, Irene thinks, even if they don't know it yet.

She leaves them to it and pads down the hallway to the toilet. She'll be up all night the way wine goes through her. On the way back, she hears laughter from the kitchen. They won't notice if she has a peek in the lounge room. Not to snoop, she's quick to tell herself. To imagine sitting in here with Flo, eating sponge cake. They always said they'd celebrate their seventieth birthdays together, but Flo missed it by a year.

Lowering herself into a soft armchair, she surveys the room. It's like something from *Better Homes and Gardens*: all neutral colours and feature furniture. It's immaculate and stylish but, like the kitchen, with its gleaming appliances and fingerprint-free cupboards, there is nothing left of her best friend. Before, she and Flo would sit together on a sagging floral sofa and talk till the cows came home. Nothing was off limits, from children and husbands to their joys and losses. Not even sex, albeit with giggles and red faces on both parts. You couldn't talk about sex in a room like this, much less have sex. The very idea makes her blush, even at her age. Rooms like this never get messed up. Do they?

'Reenie? Have you fallen in?' Bonnie calls.

Heaving herself up, Irene realises there are no photographs in the room. Not on the walls. Not on the tables. Not even one wedding photo of a smiling Matt and Amy, full of life's promise. Is this what the rest of the house is like? A show home revealing nothing but a sense of style? Poor loves, she thinks. Memories can be healing.

Unless the memories hurt too much.

Bonnie appears beside her. 'Here you are. Come on, we're about to have the mains.'

Back in the kitchen, Amy and Matt serve the next course.

'*Secondi*,' Matt announces, sounding so much like an Italian waiter that Irene giggles. 'Chicken scaloppini with sweet-a marsala; fresh-a pasta with a fall-apart pork ragú; garlicky seasonal vegetables; and thickly-sliced, toasted ciabatta. For the young lady, there's-a pasta with tomato sauce and freshly grated parmesan.'

Irene wants to taste it all, wonders how she'll fit it in, but the food melts in her mouth. She mops up the juices with her bread and reaches for more. Everyone else is doing the same – eating, talking, drinking and eating, reaching past each other.

Ashlee falls asleep in her chair, her fork still in hand. Bonnie tucks her onto the Disney princess flip out sofa she brought from home, and Amy covers the little girl with a small pink blanket that smells of mothballs. Her daughter's?

Bonnie tells Matt that Ashlee was the surprise souvenir of her backpacking adventure in Thailand five years earlier. 'A holiday fling,' she giggles, but Irene knows it was more than that. And then Amy and Matt tell Bonnie about backpacking in Thailand in their twenties; before long the three of them are trading backpacker tales and Irene feels like a plus one at a school reunion.

'It's getting late,' Irene ventures when there's a lull in the conversation. She's usually tucked up in front of the telly watching *Midsomer Murders* by now. 'Maybe we should head off.'

'The *dolci*!' Amy bounces out of her chair. 'You can't go yet. And it's only 8.30.' She replaces the flower centrepiece with a not-so-little platter, piled high with pastries. 'Ricotta-filled cannoli,' she says.

Irene's never tasted the dessert before. Following Matt's lead, she sinks her teeth in, laughing when the filling pops out the other end. The crunch of the deep-fried pastry gives way to an explosion of flavour as the sweet, creamy cheese mingles with other flavours and textures she can only guess at. Pistachio? Perhaps glacé orange peel. Either way, it's heaven in her mouth. Certainly not what Dr Ghorbani had in mind when he told her to eat healthy.

'Resistance is futile,' Matt grins, crunching into a second pastry. 'The only remedy is to eat more.'

Later, Matt clears the table and stacks the dishwasher, declining offers of help. 'Amy's cooked all day,' he says. 'Least I can do is clean up. And the birthday girl doesn't have to.'

Irene likes his style. Sid was cast from the 'cleaning is women's work' mould. He thought feminism was hogwash, and any time Erin or Bonnie talked about equal rights, he went off about 'bloody bra-burners'. He was a good provider though, and Irene hadn't minded, not really. Irene would listen to him rant all day if it brought him back. And it wasn't like she could argue with the girls. She'd never had a job outside the home – Sid didn't want her to and she'd had enough on her hands keeping up with Erin's health issues. But she would have liked one. That's why she started that grief counselling course.

'You're awesome at this, Amy. The whole themed dinner thinga-majig,' Bonnie says with wine-soaked enthusiasm.

Amy inclines her head. 'Thank you. Actually I—'

Bonnie continues, 'You should totally do this more often.'

'Funny you say that,' Amy says, leaning forward. 'I've been mulling something over for ages. I'm starting a travel-themed supper club of about six or eight people. Each month, we'll travel to a different food destination without leaving Blackwood.'

'What? Where?' Tea towel over his shoulder, Matt joins them. 'Here?'

Amy turns to him. 'No. At the café. In the event space on Monday nights.'

He opens his mouth as if to say something, and then, appearing to think better of it he nods, like something has cleared in his mind. Sid used to do that, but Irene can't remember if it was a good thing or not. 'Okay. Sure. Sounds good.' He goes back to drying the dishes.

I bet the rest of the cannoli he's less than thrilled about Amy's supper club plan.

Amy turns back to Irene and Bonnie. 'I want to call it the Around the World Supper Club. It's perfect, don't you think?'

'Totally!' says Bonnie.

'Well,' Irene says. 'There's nothing like that in Blackwood. I'd certainly come along, if it doesn't cost too much. Lord knows, this might be the closest I ever get to travelling.' Bonnie bites her lip and Irene feels guilty. It's the wine. Or exhaustion. She'd better watch her mouth.

Next thing she'll be telling Bonnie what she really thinks of that job up north.

CHAPTER TWENTY-TWO
MATT

There's a sticky note hanging precariously from Matt's work computer the next morning. A neon orange beacon from Carla: *Hope your passport is up to date. We're off to Germany.* Matt stares at it, stomach churning. It's official. He's going to the conference in Düsseldorf. It's in eight weeks. How is he going to get out of this one?

Do I want to?

The office is quiet. No one is due in for at least half an hour. Amy thinks he went in early to prepare for his Monday meeting with the boss, but really it's because he couldn't sleep any longer. When he woke at three, the first thing on his mind was Amy and how happy she had looked last night. How confident. Relaxed. The whole time, she was in her element, doing what she loved: feeding others. And the way her face lit up when she talked about this supper club idea ... it was like seeing the Amy he married all over again.

He loves her so much, even more than when he married her, if that's possible. Loves her smile, her cheeky wit. Loves the way her dinner parties are a message of love, the way she makes everyone at the table feel special, the way she goes the extra mile to create the perfect ambience. Even with everything that's happened – losing Pandora so suddenly, Amy's depression, even her self-absorption at times – he loves her. And he wants more than anything for her to accept that it's okay to be happy again, even after you lose a child. To accept that life is for living, whatever you get out of it. But he's come to see that he needs this for himself too. He needs to live for himself, not just to keep Amy alive.

So, why does he feel out of sorts? Why does he feel that his wife is slipping away?

And now there's this. A work trip back to the place that cost him his daughter and very nearly his wife. Is the sticky note on his desk a portent of doom or an opportunity?

Having heard nothing about the conference in Germany for weeks, he'd half expected head office to send someone else, but instead they chose him. Matt stares at an email from Carla. There's no way he can back out now. The airfares and hotels are already booked. The conference fee is paid. The itinerary is in his inbox. If he backs out now, he might as well kiss goodbye to any respect he's earned over the past few months.

If he doesn't, Amy will hit the roof.

He's had weeks to give her a heads-up. Weeks to tell Carla why he can't go. But he's done neither, telling himself it was pointless because, as the new guy, he was unlikely to be chosen over the others. Yet he'd known it would come to this point. Last time he talked to his mum she reminded him that sticking his head in the sand would give him nothing but sandy ears. Sooner or later, you have to face up to whatever life throws your way.

If only Amy understood that. His eyes drift to the framed photo next to his monitor: a little girl laughing. He's tired of keeping what happened to Pandora locked away like that box in the linen cupboard. He doesn't care anymore if everyone knows.

He massages a tender knot at the base of his neck, wincing. It's been knotted for weeks, since the boss brought up the conference. The thing is, if he really didn't want to go, he would have made it clear, without hesitation. Which tells him one thing: he never intended to say no.

Now he has to break it to Amy.

Matt almost told her after the dinner party, when he and Amy were rehashing the evening in bed. It all went to shit the second he brought up the supper club, even though he rehearsed it over and over in the bathroom.

'What's all this supper club business?' *No. Too patronising.*

'Why didn't you tell me about the supper club?' *Too controlling.*

'Isn't this supper club going to take even more of your time?' *Ditto.*

'It's a lot to take on. You're already doing so much,' he'd finally said. *Empathetic. Concerned.*

The instant the words were out, she got all defensive, like she thought he was suggesting she couldn't handle it. Which, in truth, was partly true. She's doing too much. Every day it becomes clearer that the café is her priority, that she's gone from one extreme to the other.

It's like the café is her child.

'I can handle it, Matt. And I thought you'd be happy that I've found something to take my mind off things.'

'I know, and I am. But I thought we agreed you'd cut back your hours. That you wouldn't rush things. Take it a bit easier.' *Still concerned.*

'I agreed not to work Sundays,' she retorted. 'And except for that time I had no choice, I've stuck to it.' She softened. 'Besides, it's not work, is it? It's a dinner party for a few people we know that happens to be at the café when it's closed to the public. We've had dinner parties before. You used to love them. What's the problem?'

He nearly flung his secret back at her then: *I've travelled overseas for work before. What's the problem?* But he zipped his lips because it was pointless to explain what he was feeling to her when he couldn't explain it to himself. Even when he pours his heart out in his journal his words make no sense.

Carla interrupts his thoughts. Her perfume dances into his nose, its exotic, spicy notes reminding him of Morocco. It's nothing like Amy's perfume, which smells of summer, of citrus and peach. 'You're in early, Matt. Meeting in ten?'

She leaves and Matt closes his inbox. Before they moved to Blackwood, his counsellor told him to step back and let Amy help herself.

And even though he didn't think she could, it's exactly what she's done. She doesn't need him to pick up the slack anymore. But along the way, something's changed between them. He suspects that Amy's moving forward in a slightly different direction to the one he expected. Where does that leave him?

Matt doesn't know where all his uncertainty has come from. All he knows for sure is that ever since Amy opened Brewed to Taste, he's felt surplus to her requirements. And it bothers him. He's grown used to Amy needing him since Pandora died and maybe it's stupid and old-fashioned, but he wants to be needed. Even if only a little.

His inbox beeps with a message from Carla. It's time for their weekly meeting. Can Matt grab two coffees on his way in? As he waits for the espresso machine to dispense the beverages, he makes a decision. Right now, work needs him more than Amy does. And they need him to go to Germany.

He'll break it to Amy tonight. There's a whole day to rehearse and he has to get it right this time.

CHAPTER TWENTY-THREE
AMY

Matt is painfully silent at dinner, pushing his food around the plate the way he does when something is on his mind. Amy watches him across the table as she nibbles the Thai-style crispy pork belly salad she's road testing for the café. It's another winner, with the tangy lime and fragrant herb dressing offsetting the salty kick from the meltingly soft pork. The crackling has the perfect crunch. Perfect for a weekend special. Even better with wine, Nick would say, but the café doesn't have a licence to serve alcohol. The paperwork alone would take an eternity.

'Not hungry, hon?' she asks when she's finished.

Matt pushes the plate aside. 'It's delicious, but I might save it for lunch tomorrow. I think I'm still full from last night.'

Nice try. Matt's got the stomach of a horse and he's never turned down pork belly before. Something's definitely bothering him. She swallows a mouthful of water before asking, 'Are you okay?'

'Yeah, fine. Tired.' He finally looks up from the table. 'Late night, early morning, you know how it is.'

Amy does know. And maybe he is tired. He's been carrying everything for so long. Maybe it's caught up with him. Guilt and shame creeps, but she brushes them away. It's easier for Matt now that she has the café to occupy her mind. She no longer sits in the dark, drowning in loss and grief until he comes home to drag her from the depths. But her gut tells her tiredness is not the reason his barely touched dinner sits between them like a roadblock and his lips are moving like he's rehearsing a speech.

'What's going on?'

Matt looks towards the window, knuckles white. When he faces her, his eyes look lost. As if he doesn't know where to start.

Amy's body tenses, but she forces herself to sound open. Approachable. 'Tell me.'

And then his words pour out like water from a burst pipe. A conference overseas. A big opportunity. He found out for sure today. A really big opportunity.

'Where?' She has a sudden instinct to cover her ears. Or run.

He coughs, then rubs his chin. 'Germany.' Her eyes open wide. 'Düsseldorf. In December.'

'What? Are you serious?' She leans forward, eyes narrowed. 'You can't. Tell your boss you can't.' Her body shakes, but with anger or fear, she's uncertain. 'You promised. You said we'd never go back.'

'You said that.' Matt stands abruptly and begins pacing, avoiding her tear-filled glare. 'I have to go, Aims. It's all paid for. All booked. I can't refuse. I mean, it's my job.'

'But if the boss knows why—'

'It doesn't matter,' his voice raises a notch. 'Look, it scares the shit out of me, to be honest. But I still have to do it.'

'Hold on. It sounds like … are you saying, you want to go to … to that place? After what happened?' *Oh my God, does he?*

He does.

He wants to go there.

His body slumps against the kitchen bench and he lets out sharp sigh, as if the air was punched out of him. 'Yes. And I want … I want you to come with me.'

What the hell?

'I can't believe I'm hearing this.' Amy glares at him. *Let him see how ridiculous this is.* 'How can you even ask me that? Are you mad?'

He comes to her then and takes her hands, but she wrenches away, her breath coming out in shallow gasps. 'It could be good for us, Aims. Closure. We could … we could visit her. And your dad. And then we could try—'

Amy never got to say goodbye to Pandora. She was still unconscious, still touch-and-go when Matt had the funeral. And as soon as it was safe for her to travel and the police gave the okay, the insurance company shipped her back to Australia for more operations and rehabilitation. She refused a window seat and never looked back.

She still feels guilty about that.

'No!' She shuts her eyes against his hopeful gaze. *Don't say it, Matt. Not now.* 'Stuff closure. I hate that word. And stuff Germany.' She spits the words out, realising too late that it wasn't about Germany, not really. Or his work. It's about Pandora. And her. What he's doing is a betrayal. 'There's no way in hell I'm going back there. No way.'

His eyes drop. For a moment, the only sound is her ragged breathing and the hum of the fridge. 'Let's talk about it later. When you've had a chance to think about it.'

She starts to back away. Reaches for the keys hanging on a hook near the door. 'I've got to get out of here.'

'What? Where are you going?'

'Away from you. I can't look at you right now.'

'Fucking hell,' he says under his breath, shaking his head like she's a child having a tantrum. Any other time, it would piss her off but she can't get any madder than she is. 'This is my job,' he says to himself. 'My job.'

'And obviously your job's more important than us.'

His eyes go black and one hand flings up like a stop sign. 'Don't even go there.'

The bedroom door slams shut.

Amy looks at the keys bunched in her hand and makes up her mind. Grabbing her coat, she jogs out to the car.

Who cares where she goes, as long as it's away from Matt?

∽

They avoid each other for the next two days. When Matt comes home from work, he goes to his study. The click of the latch snaps through the empty house. Amy has no clue what he does in there. Sometimes she hears voices. Maybe he's talking to his mother. In bed, he feigns sleep, even though Amy knows he's wide awake, like her.

Her initial shock and anger has faded, but she has no idea how to talk to him without falling apart. It hurts too much. She's scared if she starts, she won't be able to stop, and then they'll finally have to face the one thing they've never talked about.

On the third day, she takes a deep breath when his car pulls up. They can't go on like this, like they're standing at the edge of a crumbling cliff. She meets him on the back verandah.

'I'm sorry.'

He looks at her properly for the first time in days. His eyes are sad. 'Me too.'

'I know you have to go,' she falters, 'and I don't want you to. It brings everything up and I know it's all I'll think about while you're there. But … I understand that it's work.'

Matt looks like he wants to say more, but instead pulls her close. She sniffs, and then rests her head against his chest. 'But, I won't go with you. Not yet.'

She hears him swallow, hears the sound of his heart thumping. 'Okay.'

They stay like that, holding each other, until a shivering wind pushes them inside.

CHAPTER TWENTY-FOUR
AMY

On her next day off, Amy plans the first supper club evening, glad for something to focus on other than Matt's trip to Germany. But first, she cleans the house, neglected all week. Maybe they should get a cleaner. Maybe Irene knows someone who could do with the extra money. Tuning into a pop playlist on Spotify, Amy sings as she cleans. This morning when she woke, her thoughts turned to Pandora, but instead of sadness, she'd simply thought *hello*.

She takes her time dusting and vacuuming, scrubbing and washing. By the time she's finished, the clothes line is loaded, and the house smells of lemon and lavender. And she's decided that the first stop for the Around the World Supper Club will be France, landing a week from now.

She's creating an online invitation when Bonnie comes over, returning the pink blanket Amy draped over Ashlee the other night.

'Hey, Amy. Thought I'd bring this over before I fly out tomorrow. I washed it for you.'

Amy forces herself not to react. Bonnie had no way of knowing that she'd never washed Pandora's special blanket, not wanting to lose the scent of her little girl. Mothballs had long ago obscured the warm smell but she'd told herself it was still in the heart of the woollen fibres. 'Oh, thanks.'

'What are you doing? Got time for a cuppa?'

'Just working on supper club ideas. I want to have the first one next week, before I second-guess myself.' Taking in Bonnie's tired face, Amy realises the blanket wasn't the only reason her friend dropped by. 'You okay?'

'Yeah, I'm fine.' Bonnie's voice is too bright, but Amy doesn't press her. 'Want to off-load your ideas?'

Amy makes tea and they find a comfortable spot on the couch, tucking their feet under. They spend an hour talking about the supper club, before moving on to books, travelling and food.

A clap of thunder startles them. Outside, it's come over dark and heavy. Amy leaps up. 'Shit! The washing!'

They run out to the line, frantically piling clothes and towels into baskets, making it inside as fat raindrops pelt the roof. Panting, they fall onto the sofa and Bonnie starts folding the towels, as if they're her own.

'Leave it,' Amy protests. 'I can do it later.'

'It gives me something to do. If my hands aren't busy, I fiddle with things. My hair. My nails.' She holds up her hands. The nails are ragged. 'Look at this. I tell Ashlee not to bite her nails, but I'm a poor example.'

'Well, you're not folding our undies.' With a grin, Amy rifles through the two baskets and retrieves her knickers and Matt's boxers, then pushes the baskets back. 'There. That's better.'

There's a low rumble of thunder, followed by sheeting rain. Wind pushes a branch against a window.

Bonnie looks concerned. 'Crap. That's wild. Hope it clears up before I pick up Ash from kindy. Don't fancy driving in that.'

Amy can't help it. Her hands still on the T-shirt she's folding and a memory rises: another little girl in a car on a wild and woolly day.

She becomes aware that Bonnie is speaking. 'Amy? What's wrong? What did I say?'

Amy shakes her head as if that will summon an excuse. *Think!*

'Nothing. I was thinking … this top's a bit wet.' She places it to one side and reaches for another. 'What were you saying?'

'Reenie's driving back from Bunbury later. I hope she's okay.' To Amy's surprise, tears fill Bonnie's eyes and she sniffs loudly.

'What is it? What's wrong?' The irony is not lost on Amy that she's asking Bonnie personal questions, yet discourages the same.

'Oh, Amy, I'm so worried. About Reenie. She had a doctor's appointment last week and today she's having a bunch of tests. Didn't even tell me about them. I only found out because she left her diary in the kitchen.'

'What kind of tests?'

'Bloods. An ECG. Something else too. I texted her to ask what's going on, but all she said was not to worry, it was only a routine check-up. And she hasn't answered her phone since.' Bonnie sniffs again. 'What if something's wrong with her, like, really wrong? My granddad died of a heart attack. What if Reenie's got something wrong with her heart?'

'Maybe it really is routine,' Amy reassures her. Although, Irene's short of breath a lot. Amy always put it down to the older woman chasing after a little girl. Could it be her heart instead?

'Maybe. But I have to go away later next week.' Bonnie hesitates. 'Amy, I know you're really busy. But can you look out for her? Let me know if I need to come back.' She stands and paces over to the window and back. The rain is showing no sign of easing. 'I wish I didn't take this bloody job. I couldn't bear it if something happened to Reenie while I was away. I already feel guilty enough.'

Amy nods, remembering the last time she saw her grandmother. Aged eighty and still living in her Wheatbelt cottage, she'd been in her rocking chair listening to Amy pour her heart out, stroking her adult granddaughter's hair back from her face, wiping away tears that streamed down Amy's face in a waterfall of grief. Amy went back to Perth and the next day, Gran was dead. An aneurysm.

Tears threaten, and she refills their tea cups. The tea is cold. Should she make another pot? She decides against it. 'Irene raised you, didn't she?'

'That's right.' Bonnie sits. 'Has Irene told you the story? No? Well, it's like this. I didn't have the best childhood. My mum Erin – my dad was never in the picture – had mental health issues and she was all over the place, you know? I had no routine, no rules, basically fended for myself. We were living up in Perth then. Me, Mum and her boyfriend – she met him when I was about ten. He was … violent. Not to me. To Mum. But she wouldn't leave him. She loved him.'

Amy leans forward, eyes on her friend. She doesn't want to interrupt, despite questions rushing, burning like fire that's grabbed hold of dry wood. The image provokes a word she knows all too well: devastation.

'Anyhow, one day, Mum had to go to hospital. She'd overdosed. Tried to kill herself.' Bonnie's tone flattens, as if she's said these words a thousand times. Amy's heart clenches in understanding. 'And Reenie came and got me, brought me here.'

Bonnie stares at the window, swallowing heavily. Without thinking it through, Amy moves to her side and puts her arm around Bonnie. The action surprises her. She can't remember the last time she has initiated something like this, yet it feels so natural. When Bonnie looks at Amy, tears shine in her eyes.

'You'd think,' Bonnie manages a watery smile, 'you'd get used to telling the story. But you don't.'

No. You never do.

It's quiet for a few moments, save for the sound of steady rain and a shed door banging somewhere.

'But when your mum got out of hospital, when she was better, didn't you go back to her?' Amy asks, breaking the silence.

Bonnie takes a deep breath. 'She didn't. Get better. She got out, met up with her boyfriend and they went on a bender. He'd scored some drugs and she couldn't say no. They were so out of it, they stole a car. Went on a drug-crazed drive through Perth, crashed into a concrete pylon. They both … they died on impact.'

Amy can't hold back the gasp, nor her own tears, barely restrained by a gate of will, from spilling. So much in common. Her breath quickens, coming out in short pants.

It's too close. I can't do this. I need to get away.

She starts to rise, but Bonnie pats her hand, pulls her down. Fighting the instinct to run, Amy sits.

'It's okay, Amy. I've had a long time to accept that this loss is part of who I am.' She nibbles at a finger. 'I was twelve. Irene raised me from then on. I didn't make it easy for her, but she stuck by me all the way. That's why we're so close. She's like a mother to me. And that's why I can't lose her.'

Amy's throat constricts and she chokes on the sob she's barely managed to contain. She bends her head, trying to slow her racing breath. She knows what it's like to lose a mother. Her life was destroyed that day. She thought she would be broken forever, until Gran stepped in, and slowly she was put back together. Same-same, but different. But Pandora's death broke Amy beyond repair. How do you recover from losing a child? You never really do when you lose someone you love. You get up. You do what you have to. But you're never the same person. And you never forget. With your child, it feels magnified by a million.

Memories roar in her ears, fighting her efforts to calm. From what seems a great distance, she hears Bonnie speaking: 'Amy, breathe. In. Out. In. Out. That's it.'

When her breathing slows, Amy dabs at her eyes with a tissue. 'I'm sorry. Sorry for your loss. For what you've been through. And for my reaction.'

'You were having a panic attack, right?'

'Yes. I'm sorry.'

'No need to be sorry. I've had them too. Pain in the arse, sometimes.' Bonnie grins at Amy, who manages a weak smile. 'The question is, Amy, what triggered it? Do you want to tell me?' I told you my story, her eyes seem to say.

'No. Yes. I—' Fear shouts at Amy to say no, to come up with an excuse.

'You're safe, Amy. Safe.'

The words give Amy the strength she needs. 'My ... my grandmother brought me up too.'

Bonnie's eyebrows flick up slightly and then settle into a look of understanding.

Amy goes on. 'Dad left when I was eight. Mum didn't handle it well. She was depressed. Couldn't go to work or anything. We moved in with Gran – she lived out in the Wheatbelt – and she took care of everything and everyone.'

'She sounds like Reenie.'

'They *are* similar. I noticed it the first time I met Irene. But different too. Gran was more old-fashioned, less free-spirited.' Amy prepares herself for the next part of her story. 'Mum became more and more depressed. Back then, there wasn't the help there is today, not in the country. And one day ... one day she ...'

Amy falters. She's only told this story to a couple of people in her life. Matt. His parents. A friend in high school she's lost touch with. Kel. She swallows, gathers up the nerve she needs to continue. 'One day Mum took Gran's car, saying she was going into town. I remember waving goodbye on the verandah. Mum waved back.' She's strangely, unnaturally calm as the rest spills out. 'And then, on the way to town she ... she ... she drove into ... into a big road sign. It wasn't an accident.'

Bonnie gasps, but Amy is in control of herself now. 'Like you, it happened a long time ago. I was eight. But that's why I reacted like I did.' *Partly.* She decides against bringing up Pandora.

'I get the feeling you don't talk about it much.'

'No. Not for ages. I'm not very good at ... at sharing myself.'

Bonnie gives a rueful laugh. 'And sometimes I'm the queen of TMI.' At Amy's questioning look, she adds, 'TMI. Too Much Information.'

'Ah, I see.' Amy stares out the window. Sun peeks through a gap in the rainclouds, shining through the window. The downpour has eased to a trickle. She gives Bonnie a wan smile. 'We're a right pair, aren't we?' It strikes her that the warmth of friendship is starting to thaw her frozen heart. It's good to have someone to talk to, someone who understands.

Blanketed in memories, they sit side by side, sharing funny stories about the women who mothered them until Bonnie has to go. Amy watches her hurry away, then carries the clean clothes and Pandora's blanket to her bedroom. Drawers open and close, until she finds herself bending over her bedside drawer. And then it's open too, and the box Pandora decorated with gold spray-painted pasta is in her hands. They shake as she lifts out first Pandora's handprint, then a photo with bent edges.

Three smiling faces look out at her. Christmas Day, twenty-six years earlier. Three months later, the smiles were gone and so was her mother. Tears fall as she traces her fingers over her mother's face, then her grandmother's, and then her daughter's rainbow fingerprints.

'We're a right pair, aren't we,' she whispers to each of them. Maybe they can hear. Maybe not. She sniffs Pandora's blanket. It smells of lavender fabric softener now, but she tucks it under her pillow anyway.

Her mother made a choice to die. Her grandmother succumbed to age. But Pandora would be here if it wasn't for Amy. Pandora was in the wrong place, the wrong time.

Losing her hurts most of all.

You're not supposed to live longer than your kids, Amy thinks for the thousandth time. You're supposed to protect them until they're big enough to protect themselves.

She failed the biggest part of being a mother.

And in doing that, she failed Matt in two ways. She couldn't save Pandora, their little girl.

And she didn't tell him about the baby before that rainy day.

CHAPTER TWENTY-FIVE
AMY

'How do I look?' Amy's channelled vintage Brigitte Bardot for the inaugural Around the World Supper Club, albeit with brown instead of blonde locks. Her look is coquettish – a tight black off-the-shoulder top balanced by a full gingham skirt, with a red scarf looped around her neck and fastened with a ring. Her hair is artfully tussled in a *just had hot sex* manner and her eyes mimic Bardot's signature cat-eyes.

The moment she sent out invites for the French-themed supper, Amy was torn. Audrey Hepburn's classic Parisian or Bardot's bombshell?

'You'll look gorgeous whatever you wear,' Matt said, when she asked him, which was his standard response.

It was trivial compared to the logistics of organising the food and getting Matt's support, but at the same time everything had to be perfect, from the food and drinks, to the music and attire. Finding a gingham skirt in the Blackwood op shop was the decider.

Amy twirls in front of Matt, whose gaze is like fingertips tracing her skin. His hair is wet and sticking up, a white towel is draped around his waist. She bites her lip. His chest and the fine line of dark hair disappearing under the fabric is inconveniently distracting. She wants to reach out and trace her hand over the taut contours of his abdomen, up and over his nipples, which have hardened under her reciprocal gaze.

She shakes her head. *No time for that.* These days, desire catches her off guard when it surfaces. Like now.

'Do I look okay?' she asks again.

Matt's voice is low and rough. 'You look edible.' His lips are hot on her neck and Amy can't think.

'Matt! We can't. We've got to go. I've got to set up the starters.' She breathes out the words with effort. She's been at Brewed to Taste all day, cooking and decorating, and has only allowed forty-five minutes to shower, change, and get back there for last-minute prep.

He laughs. Releases her. 'I know. But I wanted to taste … dessert.'

'You're incorrigible.'

'Hungry.'

'You'll be well fed soon enough. There's enough food to feed a French village.'

'Oh, I hope so.'

The alarm on her phone peals. 'Saved by the bell,' Matt quips. He drops his towel and winks. 'Why don't I meet you down there? Unless you want me to turn up like this?'

'I'm not sure if our guests will be offended or thrilled.' Amy's gaze falls to the place where his towel should be, and then her eyes snap up. 'Hurry, okay? I'll see you there.'

'Ten minutes,' he promises. 'And Aims? You look *très chic, très sex-cee.*'

'I was going for effortlessly chic, that French *je ne sais quoi,*' she says, 'but that will do. See you!' Amy scuttles off, Matt's cheeky snigger chasing her down the hall. For someone who wasn't overly enthused by the supper club idea, he's in a good mood. That's one load off her mind.

Nick and Devi arrive at Brewed to Taste first, kissing her hand like Gallic courtiers.

'Ooh la la, Aim-ee,' Nick says, handing her a bottle of French chardonnay and a cash contribution to the cost of dinner. 'Matt won't be able to keep his hands off you tonight. You look stunning.'

'Thank you. You're looking pretty debonair yourselves. I love your shoes!'

The men are walking advertisements for layered Parisian style, with dark-wash slimline jeans, fitted tees, tailored blazers – Nick's is brown leather, while Devi's is black – finished off with scarves looped around their necks. The classy-casual mix couldn't be further from the checked chef pants, black T-shirts, bandannas and white aprons they wear while working, and Nick takes it up a notch, sporting cherry red leather brogues that look like they're fresh from a Paris boutique.

'Aren't they divine?' Grinning, Nick prances around like he's on a catwalk, hamming it up while the rest of the guests arrive, only stopping to whistle when June demonstrates *la bise*, the art of French cheek kissing, on a pink-cheeked Frank Taylor.

Watching them, Amy recalls her disbelief when Matt wanted to invite the tradesman.

'Do you think he'll fit in with the others?' He hadn't struck her as the foodie type when he was fitting out the café.

'Give him a chance,' Matt had said. 'He's a good bloke. And he's my mate.' The implication being that the other guests were *her* friends.

Amy greets them all now, delighted that everyone's dressed for the occasion. June in a blouse and skirt, with a scarf around her throat and a jaunty beret atop her grey curls; Bonnie in a little black dress, kitten heels and pearls, hair slicked back behind her ears; Irene resplendent in a vintage black beaded evening gown she says she found in the Blackwood op shop; Frank in stiff trousers, an old-fashioned paisley waistcoat and red bow tie. And Matt, Roger Vadim to her Bardot in a black turtleneck, tailored black pants, and black brogues. With his trendy black glasses he looks smart, French, and utterly kissable.

'Everything okay?' Amy asks Bonnie, who seems flustered.

'Oh my God, Ashlee chucked the biggest tantrum when I said she couldn't take Henry to the babysitter's. And then I caught her shoving Flossie into her backpack.' She accepts a flute of *Möet & Chandon* from Matt. 'I'm surprised you didn't hear her bellowing from our house.'

'Kids, hey?' Matt winks at Bonnie, and then hands the others flutes of champagne. 'To the Around the World Supper Club,' he says, raising his glass. 'To good health, food and friendship. *Santé!*'

'*Santé,*' everyone echoes, except Frank who bellows 'Cheers, mate!' and quaffs it down in one gulp.

Amy closes her eyes to savour the fruity hit, before motioning to a tray of savoury finger food resting atop an embroidered white table-cloth – crisp cheese and herb *sablés,* anchovy and gruyere pinwheels, marinated olives, and truffle and chive blinis.

'Dig in,' she tells them. Frank doesn't need to be asked twice.

A jazz rendition of 'La Vie en Rose' drifts through the café. June asks Frank to dance and he pushes his chair back, flushing. Bonnie and Irene leaf through French-inspired coffee table books; Amy hears snippets of their conversation about French lifestyles. Irene, it seems, has always wanted to live in a French village and shop at local markets, whereas Bonnie desires the romance of Paris. Frank, flushed from dancing or June's attention, asks if they've seen the television show about renovating old French farmhouses. Matt and Devi talk of backpacking in France. Why was she so anxious about everyone gelling, about the food being perfect? About proving herself. It's going better than she expected.

She scrutinises the event space. Up since sunrise, cooking and crossing items off the to-do list all day, Amy's had no time to fully appreciate her efforts. But judging by her guests' reactions, her French shabby chic with a modern twist is a winner. White enamel milk jugs filled with fresh lavender from home, tea light candles in small jam jars, a makeshift hessian tablecloth topped with a white lace runner and scattered with rose petals, and coloured glass bottles tied together and filled with voluptuous rose blooms from Irene's garden for the centrepiece. Sheer curtains hang from the street-front windows. Bonnie had offered to help set up and cook while Ashlee was at school, but Amy demurred. It seemed important to do it all herself the first time.

'What's rata-towlie?' Frank asks as she heads back to the kitchen. The creased brow as he reads the menu makes her giggle. He's in for a foodie education tonight.

Amy listens to them talk and laugh as she seasons the French onion soup and checks the *boeuf bourguignon*, the *cassoulet de lapin*, and the ratatouille. Nick joins her in the kitchen. Deftly, he slices the baguette and toasts it under the grill. As Amy ladles soup, he tops each bowl with toasted bread, grated gruyere and, without being asked, slides each bowl under the grill, keeping watch as the cheese bubbles and browns. Amy splashes brandy onto each one before she and Nick carry them to the table. The air is redolent with caramelised onion, fragrant stock, the smoky whiff of the alcohol.

Matt fills the wine glasses with a dry white, explaining the importance the French place on pairing food and wine. Frank looks mystified.

'Be just as happy with a coldie,' he says, to Matt's feigned horror.

Amy watches as her guests poke their spoons through the cheesy crust and take their first, tentative sips of the broth. The pleasure on their faces is a thing of beauty. Yes, this supper club was a good idea.

Back in the kitchen, Amy mixes the batter for the madeleines she'll serve with coffee later. The finished product looks simple, but careful attention is needed with measurements, and the butter needs to be ever so slightly browned before being added to the flour, sugar and eggs. A second's distraction will ruin the flavour, taking it from nutty to burnt. Behind her, Matt stacks the dishwasher. 'It's going great,' he whispers. 'I'm sorry I wasn't more enthusiastic about it. I should have—'

'Don't worry about it,' she says, squeezing his arm. They don't need to worry about the should haves or anything else tonight.

Back at the table, June has everyone captivated by the story of an Australian au pair who met a Frenchman with a moustache, beret, and a voice she could listen to all night. Political-intellectual lectures in Saint Germain; late-night meals in Montmartre cafés; walks along lamp-lit, rain-dampened streets; a surprise proposal under the Eiffel Tower. A dramatic break-up in the street.

'He was married,' she tells them. 'I came back to Australia, heart-broken but wiser in the ways of the world. Inherited the old house I'm living in, and eventually left city life behind for the country. Never looked back.'

'Bastard,' Frank says, summing up Amy's own thoughts. She has her own story of first love gone wrong, but it's forgotten when she catches a tender look between June and Frank. Is something going on with them? The timer goes off before she can decide.

Aromas of wine, meat, vegetables and spices waft around the table as the main course is served. *Boeuf bourguignon*, rich with nearly two bottles of burgundy, made the day before because it always tastes better the second day. A plate of sautéed mushrooms sprinkled with fresh chives is placed next to a bowl piled high with steamed baby potatoes. *Cassoulet de lapin* – rabbit stew with white beans – is set down next to a fragrant, vegetable-laden ratatouille. Hunks of bread rest on wooden planks with small crocks of French butter.

Reverting to his faux French accent, Matt introduces the wine, a full-bodied bordeaux. Frank gives this one the thumbs up, while Irene worries about the size of her glass.

'It's very big,' she says. 'I'll only have a taste. Besides, I'm driving.' Amy and Bonnie exchange glances. Bonnie had offered to be skipper, but Irene insisted.

Amy hides a smile when Devi tells Frank about true French-style rabbit cassoulet. 'They come with heads. The rabbits. That's how you buy them.'

'Heads?' Frank pushes his stew around.

'It's a law or something. To prove that you're not buying cats.' Devi's enjoying Frank's discomfort. Amy hadn't realised her sous chef had such a mischievous streak.

The others look horrified.

'Cats?' Bonnie squeaks.

'Seriously,' Devi says. He's lapping up the attention, Amy can tell. 'The French love eating rabbit heads. Brains and all.'

Frank gives Amy a questioning look. 'Are there—'

'It's okay,' Amy reassures him. 'No rabbit heads were used in the making of this cassoulet.'

'Bloody frogs,' Frank mutters.

'Frank!' June splutters. 'You can't say that!'

'No frogs were used in the making of this cassoulet, either,' Amy quips. She's light-headed and light-hearted, high on good company, food, wine, and a peculiar feeling of belonging. A shadow through the gauzy curtains catches her eye, as if someone is peering inside. She has an unsettled feeling she knows who it is. Una is back in town; she saw her in Blackwood Fresh. Pushing away dark thoughts, she turns her attention back to the table.

'Tell them how we met, Nick,' Devi's saying now.

Nick gives him a good-natured bump on the arm before telling them how he ordered *bourdin noir pommes* from a good-looking waiter, not knowing he'd ordered blood sausage with apples. 'I was showing off by pretending I spoke French. Had no idea he was a fellow Aussie on a gap year.'

Devi, who thought Nick was equally cute, had no intention of telling him until the best possible moment.

'He finished it off and asked for more,' Devi says, his words spilling out between snorts of laughter. 'You should have seen his face when I told him it was made from pigs' blood and squeezed into intestines. And of course, even though he loved it *so* much, he point-blank refused to have another bite.'

'I bloody wouldn't either,' Frank splutters. He looks at the hearty serving of *boeuf bourguignon* on his plate.

'Don't worry,' Amy whispers. 'That's beef in there. Unlike *andouillette.*'

'What's that?'

'A white sausage made from pork offal.'

Frank shivers. 'Gawd, Amy, you're putting me off the humble snag, you are.'

The madeleines are cooling on the cake rack, their buttery, lemony scent reaching through to the long table. Frank and June join Matt in the kitchen to rinse dishes and stack the dishwasher. The group members have decided to take turns washing up at future suppers. Amy's too tired to argue.

While Matt makes coffee, Frank watches, mouth agape and dishes forgotten, as Amy caramelises demerara sugar on *crème brûlée* pots using a commercial blowtorch. She lets him have a turn, guiding him to move the torch steadily across the surface to caramelise it evenly. His excitement reminds her of Pandora, back when she used to help in the kitchen. But tonight, the memory warms her insides.

Amy brings out the dessert – the *crème brûlée*, which has a layer of apples hidden beneath the crème. Madeleines, still warm, ready to melt in the mouth. Nick's chocolates. Matt pours cognac – coppery in hue, aromatic with dried fruit and hints of clove and cinnamon.

Chilled acoustic music plays in the background. The room breathes contentment and companionship. Murmurs of appreciation ripple around the table. Frank grins like Pandora used to when his spoon cracks through the toffee crust on the *brûlée*.

'These *crème brûlées* are much better than the good ones in Blackwood Fresh,' Irene says.

'These madeleines should be on the Brewed to Taste menu,' Nick and Devi tell Amy.

'I can't possibly fit in another morsel.' June takes two madeleines anyway.

After brandy, they relax in their chairs, replete. Nick and Devi leave first, insisting that it's fine if Amy comes in late the next day. She doesn't argue. Tuesdays are always slower. Everyone else leaves in an appreciative whirl of thanks and goodbyes, their voices cutting through the cool night air. Watching Irene and Bonnie walk to the car arm in arm, Amy leans against Matt and yawns. It's as if the others have taken her energy with her. She'll be asleep the second her head hits the pillow.

Matt captures her yawn with his mouth, drawing Amy inside at the same time. He tastes of brandy and as he presses against her, she remembers wanting him when he stood before her in nothing but a towel. To her surprise, she wants him still.

'You.' His eyes are shining. 'You are an amazing woman. Tonight was … it was wonderful. It was good for us. And this might sound strange, but it's convinced me finally that moving here was the right thing to do.' When she doesn't pull away, his eyes twinkle. 'Now that everyone has gone, can we go home to what we started earlier?'

CHAPTER TWENTY-SIX
AMY

The first time the man in jeans and a trendy blazer snaps a photo inside Brewed to Taste, Amy ignores it. People do it all the time in the café. Their eyes light up when they see the food and they faff around with the table so they can take the perfect snap. It used to grate on her, the way they'd whip out their phones, heedless of anyone around them. Now she grudgingly accepts that some people would rather take photos of their food than simply enjoy the food and company.

The second time the man takes a photo, she stiffens. Was that phone aimed at her? Or is she oversensitive because she's exhausted after last night's supper? Maybe she should have stayed home. He catches her eye, winks, and *snap-snaps* a few more shots in her general direction.

'Look at him,' she hisses to Troy and Devi. 'Why can't he just enjoy the food?'

'Maybe he's a reviewer?' Devi says.

'No, an influencer,' puts in Troy.

'I hate that word,' Amy mutters. 'And I'd rather he aimed his camera at food and not people,' she says. 'It's an invasion of privacy.'

'Take a chill pill, Amy,' Troy says with a grin. 'It's free advertising, yeah?'

'I suppose.' But when the man winks again as he gets up to leave, her stomach knots. Something is off and it's not her food.

The man is waiting in the carpark behind the café when Amy leaves. Goosebumps pimple her arms, but she walks straight past him to her car. If he tries anything—

'Amy Bradford?' The confident male voice rings in her ear. He's right behind her.

Amy freezes. 'No, sorry. Wrong person.'

'That's right. You go by Amy Bennet now, don't you? Eric Rolfe from *The Sunday Courier*. Got wind you were down here.'

Amy turns slowly to face him, but says nothing. *No prizes for guessing who told him.*

'I'm doing a follow-up on your story and wanted to have a chat.'

'No.'

'Come on, Amy. It's been three years. People would like to know how you and Matt are coping, what changes you've made to your lives. Human interest story. That's all.'

'No. Not interested.'

'Wait!' The reporter pushes on. 'Let's just have a coffee. In your café, if you want.'

'It's closed.'

'How about the pub?'

'No. Can you move away from my car?'

He holds up his hands and takes a few steps back. 'Honestly, it's just a follow-up piece. Your story had so much attention, people would like to know—'

'No! I said no!'

'Look, with or without your comment, we're going to—'

Her heart hammering, Amy gets into her car. 'Get out of my way.'

His eyes bore into her as she speeds away. Guilt has caught up with her and she has no idea how she's going to outrun it this time.

PART TWO

Some of us think holding on makes us strong, but sometimes it is letting go.

— HERMAN HESSE

CHAPTER 27

IRENE

Two days later, Irene fidgets in her chair at Brewed to Taste, waiting for the rest of the Blackwood Book Club members to arrive. By some stroke of luck, Ashlee didn't make a fuss when Irene dropped her off for a morning play date, the doctor was running on schedule, and there was a parking spot right out the front of the café. Her fingers tap on the table as her eyes seek out the oversized wall clock. It's nearly ten. Usually she'd welcome a few quiet moments before the others arrived, but today she wants the distraction of small talk.

The test results confirmed angina. Irene began shaking when Dr Ghorbani gave her the news, with his lecture face on. He had no way of knowing that as her fingers closed around the prescriptions he gave her, Irene's dreams of travelling slipped further out of reach.

Now she has to tell Bonnie the news. The poor lamb has been anxious and solicitous since she found out about the tests. All 'Are you sure you should be doing that?', 'Sit down and rest' and 'Would you like a cup of tea?' to the point Irene got snarky.

'Stop your fussing,' she'd snapped.

Bonnie's gone up north again, and Irene wishes her granddaughter was here, fussing around. Not too much. A cuppa now and then. But she can do that herself. What she really wants is for Bonnie to resume the lion's share of caring for Ashlee. That's all.

Bonnie still has no clue about how Ashlee plays up when she leaves. Like yesterday. Ashlee had a bad day at kindy. A quarrel with a little boy. She decked him with a book, the teacher told Irene at pick-up time. He'd scribbled on the picture of Bonnie she was drawing. They both ended up in time out. Ashlee cried and didn't eat her lunch or play with anyone else for the rest of the day.

Last night Irene found Ashlee asleep in her bed, sucking her thumb. Still tired after the supper club, she didn't have the heart to carry Ashlee back to her own room. Instead, she crawled in beside the little girl, comforted when small fingers folded around hers. Sid used to hold her hand in his sleep too. It's times like these she misses him most of all. And Flo. She always knew what to do.

'There's a time for saying yes and a time for saying no. A time for keeping silent and a time for speaking your mind,' she often told Irene. 'You need to learn which is which.'

This morning Ashlee had a meltdown because they'd run out of her favourite cereal. Was it time to come clean with Bonnie? She imagines the conversation.

'What should I do?' Bonnie would say.

'Quit your job and come home,' Irene would say, casually. She's practised it so many times. 'I don't want to spend my final years raising a child. I want to travel before I die.' It would solve a lot of problems – for all three of them – if Bonnie found a job closer to home. Amy offered her one at Brewed to Taste a while back. Maybe that's still an option.

But Irene won't say it, even though it teeters on the tip of her tongue every time Bonnie packs her bags. She's going to do what she can to give Bonnie the chance to step out on her own (with or without Jake). She'll take her medication, go back to yoga classes at the community centre, maybe even take up swimming. She'll keep going to the Around the World Supper Club dinners, even though Monday's one wore her out. It's all going to be okay.

'Irene! Where's Ashlee today?' Her friends arrive for book club in a bustle of greetings and small talk. Amy's not far behind them, notebook in one hand and a glass water bottle in the other.

'At her friend's house,' Irene says. She orders a double black coffee and a thin slice of Persian love cake, her favourite. Surely Dr Ghorbani wouldn't object to that. Fragrant with rosewater and citrus, and textured with almond and pistachio, it's cake heaven. 'Where's Una? It's not like her to be late.'

No doubt Una will be full of stories of the Gold Coast. Which will lead to the cruise she and Margaret are going on. Irene sighs. Life has a way of shoving the things you most want in your face when you can't have them. Part of her would like to tell Una all about the supper club, mouthful by delectable mouthful. See how she likes it.

'Should be here any minute,' June returns, pulling out her copy of *Burial Rites* by Hannah Kent. 'She was in Blackwood Fresh. Said to wait for her.' She turns to Amy. 'I'll have a cappuccino and the same cake as Irene.'

'There's a journalist from Perth staying at the bed and breakfast,' Margaret says after she gives her order. 'Said he's here for work but wouldn't give me a whisker of a hint. I wonder if it's about the mayor.'

Amy drops her pen and it rolls under Irene's chair. Irene fumbles for it and passes it back to the younger woman, whose fingers are shaking for some reason.

Una bustles in. 'Sorry I'm late, ladies,' she says. Her imperious tone makes it clear their time is less important than hers. Shoving herself between Irene and Margaret, Una makes a show of settling herself at the table. 'Now, let me see, what do I want today? No, Margaret, not the chocolate cake.'

Irene glances past Una and sees Sharon come into the café with a strange man. It's not her ex. Last Irene heard, he'd nicked off out of town with someone else. When Una glances across the room and gives her daughter the slightest of nods, unease ripples through Irene. The hairs on her arms quiver as goosebumps prickle her skin and she is overcome by a peculiar feeling that something big is aligning behind the scenes.

Does anyone else feel it?

Irene's eyes flick towards Amy, who is chatting with June. Amy looks up. Her expression stiffens as her eyes drift to Una and then across to Sharon and the man. Her hands still; her face and body are frozen for a few beats before she appears to collect herself.

'Yoo-hoo, Amy.' Una motions Amy to her side. 'I'll have the coffee-and-cake special.' As Amy turns to go, Una adds, 'Sharon and I figured out where we recognised you from.'

The blood drains from Amy's face and she pulls away. All of a sudden, Irene knows where she's seen her before. That same grief-stricken face stared back from a thousand newspapers for weeks. That same face everyone talked about with hushed tones: *How awful. Was she speeding? I heard ...*

'Stop,' she hisses to Una. 'This is not the time.'

Una's eyes lock on hers. Uncertainty flickers and then it's replaced with challenge. And something else. Self-righteousness. Satisfaction. Jealousy.

'Amy's the woman whose little girl died in a car crash in Germany.' Gasps whip around the table like an accelerated Mexican wave. Una continues, her voice a magnet that draws all eyes to her. 'It was all over the news, remember?'

Amy Bennet, or Amy Bradford, as the media called her, was the mother of four-year-old Pandora, killed in a horrific accident in Germany three years earlier. Amy was three months' pregnant, but the baby didn't survive. Initially, blame fell on Amy who was in hospital recovering from her own terrible injuries, before investigations revealed the driver of the other car was texting and speeding when his car slammed into Amy's. He walked away with bruises and broken ribs.

Irene remembers when Amy and Matt's story unfolded day after day. She and Sid skirted around the subject back then. It was too close to home, although Erin's death had attracted little media attention, overshadowed by news that an Austrian girl had escaped from her kidnapper after eight years. The papers were frenzied with speculation and the unfortunate deaths of two drug-addled adults went largely unnoticed.

Around her, reactions unfold in slow motion. A camera clicks in the background. Someone whispers, *I knew I'd seen her somewhere.* The glass of water slips from Amy's grasp and shatters; Irene watches helplessly as grief and guilt coagulate before Amy's face closes into itself and the ground falls from under her feet. For an instant, no one moves, as if they're all locked into place and then—

Margaret rushes off, calling for Nick.

Irene leaps up, fuming. 'How *could* you, Una?' she says over her shoulder, kneeling by Amy's side. June joins her and together they shift Amy onto her back.

'Disgraceful,' June mutters, using her handbag to elevate Amy's feet.

Amy comes to in seconds. At Nick's barked order, Devi helps her to her feet and leads her away. Troy starts clearing up broken glass, shoulders tense, his gaze flicking to Una with unconcealed contempt.

'Get out!' Nick says to Una, Sharon and the journalist, his tone one of measured anger.

'The Blackwood community has the right to know,' Sharon bursts out, but her voice lacks conviction.

'No, they didn't. It was up to Amy and Matt to decide who knew. Now, leave!' At Nick's fierce look, Sharon turns on her heel. Una snatches up her belongings and follows. The journalist looks as if he's not going anywhere, but Nick pulls himself up to his full six foot four height and the guy hotfoots it like a firewalker over hot coals. The door slams shut behind them. It seems an eternity before the silence gives way to nervous chatter, a shadow of the café's usual self.

Irene finds Amy out the back of the café, curled up in a cane chair, trembling and white-faced. A cup of milky tea is on the table in front of her. It's untouched. 'Call Matt,' Irene mouths at Devi as she wraps her arms around the younger woman, pulling her close, saying nothing.

When she feels Amy shift away, she pushes the cup into Amy's shaking hands. 'Drink.' Amy sips obediently, automatically, like a child who's too sick to fight. Her hazel eyes are red-rimmed and raw. When Irene looks into them, she sees herself, all those years ago.

'Now you know,' Amy whispers tonelessly. 'I killed my daughter.'

Irene and Nick exchange looks. 'You didn't kill her,' Irene says. 'It was a terrible, horrible accident. You weren't to blame.'

'How can you say that? How would you know? You weren't there!'

'I remember reading about the case, Amy,' Nick breaks in. 'I recognised you the first time I saw you. It just took me a while to put it together.'

'You didn't say anything,' Amy sniffs.

'It didn't matter,' he says. 'We all have stories. We take them with us wherever we go. Sometimes we share them, sometimes not. I figured if you wanted to share, you would. But, Amy,' he takes her face in his hands, 'the investigation proved it was the other driver's fault. You know this. *We* know this.'

'They were all staring at me. Judging me. Like everyone did before.'

'They were shocked. But that doesn't mean they were judging you,' Irene puts in. After the initial shock, there was sympathy. Even empathy.

But she can see Amy doesn't believe her. The stricken woman curls into herself, rocking forwards, backwards, breathing fast.

It takes Irene and Nick half an hour to calm Amy down. Thirty minutes of *Breathe with me, Amy* and *Deep breath, good girl*. Thirty minutes of stroking her arm, holding her close, until finally, she is still. When Matt arrives to take her home, she's no longer in the throes of panic, but she's wrung out like a dishrag.

Before Matt takes her away, Amy stops and looks at Irene. 'I don't understand, Irene. Why didn't she talk to me privately?'

'I don't know.' Irene's been asking herself the same thing the past hour. Embracing her friend, she feels Amy's shoulders slump. 'Sometimes people just do shitty things.'

Back at home with Ashlee, Irene can't settle. When Ashlee falls asleep with Flossie, she logs in to her clunky hand-me-down computer and googles 'Amy Bradford', aware that she's no better than everyone else in Blackwood who's doing the same. But she's not doing it to rubberneck. She wants to understand. Sifting through the results, she finds links to articles that clearly show Amy was not at fault for the accident that stole her daughter and unborn child. The other driver ended up with two years' jail after lengthy investigations and a trial.

After several hours, Irene still can't fathom why Una unmasked Amy so publicly. Una's always liked being the centre of attention, she thinks, but this? This is incomprehensible. Is she jealous of Amy? Did Sharon put her up to it? Irene remembers Amy's pain-racked face in the café – in one heart-stopping moment, she was back to the shell of a woman Irene met a few months back.

The thought of losing a daughter, plus an unborn baby, in such horrific circumstances sends cold memory shivers through Irene; the thought that some texting, speeding idiot caused her friends such agony reignites a long-dormant anger. Two years' jail. Two years. That's all the man got for the loss of two innocent lives. Apparently, he'd tried to argue it wasn't his fault. *Bastard.*

Her hands are shaking. Her breath is laboured. Irene holds the box of prescribed nitrate tablets for a long moment, before filling a cup with water and swallowing a tablet. Her eyes flick to the clock; it's too early to call Bonnie and tell her about the test results – and they seem so trivial now – so she taps out a short message asking her granddaughter to call when she's free. And then she messages Amy, keeping it brief and to the point: *I'm here when you need me.*

What else can she say to best communicate her support?

Amy doesn't reply. Her phone is probably switched off. Don't do anything rash, Irene thinks. Like pick up sticks and leave. If she has Amy pegged right, the young woman will worry that the Blackwood community will label her as 'the one who was driving when her daughter was killed', like she was labelled 'the one whose daughter was a drug addict'. Amy will worry that people will find a way to blame her. That they won't want to come to the café anymore. It's pointless trying to convince her otherwise; at least, not yet. It took years for Irene to accept Erin's death was not somehow her fault. Sid never accepted it. You never let go of the self-blame, not fully.

Exhausted by her churning thoughts, Irene drifts to the lounge room and sinks down next to Ashlee. The little girl stirs but doesn't wake; the cat makes a half-hearted meow before closing its eyes again. The phone rings, but it's not Bonnie or Amy, so Irene ignores it.

Picking up a dusty, pensive photo of Erin, Irene cries softly, silently. For Amy and Matt, and their little ones. For her husband, who wasn't the same after Erin died. And for her daughter, who was lost to her long before she passed from this life.

CHAPTER 28
AMY

A t home, Amy cries until she thinks there cannot possibly be more tears inside her. And then there are more tears, and they drip and slide as everything she's blocked for years rises to the surface in a discordant and blurry flashback montage. The media that branded Amy negligent, though it was later proven she was in no way to blame; the wrenching memorial service when they finally arrived back in Western Australia minus Pandora's ashes courtesy German bureaucracy; the day Gran, her biggest support aside from Matt, died. Even now, the details are hazy; the feelings intense.

'You can't go to Germany,' she whispers. Or did she think it?

Matt covers her with a light blanket. 'Try to sleep,' he suggests.

And she tries, but she can't switch off and her face is still wet and her nose is blocked. Matt gives her a tissue and she blows. And blows. Huffing and puffing like the big bad wolf in the story Pandora loved. She tries to slow her breathing, but instead her breath stops at a vision of a little girl sleeping eternally in a back seat. She holds her breath for as long as she can, until Matt's hand is warm on her cheek.

'Breathe,' he says.

He closes the curtains and everything is blissfully, mercifully blank.

~

Rain pelts against the windshield, smearing the scenery. The wipers flail from side to side to keep up with the onslaught. Inside the hire car, the windows are coated with a wet haze. She turns the defogger to full power. Nothing happens and Amy curses. *It's broken and there's nowhere to pull over.* With one hand on the steering wheel, she reaches for the face flannel she tossed on the passenger seat earlier and rubs at the window. The car veers to the right. Hot fear pumps through her. She corrects the steering and tightens her grip as puddles of water catch the wheels.

It's as if the rain is driving, not her.

The road straightens and Amy sneaks a quick look in the rear-view mirror. Pandora is fast asleep, her mouth slightly open, head tilted sharply to one side. How can she sleep like that? Water catches at the wheels again – *concentrate!* – and she fixes her eyes on the road, or what she can see of it through the rapidly fogging windscreen. She's driving on an unfamiliar road with her daughter in the back, and she can barely see.

As soon as there's a lay by, Amy pulls over and waits for the rain to ease. Sends her father a text: *I'll be a bit late. Raining too hard to drive.*

With any luck she'll still get there before nightfall. Amy drums her fingers on the steering wheel, thankful that Pandora is asleep. God knows what she'd do if Pandora was awake now. She'd made it abundantly known what she thought of getting in a car after the long-haul flight from Perth to Frankfurt.

'I want to go to the park,' she'd yelled, cheeks flushed with anger. 'I don't want to go for a drive. I hate cars!'

Matt tried to convince Amy not to make the four-hour drive alone. 'Come to Düsseldorf with me. We'll drive to your father's together.'

But her father was expecting her. And Amy didn't want to wait in Düsseldorf while Matt attended a three-day engineering conference. She hadn't seen her father for five years. He'd never met Pandora. He was going to spoil her rotten.

Wait till her father finds out about the baby. No one knows that news yet. Not even Matt. She was going to tell him after the conference, on their holiday. He'll be blown away, even though it was a surprise pregnancy. Matt's wanted another baby for ages. Amy was happy with one, but he wanted three or four. And now she's pregnant anyway and in six months she'll be halfway to his goal. She's less than thrilled. It's tough enough being a mother of one. There's no fail-safe recipe to follow.

Amy sighs. Dad's probably waiting at the front gate by now. And she's sitting on the side of a road, going nowhere.

The rain eases to a light drizzle and Amy gives the windscreen and windows a good wipe before starting the car again. She glides the car onto the road slowly so as not to wake Pandora. Only thirty minutes to go and then she can run around all she likes. As the car picks up speed, trees blur on the roadside and Amy opens the window a little to feel the misty air against her face, a welcome change after the stale, sweaty air inside the plane.

The other car comes out of nowhere. Slams into the passenger side of Amy's car with screeching, screaming, terrible sounds that never fade. The impact sends Amy's forehead into the steering wheel and her neck snaps back.

If Pandora is crying, Amy can't hear it. Strange smells reach her nose. Everything is foggy, as if the mist outside has coagulated into a grey mess and seeped into her car, thickening, darkening until everything goes black.

CHAPTER 29
MATT

Matt paces around the lounge room like a caged lion. With the curtains drawn, it feels like a cocoon. Airless. Smothering. But the darkness seems to have calmed Amy. She's curled in a foetal position on the sofa, having cried herself into an uneasy sleep. Her body shudders and jerks from time to time under the light blanket. Matt hasn't left her side except to answer the doorbell. It was June with a chunky vegetable soup and a fresh loaf of sourdough. She'd pushed the food into his hands with a gentle smile and left.

'Matt?' Amy's eyes snap open, but they look glazed. Unfocused. 'Where are the kids? Where *are* they? Are my babies okay? The car ... it—' Her eyes are wild as she tries to string thoughts and words together.

Matt takes her face in his hands, tilts her eyes to his, forces her to look at him. 'You're in Blackwood, Aims. In our house. You're having a flashback.'

Her head moves from side to side. 'No!' And then reddened eyes focus on him. 'It was so real. The car. The noises.'

'I know, honey. I know.' He wants to throttle Una.

He sits beside her and her head rests on his lap. They sit like that until Matt's stomach rumbles. He hasn't eaten since breakfast and that was before six, but cooking is the last thing he wants to do. Then he remembers June's soup. Thank God for community at times like these. 'I'll heat up some vegie soup and be right back,' he tells her.

When he returns with two bowls of soup and thick slices of buttered toast, Amy's dozed off again. He puts her bowl in the fridge and sinks down onto the floor beside her, propping a cushion behind his back. He wants to be there when she wakes, but he wishes he were anywhere but here. And as he eats, robotically, tasting nothing, his mind drifts to another time, another place, back to the day her heart broke and he was the messenger.

As Amy twitches on the hospital bed, Matt rehearses how to break the news. But is there ever a right way? What are the right words for something like this? Their daughter is dead. And their unborn baby – the one he didn't even know about – never had a chance to breathe.

My daughter is dead.

Amy was three months' pregnant.

Why didn't she tell me?

He'd dreamed of Pandora last night. They were at the zoo, among a crowd of faceless families, waiting for the sleeping lion to move from his sunny throne. A twitch of a whisker. The flick of a tail. Waiting. Waiting. And suddenly there was a great tearing sound that no one but he seemed to hear and he was overcome by a feeling of emptiness. Confused, he'd tried to pull his daughter close, but somehow, inexplicably, she was on the other side of the glass barrier. He shouted her name, pressed his face against the barrier, and beat the glass with his fists, but she did not answer. Instead, he watched, helpless, as she picked her way over rocks to the now awake, mane-bristling lion … and he woke, drenched in sweat.

He's sweating now as he sits in the stuffy little room, wrestling with his wretched thoughts once again.

If only Amy had stayed in Düsseldorf with him.

If only she hadn't hired a car to drive to her father's village.

If only she hadn't been driving in the rain.

As if she hears his traitorous thoughts, Amy's pulse quickens. Her eyelids flicker, once, twice, and then she's squinting like she has sun in her eyes. What must he look like? When he'd caught sight of himself in the mirror earlier, he saw a man much older than his thirty-five years. He'd had to turn away from the grief, blame and anger in his bloodshot eyes.

Is that what Amy sees?

'Hi, darling,' she says, her voice raspy and weak from disuse. She sounds the same on weekends, when he snuggles up to her in the precious moments before Pandora bounces onto the bed.

His shoulders heave. He doesn't want to look at her and yet he must. She's waiting for him to speak … and he's waiting for the penny to drop – that she's not at her father's house, but in a hospital room. He clears his throat, pushing the words upwards, but she beats him to it.

'Matt?'

Squeezing her hand, he takes a deep breath.

'Can't go.' Matt shifts position so he can face his wife. Amy's eyes are shut. Is she talking in her sleep? He's not sure. 'Can't go Doosheldorf.' The words are slurred.

Wiping his eyes, he reaches for her hand and squeezes. 'Don't worry about it now.' The upcoming conference has been floating at the back of his mind since he collected Amy from the café.

'Can't go,' she mutters again before rolling over. A light snore escapes. Maybe she's having another flashback. Remembering that day at the airport when he tried to convince her not to drive to her father's, especially since heavy rain was forecast. But maybe she means she can't go to Düsseldorf *now*. Or she's saying he can't possibly go now. Not after this.

Matt covers his eyes against the arguments and memories that assault him from all sides, like he's a punching bag in a gym. What is he going to do?

He has to go to the conference. It's work.

He can't go. Can't leave Amy like this. This could set her back months.

Can he?

Matt blinks as a question takes hold.

What if it's exactly what he needs to do?

CHAPTER 30
AMY

When Amy wakes, she has no idea of the time. Or where she is. It takes a moment to orient herself. Home. Lounge room. The curtains are pulled tight but a pencil of light tells her it's not night. Her eyes feel puffy, her head pounds. Her nose is blocked, her bladder full. Why is she sleeping in the middle of the day? And why is Matt sleeping on the floor next to her? There's an empty bowl on the coffee table, scrunched up tissues, and her phone, face-down. It's off and she powers it up, rubbing her eyes while the screen turns from dark to light. The screen flashes with incoming messages and then it comes back to her in staccato memories. Café. Una. Sharon. Journalist.

Name.

Shame.

Blame.

Easing herself upwards, Amy pads to the bathroom. Swollen, bloodshot eyes stare back from the mirror. Red blotches cover her freckles. She splashes cold water on her cheeks, eyes. Wets a flannel. Dry swallows two paracetamol. She sinks onto her bed, covering her temples with the cold compress and realises she still doesn't know what time it is. The phone is in the lounge room, where she dropped it. She can't be bothered lifting the compress to check the alarm clock.

After Pandora died, it was as if time ceased to exist. Days, nights, hours, minutes, and seconds merged into one eternal continuum. A never-ending moment in which Amy existed in another dimension. A place of screeching tyres, burning rubber, the iron tang of blood mixing with damp air. A place of darkness, horror and wails.

Time was stolen from Amy the same day her daughter and unborn baby were taken from her world. Time stopped moving. For months, Amy was immobile. A statue in a world that moved on around her, a world governed by time she no longer recognised.

People came and went, in and out of her endless moment. They stepped in and out of her static life, for who knows how long. As long as it took to feel discomfort? To realise that Amy didn't 'need more time'? She *had* time. Just not as they understood it.

To them, time was however long Amy needed to heal. To Amy, time was simply a black hole that had sucked her in. Alive. Functioning. Barely. She simply *was*.

When she finally went to therapy, Amy tried explaining it. 'You know that movie, *The NeverEnding Story*? You know the Nothing? The destroyer of imagination and dreams? It erased everything it touched.' The counsellor waited, pen twitching. 'Well,' Amy swallowed, 'to me, it's like the Nothing has erased everything good and real from my life and turned it into a lie.'

Amy remembers that conversation as she lies on her bed. And then she remembers the day the Nothing appeared.

Beep. Beep. Beep.

A noise pulls her from darkness to light. Amy opens her eyes, squinting against the harsh fluorescence above, until the white noise clears. Turning her head, she recognises her husband. She can't remember picking him up from the train station in Hamelin but she must have, because how else could he be here holding her hand?

'Hi,' she says. Why does her voice sound like it hasn't been used for days? Why doesn't he say something? Why are his shoulders heaving? 'Matt?'

He squeezes her hand, but still says nothing, though it sounds like he's trying to.

'Matt, what is it?' Waiting for him to answer, she registers beeps and drones that don't fit with the hum of a home, with where she's supposed to be. It sounds like a hospital, but it can't be. She tries to lift herself, but her legs won't move and there's a tube dangling from her arm. What the hell is going on?

'Where am I? Am I in hospital? Matt? Why can't I move my legs? Matt! Talk to me.'

'Yes, darling,' he manages. Her eyes drift towards his face. He's drained of colour, his eyes weepy and bloodshot; he looks old, but he's only thirty-five. 'Aims. You were in a car accident on the way to your dad's. Both your legs were badly broken, that's why you can't move them. Your pelvis too. You've had an operation.' He takes a deep breath. 'You had lots of internal bleeding. You've been in an induced coma for two weeks.'

Amy tries to make sense of his words. What accident? When? There's something about what he was saying that is loaded with implication, something she hasn't yet understood. What is it? The answer hits her like a clenched fist.

'Where's Pandora?' Panic rises, toppling over her like a breaking wave. 'Matt! Pandora? Where is she?'

'She's ... Pandora's dead, Amy. The baby too.'

The light snaps on overhead and Amy flinches. 'It's okay, Amy, you're safe.' Matt spoons himself around her. His hand strokes her cheek, which is wet, clammy with tears again.

'I thought I was in the hospital again. You ... you told me about Pandora. I thought it was real, it was happening all over again.' Her voice, whisper-thin, cracks into a sob. 'Do you remember what that doctor said? That I was lucky to be alive?'

She feels, rather than hears, his *yes*, and pulls back to look into his eyes, which are glassy and troubled as a spring storm.

'I hated him for saying that. Hated him. I didn't *want* to be alive. I didn't want to be *lucky*. Because Pandora wasn't. Lucky, I mean. And if being lucky meant losing her, I didn't want it. I wanted … I wanted to be dead with her. Sometimes I still do.'

It's the first time she's admitted this and Matt's face crumples. 'Don't say that.'

'It's true.'

'Don't. Don't. Say. That.' His voice is fierce.

'Matt—'

'We'd already,' his voice breaks and it's another moment before he resumes. 'We'd already … lost everything. I couldn't … I can't lose you as well.'

CHAPTER 31

AMY

Anger sets in the next day, a white-hot rage that makes Amy want to run and scream and break everything she touches. Anger at Una and Sharon for ripping her safety net from under her, plunging a knife into her grief, and destroying all hope of avoiding her pain. Anger at the journalist for not backing off. How can she face the café now? Who will come to the next Around the World Supper Club now that they know who – *what* – she is?

She finds herself jabbing at the keyboard, searching online for follow-up stories about the man who killed Pandora. His face stares mildly at her from newspaper articles, the amiable smile unpicking the stitches in her heart. It's not the face of a killer. And yet she wants to smash it to bits.

Does he feel regret? Shame? Guilt? Does he feel like a piece of shit because his actions had made Matt and Amy lose everything? The internet is strangely mute about what happened to him after he was sentenced.

Now photos leap at her: the mangled remains of her hire car and the rescue crew at the scene; herself, unconscious and almost unrecognisable in a hospital bed; Pandora smiling in a posed photo taken in a shopping centre, back when she still had life to look forward to. Amy covers her eyes and a low, keening sound fills the room. She wants the noise to stop. It's not until Matt comes in that she realises the noise is coming from her.

'Irene called,' he says.

'I don't want to talk to her. I want to talk about what we're going to do,' she says, scratching her legs. No matter how hard she scratches, the itch won't go away.

Matt pulls her hands away. 'You're bleeding,' he says, leading her to the table where tea and toast waits.

Amy picks at the toast until there's a pile of crumbs on her plate, pounding Matt with a barrage of questions and dilemmas. Should they sell up? Find somewhere else, another small town? Go quietly in the night and never see anyone from Blackwood again? It's hard to believe that only days before she was sharing a French feast with new friends, feeling like she belonged.

'Leaving won't fix the way you feel,' he says. 'But I'm taking tomorrow off so we can work out what to do about all this. And maybe you should take a step back from the café for a few weeks. Get someone else to run it. And postpone the next supper club thing for a while.'

Amy hasn't even thought about what to *do* next. She's too busy wishing she could *undo* what's been done by Una and Sharon, by that killer in Germany. But she nods anyway. He brings her a bowl of June's soup, and she pushes the spoon around the bowl.

'I'm not hungry,' she says. Matt purses his lips, but doesn't push it.

She glares at him and fight mode kicks in. Should they confront Una and Sharon? Dig up some dirt on them? Complain to the editor of *The Sunday Courier* about their invasive reporter? Even as she blurts out that suggestion, she knows complaining will only fuel the fire. More media attention is the last thing they need.

She switches tack. 'Maybe I should write a book? Turn this around and then see if Una and Sharon are still gloating.'

Matt stares at her like he can't believe what he's hearing. 'Yeah right. You'll finally talk about all of it. Just not when I wanted to. And I doubt they're gloating, not from what I've heard.' He stands. 'None of this is helpful.'

'I have a right to be angry.' She glares at him, hating that he's right. 'Why aren't you?'

'Who said I'm not?'

'You're not acting like it.'

'If you think me being angry means thinking up petty revenge strategies for those women, you've forgotten who I am.' He walks away.

She can't even think of a last word to throw after him. Anger has paralysed her tongue.

In the lounge room, she turns on the television.

'Buy today and you'll get *two* fat-busters for the price of one *and that's not all,*' a honey-voiced presenter says.

Amy's fingers tighten around her phone – she needs this fat-buster *now* – before throwing the device across the room. And then she can't breathe and the house is squeezing her, and she bolts outside for gulps of fresh air. The neighbourhood is quiet, with only birdsong, the wind in the trees, and the occasional car marring the silence. In another hour, the schoolchildren will be home, their noisy squeals, laughter and whines changing the neighbourhood tune to something more up-tempo. It's *too* quiet.

Inexplicably, she longs for the chatter and clatter of the café. Matt was right about her behaviour earlier, but she's not sure he's right about taking a break from the café. The idea of going back terrifies her, but the idea of having nothing to do but listen to her thoughts is worse. She'll take a few days. Enough to get her head together. That's all.

When Matt surfaces from the study, he finds Amy in the garden and piles of weeds strewn about the grass. He comes to her, takes her in his arms. She accepts the hug, stiffly at first, then relents and pulls him a little closer. Their embrace is brief. Amy's aware that some-thing's lacking from it, but can't pinpoint it. Perhaps they're just exhausted. Exposed.

Matt steps away. 'I meant to do the weeding,' he says. He looks tired. His eyes are squinty and red. He's been crying, but she doesn't mention it. Let things lie, she cautions herself.

But Matt doesn't want to let things lie. Over dinner, he raises the idea of talking to a counsellor again. Not *him*. Her. He thinks *she* needs a counsellor. He's nervous about bringing it up. Amy can tell by the way his jaw twists from side to side.

'I've already talked about this with counsellors,' she says. 'I don't need to go through it all again. I just need to get back to work.'

'What? I thought you were taking a break for a few weeks.'

'I never said that.'

'You need time.'

'I've had time.'

The conversation seesaws back and forth – he pushes, she pulls. He plays his trump card. 'I don't want you to have to go to that hospital again.' Like the last time her mind lost itself in an ocean of grief. She stares at him, trembling in disbelief and rage, holding the river of curses dammed by the aching knowledge that he's right. One hundred per cent *right*. She *doesn't* want to go there again.

But it's different now.

'Aims. Look at me. You need help to get through this.'

His eyes shimmer with unshed tears, but behind his vulnerability she sees steel.

'Fine. I'll talk to a counsellor.' It will keep him off her back for a while. He nods and then she plays her own trump card. 'But I'm going back to the café next week.'

She walks away before he can argue.

At night, the hours pass painfully. Amy tosses from side to side, trying not to disturb Matt. Lying still, holding her breath when his sleep turns fitful and he mutters words she cannot understand. When his breathing regulates, she turns over her pillow, seeking a cold patch; she smooths wrinkles from her sheet as though these adjustments will invite sleep. It's a fruitless endeavour. Her skin is irritated by every-thing that touches it. The sheet rubs her wrist the wrong way. The pillow pushes against her earlobe, which has begun to ache. Her hip is aching again. Uncomfortable here, there. Her breasts throb as they press into the mattress. Her head itches. Now her toe. Nerves fire, sending icicles of pain from her middle toe up her leg. She twitches. She wants nothing touching her and yet the air is frigid without some form of covering.

Matt's hand fumbles for her thigh and she stiffens. He can't want sex *now*. She holds her breath. Waits to see what his intentions are, but after a little pat his hand slides away, leaving a warm spot. Even in his sleep, he's trying to offer her comfort. Where seconds before she had winced, now she wants that comfort touch. Nothing more, nothing less. *Hold his hand*, she tells herself. And she reaches for his hand across the channel of sheets but then stops, because if he wakes he'll think she wants sex and that's the last thing on her mind. Frustration needles her out of bed, towards the bathroom and the sleeping pills pushed to the back of her cosmetics drawer. Two washed down with a gulp of water will do the trick, she tells the ghost face in the mirror.

'Will it?' the ghost asks.

CHAPTER 32

AMY

The next morning, Matt's missing. After staggering out of bed and splashing cold water on her face, Amy searches the house, cursing the chemically induced fog that's seeped into her mind, blurring her movements. There's a note in the kitchen: *Gone for a walk along river. Back soon.*

A walk where? And when did he leave? There are telltale signs that he's had breakfast and coffee – dishes rinsed and stacked beside the sink. He could have been gone for at least one, maybe two hours.

She looks around the kitchen, the beautiful space Matt dreamed into life. It feels lifeless, and sad, as if it's echoing Amy's apathy and wooden movements. They've barely used it in days, existing on the soup and casseroles June's delivered each day. It's become a zone for strained conversations, far from the warm hub it's supposed to be.

'Hello?'

Amy jerks at the sound of familiar voices at the back door. It's Bonnie and Irene. She considers pretending she's not home. If she doesn't move for a few minutes, maybe they'll give up and go away. But then a wave of shame propels her to the door, where she motions Bonnie and Irene inside.

'I know, I know,' she says to a wide-eyed Bonnie. 'I look like crap.'

'You do a bit,' Bonnie agrees, causing Amy to smile. Anyone else would have lied.

Tutting at Bonnie, Irene pulls Amy in for a hug. 'How are you, love?'

Amy hesitates. Truth? Groggy. Bone-tired. Confused. But they don't need to know that.

'Fine. How are you both? What have you been up to?' Irene and Bonnie exchange a look, but Amy ignores it. 'How's Ashlee? How's work? Aren't you back from up north early, Bonnie? Want a cuppa?'

They politely answer her questions while she makes coffee and the conversation tiptoes along like this until Irene puts down her cup. Amy swallows. Right now, the older woman has a *you can't avoid talking about this* look Amy knows all too well.

'So. How are you really, Amy?' Irene asks gently.

Amy closes her eyes. It's as if Gran is sitting in front of her. 'Fine?' It comes out as a question, and she curses inwardly.

'Amy.' Irene musters a *don't mess with me* tone. Bonnie sits up a smidgen straighter. So does Amy. 'You don't need to pretend with us.'

Amy bolts up. 'Biscuits? Water? More tea?'

'No,' Irene and Bonnie say.

Like a bird poised for flight, she perches on her chair, waiting for Irene to speak. Except it's her turn to talk and Irene's waiting patiently like Amy's counsellor used to do. 'It's been shit,' Amy blurts when she can't stand it anymore.

And then words tumble out, as if she's up-ended a laundry basket overflowing with dirty clothes. Nightmares. Flashbacks. Emotional outbursts. She tells them about pain so deep it's like a butcher's knife slicing flesh from her bones. About the moment she knew her carefully constructed walls were about to come crashing down.

'At first I wanted to run,' Amy continues. Her shoulders are slowly releasing their tension, as though each word is a brick removed from her emotional backpack. 'To pack everything ... or just leave it all here and *go.*'

'Why didn't you?' Irene asks.

The question stops Amy in her tracks. Even Bonnie looks taken aback. 'If Matt agreed, I might have,' she admits. 'But Matt ... Matt said you can't run every time something gets too hard.' A short laugh. 'My grandmother would have said the same.'

'Well,' Irene says, gently. 'It's the first resort, isn't it? To run. Or hide. Classic flight response.'

'Yeah. And then I didn't want to run. To give up what I have here.' There's a moment of silence. Amy shifts in her chair. 'So then I got angry.'

'Who with?'

'Una. Sharon. *Him*. The man responsible,' she says, pausing to collect her thoughts. Her mouth tastes like she's bitten into an orange peel. 'Angry that I didn't get to go to my own daughter's funeral. That my grandmother died when I needed her. That I had to learn to walk again. That Matt blames me, even if he doesn't say it. He'd never do that. Admit it, I mean. But I know he does. *I* would.'

Amy starts to pace. 'Angry with the police. At people who said I must have been responsible somehow.' She stops pacing. 'The other day, I wanted to scream, "Fuck you!" to all of them at the top of my voice, over and over, so the whole world could hear, but instead I screamed the words inside me. To myself.' She looks at them, searching their faces for understanding. 'Most of all, I'm angry at myself. For driving that day. If I'd listened to Matt, Pandora would still be alive.'

After they leave, Amy decides to buy groceries and pay a visit to the café. Nick needs to know her plans. She hasn't spoken to him since Una's outburst. Some kind of boss she is. Leaving them all to it without even a message. Nick's more than capable of running the place, but she can't expect him to juggle two jobs indefinitely. As she walks out to the car, she hesitates. Is she ready for this? It's not too late to turn back.

She's still wondering this when she bumps into Una Mickle at Blackwood Fresh. Literally. Amy's head is down as she scans the shopping list on her phone and she doesn't see Una round the corner of aisle one.

'I'm so sorry,' Amy spills out automatically before understanding that the disgruntled person rubbing her hip is the one person she'd rather not apologise to for anything, ever.

'Yes, well. You really should watch where you're going,' Una snaps, not looking up. 'You could have knocked me down the way you were barrelling around. You young people are always head down, goggling things on your phones. It's unnecessary and unsafe.' Her face pales. 'Oh. It's you.'

'Unnecessary?' Amy's pitch and tone amp up a few notches. *That's it. This stops here.* 'I'll tell *you* what was unnecessary. That scene in my café the other day. The insensitive, no, *cruel* way you and your … your *bitch* of a daughter played out that attention-seeking drama, even getting a journalist, for God's sake, in on the action. How would *you* like that?' Amy's so furious, she wants to shake Una to punctuate each word she spits out. 'You could have just come to *me.*'

Una lets out the breath she'd sucked in when Amy called Sharon a bitch. She squeezes her response out with effort. 'Your last name's *Bradford*, not *Bennet*. And you weren't honest with any of us, with Blackwood, with our community.'

'I don't have to tell you *anything*. All you need to know is that I'm Amy and I own the café where you're more than happy stuffing your face with my chocolate cake once a week.' Getting it all out is empowering. Why didn't she do this more often?

Una glares at her. 'You come in here, all butter wouldn't melt in your mouth, *I'm such a good cook from the city*, but you're an imposter. An upstart. You think you can waltz into Blackwood like you've always belonged, and start an elite supper club – yes, I saw you all in there on Monday – but that's not how it works in the country. You earn your place.'

'A liar? I lost my daughter and unborn baby in a terrible accident, and was wrongly blamed for it. Imagine how hard it would be living with that. Do you really blame me for wanting to make a fresh start? For not wanting everyone to talk about it, to point their fingers, to shun me and my café?' Amy takes a breath before continuing quietly. 'Una, maybe you don't know what it's like to lose a child. I hope you never have to.'

Una stares at Amy. Her mouth opens and closes, like a goldfish sucking in flakes of food. Then, making a strangled sound, she drops her basket and flees the store.

A slow, rhythmic clap makes Amy turn. A small group of eaves-droppers has gathered. 'Good one,' someone says. 'About time someone gave old Pickle what for.'

Amy pushes past them, holding back hot tears of anger, shame, relief and embarrassment as she plucks groceries off the shelf. She's gone from an emotional breakthrough with Irene and Bonnie to a much-needed confrontation with Una in a matter of hours. Empow-ered one moment, utterly drained the next.

CHAPTER 33
MATT

A few days later, Matt unrolls the Sunday newspaper he picked up from the corner shop down the road. If that bastard reporter's written a where-are-they-now story, it'll be in there today. Turning the pages rapidly, he almost misses the photo of him and Amy. Underneath is a picture of Pandora in a tutu – *God, she loved twirling about in those things* – biting her lip in a shy smile and a photo of Amy's mangled hire car. Matt swallows and skims the text.

Three years after the car accident in Germany that killed their young daughter, Amy and Matt Bradford have forged a new life for themselves in the south-west town of Blackwood.

Mrs Bradford was driving her children to visit her father when another car collided with hers, instantly killing Pandora (4) and severely injuring Mrs Bradford. She was three months pregnant.

After several months in German hospitals, Mrs Bradford returned to Perth for rehabilitation.

Police charged Mrs Bradford with involuntary manslaughter after she regained consciousness, but withdrew the charge after further investigations revealed the driver of the other car, Andreas Fechner, was texting and speeding while driving and failed to give way at a cross road.

He was fined $2000 and sentenced to two years' prison for involuntary manslaughter. Mr Fechner is expected to be released at the end of the year. He has shown no remorse publicly.

Seeking a fresh start, the Bradfords moved from Perth to Blackwood earlier this year, adopting Mrs Bradford's maiden name, Bennet. Mr Bradford, an engineer, works at Timbertop's lithium mine, while Mrs Bradford owns a popular Blackwood café and hosts a themed supper club.

Although she had no idea about the Bradford's tragic past until last week, Blackwood CWA President and friend Una Mickle said the couple appeared to have embraced a new life, and were known in town for hosting travel-themed dinner parties.

'Of course, I was shocked when it all came out,' she said. 'We all were. We had no idea they had gone through so much.'

'You wouldn't know it to look at them. Amy's a regular at the local farmers markets and is known for hosting lavish dinner parties and you can't do that with a sad face, can you. I don't know how she does it.'

She added that the couple had also been renovating their home.

'Don't be surprised if there's the pitter-patter of little feet in that household soon,' she said.

The Bradfords declined to comment.

A bitter laugh escapes as Matt finishes the article. Nothing new there – most of it is common knowledge. Hope flares when he reads Una's final remark, but turns to cold anger. What would she know? Una's made that up, or been led on by that journalist twat. How ludicrous to link a kitchen renovation to future children. Still. He can't help wishing there was truth behind it.

He scrunches the article into a ball and bins it. Shoving the rest of the newspaper aside, he reaches for the travel lift-out and finds a distraction in a feature on Windy Brook, a nearby tourist town. His interest is piqued by images of its picturesque main street, complete with antique shops, restored historic buildings and a background of rolling hills and forest. The accompanying article describing the town as the heart of the food and wine region, almost has him reaching for his keys. That's where he'll take Amy today. Get her out of the house for a bit.

If she's not up to it, he'll take himself for a bushwalk. Lately, nature has been his refuge. Locking himself in his study gives him space, but it's not the same. He's always aware that Amy's somewhere in the house. In the bush, he can be alone with his thoughts. Which are starting to bother him.

The other day, he'd bumped into Frank down by the river. Straight up, Frank had asked how Amy was doing. How Matt was coping. He'd really seemed to care, rather than asking out of polite curiosity. He asked, then waited for an answer. Even invited Matt out for a drink at the pub one night.

'Us blokes, we've gotta talk sometimes,' he'd said. 'Women have got it right the way they gasbag on with each other, but it's bloody good for blokes as well.'

Matt still isn't sure about the *talking with other blokes* bit. It was one thing to talk with his counsellor about all his shit – he was paid well to listen. With your mates, you didn't talk about the tough stuff. Did you? It's been so long since he's hung out with a mate. Hell, the last time was probably before the accident. A beer with Frank would be nice, he muses.

Suddenly, the urge to speak to his counsellor is strong. Maybe he can tell Matt why there's a thick fog over his feelings. Why he feels like he's spiralling to the depths of the ocean while Amy's rising higher every day. He locks the study door, hoping Amy doesn't hear. She asked what he was hiding the other day. And then her mind went off on all sorts of tangents, and it took ages to sort that out. Why doesn't he tell her? He knows the answer. It's twofold. One, he doesn't want to look weak. Two, it's something that's only for him.

Taking a deep breath, he makes the call. There's no answer. The counsellor is offline. He's disappointed, but he shouldn't be. It's Sunday, after all. The man is probably spending time with his family. Maybe his kids are climbing all over him. Maybe they're eating pancakes in the kitchen, like Matt used to do when he had a family.

Amy stumbles out of the bedroom when he's on his way back to the kitchen, her face pillow-wrinkled, eyes sleepy. He's always loved Amy this way, morning mussed, before the smoothing out, covering up process begins. When he gathers her to him for a kiss, he's surprised that she doesn't pull away. Once the kiss would have turned into sex, back in the bedroom, or even right there in the kitchen, fast but sweet. He's under no illusion that's on the cards today, although the thought stirs him to life, and he moves away in case Amy thinks that's what he wants.

She sinks into a chair, yawning, and flicks through the newspaper without reading, while he makes her coffee and toast, hoping she doesn't ask if there is a story about them. She doesn't, and her appreciative smile gives him the confidence he needs to unveil his get-out-of-the-house idea.

'Aims,' he starts. 'Want to go check out Windy Brook?'

She blows on her coffee and considers. 'Yes,' she says, surprising him for the second time that morning. 'Nick's told me there's a café there with amazing food. Waffles every which way.'

Perhaps he was too quick to dismiss the sex-in-the-kitchen idea.

Windy Brook has a charming but touristy feel, an almost too-perfect atmosphere, with its specialty shops aimed at visitors with open wallets, and an overabundance of cafés and gift shops. Amy loves it, Matt can tell. Even behind her sunglasses, her face lights up when they walk down the pretty, tree-lined street, past a goldsmith, an aromatherapy shop, several art galleries, and an alpaca shop. The café Amy's chosen is full. Will they even get a table?

After ordering the café's signature dish – waffles with buttermilk fried chicken and chilli maple syrup – they find a table in the al fresco courtyard. Matt glances at his wife, whose profile is etched in sunlight as she gazes around. When she catches him watching, her mouth opens and he knows she's self-conscious and about to say

'What?' like she always does when she catches him staring. He's about to tell her he loves her when the delivery of food swallows the moment.

The food lives up to the hype. The crunchy chicken gives way to tender, fall-apart meat. The chilli maple sauce has enough bite to awaken their taste buds, but not enough to deaden them. Amy dives in as if she hasn't eaten for a week. Good food brings out the teenage girl in her, and as she 'mmms' and 'yums' her way through the dish, his shoulders let go.

'How do you feel about going back to work?' Matt asks between mouthfuls.

Amy looks uncertain, but when she speaks, she's calm. 'I need to,' she says. 'Being locked up in the house is no good for me. It'll be good for you, too. Going back to work, I mean. Getting back to routine.'

He agrees. Una and Sharon's ploy had knocked her over, but she's pulling herself back up faster than he expected, the way she used to when life threw a curve ball. As if she's becoming more resilient. How long until she falls again?

They leave the café hand in hand, and browse through the small town's shops, like tourists having a day out, not the couple whose children died. Amy buys an overpriced but pretty Italian brass photo frame from a stuffy antique shop. Matt buys matching alpaca wool beanies for them from the alpaca shop. But it's the goldsmith's shop that makes their eyes glitter. It's an Aladdin's cave of sparkling treasures. Amy's eyes linger on an ornate 1920s-style, heart-shaped silver locket that echoes the elegance of the Jazz Age. Matt imagines Pandora's photo in there, nestled close to her heart. When Amy's distracted, he buys it. He'll give it to her when the time is right.

They buy salted caramel donuts and head to the river, where they eat the decadent treats, licking sugar from their fingers and ignoring the friendly ducks who are eager for a taste. When they've finished, Matt drapes his arm around Amy and she leans into him. Her hair smells of apples and he closes his eyes, breathes her in. He wants to bottle this feeling, this connection of two people who've been through hell but still have love. And then he realises it's everything, but not quite enough. Is now the time to bring up what's been on his mind since they moved here? How should he word it?

His counsellor's words echo in his mind. 'Have you told Amy how you feel?'

'She doesn't want to hear.'

'Have you tried? Sat her down and told her everything you've told me? Or are you holding all that pain and bitterness inside?'

'This was a good idea,' Amy says, breaking into his thoughts.

Matt kisses her forehead. 'Yeah. Thanks for coming out with me.'

'We both needed it, I reckon.'

'Yeah.'

She pulls away slightly. Hugs her arms to her chest. 'I read the article.'

Matt stills. *So much for relaxation.*

She looks at him sadly. 'I found it in the bin. It was sticking out.' She pauses, like she's searching for words. 'It was pretty tame. I thought … I expected worse. More sensationalism. More holier-than-thou comments from Una.'

'Maybe they were edited out.'

'Maybe. You know, after I read it, I nearly changed my mind about going out today. I was scared people would recognise us. That we'd come here and people would look and know we were those people whose daughter was killed by their … in a car accident.'

'I know what you mean.'

Amy looks at him. Her shoulders relax and a half-smile crosses her face. 'But they didn't.' She leans into his chest. 'They didn't. And just for today, it was nice to be Matt and Amy. Not *those people*, or those *poor people*. Or *that woman*. You know?'

'Yep.' He does know.

'Although,' she continues, 'the pitter-patter of tiny feet part in the article bothered me. Why would Una say that? I mean, it's the last thing on my mind. I'm thinking of looking into the Mirena so I can get off the Pill. Bonnie says it's great.'

'Wait. You're on the Pill?'

She gives him a strange look. 'How did you think I was—'

'I don't know. I thought …' Matt scratches his head. 'What's the other thing?'

'It's an intrauterine device. Prevents pregnancy for about five years.'

'Five years? But—'

'What? Right now I can't imagine ever being a mother again, so—'

Matt pulls away sharply, trying to process her words. 'What? Never?'

'That surprises you?'

'Well, yeah, it does. I mean … I knew you weren't ready *yet*, but I thought …'

'That we'd replace our daughter?'

'No! I don't want to replace her. But I thought we'd try again one day. One day soon. That's why we came here. To try again. That's why I've been stressing about your hours. And you doing too much.'

'Really? I thought we came here to work on *us*.' Amy sucks in a breath. 'I'm nowhere near ready to think about a baby.'

When she tries to close the gap between them, he shifts away, feeling like a cork about to explode from a bottle. The last time Amy said she wasn't ready Pandora was a toddler. A year later she was pregnant and he didn't know until it was too late. He hadn't wanted to rush into having children after that. But it's been three years and he's pushing forty. He wants to be a father again.

'Did you mean what you said before?'

'Which part?'

'You can't imagine being a mother again.'

She's silent for a long, hope-crushing moment. 'I don't know. Maybe.'

CHAPTER 34
AMY

They tiptoe around each other the rest of the afternoon. Matt makes excuses not to be in the same room as Amy. The more distance he puts between them, the more Amy tries to draw him close, seeking him out to ask if he'd like coffee, toast, or help in the garden.

'I need some space,' he finally says.

Hurt, she backs off, wondering if his self-imposed detachment is safer than the alternative – having to talk about things she wants to leave in a box, buried deep somewhere unobtainable. It's better than him being angry with her; easier than wearing his disappointment and blame like a tattoo branded on her skin. Isn't it?

'For fuck's sake!' The tone more than the expletive startles Amy from her reading. Matt is wrestling with the tangled extension lead for the vacuum cleaner, teeth clenched as he untwists the cord. He catches her watching.

'Could you roll it any tighter? When you do it tight like this, it always tangles. Geez!' The last word whooshes from gritted teeth.

'Sorry, hon,' Amy says, thinking he was the one who used it last.

'You always say that,' he grunts, still yanking at the cord.

Amy inhales at the double-edged comment. As the afternoon has worn on, his distance has turned to mounting irritation. Swearing. Muttering. Banging doors. Biting back won't help, but it's getting harder to keep her thoughts to herself.

'Matt, hon, you okay?' She cringes as the words hang between them. Stupid question. Of course he's not.

'Fine. Pissed off about this bloody cord,' he retorts, yanking the cord. 'Or maybe it's my time of the month.'

It takes all the grace she has not to react. 'Do you want to talk?'

'No. I'm busy.' He storms off without making eye contact, leaving the vacuum cleaner stranded. The screen door slams behind him and then the car starts, and he's gone who knows where.

Amy watches him go. Matt rarely behaves like this, like a petulant adolescent, all slamming doors and glowering eyes. It's not his style. He's more the brooding, keep-it-inside type. She has no idea what to do except leave him alone.

'Fine,' she says to the air. Thank God he's going back to work tomorrow, and she'll start back on Tuesday. The past week has turned the house into an emotional vacuum, sucking the marrow from their marriage, paralysing them. Distance will do them good. Having something to do rather than prop each other up.

It's strange. Whenever they argue, she usually ends up in a puddle of angry, helpless tears. Right now, her eyes are dry, her mouth set. She puts the vacuum cleaner away, taking care to roll up the extension lead the way Matt likes it.

'Aims? Sorry for being a prick.' Matt's standing in the bedroom doorway, holding a bulging hessian shopping bag. Before she says anything, he hands her a bottle of white wine. It's one of her favourites – a Leeuwin Estate Art Series riesling she loves for its dry, delicate flavour. 'Let me make it up to you by cooking dinner? I thought I'd cook that Thai stir-fry, the chicken and basil one you like.'

After a beat, Amy opens her arms. They stand together for a few moments, holding, not speaking, until Matt pulls away. Gently, he takes Amy's face in his hands, those large hands she used to love trickling over her whole body; he looks as though he's about to say something but then thinks better of it.

'I'm going to get started on the cooking,' he says, shaking his head when she offers to help.

Later, when they go to bed, she hesitates and then reaches out, running her fingers up and down his back the way he loves. He lies still, but his breathing quickens slightly and she knows he's waiting to see what she'll do next. She continues what she's doing, unsure of what she wants, but knowing that this is what he needs.

After a moment Matt rolls over, into her arms. The sex is frantic; the release of pent-up sexual frustration for him, she suspects, and her urgent desire to feel as close to him as possible. It's not about lust or physical release but about craving Matt closer and deeper. About their minds and hearts connecting once more. She wraps her legs around him, spiralling him out of control; she doesn't come but doesn't care.

Rolling away, Matt's asleep within minutes, one leg outside the light blanket they're using now it's getting warmer. Usually he's snuggly after making love, and it occurs to Amy that no matter how close their bodies were moments before, Matt was not fully present. He was there in the bed, having sex with her, but he did not make love to her. It's as if he was just going through the motions. Is this what their marriage has come to? Brooding over this, Amy reaches into her bedside drawer for her contraceptive pills. Popping one out, she rolls it between her fingers for a long second, then swallows it.

It feels like no time has passed when she jolts awake from a dream where Matt was singing softly, strumming a guitar. It was like he used to do when they were newlyweds, except he was perched on the edge of a cliff, and the stone was crumbling around him. The song's distinct melody stays with her as her heart rate slows and her eyes adjust to the inky darkness, and she recognises it as Simon & Garfunkel's 'The Sounds of Silence', Matt's favourite. He's always had a thing for the duo – when he's happy, he sings along with them, adding his own harmony to theirs. Amy hasn't heard Matt sing for ages, but as her mind wakes, the song lingers. The music is real and it's coming from somewhere in the house.

Reaching out for Matt, she realises his side of the bed is empty. She tiptoes through the house, in case he's crashed out on the sofa, but stops short at his study. The door is open and Matt's listening to the Disturbed cover of the classic song, eyes closed, tears streaming down his face.

She backs away. Back in bed, she moves restlessly from side to side before whispering an affirmation her old counsellor suggested: 'I deserve sleep. My body deserves sleep.' Nothing happens. It never does. Her eyes remain stubbornly open.

What that counsellor never said is that when you lose someone you love, the grief lasts a lifetime. And you also lose part of yourself.

What if she's also losing Matt?

CHAPTER 35
MATT

The way everyone looks at him when he gets to work almost has him walking out the door. Searching. Accusing. Sympathetic. But he needs to be here. At home, he feels like a toddler in a safety harness, straining to break free but invisibly connected to his wife. Here, he walks around wearing an invisible 'My daughter died' badge over his heart, but at least he can breathe.

'Sorry about your daughter, mate,' some say. Matt appreciates their sympathy, but when it's clear he doesn't want to talk, they fade away like ghosts at dawn, leaving only a trace of disappointment in their wake.

Carla summons him the second his bum hits the seat. They're waiting in her office – Carla and someone from HR – and Matt's heart sinks. Duty calls.

'I'm so sorry for your loss,' Carla says, leaning forward and lightly patting his hand. 'I had no idea.'

The HR manager rolls out a few well-meaning platitudes. Matt nods and murmurs 'thanks' here and there, keenly aware he's not the only uncomfortable one in the room.

'If you can't go to Düsseldorf, it's fine. Perfectly understandable,' Carla adds.

'No, it's all good,' Matt says, surprising himself. Driving from Blackwood, he'd been undecided. When he walked into this room, he was no closer to an answer.

Last night he'd dreamed he was walking on a limestone path that curved like a wiggling snake. Feet and back aching, he plodded along until the path became two: one way led to the cliffs; the other to an idyllic beach. His feet rejected the beach track, instead carrying him along the cliff walk, traversing heathlands as the path steered closer to granite outcrops and sheer limestone towers dominating the white sand far below. Now and then a bobtail lizard scuttled across the path, a red-winged wren darted in front of him, and a little eagle hovered above. And then he was standing at the verge of earth and air, eyes drawn to an endless, blurred line of blue. There was no sound – no singsong bird call, no rushing wind, no crashing waves – as if nature had conspired to give him a moment of the purest peace. His foot lifted, hanging in the air just past the cliff edge. He lifted his arms and leapt.

It's time to leap for real. Whatever happens.

'It's all good,' Matt repeats. 'I want to go.'

I have to.

Carla and the HR guy exchange looks. 'If you're sure,' Carla says. She looks relieved.

The HR guy leaves. He's addressed the issue, now he can move on. Matt shifts in his seat, unsure what to do next. *Can I leave?*

As if she heard his unspoken question, Carla nods; he moves before she changes her mind.

'Matt.' He turns; she's followed him to the door. 'If there's anything I can do, come and see me.' Carla touches his arm, and Matt almost breaks.

Work, home, dreams – his ghosts trail him wherever he goes.

'Thanks,' he says, backing out of the room before the walls close in.

As the day wears on, it's easier to disconnect work from home. With hundreds of red-flagged emails clamouring for Matt's attention, there's only one thing for it – head down and focus. The initial awkwardness dissipates as Matt gets stuck into catching up, and by lunch, it's as if he hadn't had time off at all. And he feels lighter. Purposeful. Until he gets into his car and the heaviness blankets him once more.

What am I going to do? His heart tells him it's not the conference he's thinking of.

Amy's curled up in child's pose when he gets home. His gut churns. Not today.

But then he hears ambient meditation music in the background. Yoga. She's dusted off her mat and is practising yoga.

'You okay?' he asks, hoping it's not the wrong question.

'Meh. My hip has flared up again. Want to make sure I'm good for work tomorrow.' She unfolds and lies flat on her back, moving into the stretching routine a physio taught her. 'I'll be done in a minute if you want coffee. I made scones.'

In the bedroom, he sheds his work clothes and pulls on shorts and a T-shirt. Amy joins him a moment later.

'How was work?'

'It was okay. Bit tough at first. Awkward.'

She nods. 'I suppose they wanted to talk about—'

'Yeah.' Grabbing his dirty clothes, he heads for the laundry. Should he wait to tell her he's still going to Germany? No. Get it over with.

Amy appears beside him. She's changed into a short loose dress. It looks like the nighties Pandora used to wear.

'About the conference,' he starts.

'Yeah, what did they say when you told them?'

'When I told them?'

'That you can't go.'

Shit.

'That's the thing. I'm still going.'

'What? I thought we said—' She stares at him. 'I mean, I assumed …'

'No. We didn't say anything. And you assumed.' He steps around her. Walks to the kitchen. She follows.

'But I—'

'You don't get to make all the decisions, Amy.' He takes a too-fast sip of water. When he finally stops spluttering and clearing his throat, he says, 'I'm still going.'

She walks to the window, shoulders tight. He steels himself for a fight.

'Okay,' she says, without turning around.

He doesn't know what's worse. Amy giving him a serve. Or giving up.

Later, they eat in front of the television, not talking, watching some Netflix show Bonnie suggested. Amy seems to like it, but Matt can't get into it.

'Going to give Mum a ring,' he tells her, collecting their dishes. 'Forgot to call her on the weekend and she's been texting all afternoon.'

Amy nods, eyes on the screen. Is she still pissed with him or did she mean it when she said 'okay'? He can't tell.

His mum's easier to work out. 'Are you sure it's a good idea, Matt? Going to Germany now? What does Amy think about this?'

'She's fine, Mum.'

Helen sighs. 'Well, if you say so.' She hesitates. 'Matt, do you and Amy talk about it now? About Pandora?'

'If you count the past week, yeah.'

'What about … what about having another baby? Have you talked about that?'

'Yeah. We're not ready.' Matt doesn't know why he's protecting Amy. 'Mum, we're just trying to settle here. Work on us, you know?'

Are we? I mean, is it working, all this?

'Mmm.' Helen loves kids. She won't put pressure on, but it doesn't take a rocket scientist to know she thinks a new baby would help. 'How is that going?'

'We're getting there,' he says. Then, 'Actually, we seem to argue more since we moved here.'

She's quiet for a moment. 'You know, when you were a kid and you got sick, I always knew you were getting better when you started giving me lip.'

'Are you saying this is healthy?'

'I'm saying this sounds like progress. Six months ago there was no fight in Amy at all.'

She's right about that. But Matt's starting to wonder if he and Amy are making progress or rapidly losing ground.

CHAPTER 36
AMY

Days later, discomfort gnaws at Amy like a dog with a bone. It's as if Matt and she are on opposite sides of a chasm that is widening by the hour, day by day. If he's not irritable, he's polite and reserved, as if she were an acquaintance, not his wife.

She's tried to bridge the gap by cooking his favourite meals, initiating sex, and encouraging him to talk. But he continues to shut her out.

'I'm fine. Tired,' Matt tells her when she asks. 'Work's been a bitch. Lots to do before I go away.'

Every part of him looks exhausted. He's still not sleeping well, but he keeps putting it down to work, as if that's the answer to everything. Amy knows there's more going on, even if he won't admit it.

Sometimes she catches him looking at her and it's like he's fighting with himself. He goes to work and she goes to work, and they have coffee together before dinner, and it's like nothing has changed.

Except it has. They want different things.

She has no idea what to do about it because either way, one of them has to give up something.

But she can't have another child.

She can't, because she doesn't deserve it. She had her shot at motherhood. Loved Pandora for making her a mother but resented Pandora because Amy thought being a mother compromised her sense of self. Who does that? When she found out she was pregnant again, she wished she wasn't. She'd reached a happy medium – part-time work, where she could be Amy; part-time stay-at-home mum. Changing that wasn't the plan.

If she hadn't wished that pregnancy away, no matter how briefly, would Pandora still be here? Would she be a mother of two, maybe three by now?

Matt wouldn't understand. He'd try to convince her that she was projecting her fear of losing another child onto the future. He has no idea of the shame she feels for her selfish thoughts while staring at a pregnancy test in her grandmother's bathroom. For resenting a life they had made because it would affect her career.

Now she has a career and no children.

Some might say she got what she wanted.

If home is a silent battlefield, Brewed to Taste is her surprise sanctuary. The first day back at work, Amy expected the worst. A panic attack. No customers, or worse, people coming in to judge and point, whisper and blame. People always blame the mother. And perhaps some still did, but if so, they kept it to themselves. Since she walked back into the café, a steady stream of customers has kept Amy and her staff on their toes, and she knows she made the right choice to come back. As for Una and Sharon, they haven't set foot in the café since Nick turfed them out. Amy still doesn't know how she'd react if they turned up.

Sitting in the café alone after closing up, Amy mulls this over while she works on a summer menu for the café – mango and avocado salsa with grilled tiger prawns? A roasted nectarine and mascarpone tart? After this, she needs to plan for the upcoming Around the World Supper Club. Next stop, Morocco. A tagine of some sort. It's hard to think of food when her husband has buried himself. Who will emerge once he's sorted out whatever is going on inside his head? Losing a child changes you; Amy's living proof. It's changed him too. He's quieter. More introspective. But Matt has always been her abiding rock, her ever-present supporter. Her indestructible, indefatigable, perceptive husband. Until now.

Her phone buzzes and she snatches it up. Is it Matt? He's out walking. Again. But, no, it's Bonnie. And she's called three times. Amy's about to hit redial when the phone buzzes again.

Bonnie wastes no time on greetings. 'Amy. I need a really big favour. I don't have anyone else to ask right now.'

'What is it? Is everything okay?'

'Yes. No. I mean, it should be. It's Irene. She's in the hospital. In Bunbury.'

'What? What happened? When? Is she okay?' Amy's chest constricts as the questions spill out.

'I think so. I don't know. She went to Bunbury with Ashlee for the day and she started having chest pains—'

'A heart attack?' Amy interrupts. *Not Irene. No.*

'I don't know. They've got her in Accidents and Emergency now. It's probably her angina.'

'She has angina?' So much has happened since that day Bonnie said she was worried about Irene. Amy didn't even ask about the test results last time Bonnie and Irene visited. Too caught up in her own drama.

'Yeah. Didn't I tell you? Oh, right.' Bonnie goes quiet. 'Well, thing is, she's in A&E and Ashlee's with her, but I'm up north and I can't go get her. I'm at the airport now, but—' She hesitates. 'Can you pick her up? Bring her back to yours?'

'Of course,' Amy says, without thinking. Once the words are out, nausea rises. She wants to be sick. Pandora was the last child she's had in a back seat. Her heart races and she grips the phone so hard she thinks it will snap. She can't do it. There has to be someone else. 'I don't have a car seat.'

'There's one in Irene's car. I've got to go. My ride is here. Flight's at two. I'll text when I land.' The phone goes dead.

Amy stares at it, then texts Matt: Irene hospital. Bunbury. Have to get Ashlee.

He probably won't even notice.

Amy hears Ashlee before she sees her. The little girl is sitting next to Irene's bed in A&E, chattering nonstop to a nurse writing in a folder.

'Amy!' Ashlee squeals. 'I haven't seen you for ever and ever.' She sticks her fingers in her mouth. 'Look! I losted my tooth but the tooth fairy buyed it from me for a hundred dollars and a singing toothbrush!'

'Really?'

'It was *one dollar* in five cent coins.' Irene breaks in, giving Amy a weak, self-conscious smile. 'Hello, love.'

The nurse squeezes past and Amy bends down and kisses Irene's cheek, hiding the shock she feels at her frail appearance. Leads snake from her chest to the monitor measuring her heart rhythm.

'How are you? Any news?'

'Not yet. It's probably my angina flaring up. They want to keep me in overnight, at least.'

'I'm coming to your house and so is my singing toothbrush,' Ashlee interjects. 'It sings "hot potato, hot potato". Do you know that song? I can teach it to you, Amy. It's really, really fun. We can sing it all the way home because it's a very long drive. Can I have a Milo in the cat cup when I get to your house?'

Amy winces at the sudden lump in her throat. Pandora loved that song. She'd sing it over and over until Amy asked for five minutes' peace. And then she'd start all over again.

'Mrs Knight?' A thirty-something woman enters the cubicle. 'I'm Dr Liu.'

While the doctor chats with Irene, Amy takes the chance to collect Ashlee's car seat. Ashlee wants to come too and keeps up a lively stream of chatter as they find Irene's car, remove the car seat, and carry it to Amy's car, which turns out to be only three cars down. Her fingers fumble as she fits the seat into place. Ashlee bounces on the front seat, giving helpful instructions. It's all Amy can do not to cry. But then it's done and they head back inside.

'What did the doctor say?'

'It's angina. But they still want me to stay in. Apparently it's unstable, whatever that means. I've a good mind to go home anyway. Other people could use this bed.' Irene tries to get up, but then falls back against the pillow, wheezing. The machine next to her beeps. 'Maybe not.'

'How long will you be in?'

'Couple of days. Not sure. Bonnie will let you know.'

A nurse checks the machine. 'I hope you're not exerting yourself, Mrs Knight.'

'Fuss, fuss,' Irene jokes.

The nurse doesn't smile. Instead she gives Ashlee and Amy a pointed look. 'I think Mrs Knight needs to rest.'

Amy swallows. She can't put off the drive any longer. 'I should get Ashlee home.'

'Will you be okay?'

Amy knows what her friend is really asking. 'Yes, yes, I'll be – *we'll* be fine.'

'Of course you will. Now, listen, here's the spare key if you need anything from the house. A change of clothes. Whatever. And if you could feed Piglet, Flossie and Henry, that'd be great. The food's all in the laundry.' Irene pushes a key into Amy's hand. 'Bye, Ashlee. Going to come give me a hug?'

'No. I've had enough of hugs for today. Bye, Reenie.'

'Fair enough. Bye, girls. Take care.'

Amy's heart thumps like a drum all the way out to the carpark. Hands shaking, she buckles Ashlee in, then slides into her seat and grips the steering wheel so hard her knuckles ache. She debates marching back inside and telling Irene she can't do it after all, but a little voice from the back seat stops her.

'Amy? When are we going? Don't you know about driving? It's really, really easy. You turn the key and then you turn the wheel round and round and that's driving.'

Amy's fingers relax on the steering wheel. She starts the engine, but leaves the car in park.

'Come on, Amy. You can do it.'

Come on, Mummy. You can do it.

Taking a deep breath, Amy shifts the car into drive.

CHAPTER 37
AMY

'You forget how exhausting it is,' Amy tells Matt a few hours later, filling a water bottle. Bonnie texted half an hour ago to say her plane had landed, but it'll be at least three hours before she arrives, and Ashlee's energy seems boundless. And Amy will be happy never to mention, let alone eat, a hot potato again.

So far, they've watched half of *Frozen 2*, made Milo twice, brushed Ashlee's teeth with the awful singing toothbrush three times, and baked jam drops. Ashlee's run next door to say hello to her pets, drawn seven pictures for Irene, and eaten four pieces of toast, an apple and two biscuits. She's hungry every five minutes and doesn't sit still for more than two. Even when she watches her movie, she's upside down and rolling around. Now Amy and Matt are taking the little girl to the park.

Matt helps Ashlee put her shoes on while Amy adds a small plastic container with sultanas to her bag, in case Ashlee wants more food. Amy steals a look at her husband. He's tying up Ashlee's laces, with an intent look she remembers well. A twinge of guilt pulls as she watches him ruffle the little girl's hair and pretend to steal her nose. From the way Ashlee stares at him, she's in love.

Matt grins at Amy as he hides a yawn from Ashlee. *I'm shattered*, he mouths. 'Ready to go for a walk?' he asks the little girl.

Henry honks as they walk down the driveway, Ashlee skipping ahead. Amy rubs her bum, remembering Henry's sharp beak. They'll have to feed the goose later and she's not looking forward to it. Maybe Matt will do it.

'Quiet, Henry!' Ashlee shrieks. 'You'll wake the whole street, you naughty goose!' She looks at them, exasperation bouncing from her freckles. 'She always does this. She's so naughty. Sometimes I call her Honking Henry, don't I, Henry?' She shouts the last bit at the fence and grins when she receives an answering bray. 'See? She likes it. I made up a song about Henry.' She sings her song to the tune of 'Frère Jacques'.

'It's a wonderful song,' Amy agrees.

'I've got a great idea! Let's sing it all the way to the park!' Ashlee starts singing loudly. When Amy and Matt don't join in, she squints at them crossly. 'You're not singing.'

Dutifully, they start to sing. Amy is wondering how long they have to keep it up when Matt grabs her arm, laughing. Henry is waddling down the path behind them. Ashlee squeals and runs to her pet, throwing her arms around the bird's neck. Amy keeps her distance.

'She mustn't have shut Henry's pen,' she says to Matt, shaking her head.

'Henry wants to come to the park too!' Ashlee's voice is feather-muffled.

'Well, she can't,' Amy says. 'We have to put her back.'

Ashlee plonks herself down in the middle of the path. Henry hisses.

'Come on.' Matt takes Amy's hand. 'We've got this.'

And so, they resume the singing walk to the park with a little girl and a goose, and Amy wonders what the neighbours must be thinking.

When they get back, and Henry, Flossie and Piglet are fed, Ashlee announces that she's hungry. 'But not for fruit. And after I've eaten, you can read me a story,' she tells Matt. 'I bringed my favourite book.'

'How about some sandwiches?' Amy asks, realising that she's hungry, too.

'Only if they are cheese and tomato. And they have to be triangles, not squares. And no crust. Crust makes your hair curly and I don't want curly hair.'

'As you wish, Miss Bossy Boots Pandora.' No sooner than the name is out, Amy wishes she could suck it back in. For a moment, it was as if Pandora was here, had never left. Matt raises his brows. Amy ignores him. Did Ashlee notice? 'Do you want tomato sauce on your sandwich or no sauce?'

'Who's Pandora?' Ashlee tilts her head to one side and looks quizzically at Amy.

Avoiding Matt's gaze, Amy concentrates on slicing tomatoes. 'She's my ... she's a little girl I ... I used to know,' Amy says. 'I was seeing if you were listening.' Betrayal slices like a knife, but Amy can't have this conversation now. 'Do you want sauce?'

'Sauce on the plate, but not on the bread. And Mummy always makes a smiley face with the sauce,' Ashlee instructs. 'When can I see her?'

'Mummy will be here soon,' Amy says, glad they're back on safe ground.

'Not Mummy. The little girl. Pandora.'

'Oh. Well, she's not ... she's not here anymore.'

'Is she on an adventure like Dora the Explorer?'

'No.' Her throat swells as she pushes down the words that want to flow. Matt comes to stand beside her, still her rock.

'Well, where is she then?'

'She's ...' Amy swallows. Her eyes ache with the sting of tears. To collect herself, she places the sandwiches on plates, squeezes a tomato sauce smiley face on Ashlee's plate, and sets down the plates at the table.

Matt squeezes her shoulders and she knows what she has to do.

'Come here,' Amy says, patting the chair next to her. When Ashlee is settled, she goes on. 'Pandora was our little girl. We loved her very,

very much. But one day, a very sad day, she was in a car accident. It was so bad that her body stopped working and she died.'

Ashlee stops chewing and looks at her. 'Pandora died? Like Grandpa Sid?'

'Yes.'

'Oh. I miss Grandpa Sid.' She dips her sandwich into the sauce face and changes the smile into a frown. 'Why don't you buy another baby?'

'Well, you don't buy babies, Ashlee. They come when they're ready.'

'When will a baby be ready?'

Amy drops her eyes from Matt's burning gaze. 'I don't know.'

Ashlee screws her face up. 'I hope a baby comes soon. I like babies. Except when they poo. Did you know Mum used to call me Stinky-poo when I was a baby? It's because I did poos and they were stinky.' She giggles and pushes her plate away. Three of the four triangles remain. 'I'm finished now. Is Reenie going to die?'

Amy hides a smile. Pandora had been the same, switching from one intense topic to another in the blink of an eye. 'I'm sure she's not. The doctors will make her all better.'

Reassured, Ashlee turns to Matt. 'Will you read me the story now?'

Twenty minutes later, Ashlee is asleep on the sofa, halfway through the second reading of *My Silly Mum*. Listening to Matt read the book that was also Pandora's favourite, Amy is mystified. Why is the universe conspiring to bring Pandora, and Matt's desire for a baby, to the forefront of her mind?

She snorts. The universe. God. Does she even believe there's something or someone working behind the scenes anymore? If she does believe that, does that mean what happened to Pandora was not an accident?

Amy sinks down next to Matt, who's lightly snoring. Ashlee's feet are on his lap. Her heart squeezes at the sight of them, eyes closed, breathing in and out. It's been a day of mixed emotions. Driving with a child in the car. The aching reminder of the busyness of motherhood. The tiredness at Ashlee's constant need for attention mixed with delight at her childish innocence.

Ashlee brings life into the house.

An hour later, Bonnie taps at Amy's back door. 'Hey. How'd you go?'

'Great. Ashlee's asleep on the sofa,' Amy says. 'She bombed out after we went to the park with Henry.' She wipes her hands on a tea towel. 'Do you want a cuppa?'

'No, I grabbed a coffee for the drive home. I'll get Ashlee home. She's got kindy in the morning.'

'Any news on Irene?'

'Not yet. I mean, it's her angina, not a heart attack, thank God. I'm going to see her tomorrow. And then I'll figure out what to do.' Bonnie sighs loudly. She looks wiped out. 'I reckon I might quit the FIFO job. I told Jake I'm thinking about it. He's pissed, but too bad. I need to be here.'

Amy nods. 'Let me know how that goes. And if I can help ...'

'Yeah. I might come back to you on that once all this is sorted.' Bonnie follows Amy to the sofa where her daughter is sleeping. 'Thanks so much, Amy. For looking after Ashlee.' She pauses. 'She thinks the world of you, Amy. Totally worships you.' Her eyes travel to Matt. 'Look at him, all flaked out. I bet he was a great dad. I'll bet you were a great mum too.'

CHAPTER 38
IRENE

'Reenie? Where are you?' Irene startles awake. She must have dozed off while waiting for Bonnie to drop off Ashlee at the babysitter's. Footsteps click-clack down the hall.

Disoriented, Irene heaves herself out of the sofa's embrace. 'In here.'

She's barely smoothed out her hair when Bonnie's head pops around the door frame. 'You okay, Reenie? You having a nanna nap?'

'Don't you worry about me, love,' Irene says. 'A little lost in thought, that's all.'

Bonnie squints at her. 'If you say so. You good to go? Are you sure you're okay?'

'I'm fine. Stop your fussing.' Bonnie's been like this since Irene got home from hospital. But this time Irene doesn't mind so much. Bonnie's thrown in the towel on that FIFO job, once and for all. They'd talked about it while Irene was in hospital. Doctor's orders.

'Bonnie. I need to talk to you about something,' Irene had said. She'd rehearsed the speech so many times but couldn't remember a word.

'What?'

'The doctor says I need rest. He said I ... he said I shouldn't be

229

looking after Ashlee on my own anymore.' Bonnie was silent and Irene was quick to fill in the gap. 'I need you to come home and look after your daughter. It's time I looked after me.'

'I know.' Whatever Irene had expected, it wasn't that. 'I've been thinking about it for ages, actually. But Jake—'

'You're a mother first,' Irene interrupted, gently. And as she told Bonnie the truth of how Ashlee had reacted, sadness and shame gathered on her granddaughter's face.

'I feel awful. Like, all along I've missed Ashlee. And you. And I kind of knew what was happening with Ash, but I kept telling myself that you'd sort it out. Because you always do.' Tears slid down Bonnie's face. 'I let myself get so distracted by Jake and what he said we wanted, and never stopped to ask if that's what *I* wanted. Or what you, me and Ashlee needed.' Her voice broke. 'I'm sorry. It totally wasn't fair of me to put this on you.'

Turned out they were both reluctant to say no to someone they loved. And now Bonnie's jobless, but back home. Irene privately thinks her granddaughter needs to quit Jake too, but one thing at a time. It looks like it's on the cards. She hasn't said much about him lately and as far as Irene's concerned, the less said, the better.

Bonnie chats idly as she drives them into town, but Irene hardly takes in a word. Now that Bonnie's back, Irene's desire to travel is no longer a guilty secret. While she was in hospital, she got hooked on travel shows after Bonnie set her up with Netflix and an iPad. She imagined it was her, not the bubbly hosts, cruising down the Rhine, gazing at paintings in Florence, wandering through gardens in England, licking a gelato while walking the Cinque Terre, dancing in a *biergarten*, and staring open-mouthed at ancient buildings and towering mountains. But imagination can only take her so far. She's ready to feel the essence of another culture seep under her skin, and listen to the sound of multiple languages competing to be heard. To learn about customs and quarantine, and sit on a crowded, stuffy airplane for twenty hours.

Sure, she's heard many a holiday horror story. Una loves these stories, loves the theatre of describing disastrous flights to London and New York on planes filled with screaming children and sweaty, rude passengers, while relishing the fact that she's more well-travelled than most of her friends. But if Irene looks after her health and plans well, Dr Ghorbani says there's no reason she can't find out for herself. Bonnie doesn't know yet, but next week, Irene's meeting a travel agent. Next year, she's going to Europe to see beautiful gardens.

Irene sniffs spice scents floating on the air before she gets inside Brewed to Taste. She spies Matt first. His posture seems stiff, like he's on guard, but when he smiles Irene tells herself she's imagining things. Inside the café, the air is fragrant with cumin, coriander, cinnamon, chilli and other aromas she can't define. She follows Bonnie to the long table; Nick, Devi, June and Frank are already seated. After kissing Amy on the cheek, she sinks into a chair, unable to stop a groan from slipping out.

Moments later, Matt passes around amber handpainted Moroccan tea glasses, each one filled with a spice-infused drink. It smells like liquorice and tastes of star anise, citrus and cinnamon, refreshingly cool at first, but warming as the alcohol kicks in. Irene leans back in her chair while the others chatter and help themselves to flatbread, hummus, Persian feta and juicy marinated olives.

Two soft mosaic lamps and tea light candles in coloured glasses send soft light around the café. The effect is warm and comforting. Irene closes her eyes and focuses on the background music. Moroccan or at least Moroccan inspired, it's haunting at times. Hypnotic. She almost dozes off again, but Bonnie sits next to her and her eyes snap open gratefully. Bonnie's holding an iPad across which images float – deserts, markets, towns built into hills, colourful rugs, camels, date palms, mountains and strangely shaped cooking pots. One thing stands out: colour. Clearly, Morocco is no bland, featureless country. The images, the music, the aroma of Amy's cooking, and the brightly coloured bowls are transporting her to a world she knows nothing about.

Matt joins them. 'You've found my slide show,' he says, pointing at a picture of the markets. His face lights up as he talks; he sounds more confident than usual. 'My favourite thing was wandering through the *souks*, the markets. There's nothing like it here. Everywhere you look there are cone-shaped towers of brightly coloured spices. The smell – it's a mixture of earthy, spicy and sweet all at once. And the noise. It's chaotic.'

He sips his drink and goes on. 'The *souks* are like labyrinths, with alleyways twisting here and there. You never know what you'll find when you go around a corner. From soft-as-butter leather slippers to touristy knick-knacks, from hand-painted pots to carpets, from sticky sweets to meat hanging from hooks. And everywhere you look, there are stray cats. I had to stop Amy wanting to adopt them all.' When he looks at Amy, who is ladling what looks like soup into bowls, his expression is hard to read.

'It sounds wonderful,' Irene says.

'It is. But it can be overwhelming. Smelly, sometimes. And you have to learn to haggle, and not cave every time someone says, "I give you good price, lady".'

Irene's almost disappointed when Amy tells them the first course is ready. She wants to hear more of Matt's stories, but when she's handed a bowl of cauliflower soup garnished with toasted almonds, teasing her nose with whiffs of cumin, cinnamon and coriander, she decides stories can wait. All around her, spoons clink into bowls. The soup is smooth and perfectly seasoned, with a rich smokiness Amy tells them comes from the almonds.

'I'd never have thought of this combination,' she tells Amy, licking her lips.

Amy smiles gratefully. She looks beautiful, dressed in a colourful shirt and white Capri pants, but Irene knows her friend is not fully relaxed by the way her shoulders tighten when she thinks no one is looking. Is Amy tired or is something bothering her? Has she argued with Matt? Looking at him now, she wasn't imagining it; there is a certain stiffness to his demeanour tonight, and none of his usual affectionate manner with Amy. What is going on with them?

Not wanting them to catch her watching, Irene shifts in her chair.

'You're very quiet tonight,' Bonnie whispers.

'I'm happy listening.' She pats her granddaughter's hand reassuringly and turns to June. 'You two are getting chummy,' she teases, nodding at Frank, who's devouring his second bowl of soup. 'Anything you want to tell me?'

June blushes. 'Maybe.'

'I've got my eye on you, Miss June.'

Pitchers of mint water are placed on the table, followed by an abundance of food. Amy announces each dish as she and Nick set them down: 'Mint tabouleh. Homemade labneh – that's cheese, Frank. Tagine of chermoula-drizzled lamb meatballs in a spicy – not too spicy – tomato sauce.' She pauses to catch her breath. 'Chicken on the bone with olives and preserved lemons. Israeli couscous. Cucumber, green capsicum and tomato salad. Baby carrots. Mashed sweet potato with a smidge of ginger.'

The room swims with the heady perfume of the feast before them. Irene breathes it in. She doesn't know where to start, and she doesn't want this cultural immersion to end, so she waits for everyone else to serve themselves first.

Frank pokes at the couscous June has spooned onto his plate.

'It's not my kind of food,' Irene hears him whisper.

'Try it anyway.' They sound like a married couple, Irene thinks, watching Frank taste the meatballs tentatively.

To be fair, Irene thinks, Frank's not the only one feeling apprehensive. She's been wondering how her palate would take to the spicier foods on the menu. But the sweet potato mash, its sweetness tempered by the unexpected heat of ginger, sings to her tastebuds.

'Oh, it's a stew,' Frank blurts out. 'Hey, I know what would be good. German food. Reckon you could do that, Amy?' Matt gives him a tight smile. 'Ah, crap. Put me foot in it, didn't I?'

Not wanting to see him squirm, Irene focuses on her chicken. She's eaten lemon chicken from the Chinese place in town, but the lemon flavour in this dish is complex; delicate and yet bold at the same time. She makes a note to make some preserved lemons. 'I might never feel the Moroccan sand beneath my toes, but I feel like I'm there,' she says to no one in particular.

Later, Irene stifles a yawn. The table has been cleared again, ready for dessert. The teasing melody of Nick and Devi's banter rises above the muted table conversation as they wash dishes. Frank and June's noses are almost touching. Is Frank's hand on June's leg? That explains June's uncharacteristically soft smile lately. Irene recognises the glow of early love and smiles to herself. For as long as she's known June, there's never been a man in her life; the only one she knows about is the married Frenchman in Paris. That cheating bastard missed out on a great catch, she thinks. I hope Frank realises what a gem he has.

Bonnie's chatting with Amy, something about Ashlee; she's laughing, so it must be a funny Ashlee story. Amy's smiling, but when she turns her head, Irene catches a flicker of sadness before Amy fixes her face into a smile once more. Probably thinking of her little one, poor love. She remembers the way Amy looked at Ashlee when she stopped by with leftovers from the café on Saturday. A mix of grief and loss and yearning all at once. The look of someone who wants nothing more than to be a mother. Even if she won't admit it.

Irene thanks her lucky stars Bonnie's home for good. It's all worked out for the best. Ashlee is sleeping in her own bed again, and she's not acting up near as much. All Bonnie needs now is a job. She wants something between school hours so she can do the school run.

'Why don't you ask Amy if she's got any work?' Irene asked Bonnie a few days ago. 'She offered it before.'

Bonnie was noncommittal. Too busy messaging that Jake again to think about work.

'Who's ready for dessert?' Amy calls out, bringing over a coiled pastry that looks a little like baklava, has a light dusting of powdered sugar and is sprinkled with what looks like pistachios. 'This is *M'hanncha*. Filo pastry filled with fig and almond paste.'

Irene's never heard of it, but it looks impressive. Almost like a snake. Amy passes around shots of coffee-flavoured liqueur and tells them to dig in. The pastry is infused with an orange blossom and honey syrup, yet the filo has a satisfying crunch. How does she cook like that? Una thinks she's the best cook in town, but she's got nothing on Amy. She sips the liqueur; bold and sweet, with a bittersweet dark chocolate-vanilla flavour, it's a perfect match for the pastry.

'Mind if I have some more stuffed snake?'

'Frank!' June covers her face when everyone bursts into laughter.

'What? That's what it looks like.'

Laughing, Irene considers this unlikely group of friends, all so different and yet, like ingredients in a recipe, together they bring out the best in each other. Frank and June, chalk and cheese. Bonnie, light of her life. Nick and Devi, in their element as they talk food and travel. Amy and Matt, new friends introducing her to new things. There's a contented smile on Amy's face, as if the tension of earlier has gone. Perhaps she was simply worried about her cooking, not that she needed to be. A little flustered by trying to make everything perfect. Relaxed now that the evening's almost done.

Silly old woman, imagining things.

And then Irene's eyes fix on Matt, who's drifted off into another world. Sadness steals a path across his features, before he snaps out of that otherworld, into the room, his eyes on his wife.

That's when Irene knows she's not imagining the couple's tension. And she knows something else too.

Amy's not the only one who wears a mask. Don't they all?

CHAPTER 39
AMY

A week later, Amy drops in next door on her way home from work. It's time to renew her offer of employment to Bonnie. The summer school holidays are six weeks away and if she doesn't do something about Brewed to Taste's staffing now, she'll be hard pressed to get her Sundays off. Nick reckons tourists flock into Blackwood like sheep to green pastures.

Bonnie's not home, but Irene's resting in a cane chair on her back verandah, an empty tea cup by her side. Her eyes light up when she sees Amy. When was the last time Matt had looked at her like that?

'Good to see you resting, Irene,' Amy tells her.

'Don't you start. I get enough of that fussing from Bonnie and Ashlee. Did some weeding earlier and Bonnie nearly wore my ear out.' Irene sighs, waving her hand towards the backyard. It's bursting with flowers, but the grass is in need of a trim and piles of weeds are scattered around the garden beds. 'I can manage the weeding, but Frank's coming to mow my lawn and do some pruning on the weekend.'

'Is he? That's nice of him.' She'd been thinking of asking Matt to give Irene a hand. And if Henry wasn't poking around the weeds, Amy would scoop them into the bin.

'Ah, Frank likes my scones, so it's not hard to twist his arm,' Irene laughs. 'Not usually, anyway. Getting him away from June is proving tricky.'

'Frank and June? They're officially a couple now?' How did she miss that?

'Oh, yes. It's rather sweet. They've both been on their own for quite a while, you know. Well, June's never married. And Frank … well, anyway, that's another story. By the way, Frank wants to go to Vietnam next.'

'Does he? Vietnam's great. He'll love the food, although it might be a bit spicy for him.'

Irene laughs. 'No, not for a holiday. He's suggested Vietnam for the next supper club.'

'Oh, the supper club. Of course.' She straightens in her seat as her mind flicks to pho, sticky rice and freshly rolled rice noodle rolls. Matt loves that food. But will he be home from Germany? She tries to calculate the dates, but Irene keeps talking.

'Actually, love, would you mind if we bring the date forward a week? It clashes with the Christmas concert at Ashlee's school.'

'Oh.' Amy falters. Matt will definitely be away. Pity. He loves Vietnamese food.

'We could put it off until January?' says Irene.

'No, it's not a problem. I'll make a note in my diary when I get home.' Right next to *Matt: Düsseldorf*.

She lifts her head at the sound of a car pulling into their driveway, then glances at her phone. Why is Matt home this early on a work day?

'Are you okay, love? You seem a bit distracted,' Irene says, patting her arm.

'Oh, I'm fine. Fine. A bit tired after work, that's all.' Is Matt sick? With effort, she turns back to Irene, who looks as if she wants to press further and then thinks better of it.

'Well, now, Frank has offered to bring spring rolls to the supper club.'

Visions of tiny, bland supermarket spring rolls fill Amy's head. 'Oh, that's not necessary—'

'His late wife showed him how to make them,' Irene interrupts, gently but firmly. 'They're pretty good. Very good, actually. Go down a treat at the pot luck dinners we have on barn dance and quiz nights.'

Amy relents. They have barn dances in Blackwood? 'Well, okay. I'll focus on the mains and desserts then.' She stands to go. 'Can you tell Bonnie I was looking for her? Or I can message—'

'I think I can remember,' Irene says, winking.

Walking down the driveway after another ten minutes' talking, Amy fights resentment towards Frank. She's the cook, the organiser of the supper club, not Frank. Seconds later, she gives herself a mental kick.

You don't have to control everything.

Her self-talk is forgotten as soon as she bounds up the stairs. The unmistakeable screech of metal boring into plaster assaults her ears.

A drill? What is he doing?

Matt's in the long hallway near the front door, lifting a photo of Pandora onto the wall. Lined up on the floor are three more photos, all of Pandora: laughing, serious, playful.

'What are you doing?' she asks, although by now it's obvious. What she means is *why*, and that's obvious, too.

'Hanging Pandora's pictures,' he says. He glances at Amy, his expression inscrutable, then at the floor before striding to the study, leaving her to follow. 'I forgot the tape measure.' She wrenches the frame from the wall, scoops the rest from the floor, and stalks after him, body bristling with anger.

On his desk are more framed photos of their daughter. A happy, gummy baby. An inquisitive toddler. Averting her eyes from them, Amy plants the frames she's holding face down on the desk, and faces her husband, hands on hips.

'We haven't talked about this, Matt. I thought we'd at least discuss if you were going to hang things on the walls and … and redecorate.'

'Of course, decorating is your domain, isn't it? I can't change a thing without your permission.' Amy grits her teeth at Matt's sarcastic tone. 'Well, in case you forgot, this is *my* study. And as for the wall out there,' he says, quietly, 'it's time.'

Amy looks away, shaking her head. *No, no it's not.* She fights a sudden urge to burst into tears. If she does, Matt will think she's manipulating him. But she's not.

'No!' she shouts. 'No. I don't want to be reminded of her every day. Don't make me. Please.' She takes a breath, forces her volume down. 'I thought we agreed—'

'Agreed?' Matt's laugh has a bitter edge of disbelief. 'I've gone along with what *you* wanted. For three years. And I'm over that. It's not all about you. I've said it before and I'm saying it again: *you* don't get to decide how *I* deal with this, how I grieve, or remember our daughter.'

She stares at him, too stunned to speak. He's never spoken to her like this before. His words are measured, like he's been rehearsing lines. Is that what he does when he locks himself away? How long has he been planning this?

'I've never—'

He interrupts. 'It's always been about you. About supporting you. Protecting you. About walking on fucking eggshells so you can walk on soft sand. All of this, this move to Blackwood, it's all been about *you.*'

'You wanted to move!'

'For *you,*' he grinds out. 'I wanted to move here so *you* could find a way to deal with what happened, away from everyone who knew, and then put your focus onto *us.* That's what we talked about. But it's like my needs and wants and opinions are less important than yours.'

He walks away, looks out the window, shoulders heaving. Silence fills the room.

'Amy ...' he falters and then surges on, 'we have to find a way to compromise on this. We've done it your way. But I can't do that anymore. It's time, Amy. I want to talk about our daughter. And the baby we lost. The one we never talked about. I *need* to. I want to see Pandora's face so I can remember her the way she was. Look!' He picks up a frame from his desk and thrusts it at Amy's face.

Flinching, she flails at his hand, knocking the frame onto the wooden floor. Glass shatters.

For a moment they say nothing, staring at the broken glass,

breathing heavily, like boxers taking a rest between rounds. And then he says the words that split her heart all over again.

'I think we need a break. From each other.'

Amy gapes at him. How did they get to this place?

'Don't be ridiculous.' It's the first thing that comes to mind, but the second the words leave her mouth she wants to stuff them back into the darkness where they belong. Flinty eyes shrink her to the size of a flea. She takes the high road. 'Matt. We'll talk about this later, when we've both calmed down, okay?'

Without waiting for an answer, Amy slides past him and heads for the shower, thoughts curdled with indignation, hurt and anger. She can't get past the careless way he'd flung the words at her: 'I think we need a break.'

If it means that bloody much, he can hang the photos in the study and shut the door.

Caught up in anger, she ignores the sounds of separation: drawers opening and shutting, a door slamming, the car backing out of the driveway. Even when Amy stands in the empty carport, stomach churning with shame and fear, she refuses to believe that he's actually gone through with it.

He's just gone for a drive, she tells herself. He'll be back in a couple of hours and he'll say sorry and I'll say sorry and everything will be okay.

Hours later, Matt hasn't returned her calls or messages. His phone is off. She has no idea where he is, but has a pretty good idea that he won't be back tonight. Between bouts of crying and rushing to the loo with bowel spasms, she paces until her phone finally pings with a message and her world tilts sideways.

Staying at hotel. Don't call. Will talk on weekend.

CHAPTER 40
MATT

M att shuffles on the single bed, turning fitfully from side to side. The mattress is old, and it feels like a spring is about to break through under his butt. He hasn't slept on a bed like this since he was a kid, but when Frank offered, he couldn't say no.

Frank had unexpectedly turned up at the Timbertop Hotel where Matt was booked in for the rest of the week. Nursing a cider, Matt had been lost in thought until Frank slapped him on the back with a hearty, 'Mate, what're you doing here?' Curiosity was scrawled on his face.

'Felt the need for a brew,' Matt had answered. 'What are you doing here?'

'Doing some work out back. Was just about to have a counter meal and get home.' Frank ordered a beer and the chicken parmy special, then turned back to Matt, brows furrowed. 'You okay, mate?'

'Yeah, course I am,' Matt lied. And then, without knowing why, he added, 'Staying here a couple of days. Putting in some extra hours ahead of that conference I told you about.' He's not lying about that part, but he could tell Frank wasn't buying it.

'Tell you what,' he said. 'Save your money and come back to mine.

I'm only fifteen minutes from your work, give or take. Little house on a couple of acres. Nothing flash, but it does me fine.'

Shifting restlessly, Matt sighs. Frank's not stupid. He knows something's up. Can probably guess what it is, too. Matt's shared bits and pieces with him when they've been out walking. But at least he didn't ask questions. When they got back to Frank's, they drank beer and talked footy and politics, good-naturedly sledging the other's team. It was nice hanging out with Frank, bloke to bloke. No tiptoeing around, wondering what might set Amy off.

Amy. He squeezes his eyes tight, as if to force her from his mind. Even while he was drinking with Frank, she hovered at the edge of his thoughts, thanks to at least ten messages and as many missed calls. He'd switched his phone off; couldn't deal with it, with her, any longer. Now his stomach churns. Leaving while she was in the shower was a shit thing to do. He's never done anything like that before. Then again, he's never needed to reconsider his marriage before.

He almost called earlier, but took the cowardly way out and texted instead. Said just enough to stop her worrying. She probably would have rung all the hospitals otherwise. But he hasn't told her his plans changed. She'll freak if she realises he's at Frank's.

You're such a bastard, he tells himself. Amy must be feeling like crap. The accusation is nearly enough to make him call her, but then anger stirs again, an angry hornet buzzing in his chest.

Amy's got to get her shit together. And she's got to realise that it takes two to make a marriage work. And if she can't do that, then I'm done.

Even as the idea seeds, he wants to blow it away before it takes root.

Not yet.

Despair blows from his lips in a gusty sigh. He reaches for his watch. It's nearly midnight. And sleep is nowhere in sight.

'Shit.' The word bursts from him through clenched teeth. Even when he's nowhere near his wife, even when he's not walking on broken glass, he can't relax.

Work is Matt's saving grace. He's swamped from the moment he arrives, bombarded with questions and emails all day, every day, one thing after another. It's relentless and would usually piss him off but doesn't faze him now; instead, it takes the focus off Amy, their marriage, and what the hell he's going to do. The only plan of action he's settled on is taking time out. Giving them both breathing – and growing – space. Work gives him that although, if he's honest, it always has. Who doesn't sometimes go to work and breathe a sigh of relief at leaving home and responsibility behind?

At night, in Frank's spare room, it's a different story. When he stops surfing the internet, or snaps his eyes open after falling asleep from repeatedly reading the same page of whatever action thriller he's plucked from Frank's surprisingly well-stacked bookshelf, his mind clicks into action, like it's stuck on repeat cycle and the off switch is stuffed.

It's been four days since he walked out but he feels no lighter. And now he's got to face Amy. Out of courtesy, he'd texted her earlier to say he was dropping by, using the pretext of picking up more clothes. She'd responded immediately: Fine. One word. She hasn't called him since the night he left. He misses her more than he wants to.

At 3 p.m., Matt shucks off his lab coat and clocks off, mouthing 'See you tomorrow' to Carla, who's on the phone. Walking out to the car, he rolls up his shirtsleeves. The air is warm and heavy; sweat pools under his arms. Summer's just around the corner, but it's unseasonably warm for the time of year, according to his colleagues. Inside his car, he leaves the door open to let the heat out. His hand hovers over the ignition and he hesitates. Delaying the inevitable. If he didn't have to get clothes, would he bother? The next few hours will be rough and he can't escape it.

Matt plugs in his phone and searches for *Queen's Greatest Hits*. The opening lyrics of 'Bohemian Rhapsody' swell in the small space as he heads towards Blackwood. He knows the words to the masterfully absurd rock opera by heart and belts out the song with Freddie, Brian and Roger. The irony of the opening lines – 'no escape from reality' – is not lost on him. When the bass riffs of 'Another One Bites the Dust' subside, he mutes the sound so he can figure out what he's going to do when he gets to the house.

Trees flash by in a blur. His shoulders tighten as he travels closer to recriminations and tears, knowing the chance of a quick exit is slim. Amy will be in the house and he can't exactly ignore her, not that he wants to. He imagines the conversation, but it's coloured by how he hopes things go, not by how he knows they'll go. His counsellor's voice pops up: *Just stay calm. Explain that you want to talk but you need a few more days to think things over.* Like he hasn't been thinking things over every night.

Driving into Blackwood, he recalls the blanket of fog that wrapped the town the day he and Amy moved in; it was especially murky at the crossroad that led to their new home. Matt was full of hope. Amy was full of fear. She didn't have to say it out loud. And now look where they are. Another crossroad. The sky is gloriously blue, the town looks as though it has opened up, but instead of hope, there's trepidation. He no longer knows what lies ahead. And somehow the town feels like home, but not like home. Surely he can't feel disconnected from Blackwood already? It's only been a few days. Maybe it's just him, feeling disconnected from life.

He parks out on the street and takes a moment to collect himself. *Be strong. You can do this.* He repeats this as he makes his way up the back steps, aware that he's not only strengthening himself for the inevitable confrontation, but against his desire to see and hold his wife again.

'Amy?' His voice echoes. 'Amy? It's me.'

Her car's in the carport, but she's not home. The heart-punching realisation that the house is empty, that Amy has chosen not to see him, hits harder than expected. Instead of relief, he's crushed. His emotions are two clashing tunes banging about in his mind; he shakes his head, as if to dislodge the discordant reaction. Rubs his eyes, as if that will make him see his heart clearly. It doesn't make sense. He wanted to avoid the hurt of confrontation, but a small part of him was willing to endure it because it meant seeing Amy.

Where is she? I'm flying out in a week.

Something essential is missing from the house. It looks the same as when he left, but it's as if all the heart has leached out of the walls, leaving only a sad shell. His footsteps echo as he walks on the floorboards towards the linen cupboard. The doors squeak when he opens them to remove a suitcase. There are no homely sounds to muffle the noises he's making, even though he's practically tiptoeing through the house. No washing machine. No cooking sounds and smells. No birdcall floating through open windows. The only thing alive and ticking is the grandfather clock Amy inherited from her grandmother.

At the bedroom he stops, feeling like a stranger invading someone's space. The bed is neatly made, but the room smells faintly of peach, vanilla and musk. Amy's perfume. Get a grip, he tells himself. He fills a suitcase: shirts, trousers, T-shirts, shorts, underwear. In the bathroom he collects toiletries, averting his face from the sharp slap of birth control pills on the countertop. *She's not even trying to hide it.* The scent of Amy's body wash lingers in the small space. Matt breathes in the vanilla scent and is hit with a sudden longing for his wife, for things to be normal, to be the same as they once were. Except they won't be. They want different things now.

Before he leaves, he takes the photos of Pandora from his desk. He doesn't know what Amy's done with the ones she slammed onto his desk days earlier. He hesitates before adding a silver-framed portrait of Amy – laughing and relaxed on their wedding day – to his bag. The last thing he does is leave a note for Amy. He keeps it simple: *Hope you're well. Let's talk on Sunday.* If she takes the day off.

It's not until he's halfway back to Frank's place that he remembers his journal. He doesn't want Amy finding it, but at least it's locked away. He's left the key to his desk in a jarrah trinket box on his bookshelf. Amy had bought it from a woodcraft gallery down south years ago and given it to him, saying the yin and yang design, with two separate compartments, represented them both. As well as the key, Matt keeps Pandora's first locks of hair in there.

He'd found them before they moved to Blackwood, packed in tiny labelled ziplock bags inside a box full of photos and baby clothes. Pandora's box. He remembers the day they moved in, when Amy told him to get rid of it. As if the memories of Pandora were no longer worth holding on to. The box is at the top of the linen cupboard. Out of sight, but not out of mind.

Tonight will be the last night he stays at Frank's, he resolves. Frank says Matt can stay as long as he needs, but while Matt appreciates the offer, he wants and needs space more than anything. And the mattress is hell on his back. He'll talk to Frank tonight and then he'll phone the hotel and book a room until he leaves for Germany. But before he goes, he and Amy are going to talk.

CHAPTER 41

AMY

A my doesn't tell anyone that Matt's left. She barely wants to admit it to herself, but the deep down knowledge eats at her, as does the lie – 'he's working away at the moment'– whenever anyone asks. She keeps her voice breezy, as if Matt were still a FIFO worker like many of the people living down this way. It surprises her how easy it is to lie – to herself, as much as the people she calls her friends. After all, nothing is settled yet. It's just a break.

They haven't talked since he left a week earlier. A few texts here and there. Impersonal cyber messages. Amy aches to talk to him, has to force her fingers not to press send on the messages she drafts. One week. One week since he'd walked out while she was in the shower. She doesn't even know where he is staying.

Not talking to him is killing her. And yet, like a coward, she'd hidden next door when he came to collect his clothes. It was easier to hide than face him, to watch him pack his bags. Over Ashlee's chatter, she'd heard Matt's car pull up. Imagined the back door open, his footsteps and voice echoing through the empty house. When he drove away, the wheels catching on the gravel like they always did, she felt as though her heart was pulled from her body.

Now, she regrets hiding. Matt's presence still lingers in their bedroom, where half the drawers are now empty. She wishes she'd been braver, even if her heart was torn apart all over again. She wishes a lot of things now there's no one to talk to.

It's not so bad during the day. Brewed to Taste keeps her busy. When she gets home, she bakes cakes she doesn't need and won't eat. But at night, she switches on the television to drown out her clamouring thoughts. It helps for a while; staring at the screen, watching earnest actors tell their stories, she can dissociate from the questions that plague her once she's in her bed. Lying there in the dark, she forces herself not to email, text or phone Matt; to give him the space he wants, even though she doesn't quite understand why. All this over some photos?

Some nights she rolls over and buries her face in Matt's pillow, breathing in his scent. Other times she replays the *we need a break* scene over and over, wondering how it could have gone differently. She's like a director, moving characters into position, calling for more of this and that, but every time, no matter what she does, the ending's the same.

The night he left, after the tears had run dry, she wandered through the house on autopilot, her mind and body numb. How could he leave after all they'd been through? How can she do this thing called life without him? And when the numbness wore off, after he'd sent her a message saying 'Don't wait up' – he'd *known* she would – she wanted to smash something. To throw plates on the ground and watch them shatter, like her world was shattering once more. Her mind had raged and roared and screamed and cried all night and the next day, exhausted from no sleep, she'd dragged herself into work and somehow found the autopilot switch once more.

It's the only thing that's getting her through the week. And Matt's restrained note promising they'll talk on the weekend.

Matt calls on Sunday morning; she grabs her phone like a love-struck teenager. His tentative voice makes her simultaneously excited and wary. Is he ready to come home?

'I was thinking I'd come over later, if you're home,' he says, as if he needs permission. 'Around one. We need to talk.'

Unease trickles through her veins. Matt once said men feared that phrase. It set off all manner of anxieties, because it meant that something the woman had been thinking about for days was about to be thrust upon them with no warning. Is that what was happening here?

'I'll see you later,' she agrees, more lightly than she feels.

Amy throws the sheets in the wash, makes up the bed with fresh ones, and spritzes the room with an orange and lavender mix. In the kitchen, she mixes up Matt's favourite chocolate-chip biscuit dough and tidies the kitchen while the cookies bake. The brown sugar smell wafts through the kitchen. While the biscuits are cooling, she speeds through the rest of the house dusting, vacuuming, perfecting.

With half an hour to go – Matt's never late – she straightens her hair, flicks on mascara and swipes her lips with a tinted lip gloss. Taking a step back, she stares at her reflection. Why is she doing this? Trying to create the illusion of the perfect wife and perfect house? He's given her no clue about what he wants. Apart from the pointed remark about being home, he sounded professional, like he was talking to a client, or a colleague. It was as if his husband voice, the real Matt voice, had rusted into disuse.

When she hears the hum of Matt's car, she leans against a door-frame, trying to appear relaxed. But his footsteps jolt hopeful anxiety to her heart; she startles at the rap of his knuckles on the back door. Somehow her feet move and her shaking hands turn the handle, and there he is – his tired, pale face echoing her own. It takes all of her strength not to throw her arms around him.

'Hi, Amy,' Matt says, neutrally. Still no clue. He follows her to the kitchen, declines coffee, but accepts water.

Amy puts the kettle on anyway, and fishes around in the pantry for camomile tea while he makes small talk. She tries to sound cool and measured, but her heart is hot, jackhammering in her chest. When will they get to the real stuff? Pushing a plate of biscuits towards him, she answers his questions about the supper club, about Frank and

June's fledgling romance and the café's new menu, her short answers matching those he gives her questions.

Finally, Amy can't bear it any longer.

'When are you coming back?' It wasn't what she'd intended to ask, but what her heart sought.

He looks down at his glass. 'I don't know.'

She stares at him. 'What kind of answer is that? Why? Why don't you know?' When he doesn't meet her eyes, more questions barrel out. 'Why did you just walk out like that? When I was in the shower? Why didn't you talk to me?'

Matt looks at her like she's a petulant child refusing to understand. 'I tried to talk. You didn't want to listen.'

'You didn't try hard enough,' she throws back.

He looks skyward, the way he does when he's frustrated. 'I've been trying to tell you how I've been feeling for ages. But you don't want to hear what I'm saying.'

She ignores the inner voice urging calm and patience. She's suddenly furious with everyone who has left her. A long-buried anger dislodges years of dust and bondage, and takes aim at the man she loves.

'What? What are you trying to say?' When Matt doesn't answer immediately, she carries on. 'Is this about the photos? Look, keep them in the study. It's fine. Whatever. It's your space, I get it.' The words tumble out.

Incredulity washes across his face. 'You think this is just about the photos? Geez, Amy. Shit.'

Matt paces around the kitchen, his shoulders tense. When he turns, his voice has changed, has taken on a harder tone. 'It's *not* just about the photos. It's about us. About me needing to grieve *and* to remember. And *you* not letting me. About our future and what that means to us.'

'What are you talking about? I let you *remember*. Don't—'

'No. You don't. Not really. Only in the way that *you* want to do it.' He holds his hand up when she tries to interrupt. 'And in your case, it's boxing Pandora away, so you don't have to think about her at all.'

His words crush her. She spits her words out, trying to hang on to calm.

'I think about her every day. Every. Day. How dare—'

'So do I. But I need to grieve, Amy. I've never had the chance to do it properly. Unlike you, who's trying to remember nothing, I want to remember the good, not just the … the bad. I want to see her little face —' Matt's voice breaks. He turns away, shoulders heaving.

'Matt—' Amy reaches out. He jerks away, knocking Pandora's special cat cup to the ground. It breaks in two.

Amy stares at it, before reaching into the pantry for the dustpan and brush.

'Leave it,' he says, through gritted teeth.

She draws back, helpless. Unable to help him, to help them. Not ready to entertain the thought that he might just be right.

'I can't be around you right now,' he blurts. 'I just … I just can't. I don't know what to say to you to get you to understand. The more I try, the more it feels like we're pulling apart.'

'I know you want a child.' Keep him talking. Keep him here. 'But you don't want to listen to my side, either.'

He cradles his head in his hands for a long time. 'There's something I've always wanted to know. Why did you keep it from me?'

'What?' *The baby. He means the baby.*

'Why didn't you tell me about our baby?'

A tear slides down her face and she swipes at it. If she starts crying now, she won't be able to stop. 'I wasn't ready to tell you.'

'Why? I'm your husband.'

'Because of the way you're looking at me now. Like I'm despicable. Selfish.'

'I'm not.'

'You are. And it's true. I am selfish. I didn't tell you because I freaked out, okay? We weren't planning another baby yet.'

'But it happened anyway, so why—' Horror crosses his face. 'What were you going to do, Amy?'

'Nothing! I just needed time to think. I wanted things to stay the way they were a bit longer, you know? I'd just gone back to work.

Pandora was starting school the following year. And they'd offered me the head chef job at that East Perth café, do you remember?' Matt nods. 'Anyway, I was going tell you while we were in Germany. Tell my dad while we were there.'

'Except you didn't. And we never did talk about it.' Matt stands. He's never said he blames her, but she feels it now, the silent accusation seeps from him: *I hold you accountable for all of it.* 'I have to go. I'm flying out on Friday. We'll talk when I get back, okay?'

Amy busies herself with cleaning up the broken cat cup so he can't see her face crumble when he leaves for the second time in a week. Arms wrapped around herself, she watches his car slide away.

Anger tears her from the window. Once again, she wants to smash something. To hurl plates at the wall and watch their shattered bodies fall to the ground. To open the glass cupboard and swipe its contents onto the floor. Just for the sound. Because her heart is breaking all over again and she doesn't want to be the only one in pieces.

She resists. Just. Hot and sour tears stream down her face as she alternates between yelling and weeping. Wiping her face on her T-shirt she storms into the study, intent on planting the pictures of her daughter face up on Matt's dusty desk. They're nowhere to be seen. Matt must have taken them.

She's overcome with an urge to ring Gran, but since she doesn't have a direct line to heaven, how can she? She swears and kicks out at furniture that gets in her way as she stumbles to the lounge room. Collapses onto the armchair and lets her thought-storm rage until, finally, the fury peters out and the questions roll in.

Was it a mistake moving to Blackwood?

It seems to have torn them apart rather than knitting them closer together. What would have happened if they'd stayed in Perth? Would they still have reached this point? Has Blackwood been the catalyst or was their marriage on course for implosion no matter what? Even if Pandora had lived, would Matt and Amy have made it?

She sits for hours. Only when her bladder urges her up does Amy ease from the chair. Her entire body cries in protest, her joints stiff from sitting too long.

Darkness has folded the house into its embrace, blanketing the rooms in gloom. Amy catches sight of her face in the mirror. The whites of her eyes are red. As if she's cried rivers of blood instead of salty tears, draining the warmth from her, leaving her cold.

Amy wanders through the house like a robot. Except unlike a robot, she has no focus. Darkness has her in its grip. When words do come, they are names. Matt. Pandora. The Baby. Gran. Mum. People she has loved and lost. These names swirl around in her mind and she can't make them go, not even when she shuts her eyes or blocks her ears or screams.

She stands in front of the 1930s walnut cocktail cabinet in Matt's study. He'd found it in an antique store in Fremantle.

'Imagine the stories this could tell,' he'd exclaimed when he brought it home.

Amy fingers the lid, lifts it and stares at the mirrored serving area. They'd used it for parties in the past. It would have been perfect for the French supper club night; that night Matt was the perfect host and she saw a future in Blackwood.

She opens the two doors at the bottom of the cabinet. On the left is an assortment of bottles – gin, vodka, rum, whisky, cognac. Amy fingers the glasses on the other side. A drink? Just one? She rarely drinks alone, except for the occasional glass of wine. She doesn't want to end up like her mother. But now, the urge to reach in and grab a bottle, any bottle, and swallow certain oblivion is overwhelming. Forget the glass. Tip the bottle up and let the fiery liquid slide down her throat.

Just this once. It'll help.

She's so close. The bottle is in her hand. Her fingers shake on the lid.

CHAPTER 42

MATT

'Did you know that one in fifty people meet the love of their life on a plane?' Bumping Matt's elbow, Carla points to a headline in the inflight magazine she's reading.

'Yeah, and the other forty-nine just annoy the crap out of them,' Matt says, inclining his head towards the obnoxious lout on the other side of her. The man was exactly the kind of boorish bloke Matt had never connected with. The kind of guy who drank too much, laughed too loudly, and flirted with the flight attendants in a manner bordering on harassment. Even tried it on with Carla, but she'd put the jerk in his place with a withering look. Matt smiles at the memory. The twenty-hour flight would have been torture without Carla's company.

It came as a surprise to Matt that he and Carla were seated together; he'd expected her to fly business class or premium economy. He'd thought it would be awkward – after all, aside from work, they barely knew each other. But it wasn't awkward at all. Instead, they fell into a conversation that lasted for hours. Turned out they'd gone to the same university, had several mutual friends, and lived in the same suburb growing up, but somehow had never met before Matt came to Timbertop.

As the plane makes a smooth landing at Frankfurt Airport, Matt reflects on what he's learnt about Carla. She's witty one minute, insightful and kind the next. Talking to her is easy. There's no history, nothing to trigger upset. Her cheerful chatter kept his mind from drifting to Amy and their fragmented marriage. To the what-ifs and what-nows. To the future that lay behind curtains of uncertainty. And Carla listens, really listens, like Amy used to do when they first met. When exactly did that change?

'Matt?' Carla's standing, her carry-on slung over her shoulder. How long was he zoned out? 'We have to get a move on if we want to make our train to Düsseldorf.'

It's 4 p.m. when they finally check into the Tulip Inn at Düsseldorf Arena. Carla wants to go somewhere for a drink and food, but Matt demurs. Instead, he goes straight to his room, sets an alarm and passes out on the bed without bothering to change.

After breakfast the next morning, Matt rugs up and walks alone to the CCD Congress Centre where the conference is being held. The wind needles his face, but he feels alive. By the time he arrives, he's ready to face the throng – more than four thousand people from seventy-five countries.

Day one of the conference passes in a mind-numbing blur. It's exactly what Matt needs to take his mind off his messy life. And if it has to be jargon-loaded presentations about innovation, application, sustainable industrial processing and emerging technologies, that's fine with him. He concentrates as best he can, mingles with people he'll never see again after the conference, and wishes he had the guts to play truant and explore the city instead.

The first night after dinner he walks back to the hotel, shunning the after-dinner drinks, despite Carla's entreaty. It's only a kilometre and although the outdoor temperatures are near freezing, the wind cutting and the sleet stinging, he welcomes the feel of it on his skin. But back in the comfort of his room, where photos of Pandora and Amy awaken his sadness, he can't relax. Was he too quick to dismiss the ritual of drinks and small talk? On the one hand he has no desire to hang out with virtual strangers. On the other, he craves human contact. Should he put himself out there more? Don a mask and pretend he's someone else for a while?

'Stay for drinks tonight,' Carla urges after dinner the second night. Matt hesitates. It's been a long day and he's all peopled out. 'It's just a few of us, we're going to the taverna down the road.' She tilts her head and smiles up at him. 'Come on. Live a little.'

When he agrees, her face lights up and she claps her hands like a little girl.

Carla's idea of 'just a few' is the opposite of his; as soon as they walk into the taverna, she's surrounded by people. Drinking beer from the sidelines, Matt's amazed by her seemingly limitless energy for being the centre of attention, especially with men. It shouldn't bother him, but it does, and it bothers him that it does. Unsettled, Matt chugs down the rest of his beer and gets to his feet. He shouldn't have come. This is not his kind of place; it stopped being that years ago, when he met Amy.

Weaving through the crowd, he goes in search of Carla. She's on the dance floor, alone, eyes closed. Forcing his eyes away from the sensual sway of her hips, he taps her shoulder.

'Come to ask me to dance?' Without waiting for an answer, Carla reaches for his hands and pulls him close. Too close. Discomforting heat rushes through him, unbidden and unwanted. Thoughts fire like bullets.

She's tipsy.

She's not Amy.

It's just a dance.

With effort, he releases her hands. 'I'm going back to the hotel. Will you be okay to get back?'

Another man takes her hands and spins her round. 'I'll get an Uber,' she says over her shoulder. Her fingers trail up the other guy's arm. Matt wishes those fingers were running up his arm and then wishes that wish away. Back in his hotel room, he sits on the edge of his bed, head in hands, until the shame fades.

On the final day of the conference, Matt avoids Carla, but it seems that whenever he turns around, she's there. More than once, her eyes meet his – across a table, across the room, across the crowded foyer – then dart away. As lunch approaches, his stomach flips. They've sat together for the past two days. He's not sure he wants her that close now. Maybe he's imagining things, maybe he read Carla wrong last night – he *wants* to be wrong – but he's ninety-five per cent sure he's got a situation on his hands that he can't avoid forever. So when a competing lithium mine owner invites him to lunch away from the conference centre, he doesn't hesitate. By the end of the lunch, his stomach is curdling, and not because of Carla. He's been offered a job. In London. At double his current salary and all relocation expenses covered.

Back at the conference centre, Matt tunes out the closing speeches. Possibilities swirl in his mind. What should he do? So many what-ifs he could write a book. London was a coup. The golden ticket. Some would say he'd be a fool to turn it down. But until things with Amy are sorted – one way or another – how could he even entertain the idea?

'Matt?' Carla's standing at the end of the row. The room is near-empty. 'You okay?'

'I'm fine,' he says, pulling himself out of his seat and stretching. 'Bit tired, is all.' He bends down for his backpack. 'Going to skip drinks tonight. Got an early start in the morning.' Guilt rises anew. Amy knows he's here for the conference. What she doesn't know is where he's going next.

'Me too,' Carla says, moving closer. She smells like temptation; he breathes it in. 'I've got to pack. I'm catching the eight o'clock train to Paris. Wait for me – I'll walk back with you.' She darts over to two women and says something. He tells himself to walk away before she comes back, but his feet don't move.

When they get to the hotel, Carla invites him into her room.

CHAPTER 43
IRENE

The smell of fresh chilli, onion, garlic and coriander tickles Irene's nose when she walks into Brewed to Taste. The Around the World Supper Club is meeting tonight and she's come in early to help Amy prepare. When Amy took her up on the offer, Irene was taken aback. Amy's always struck her as someone who likes to do it all herself, so it's just right. Irene understands that. It used to be her way, too, until her health problems took care of that.

The dynamics will be different tonight. Matt's overseas. In Germany, of all places. They'd kept that quiet.

'How do you feel about that?' she'd asked when Amy mentioned it.

'Oh, you know, it's work. Gotta do what you gotta do.'

Something about Amy's overly cheerful tone had pinged Irene's inbuilt lie detector. What was going on with Amy and Matt? Something was off, that was certain. She'd bumped into Matt in Blackwood Fresh a week or so ago, filling a basket with pre-made gourmet meals for one – Thai green curry with rice, butter chicken, that sort of thing. And then June let it slip that Matt was staying at Frank's for a few days. Irene doesn't want to push it, but with Amy acting like it's business as usual, she can't help wondering what the story is.

'What's on the menu tonight?' she asks Amy. Not too spicy, she hopes. Some foods react with her medication, giving her all manner of discomfort.

'Frank's bringing spring rolls.' Amy is still unable to mask her scepticism. 'And I'm – we're – making a sweet and sour soup, lemongrass chicken skewers, five-spice caramel pork, *bun cha*, and banana coconut tapioca puddings. I've already made the *nuoc chan* – dipping sauce – and a pickled vegetable salad.'

'*Bun cha?*'

'It's a popular Vietnamese street food. Noodles, herbs and grilled, marinated meat – usually pork. It's a really good food to enjoy together. You'll love it.'

'It sounds delicious. It all does.' Irene rubs her hands together. 'So, where should we start?'

'A lot of this food has to be cooked just before serving, so we're going to focus on the prep.' Amy gestures to the stainless steel bench, which is loaded with ingredients organised into groups, one for each dish. 'And then we can set the table.'

Irene spies tomatoes, mushrooms, vegetable stock and a few ingredients she doesn't recognise. While Amy pours them chilled lemon mint water, she wanders over to the table for a closer look. Tamarind paste, star anise and some sort of strappy leaf that feels a little like lemongrass. Amy appears beside her, handing her a glass.

'You can find most of these things in Blackwood Fresh. Except for the pandan leaves. I picked them up at Bunbury Farmers Market yesterday. We're adding the puddings to the summer menu at Brewed to Taste. The leaves add flavouring.' She screws up her nose, as if searching for words. 'It's hard to describe, but it's intensely aromatic, a little bit sweet, a bit grassy.' She looks at Irene and laughs. 'You'll see for yourself.'

Irene sets to work preparing the soup ingredients. Each item is chopped or measured and placed into separate glass bowls so later they can be added to the broth in order. Amy marinates the pork and chicken. As they work, Irene asks Amy about Vietnam. Amy's face lights up as she recalls wandering around busy markets and tasting different street foods. Her voice is wistful with nostalgia.

'Did you go with Matt?' Irene asks, wondering who she could go to Vietnam with. Bonnie and Ashlee? Is it a suitable place for a child?

'No, that was before I knew him. I went with Gran, actually. I was sixteen.'

'How *is* Matt? Such a shame he's away,' Irene puts in as casually as she can, wiping down the bench.

'Fine, he's good,' Amy says, not looking up.

'You must miss him,' Irene presses.

'Yes, of course. But he used to work fly-in, fly-out, so I'm used to it, you know?' She wipes her hands on a towel. 'So, while I was in Hanoi, I came across this little old man in the street markets. He was selling the tastiest crepe-style filled rolls and had the cheekiest smile. He was flirting with Gran and she loved it, even though she couldn't understand a word.'

Irene never ceases to be amazed by Amy's smooth transition from one subject to another. They stack the fridge according to Amy's precise instructions – ingredients for each dish are placed on trays on separate shelves, ready to pull out for last-minute cooking. When Frank calls, asking if he can deep fry the spring rolls there, Irene wonders what he knows about Matt and Amy.

Lord, I'm as bad as Una Mickle.

She's about to go home and shower when Amy calls out, 'Wait, I almost forgot something.' She runs out the back and reappears holding packets of colourful, paper lantern string lights, and a calico tote bag. 'Found these in the two dollar shop,' she says, off-loading the items onto the bench. She drapes a string of lights around the chalkboard. Switching them on to test, she smiles. 'Pretty. Irene, there are some loose lanterns in the bag. Can you scatter them on the table? They won't light up, but they'll look nice.'

Another lantern string is draped on the side buffet. Irene and Amy finish off the decorations with tea light candles in jars and a tall vase bearing a single stem of Singapore orchids.

'Not quite right, but they'll do.' Amy's head is tilted to one side as she assesses their work. 'So, what do you think?'

'It's all lovely.'

'Yes …' Amy sounds unconvinced. 'I want it to be an experience.'

'Amy, it really is. We all love what you do, especially the food. Don't worry so much. You don't have to try so hard to be perfect.' Irene pats Amy on the arm. Are there tears in Amy's eyes?

Amy shifts away. 'Look at the time. We've got to get home and change. Oh, bummer, I meant to put some lemongrass oil in the diffuser.' She dashes to the sideboard, but Irene doesn't miss the way Amy dabs at her eyes when she thinks Irene can't see.

The opening riffs of 'Fortunate Son' by Creedence Clearwater Revival fill the café when Irene returns with Bonnie an hour later. Sid loved this song. He didn't go to Vietnam. Did his two years' National Service, but a broken leg from a motorbike accident prevented him from being called up. He'd always resented that he missed out, as if it made him less of a man, but Irene had secretly been glad. She finds herself bopping along to the music just as Frank and June walk in with a foil-covered tray of spring rolls ready to deep fry, and Nick and Devi arrive, bearing bottles of rosé.

'Nice moves, Irene,' June teases, but she drops her handbag on a chair and joins in. June certainly has the moves. Frank can't keep his eyes off her. At the end of 'Bad Moon Rising', Irene raises her hands in defeat. She's puffing and needs a rest. And a quick sniff of her nitrate spray. Leaving June to it, Irene makes her way to the café kitchen where Frank is now showing Amy his perfectly formed spring rolls.

'They're amazing,' Amy tells him.

Frank grins. 'My late wife taught me,' he says, plugging in the deep fryer. 'She was Vietnamese.'

Irene watches surprise and guilt scrawl across Amy's face. Of course, she hadn't known Frank's wife was Vietnamese. Irene takes the soup ingredients from the fridge and lines them up on the bench in the order they need to be used. Pretending not to listen. To be invisible.

'How's Matt?' Frank asks Amy. His voice is quiet, but Irene hears every word.

'Yeah, he's good. In Germany, actually. Did you know?'

'I did.' From his tone, Frank knows more than that. 'He crashed at mine when he was doing that overtime before he left.'

There's a pause. 'Oh, right, of course he did. Completely forgot about that, it's been so hectic.'

Ten minutes later, Amy carries steaming bowls of soup to the table. Frank follows with a platter of golden-crisp spring rolls. The soup's sweet-sour perfume teases Irene's nose, although she's not sure if she wants to taste the broth first, or bite into one of the spring rolls. She opts for the soup. The tangy broth has a rich, bold flavour that belies its watery appearance. She almost giggles at the sound of slurping, and reaches for a spring roll to distract her, biting through the crunchy but delicate wrapping to the vegetable, pork and vermicelli filling.

Nick groans. 'Mate, these are fantastic,' he says to Frank. 'It's like I'm eating in a Vietnamese market. How'd you learn to make these?'

Frank beams with pleasure. Setting down his spoon, he leans forward. Irene reaches for another spring roll and winks at Amy. This could take a while.

'Well,' Frank begins. 'My late wife, Lien, showed me how to make these rolls years ago.' He pauses and June squeezes his hand. 'When she first made them, I was worried, I have to say. They looked good, but I was worried about what was inside. Hadn't even tasted Chinese food back then. Grew up on the old meat and three veg, I did. But I gave them a go and, by golly, they were bloody good, full of pork mince, prawns and noodles. Crabmeat, when we could get it. Carrots, garlic ... and seasoning. Fish sauce. Pepper. Lien told me off for eating too many the first time. Think she was supposed to take them to some pot luck dinner down at the church.'

Irene's hand hovers over the spring rolls. Has she had three or four? She's supposed to be watching her diet, but these are too good to ignore.

'Go for it, Irene,' Frank booms, helping himself to another two. 'Oh, geez, my soup's gone cold.'

Amy offers Irene more soup, but she demurs. 'I'm saving myself for the rest.'

'Ever tried *bun cha*?' Devi asks. Irene shakes her head – her mouth is full of spring roll. 'It's so good. When I was in Vietnam I couldn't get enough of it, especially in Hanoi. It was my lunchtime go-to meal. Tasty, filling and cheap. I'd just buy it from street vendors and the markets.'

'Weren't you worried about getting Bali belly or something like that?' June puts in.

'Bali belly in Vietnam? Nah, not really.' Devi grins at June. 'I admit, I didn't really give it a lot of thought back then. It must have been fifteen years since I've been there. And I've got a cast-iron stomach. Unlike Nick here.' He pats Nick's knee.

Amy and Bonnie disappear into the kitchen to cook the main meals. Irene watches them go with pleasure. Bonnie's starting work at the café tomorrow and it's all she's been talking about. It's taken her mind off Jake, who dumped her by text message a week earlier. Irene consoled her with hugs and kind words, but inside she's jumping for joy.

Nick and Devi share travel stories – Frank and June are captivated – but Irene's mind drifts to Amy. She senses whispers of loss leaking from underneath her friend's smile, like a hole has been torn in her side. Irene knows that feeling. Sid left once. Life was all too much for him. A combination of work pressures and the issues with Erin and, later, Bonnie. Their marriage nearly ended over it. They'd both changed so much and had to get to know each other all over again. Losing a child does that. It shatters everything you have, everything you are. Everything you thought you wanted.

She's jolted from memory lane when Amy and Bonnie place the mains on the table.

'Lemongrass chicken skewers, *bun cha* and five-spice caramel pork,' Amy says.

Frank claps his hands. 'Blimey, what a feast. Reminds me of how Lien cooked on special occasions. Still miss her, you know.' He gives June an apologetic look.

Irene does know. The missing never ends.

'How did you meet her?' Amy asks. 'If you don't mind, June?'

'We've all got our stories,' June says, sipping her wine.

Frank leans back in his chair. 'My brother went to Vietnam. Only lottery he ever won. He thought he was lucky. I was bloody mad that my number didn't come up. I idolised my brother.' He squeezes June's hand before continuing. 'Turns out he wasn't so lucky. Jim didn't come back. A mine got him. They reckon he didn't feel a thing.'

Irene is spellbound. She'd heard, of course, what happened to Jim but she'd never heard Frank mention it.

'I was eighteen when Jim died. Eighteen and angry. At the war, at the government, everything. And back then you were either for the war, or you protested against it. It's funny, in hindsight, that back then I would have done anything to be called up like Jim, but after Jim died, I swapped sides. Couldn't see the point of war. Long story short, some mates and I started protesting against Viet-bloody-nam. I even spent a year in a hippie commune.'

Frank in a hippie commune? Irene can't imagine it.

'Yeah, yeah, I was in a commune. Make love, not war and all that jazz.' Frank laughs. 'Anyway, I met Lien in Sydney in the late seventies. She was a refugee; came over on the boats when the Communists took over. God, she had such a rough time.'

This Irene can imagine. She watched a documentary on Vietnamese boat people once. It had horrified her.

Frank continues. 'Lien was working at a hot bread shop – they were springing up all over the place back then and they made the best rolls. Used to go to that shop every day for a couple of bacon and cheese rolls. It wasn't just for the rolls either. There was something about her that made me keep going back, day after day, and after about a year I asked her out. I was gobsmacked when she said yes. I'd never had a girlfriend before her, you see.'

Irene glances around the table. Everyone is as hooked by Frank's story as she is, leaning forward in their chairs, transfixed. Even Amy has stopped fussing about.

'Anyway, as time went on, Lien told me what it was like for her family in Vietnam after the war. They had a business but they were living in fear of the Communists and couldn't trade, so her father told them they had to try to escape. And so the whole family – there were nine children – tried to escape, but two of her brothers were caught and jailed. One of them paid corruption money to escape and the other was killed. The rest of the family got on a boat. They were packed like sardines. They were told they would be transferred to a bigger boat, but it was lies. And so they were stuck on this unseaworthy boat out in the ocean, jam-packed, hungry and sick. But what could they do? They couldn't go back. The engine broke down and they had no sails or paddles, so they just drifted until finally, their boat came ashore in Malaysia. It took almost a year before they were allowed into Australia.'

Unbelievable.

'So, eventually Lien and I got married. Caused quite a stir, that did. Her parents didn't want her to marry an Aussie. And we copped lots of flak in the early years. Some people, even some of my relatives, called me a traitor – and worse – for marrying a Vietnamese woman.'

'That's horrible!' Bonnie exclaims.

'The way it was, Bonnie. Not the first time it's happened, won't be the last. Those first few years weren't easy, I can tell you. Especially when we moved here. Some of the women in Blackwood wouldn't give Lien the time of day. They had husbands who were Vietnam vets, you see.'

Irene remembers. Una was behind that. Bob Mickle was a changed man after Vietnam, and she knows Una bore the brunt of it. But Irene could have done something. Stood up for Lien. Befriended her. Instead, she'd avoided the flak by withdrawing into her own messy home life. Tears prick her eyes. Often, you don't realise how you foster hurt by saying nothing, until it's too late.

'But Lien and me, we made it work, despite the prejudice. We had thirty years together. And then five years ago, Lien got pancreatic cancer. She died within a year of diagnosis.' Frank clears his throat. 'That's why I chose Vietnam for tonight's country. To honour Lien, who gave me so much and taught me to forgive.'

Irene sniffs, and fumbles for a tissue. Around her, Amy and Bonnie are wiping away tears with napkins. Even Nick and Devi's eyes are shining, although it could be the lighting. Frank hugs June, who wipes a stray tear from his cheek. The tenderness between the couple brings a lump to Irene's throat.

'We've all been there, one way or another,' Frank says, suddenly, his eyes drifting around the room before settling on Amy. 'We're all just making it through life as best as we can.'

CHAPTER 44
AMY

B ack at home, Amy checks WhatsApp for a message from Matt. Nothing. She logs into her email account. Nothing there either. She hasn't heard from him in days. Things were strained when he left, but it was out of character for him to close communication like this. Earlier in the night she'd had to force herself not to keep checking her phone, just in case. Frank's love story distracted her for a while, thank God. Stopped her from bobbing up and down like a duck on a pond.

Frustrated, she turns her thoughts to Frank. When she met him months ago, she thought he talked too much. She would never have imagined he'd be counted among her friends. Frank revealed a different side tonight: a loyal, strong man who took a stand against prejudice to be with the woman he loved. A man who lost his wife to cancer but chose not to give up on life. A man who is opening his heart to someone else. Amy shivers, remembering the way his eyes locked on hers when he'd talked about 'making it through life'. She'd practically flown to the kitchen to get dessert after that.

If only Matt had been there tonight. The evening had still gone well – especially after people stopped asking how Matt was – but it wasn't the same. He would have loved everything about it. The food. The music. Frank's story. If he didn't know it already. She can't believe he stayed at Frank's house after he walked out and didn't tell her. Did everyone know? And what exactly had Matt told him? She'd been unsettled the rest of the night once Frank let it slip, but fortunately no one seemed to notice.

She pauses. Except Irene. She'd felt her friend's eyes on her all night. Irene knows something is up. She's probably dying to know, but what's there to tell? Matt's away. He'll be back. And then they'll sort it all out.

God, she misses him. If he were here, they'd be talking about the supper club now. Perhaps making love. She misses that, too. Back when she and Matt were first together they couldn't get enough of each other. But after the accident, that part of her died, along with half of her heart.

She looks at her phone. Still nothing. He's probably asleep. Turning the phone face down, she stares at the ceiling.

Does he lie awake at night, thinking of her?

CHAPTER 45
MATT

'I can't.' Matt's eyes meet Carla's. He's never cheated on Amy and he won't start now. 'I'm not free.'

Carla holds his gaze for a long moment. He reads disappointment in her eyes, but understanding too. Or at least, that's what he wants to see. 'I get it,' she says, stepping back. He opens his mouth to say something – *I'm sorry* – but she holds up her hand. 'Don't say anything. Let's just leave it here.' She opens her door, then pauses. 'You're a good man. Decent.' The door closes behind her.

In his room, Matt slumps onto his bed. Is he a decent man? Not getting what he wants and needs from Amy is no excuse for allowing himself to get this close to the cheating zone. In that moment, he hates himself for betraying his wife, if only in his mind. For wanting someone to want him.

That night he dreams that his feet are stuck in mud, except he's not Matt the man, but a child; he can't move, and Amy is pulling one arm, Carla is pulling the other, so hard he fears he will split in two. He wakes, sweating, knowing an impossible decision awaits, but not between two women. It's about who – or what – he wants to be.

∾

The next morning, Matt catches a train to Hamelin. The landscape flashes past in a blur as he mulls over what happened with Carla. She was gone before he went downstairs for breakfast, and he was grateful for the space. But they still have to work together. Can they put this aside? By the time he alights at Hamelin, his mind is no closer to settling, but he pushes his worries aside as he walks towards Amy's father, Dominic.

'Matt, mate, it's good to see you. Come on, let's get you to the car. It's freezing.' Matt is pulled into Dominic's warm, hearty embrace and when he's released he sees tears in the older man's eyes. His own eyes reciprocate, filling with a mixture of pain, regret and guilt.

The last time they saw each other was at Perth airport; Dominic was about to fly back to Germany after visiting Amy. Back then, they were still grief-shattered and broken. When Matt contacted Dominic to arrange a visit, the older man had insisted Matt stay with him and his partner, Margit. Shrugging away his fears, Matt had agreed. He'd always liked Dominic. But the shadow of loss would make the reunion emotionally rough.

As Dominic makes small talk in the car, Matt fidgets with his fingers, his sleeve, his phone. Is he strong enough to do what he's here for?

'Amy doesn't know I'm here,' he confesses when they arrive at Dominic's home.

Dominic hesitates before nodding. 'Come inside. Margit will be waiting with coffee and cake. We'll talk later.'

Inside, as Margit fusses over Matt, telling him in heavily accented English that he's too thin and looks too tired, Matt's taut posture loosens. Margit reminds him of his mother with her loving hustle and bustle, and need to fix men and children's hearts with food. He sips milky coffee and spoons mouthfuls of Margit's *apfelküchen* – apple cake – into his mouth, accepting another oversized piece even though he's full. Her cake, embellished simply with a cinnamon crumble, is like a warm hug. It reminds him of childhood, of coming home from school to freshly baked treats on the kitchen bench. It reminds him of Amy.

When Margit catches him yawning, she hustles him to the spare room, pointing out the bathroom on the way. 'Rest,' she tells him, handing him a towel and face cloth. 'You need long sleep and good German food. Is good you are here. We will look after you.'

The door closes. Matt falls onto the bed and into the deepest sleep he's had in years.

When Matt wakes, Dominic and Margit are eating breakfast. Embarrassed that he's come to their home, eaten their food and fallen asleep for fifteen hours with barely a word of explanation, he hesitates at the door. Margit spots him first. She waves him in, getting up and pushing him onto a chair.

'I will get you breakfast,' she says.

He tries to protest, but Margit dismisses his feeble attempt at independence with a look.

'You sit. Drink *kaffee*.'

Dominic grins and passes the coffee pot. 'You'd better do as she says. I find it's easier when I do. How did you sleep?'

'Good. It's a comfortable bed.' Matt pours coffee and adds milk. 'I'm sorry I flaked out last night.'

'Don't worry about that. You needed it.'

Margit plonks a plate in front of him. It's piled with slices of cheese and salami, a ramekin of liverwurst, and two fat white sausages. 'Bread, butter, mustard and jam,' she says, pointing to a basket of fresh rolls and tray of condiments. Matt's forgotten how much Germans love their breakfast. He usually makes do with cereal on weekdays.

'Eat,' she says, and sits down to make sure he does.

He spreads butter on a roll, inhaling the yeasty scent before adding cheese, salami and mustard. Biting in, his shoulder muscles soften as he eats. The food is simple but good. He manages to polish off three salami and cheese rolls, the sausages and egg. He leaves the liverwurst untouched – he could never stomach it.

'You need more rolls for your liverwurst?' she asks. 'Or perhaps some crackers?'

'Oh, no, it's fine,' he demurs.

She gets up anyway. 'No one going hungry in my house.'

Dominic laughs. 'Matt's my ally against the horrible liverwurst.'

Margit glares at Dominic and it's like Matt's been captured in a surreal moment of time. As if he's listening to his mother and father bicker lovingly. A child, safe and sound at home, where minor scrapes and hurts were healed with a kiss, and aches were eased with a hot water bottle. He pours another coffee and lets the warmth of the moment blanket him. And then he bursts into tears.

Years of suppressed grief pours from him, a waterfall of emotion. Pulling his chair closer, Dominic places an arm around Matt's shoulders. Margit fetches a box of tissues and a fresh pot of coffee. In this homely kitchen, with two kindly near-strangers, Matt empties himself of tears until, finally, the well dries up. Margit says something to Dominic in German and makes herself scarce.

'You've been holding that in a long time.' Dominic's look is gentle.

Matt blows into a tissue, embarrassed and drained. 'Sorry about that. Don't know what came over me.'

'No need for sorry. You needed to get that out. It's not good to hold it in.'

'No.' Matt doesn't know where to start.

'Seems to me like there's more where that came from,' Dominic prods, handing Matt another coffee.

With Dominic's gentle urging, Matt's story comes out. 'I feel like I've locked away my grief for so long,' he says. 'There's always been something to do, like organising the funeral here while Amy was in hospital and then, helping her deal with *her* grief. Her depression and when she tried to—' he stops short. The memory of Amy's suicide attempt is still too fresh. 'It's as if dealing with Amy has stolen my time to grieve.'

Dominic makes a noise of agreement. 'Incomplete grief. It takes its toll.'

'Yes.' Matt twists his cup in his hands. 'It's like I'm always trying to outrun my grief, because if it catches me, I can't be there for Amy. But—'

'Go on. Let it out. You're safe here.'

'I resent her. I know I shouldn't, but I do.' As his truth spills out, Matt feels inexplicably lighter. 'I want to be a father again. Amy doesn't want more children. I don't know what to do.'

Dominic listens without judgement, offering no advice, only compassion. 'Rest now,' he says, squeezing Matt's hand when the words finally dry up. 'Tomorrow we'll go to Deister Freidhof cemetery and visit Pandora.'

It's always saddened Matt that his daughter is buried in another country, but with Amy in an induced coma and critical condition, there was no choice. German funeral laws were tight, the costs exorbitant, and there'd been little say in how Pandora's remains were handled. She had been cremated, her urn buried in a small plot.

All Matt remembers of the funeral is a grey haze and feeling of emptiness. His wife, not by his side, but in an intensive care unit. And drizzling, cold rain. Today is overcast and the wind bites through the layers, but there's no rain. Snow is possible later, Dominic tells him. So, when Dominic drives into the cemetery, Matt's surprised that it's so green, despite the naked trees. The cemetery is set in verdant parklands, beautifully tended. His heart thumps with apprehension as Dominic parks the car and looks across at him.

'Ready?'

'Yes.' It's not true. Matt will never be ready, not really.

Dominic leads the way to the plot. Matt follows slowly, knowing that every step is another closer to falling apart again. They reach the plaque and Matt looks down. The plot has been tended by someone, probably Dominic. Matt focuses on words engraved on the plaque. Hot tears blur his daughter's name. He wipes his face with a sleeve.

'Do you want me to wait at the car?' Dominic breaks in hoarsely.

Matt thinks about it, weighing up potential embarrassment versus support. 'Stay.'

'I'll be under that tree.'

Matt takes a steadying breath. Turns back to the plot. Clears his throat.

'Hello, Panda-Bear.'

When they arrive home, Margit is waiting with a comfort-food feast of cold meats and soft poppy seed rolls, potato salad, slabs of schnitzel, and red cabbage with apple. Looking at Dominic's rounded belly, Matt realises Margit was not joking about putting some 'meat on his bones'. She'll succeed, for sure. Margit's food is so moreish. And so good.

The rest of the week passes with more of the same: food, talk, comfort and rest. One day they visit the Hamelin Old Town, with its quaint architecture and cobblestoned streets speckled with brass rat plaques in a nod to the Pied Piper fairytale. After visiting the museum, they join the crowd in front of the stunning, gabled *Hochzeithaus*, just as chimes tinkle from somewhere overhead. Matt breaks into a smile as two bronze doors ease open and a miniature mechanical ballet tells the tragic story of Hamelin; glockenspiel music plays as rats and children follow the Pied Piper round and round. An excited squeal diverts his gaze to a man standing nearby with a little girl on his shoulders.

'*Nochmal! Nochmal!*' she cries. Again, again.

His heart squeezes. Pandora would have loved this too.

Dominic follows his gaze. 'Let's go. It's time for *kaffee und kuchen* – a German tradition you must not miss.'

In a too-warm café, they drink steaming coffee and eat cake – Dominic opts for a simple cinnamon crumb cake, but Matt can't resist the lure of the chocolate-raspberry buttercream layer cake that reminds him of one of Amy's creations. He bites in – how can a cake be fluffy and fudgy? Dominic was right, this was a tradition not to miss.

Later, Margit insists on taking Matt to the Christmas markets. She's more excited than him – the reality of what this Christmas will likely be is not one he's ready to consider yet – but he can't resist buying gifts. Handpainted glass tea light holders for his mother and Amy. A wooden music box that doubles as a nativity scene. A selection of hand-blown glass ornaments. They drink mulled wine, eat potato pancakes and sausages with curry sauce, and scoff handfuls of sugar-coated roasted nuts. Before they turn in, Margit hands Matt a tissue paper-wrapped parcel.

Unwrapping the parcel, he finds a fine crystal crucifix with a basin big enough to hold a tea light candle. He can't speak.

'You light a candle in this for your *tochter*,' she says. His daughter. 'On special days to remember her.' She submits to his hug for half a minute. 'Sleep well, Matt.'

The next day, Matt visits the cemetery once more, by himself this time. When he gets back to the house, he tells Dominic about the job offer in London. He has six weeks to decide. What should he do? Dominic shares his own story, which is as full of twists and hurdles as Matt's.

'Look into your heart and do what's right for you,' he finishes. 'That's all the advice I can give. But, mate, you need to tell Amy. About coming here, the cemetery, everything.' Matt's heart lurches, but he knows the older man is right.

When he leaves, it's with the knowledge that someone shares and understands his pain. Whether or not he sees Dominic and Margit again, he will always be grateful to the couple for what they've done. For allowing him the freedom to grieve Pandora. For space to think things through. And hope. Hope that he will find the way to live life differently.

Whatever that means.

CHAPTER 46
AMY

Summer has arrived in Blackwood, bringing the smell of backyard barbecues and sunscreen, the sounds of shrieking children leaping into swimming pools, and the evening chorus of crickets. Christmas has also come to town. Strings of coloured lights appear over the main street and around tree trunks. Houses are draped with flashing fairy lights reminiscent of icicles, and gaudy inflatable Santas and snowmen appear in sunburnt gardens. Every night, as flies give way to mosquitoes, and the sun dips over the hill, families emerge from their cool sanctums to promenade the streets in search of the best decorated house.

Amy observes the town's transformation with detachment and trepidation. She hasn't had the will or energy to celebrate Christmas for years, but Bonnie begged her to decorate the café, so she gave in and let Bonnie go for it. Strangely, it's growing on her, all the lights and tinsel and carols. It's caught her off guard.

The first Christmas after losing Pandora and the baby, Amy was in hospital, sedated and lethargic. After that, celebrating without her daughter seemed like a betrayal. What did the holiday matter without Pandora's little face lighting up as she tore wrapping from gifts? Since then, Amy and Matt have dutifully gone to his parents' for Christmas dinner every year, but otherwise they pretended the holiday didn't exist.

Well, Amy did. Matt wanted to put up the tree last year, before they had moved to Blackwood, she recalls now.

'What's the point?' she'd asked, and turned away. *Who would see it?*

He gave her a painting. Two poppies in a field. She hadn't bought him anything, had mumbled something about how she thought they weren't doing presents anymore. Pretended not to see the hurt in his eyes.

Amy sits in the rocking chair on her verandah as the sun sets on another day without Matt. What will they do this year?

Will she and Matt still head up to Perth for Christmas dinner with his parents? Has Matt told Helen and Stan what's going on with them? Do they know Amy and Matt are having a break?

Guilt flares, flushing her cheeks. Amy hasn't talked to her in-laws for weeks. Months. A quick chat with Helen when that journalist came to town. Before the accident, she and Helen had connected well, but afterwards Amy had shut down. Because of her, they'd lost their only granddaughter. Amy's guilt kept them at arm's length, but now it shadows fresh insight. She's been so caught up in her loss and shame that she's been blind to their pain.

She still hasn't told anyone that Matt's walked out. Irene, Bonnie, Nick … they all think Matt's away for work. *Well, he is,* she defends. But Amy knows she's lying to herself, and she needs to prepare for the inevitable.

What if Matt can't forgive her?

What if moving on means life without Matt?

The next day, Amy checks her messages as soon as she wakes up. Nothing. She calculates the time in Düsseldorf. It had been early afternoon Düsseldorf time when she'd sent it. Why hadn't he answered? And then it strikes her that conferences rarely last more than a few days. She googles the CCD Congress Centre and a few clicks later has confirmation that the conference ended a week ago.

Unsettled, she snaps out a terse WhatsApp message: *Where are you?* Amy waits for an answer, but gives up after a few minutes. Waiting for a message is like watching water boil. Questions fly at her: Is Matt still in Düsseldorf? Is he sightseeing?

Is he coming home?

Annoyed, she heads for the bathroom to shower. Nick and Bonnie have warned her Brewed to Taste will be busy, so she's going in for a few hours. It's the day of the annual Blackwood Christmas Fair, which attracts stalls from patchworkers, woodcarvers, weavers, toymakers, and other talented craftspeople in the region. Bonnie has been knitting multicoloured beanies and funky goose and cat tea cosies for weeks – turns out, she was responsible for the rainbow ones Irene, Ashlee and Bonnie wore all winter. Irene will be selling them alongside her jams. As Amy drives into town, she decides to stop at the fair after work and buy Christmas presents for Matt's parents. Something for Matt, too. Maybe.

She tries to hide it, but Nick picks up on her irritation as soon as she walks in.

'Everything okay, Amy?'

'Yeah, all good,' she says, automatically. 'Just running a bit late.'

'Not long till Matt gets home, hey?'

'Later in the week.' His penetrating gaze unnerves her and she looks away. Changes the subject. If she can pretend everything is okay, it will be.

During her break, she calls Matt's work. Someone there will know where he is. A simple explanation. A work thing, something tacked on after the conference. It's happened before. But his number is diverted to the switch. Giving a fake name, she asks for Matt. He's on annual leave and due back next week, the duty receptionist informs her. Does she want his email address? Amy barely manages a polite 'no thanks' before disconnecting.

Annual leave? What the hell? Where is he?

~

After the café closes, Amy drives to the town hall, bearing takeaway coffee and apple crumble muffins for Irene and Ashlee.

'Go check out the stalls,' Irene urges, taking the coffee gratefully. 'They're closing soon.'

Amy wanders around the displays, surprised by the range and depth of creative talent on offer. She buys a cloud-soft alpaca scarf for Helen and a chunky beanie for Stan, who's been losing his hair for as long as Amy has known him. Pandora used to rub his shiny scalp and wish on it, Amy remembers, smiling at the image.

She lingers over a multi-drawer she-oak box at a woodcraft display, running her fingers over the smooth, rounded edges, marvelling at the reddish-pink grain. It's like nothing she's seen before and yet it reminds her of the yin-yang trinket box she gifted Matt once. It's in his study. The craftsman shows her a hidden compartment. Matt would love it, she thinks, and hands over her credit card, adding a banksia-handled magnifying glass at the last minute.

As she's walking back to Irene's stall, she hears Una's name mentioned, and stiffens. She hasn't seen Una or Sharon in ages and she doesn't really want to now. Eager to get away, she steps around the people – an older couple she's seen around town – but stops when she hears the words 'accident', 'badly hurt' and 'might die'. What on earth?

'Irene? Have you heard anything about Una and an accident? I overheard some people talking—'

'I just heard. June called.' Irene's face is pale. 'But it's not Una. It's Sharon. Her car ran off a road two nights ago and hit a tree. She's in a critical condition in Bunbury Hospital. Her kids are fine,' she adds. 'They weren't in the car. Sharon was on her own. Fell asleep driving, apparently. She had to have an emergency operation for swelling on the brain, plus she had her spleen removed. And her lung was punctured. Oh, and broken ribs and a broken collarbone. The doctors are confident she'll pull through. But it's still a shock when it's someone you know.'

Amy doesn't like Sharon – or her mother – but wouldn't wish anything like this on them. 'I can't believe it,' Amy says, not sure what else to say. 'What about the kids? I mean, I know they're not hurt, but who's looking after them? Sharon's husband? What's his name again?'

'Shane,' Irene says dismissively. 'He's the grandson of Flo and Bill – the people who used to own your house – but he inherited none of their responsibility genes. He took off a while ago. June says he's got a new woman and is refusing to take on the kids. Una's looking after them. She's been a mess, apparently.' She shakes her head, before offering a rueful smile. 'Hard to imagine Una a mess, but who wouldn't be, with that going on.'

Amy remembers Gran visiting her in hospital in Perth. It was after the accident, after they'd returned to Perth from Germany. After Amy tried to take her own life and had her stomach pumped. When she woke, Gran was there, white-faced with pink-rimmed eyes. Lost in the abyss of grief and pain, Amy had barely acknowledged her. She'd taken the comfort on offer, but had given nothing back to acknowledge her grandmother's pain.

Amy helps Irene pack up, turns down Irene's offer of a cuppa, and walks to her car. By the time she gets home, she's made a decision. It's time to start giving back.

The next day the café is closed, so Amy drives to Bunbury after lunch. She tries not to think about Matt, who still hasn't responded to her message, and fails. His lack of communication is really starting to piss her off. Sometimes she thinks it would be better if he didn't come back at all. She's doing fine on her own. When her mind starts working through the legalities of separation, she changes tack. What if they simply rip this chapter from their story and pretend it never happened? Go back to how things were, because the alternative is unthinkable. Except she knows that's not how it works. You have to go forward, even when you don't know where the path leads.

At the hospital, Amy parks and lifts a gift hamper from the back seat. Inside, she follows a sprightly hospital volunteer to the trauma centre, ignoring the pounding of her heart that shouts with every step. Amy peeks around the door. Sharon is in a bed near a window, watching television. Amy pulls her head back and hesitates.

'Are you right there, love? Looking for someone?' A nurse on a mission throws the questions over her shoulder but doesn't break her stride.

Amy leans against the wall, summoning up strength. Does she really want to do this? She makes a snap decision and walks into the room, towards the bed.

Sharon turns her head. 'Amy? Why are *you* here?' There's no animosity in her tone. Her voice is weak, roughened from having a tube thrust down her throat. There's a bandage around her head. Half of her hair has been shaved off where surgeons operated. Drips and lines lead from her body to beeping machines framing the bed. She looks like a shrunken version of the woman Amy knew.

Amy shrugs. 'I know what it's like to be stuck in a hospital bed.' She places the hamper on the bedside table. It's filled with gossip magazines, a new release from a popular Australian author, chocolate, a lavender-filled sleep mask, colouring book and pencils, lip balm and a cooling facial spritz.

Touching her head self-consciously, Sharon looks towards the hamper and chews her lip.

'Mind if I sit?' At Sharon's nod, Amy pulls the visitor's chair closer. Sharon makes no move to speak. Amy waits. Did she make the right choice to come? She'll give it five minutes.

'What can I do to help?' she asks, remembering how much she'd hated being asked how she was feeling. The answer was always the same: *Like shit.*

'Why are you being so nice to me?' Sharon blurts out, taking Amy aback with its suddenness. 'I wouldn't blame you, you know, if you thought I had it coming.'

'I wouldn't wish it on anyone.' She'd wished for karma to pay a visit, but not like this.

Sharon's silent for a moment. Her mouth works as if she's squeezing words inside. When she meets Amy's gaze, her eyes are full of tears. 'For what it's worth, I'm sorry. You didn't deserve what happened. What we did. I've had a lot of time to think about it.'

Amy regards Sharon for a moment. The apology seems genuine. 'Thank you,' she says, pushing back the inner snarky voice that asks, *So, why did you?*

Sharon answers Amy's unspoken question. 'I've really got no excuse. Except maybe jealousy. You moved into Blackwood and it looked like you had it all. Good husband, lovely home. You're a chef, you've travelled … I've never done anything but spit out kids and try to keep my marriage together. I wanted to be an investigative journalist. I love my kids, but …' Her voice is bitter, but Amy senses it's not directed at her. 'Shane and I, we've been having problems for a long time. And you know how people talk in a small town. That's why I bailed. Did you know? No? I guess you've had your own stuff to think about. A few weeks ago, I moved to Bunbury to start over. Somewhere bigger, where I could just blend in. I know what people are saying. That I've got another man. It's not true. It's just a rumour Shane started so he could save face. He was the one cheating, having it off with some younger chick in Bunbury. Hasn't even come in to see me, the bastard. I don't even know what's going to happen when I get out of here.'

'That's rough,' Amy says. She can relate in a way. She has no idea what's in store for her and Matt. What she'll do if her marriage really is over.

When Amy leaves half an hour later, she knows one thing: she and Sharon will never be friends, but they have reached an understanding.

She's passing the nurses' station when Una appears with three children at her heels. The older woman's mouth purses in a silent 'o'. She gives the children a gentle nudge.

'You go ahead and see your mother. No, you can't have something to eat, you've been eating all morning. Go on.' She turns to Amy. 'I must say, I'm surprised to see you here.' There's no trace of sarcasm.

'I'm kind of surprised myself,' Amy admits. She falters and surges on. 'I know what it's like to be in there, to wonder what's going to happen next.'

'Yes,' Una says thoughtfully. 'I'm sure you do.' She looks away, as if she's considering what to say next. 'Thank you. You didn't have to. After all … after all we did.'

Amy's not sure how to respond to that. 'It's okay,' she says finally.

'No.' Una meets her eyes. 'It's not really. What we did was cruel. I knew it and I still did it.' She hesitates, looking towards the room where her daughter is lying. The excited sounds of chattering children filter down the hallway. She looks back at Amy. 'I'm sorry. For opening those wounds, for causing that pain. I've had a lot of time to think that over, especially since Sharon …' she gulps and swallows before collecting herself. 'I thought I'd lose her. I've already lost one child, you know. My son, Thomas. He drowned. When he was two.'

Amy hadn't known. It's on the tip of her tongue to ask what happened, but she resists. There are some stories she doesn't need to know. She finds herself putting an arm around the woman who has been a thorn in her side since moving to Blackwood. Una stiffens but allows a short embrace before pulling away and sniffing. 'I'd best go see my daughter. Make sure my grandkids aren't climbing all over her.'

'If there's anything I can do—' Amy offers.

'Thanks. But we've got it covered. I'm moving in with Sharon for a bit so I can take care of her and the kids. Not that I've told her yet, mind you. But she'll have to deal with it, won't she. Needs must.'

Amy dips her head in agreement. Strangely enough, she thinks Sharon is lucky to have a mother like Una. She bids Una goodbye and walks back to the car, lost in thought. Today has not turned out the way she'd expected.

She plugs her phone in so she can listen to music and that's when she sees a message from Matt. He's on his way home, at last.

CHAPTER 47

MATT

A scorching, dry north-easterly wind smacks Matt in the face as he walks out of Perth International Airport, and with it the reminder that things are about to heat up on the home front. In the long-term carpark, he waits for hot, stale air to vent from his car and considers sleeping off his exhaustion in air-conditioned comfort at one of the nearby hotels. But five minutes later, he turns onto the freeway that will take him and his problems back home.

The closer he gets to Blackwood, the more worked up he feels. There's so much to sort out. His marriage. The London job offer. And in the short-term, what will he and Amy do about Christmas? Amy messaged him about it and he hasn't answered because he doesn't know what to say. He hasn't told his parents about the separation yet.

Suddenly claustrophobic, he opens his car window and gulps big, deep breaths. But his mind continues to rush like the hot wind on his skin. If he doesn't take the London job, and he and Amy split for good, will he stay in Blackwood? He can't stay in a hotel forever. There might be a donga free at the mine's staff accommodation, but Matt's not sure that's what he wants to settle for.

At Timbertop, he books a room at the pub. Jetlagged or not, he's got work in the morning, and even if he drives the extra twenty minutes to Blackwood, where would he stay? After showering away the stale plane air, he falls on to the bed and into a dreamless sleep.

When Matt wakes he's in a foul mood. He orders room service breakfast and immediately wishes he hadn't. He's famished, but the bacon and eggs, served with barely toasted white supermarket bread, look far from appetising. The eggs are overcooked and rubbery, the bacon dripping with fat, the bread sugary. His stomach rolls. After a few bites he pushes the food aside, cursing. Even one of Margit's hearty breakfasts would upset his stomach today.

At work, he steels himself to face Carla. She calls him into her office first thing and he trips over his words in an effort to get them out first.

'About the conference—' he begins, sitting opposite her.

She gives him a gentle half-smile. 'Water under the bridge, Matt. Let it go.'

'I'm sorry.'

'Don't be.' She leans forward. 'But there is one thing I do need from you.' He stills and she laughs. 'A report on the conference. The higher-ups want it by the end of the week.'

Matt waits until he gets back to his desk before releasing a sigh of relief. That went easier than he expected. He decides to let it go, like Carla suggested. But when his gaze drifts to the wedding photo of Amy he keeps on his desk, next to a collage frame holding photos of Pandora, indecision claws at him. Is he ready to let go of his marriage?

Blackwood is a familiar stranger. Matt knows it's an oxymoron, but it's the only way he can make sense of the feeling he has when he drives into the town later that day. Do I still have a place here? A bitter laugh escapes as he imagines his counsellor's response: *You're putting up barriers to make it easier if you decide not to stay.*

The town is wreathed in Christmas. He envisions it sparkling with fairy lights – it doesn't compare to the splendour of the Hamelin Christmas markets, but he imagines the joy on the children's faces to see their town in celebration mode, to see the shop windows bearing Christmas scenes of all varieties.

Parking in front of his house, he takes a moment to look it over. He fell in love with it immediately. Deep down, this is what he still wants. A life here with Amy. But what will happen if he and Amy can't work things out? If she's dead against having another child, can he accept that? Exhaling in frustration, he steps out of the car and stretches his arms and legs. Ashlee is squealing somewhere and Henry is honking in answer. It makes his heart flutter.

'Matt!' Bonnie calls from next door. She appears at the hedge separating their houses. 'It's good to see you! Did you just get back?'

'I've come from work. Landed yesterday afternoon; stayed in Timbertop last night.'

'You must be exhausted. And looking forward to seeing your wife.' She gives him a cheeky wink. 'Surprised you didn't come straight home.'

Hasn't Amy told Bonnie anything? 'Yes, well, it was late ...' It's been three weeks since he and Amy have spoken, but the thought of her in his arms still has a certain effect.

Bonnie continues. 'You'll have to wait a bit longer. Amy's not home. She's gone to Bunbury for the day.'

His face falls. It's her day off. He'd expected her to be home. But why should she wait around for him? 'Bunbury?'

'Yes, she's visiting Sharon Thompson. She told you about the accident, right?' Her forehead furrows at his confused look, then she continues. 'No? Don't you two FaceTime? Okay, well, Sharon had an accident about a week ago, a bad one. Hit a tree.'

Bonnie fills in the details, but Matt hardly takes them in. 'You do mean *Sharon*, the one who—'

'Yes. Bloody cow.' Bonnie colours. 'That was harsh. I'm glad she's going to be all right and all, but I'm still pissed off with her for what she and Yoo-hoo ... her mum did to Amy. And then— Ashlee! Stop painting Henry with your watercolours!' Giving Matt a look of exasperation, she adds, 'Duty calls. Catch you later. Ashlee!'

She jogs towards her daughter and a paint-splotched goose; Matt can't help watching Ashlee's animated expressions and gestures as she presumably explains why her goose needs to be rainbow coloured. He's missed Blackwood life.

Walking around to the back door, Matt lets himself in. He stands in the kitchen and looks around the room bristling with memories. A lone cup and plate are stacked in the dish drainer. A well-thumbed book lies open on the kitchen table: Amy's worn copy of *Rebecca* by Daphne Du Maurier. A notepad and pen lie on the bench, next to a daily planner. On today's date is scribbled: Bunbury Hospital. Sharon. Below that, Amy's written, Matt back today? He stares at the question mark through a film of tears. Does he belong here anymore? Does he want to? Does she want him to be?

Wiping his eyes, Matt pulls the notepad to him. He wants to leave Amy a note. What should he write? *Dear Amy? I want to be here, but I can't until we sort things out.* In the end, he keeps it simple: Dropped in to see you. Will call later tonight.

He's washing three weeks' worth of clothes at the laundromat in Timbertop when his phone rings. It's Amy.

'I'm sorry I wasn't home. I was in Bunbury when I got your message.' She sounds upset. 'I wanted to see you.' She lets the words hang. He's about to say something when she continues. 'Are you still in Blackwood?'

'No, I'm at the laundromat in Timbertop.'

'You could have washed your clothes here, you know that,' she says.

'I know. I …' he falters, not wanting to tell her how it tears him apart to come back and go again. 'Anyway, I'm sorry I missed you too.' The words linger. He hears her breathing. Waiting. 'I saw Bonnie. She said you went to see Sharon in hospital.'

'Yes, I did. I'll have to tell you what happened when you get home.' Her voice sharpens. 'Matt, where have you been? I called your office. They said you were on annual leave, and conferences never go for more than a few days, and you didn't answer your emails, and—' She stops. 'I'm sorry. I'm babbling. I don't know why.'

Glad she can't see the guilt on his face, he tells her that extra meetings were tacked on after the conference. He holds back the job offer and visiting Dominic and Margit. He wants to do that face to face.

'What's the deal with Sharon?' he asks, changing the subject before she can ask more questions. As she updates him about Sharon's plight and the unexpected apologies she received, he scratches his head. 'Think they're the real thing?'

'I do, yeah.' The admission takes him aback. He didn't see that development coming.

The washing machine beeps and he tucks his phone between his ear and neck while he transfers the clothes to the dryer. Life in Blackwood has continued without him. It makes him wonder. Will Amy keep moving forward with or without him?

'Matt? You've gone quiet.'

'Have I? Sorry. I was putting the clothes in the dryer. You were saying?' He shifts the phone to his other ear, wincing as his neck twinges in protest.

'It's okay. It's not important.' Amy falls silent. 'Matt? Are you going to, I mean, are we going to, you know ...'

He knows what she's asking. Part of him wants to scream *yes*. That part of him wants nothing more than to toss his suitcase in the corner of their bedroom, pick up his wife and lay her on the bed. Make love to her all night. The other part pulls the *yes* back into his throat, reminding him with a short, sharp tug that things need to change. Amy needs to get it, to get *him*, to understand that they are on this life train together ... or on different trains with different destinations.

'I need more time,' he says, when the pause becomes uncomfortable. He imagines her nodding, her eyes tearing up, and wants to take the words back, but he can't. He doesn't know why.

'Okay,' she manages, her words choked. 'Okay. You just let me know when you've had enough. Enough time, I mean.' She disconnects, but not before he catches her choked words: '*Stuff you!*'

The silence is a slap.

CHAPTER 48
AMY

When Irene invites Amy and Matt for a Christmas Eve supper, Amy hesitates. She wants to go – it's better than sitting here alone – but she hasn't yet told Irene about Matt leaving. Not that it's an official separation, she reminds herself. A break.

'I'd love to,' she says, thinking fast. 'But I'll check with Matt first, in case he wants to drive to his parents that night instead of on Christmas Day.'

'No problem. It's nothing formal anyway. Just Bonnie, Ashlee and me. We thought we'd have a meal and then take Ashlee for a walk to see the Christmas lights.'

Amy remembers doing that with Pandora. Her baby face alight as Matt carried her on his shoulders. How will Amy feel watching another child experience the magic of Christmas? She dreamed of making magical Christmases for her daughter, the way Gran had for years, even after she lost her own daughter. Amy claps her hand to her mouth.

Gran lost her child, but still carried on. So did Irene.

Christmas would have been bittersweet for both of them – missing their daughters, but keeping the joy alive for their granddaughters. Why can't she help bring the joy to another little girl?

She messages Matt, asking if he will join her at Irene's for Christmas Eve. A tense hour passes before he responds: *OK.*

Two days before Christmas, Amy hovers next to a stand of potted live Christmas trees at Blackwood Fresh. She hasn't bothered to decorate the house – why would she, with only her to see it? She's got no decorations in storage anyway. They left them behind when they moved to Blackwood. Amy picks up one of the pots and peers at the label. It's a Colorado Blue Spruce, a pyramid shape with dusty blue leaf-needles. She imagines it as a centrepiece on her dining table, adorned with simple, not garish, decorations. But the needles are sharp to the touch so she puts the plant down and rolls her cart away. Seconds later, she's back, lifting the plant into her trolley. She'll find a place for it in the garden once the holiday season is over.

She stops in at one of Blackwood's gift shops and selects two etched glass candle holders, a roll of hessian ribbon, a silver bow, and a dozen ornaments – lacy silver stars and snowflakes, and delicate glass baubles. She's about to pay when she catches sight of a rustic star-shaped wreath made of recycled wooden rulers, and decorated with a central circle of snow-sprayed grapevine twigs, tiny matte red, green and ivory berries, and a loopy hessian bow. The whimsical design, and its almost-but-not-quite knocked together look, reminds her of the presents Pandora made her at playgroup. She adds it to the pile on the counter and tries not to flinch at the cost.

At home, Amy opens windows to let in fresh air, unpacks her groceries, and puts on a load of laundry. When she's done procrastinating she spreads a white, lace-edged tablecloth over her dining table. It had been Gran's best tablecloth, only brought out for special occasions like birthdays and Christmas. She places the little Christmas tree onto a plate before moving it to the centre of the table, remembering tree-decorating days with Gran: freshly made gingernut cookies on a plate and Christmas carols playing on the record player – Gran resisted CDs for as long as she could. They wound the lights around the tree together, laughing when they got tangled up, and

Gran told her the stories behind the 'special' decorations, including ones Amy's mother, and later Amy, had made at school.

Amy wishes she hadn't been so quick to get rid of her decorations. She opens a packet of gourmet gingernuts from the supermarket and finds a Christmas playlist on Spotify before hanging the new decorations on her tree. They're part of her new chapter now. Placing the candle holders on either side of the tree, she finds matches and two tea light candles in the buffet drawer. The effect is simple, but elegant. And then she fixes the wreath on the front door. It's not much, but it's a start. What will Matt think?

Hopes for a slow Christmas Eve day at Brewed to Taste are dashed early. It's not just the local last-minute shoppers – there are plenty of out-of-towners making a coffee stop on their way south for the holidays. But there's an infectious exuberance in the air. Bonnie's bought them all Santa hats and Amy finds herself caught up in the Christmas cheer, joining in an impromptu carols medley, and dishing up each meal with a sprinkling of well-wishes.

When Brewed to Taste closes at two, Nick and Devi linger. 'We have something for you,' Nick says. 'Wait here.' He disappears out the back.

Amy scans her café, savouring the quiet. Brewed to Taste will only be closed on Christmas and Boxing Days. Any longer and they'll fail to capitalise on the tourist trade. In just six months the café has become everything she dreamed it would be. At first it was a distraction from painful memories, something to keep her busy. Now she sees how it has restored her love of food and cooking. Nick once asked if she'd be able to find her passion for food again. Somehow, it had stolen its way back under her skin.

'Here.' Nick hands her a wrapped gift. 'This is from everyone at the supper club. Go on, open it.'

Self-consciously, she peels away the layers of paper, revealing an exquisite wooden box. She bites her lip as she runs her fingers over the marquetry lid, inlaid with different wood types to create a story-scene. Her breath catches as she recognises a smiling toddler, skipping along a pathway that starts on the front of the box, and weaves over a stream and far-off hills, disappearing into finger-of-God sunbeams that peep from clouds. Wiping her eyes on her wrist, she lifts the lid. Inside is a soft velvet cushion holding an old-fashioned key, and as she looks at the inner lid, she makes out a name: Pandora.

Amy can't speak.

'It's a memory box,' Nick says gently. 'You'll know what to put in it when the time is right.'

'Thank you,' she says and bursts into tears. It's the most beautiful thing she's ever been given, apart from her daughter. It's also the scariest thing. Because opening it means opening something she's hidden for a long time.

At home, Amy takes the gift to her bedroom and clears a space for it on her chest of drawers. She runs her fingers over it, tracing the little girl outline, imagining baby-soft skin, before heading outside to water the garden. There's always something to look after, even when you think you have nothing left to give. But it's been a hot day and the garden needs her help; the plants are parched, and the slow-sinking sun still holds a bite.

The scent of barbecued meat wafts on the warm breeze. Amy pauses on the verandah and listens to the sounds of people celebrating family and friendship. Music, voices; people laughing, singing. Bottles clinking. Softly lit gardens are churches for carolling crickets. It's warmly familiar. But it's not the same when there's no one to share it with.

Back inside, Amy undresses and stands in front of the bathroom mirror, her face as naked as her body. Her eyes are still puffy and red-rimmed, her cheeks blotchy with emotion. She runs her hands over the scar on her belly, feeling the silent badge of her daughter's birth. And then a sharp pain almost takes her legs out from under her, and she clutches at the stone bench, gasping as the pain recedes as fast as it appeared. It's a throwback to the months after the accident, when she had to learn to walk all over again. Is that what she's doing now, psychologically?

After showering, she covers her puffy eyes and cheeks with make-up as best she can, slips into a floral maxi dress and collects the presents she's wrapped for Bonnie, Ashlee and Irene. A funky cat cup and spoon set for Ashlee; the spoon has cat paws that rest over the lip of the mug. Some bright coloured arm warmers and a selection of aromatherapy oils for Bonnie. A leather-look travel bag for Irene. She carries her gifts for Matt to the kitchen and leaves them under the tree. She'll give them to him in the morning if he stays. Tonight, if he doesn't. Glancing at the clock, her stomach flutters. It's just after six, and she's all jittery, like she's going on a first date.

When the doorbell rings, she has to stop herself from running to the door. And when she sees Matt's face, it's all she can do not to reach out and stroke it, as if seeing it for the first time. His smile gives her hope.

They walk next door, making small talk. In another time, they would have held hands, linked together by love. Amy yearns for Matt's hand to curl around hers. It's that teenage crush feeling all over again. But his hands stay by his sides; one carrying the bag of gifts, the other swinging lightly. When he ruffles Ashlee's hair moments later, and hoists her onto his lap, Amy is torn between jealousy and pride. Bonnie was right. Matt *would* make a great father.

He was *a great father.*

At Ashlee's order, they sing carols before exchanging gifts in front of Irene's Christmas tree, which is covered in homemade decorations, tinsel and fairy lights. Amy chokes up when Ashlee hands her a parcel wrapped in newspaper and containing a paper plate angel.

'I made it for you,' Ashlee tells her. Her aliveness tugs at Amy's heartstrings. 'Because you don't have a little girl.'

The adults eat far too much and drink enough to get the giggles. After a short Christmas lights walk, Ashlee falls asleep on the sofa, the fairy lights from the tree glittering her face. But for Amy, the moment that stands out the most is when Matt's hand steals onto her thigh; his touch burns into her, branding her as his. And for the first time in ages she believes, really believes, that things are going to be all right.

That they've been through a rough patch, but nothing that can't be smoothed out.

They walk home again, hand in hand this time. And when they get home, wine-chilled and desire-heated, they tumble onto the bed, their mouths locking and bodies arching frantically to feed the hunger they have starved for too long.

CHAPTER 49

AMY

On Christmas morning, Matt and Amy drive to Matt's parents' house in the Perth Hills. Matt's quiet, his festive cheer washed down the plughole with the long shower he'd taken. Amy watches his hands grip the steering wheel, white and tight. His cheek is twitching, a telltale sign that he has something to say.

'What are you thinking?' she ventures, dreading the answer. He takes his eyes off the road briefly. Looks back at the road and swallows. Is he going to tell her it's over for good? Surely not, after last night? Her heart quickens as her mind tears through possibilities.

'I went to see Dominic and Margit after the conference. Stayed with them a few days,' he says, finally.

'You went to see my *dad*? Without me? Why?'

'There were some things I needed to do. For me.' Matt sucks in a breath. 'I went to Pandora's grave.'

Chewing her lip, Amy stares out the car window, concentrating on everything else and nothing at all. Tears pool, spilling over in plump pain droplets.

'I needed to. Amy, I had to do it for me. I needed the closure. For *me*.'

She swings her head from side to side in violent disbelief. 'Why didn't you tell me earlier? About visiting dad. And … Pandora. Why didn't you tell me you were planning to do that?' He flinches at her accusing tone.

'Because I knew how you'd react. Because you would have wanted to know why. And because I didn't know myself until the week before.'

Amy mulls this over, trying to overpower the rising defensiveness and hurt. He's right. It's true. She would have questioned him, made him account for his motives.

'What was it like?' she asks after a while.

'Which part?'

'I don't know.' She grasps for something, anything to delay hearing about the cemetery, even though part of her wants to know. 'How was Dad? And Margit?' When did she speak with them last?

He tells her how Margit insisted on fattening him up and her dad took him on long walks that always ended with *kaffee und kuchen.* Amy absorbs this new information. If she's honest, she's a little jealous. She hasn't seen her father in years. If Matt had asked her—

'The grave,' he says, cutting into her thoughts. 'Your dad's been looking after it. It's in a park. I'm glad I went. I sat and talked to Pandora, Aims. It was … it was … I can't describe it. Peaceful. *Right.*'

She tries to picture it in her mind. She can't quite see what he's describing, can't juxtapose the word peaceful with death.

'You should go.' He reaches across the car for her hand, squeezes it. 'Go and visit her, too. And your dad and Margit. They'd love to see you.'

If I do, will you come with me?

It doesn't sound like a plan for two. Matt switches on his music. Amy looks out the window at tear-blurred trees and cows and pastures until the concrete jungle tells her they are nearly at their destination.

Christmas at Helen and Stan's is the same every year. Same decorations. Same food. Same Christmas tree. Helen welcomes Matt and

Amy with warm, ample-bosomed hugs, before disappearing to the kitchen, waving off Amy's offer to help. Stan brings them drinks. A cold Stella for Matt. A crisp pinot gris for Amy. They make small talk for a while, but once the conversation turns to vintage car meets, Stan's favourite topic, Amy wanders off in search of Helen.

'Are you sure I can't help? I need something to do,' she says.

Helen points out dishes of food to be carried to the dining table. Amy busies herself setting out the side dishes of steamed asparagus with toasted almonds, honey-glazed baby carrots, and potato salad with peas and mint. She carries in a tray of crisp roasted potatoes and Helen follows with her signature dish – a maple-glazed ham – before calling the men. Stan affects a mischievous glint as he sharpens the carving knife and Helen, rolling her eyes, tells him to settle down and say grace. They pull the bonbons, dutifully plonk the tissue paper hats on their heads, and read out the bad jokes. Stan loves them. Every year he tells Amy he could get a job writing those jokes. This year is no different.

Amy picks at her food. It's tasty, as always, but her stomach is jumpy. It's not just the fact that Matt went to Pandora's grave without her. It's that she still, even after last night, has no idea where she stands with him. Where their marriage stands.

After lunch, Helen grabs a bottle of rosé and two glasses, and pulls Amy outside to show off her newly landscaped garden. Gone is the patchy lawn Amy remembers from last year. In its place is a decked area with a sunshade, a water feature and an outdoor furniture setting. The garden has been transformed into a Zen-like Japanese-style oasis with a pond, pebbles, moss, bamboo fences, oriental statues, and ornamental grasses and trees.

'It's stunning!' Amy tells Helen. She had no idea they'd been working on this. What else has she missed? Helen's only too happy to update her and then it's Amy's turn.

Amy tells her about Brewed to Taste and the Around the World Supper Club, leaving out the news that her marriage is a mess. Moving to Blackwood is the best thing Amy's done in years, as far as Amy wants her mother-in-law to know.

'But how are you really, love?' Helen asks.

'Good. I'm fine.'

Helen turns don't-mess-with-me eyes on her daughter-in-law. 'You always say that.'

Amy's shoulders tense. Why does she feel like an ambush is coming?

Helen tries again. 'Matt told me he stayed with Dominic in Germany. And visited Pandora's grave.' Her voice stumbles and she collects herself. 'He told me before lunch that you didn't know until today. That would have been a shock for you. It was for me. I suppose I thought it would be something you'd do together.'

'Oh, it's fine,' Amy lies. 'Matt was in Germany anyway, so it made sense.'

'Hmmm.' Helen finishes her wine. 'Well, as long as you're okay with it. I know it's been stressful for you both, what with moving and all that.'

'Yes, yes, it was, but it's all good.' Amy reaches for the wine bottle. 'Um, did you want another—'

'I just want you to know,' Helen interrupts, 'that Stan and I are here for you. No matter what.'

Amy says nothing.

'We're family. You don't need to keep shutting us out,' Helen continues. There's a hint of frustration now. 'Why do you do that? Why?'

'You were angry with me.' Amy whispers the words.

'Oh, love. We were angry, yes. But never with you. We never blamed you. It wasn't your fault. It was all so terribly, terribly sad.' Helen pauses. 'And there's something else I should have told you long ago. You were a great mother to Pandora. Don't ever doubt that.'

'Thanks.' How else can she respond? Amy tries to sip her wine, but there's a lump in her throat.

'And, Amy, if you and Matt decide to try again – not that I'm inter-fering one way or the other – if that's what you decide, you will be a great mother to whoever else comes along.'

Amy blinks. Has Matt told Helen about this too? 'You don't know that.'

'I know it like I know my own son. But either way, it's your and Matt's decision.' Helen pats Amy's arm, then looks at her watch. 'Goodness me, is that the time? I'd better get dessert ready. You stay out here, love, and relax. I'll call you when it's ready.'

That night, Amy and Matt spend a restless night in Helen and Stan's spare room. With the ceiling fan at full blast they lie side by side, heavy with too much rich food and wine.

Amy wants to touch Matt but she doesn't want to, and she lies with her hand inches from his, feeling his body heat under the sheet. Eventually he sighs and pulls her close. She sags against him, needing the embrace, but wanting so much more. Not sex. Just him. But it's too hot and he soon rolls away.

She wakes, tangled in sheets, exhausted and grumpy. After breakfast with Helen and Stan, Matt stands to go. 'We've got a long drive. And Amy's got work tomorrow.' It sounds like an accusation.

Out at the car, while Matt loads the overnight bags, Helen draws Amy close. 'Remember what I said,' she whispers.

Amy mulls this over as Helen hugs Matt. Does Helen mean the part about being family? That's bound to change if Amy and Matt split. Or the part about being a good mother? Or both?

'That was nice,' Amy says as Matt weaves the car through the suburbs. He's barely said a word to her all morning.

'Yes, it was.' Matt keeps his eyes on the road. His fingers tap the steering wheel and for the second time in as many days, Amy senses he has something to say. She twists her hands in her skirt, waiting for him to speak up.

'I've been offered a job,' he blurts out when they're on the South Western Highway. 'In London.'

She looks at him, eyes wide. '*London?* As in London, United Kingdom?'

'Yes. That London.'

'Wow,' she says. 'London.' There is so much more that she wants to say, but all she can think is *London*. She waits for him to elaborate, but he doesn't. 'When ... what did you tell them?'

'I told them I'd think about it. I'm supposed to answer by the end of January.'

'But ... but we've only just got here. To Blackwood, I mean.'

He looks across at her then, his eyes unreadable. 'How's that worked out for us?'

Her mind reels with the implications of what he's saying. 'Are you saying moving to Blackwood was a mistake? Or that you want us to move again? Or that ...' her mouth grabs for the words her heart doesn't want to say, 'or that *you* want to go. On your own.'

'Yes. No. I don't know. I'm just ... I don't know.'

'Do you want to go?'

'No,' he says, too quickly. 'I don't know. It's *London*, you know.'

She sighs, frustrated by the circular conversation. 'Well, *I* don't want to go. We've just moved and we've just started to fit in.'

'Have *we*? Or have *you*?'

'God, Matt!' she bursts out. '*You* were the one pushing me to buy the café, make friends, all that. And the second I did, you weren't happy.'

'I am happy for *you*. But I keep wondering where *I* fit in.'

'You're my husband!'

'Yeah. But I haven't really felt that for a long time. We want different things.'

She stares at him, dumbfounded and stung. 'I'm trying. I know I haven't been there for you. I've been caught up with the café and the supper club. I know you want a baby. You've made that clear. It's all I've been thinking about for weeks. But London? You're seriously thinking about this?'

Matt says nothing.

'How long have you known about it?'

'Since the conference.' A few kilometres pass before he speaks again. 'If I accept, they want me there by the end of February.'

I, not we.

'Seems like *you've* got some thinking to do,' Amy says, finally, unable to stop the emphasis on *you*.

The air in the car is thick with brooding. Amy forces choking sensations deep down. When they arrive home, she gulps great mouthfuls of Blackwood air, as if it will mend the fresh rips in her heart. He leaves his overnight bag in the car and places hers on the kitchen table.

'I guess I'd better get going,' he says. Uncertainty stains his voice.

'Yes, suppose you should.' Amy's tone is offhand, like it doesn't matter when it really does. She gazes out the window, willing herself not to ask where he's staying tonight. His parting kiss is perfunctory, lips dry on her cheek.

Only when the screen door snaps shut behind him does Amy turn back to the table, where two unopened gifts wait under the Christmas tree.

In the blink of an eye, Christmas is over.

Why does she feel like her marriage is over as well?

CHAPTER 50
IRENE

I rene pinches a weed between her thumb and forefinger, tugging it slowly out of the dry earth. She drops the weed – a flower growing in the wrong place, Bonnie likes to say – into a bucket and reaches for another. Sid hated weeding, always cursed at the way weeds got out of control, but Irene's always found a sense of satisfaction in the job. It gives her time to think, to filter out the unnecessary worries that fill her head at times. And this morning she's had a few things on her mind. The European trip she keeps putting off booking. Her back, which she put out straight after Christmas when she picked up a toy, and still isn't a hundred per cent. Bonnie and her Jake soap opera. Ashlee, who's on summer holidays and back under Irene's watchful eye whenever Bonnie's at Brewed to Taste. And Amy and Matt.

It's none of her business, she thinks, glancing in the general direction of their house. But she cares a great deal for the couple, and Irene knows they're struggling, even though Amy won't admit it. She's never told Amy she knew Matt wasn't simply out of town for work all that time. That she knows he's been bunking down at a hotel in Timbertop since Boxing Day. Frank told June, who told Irene. It surprised her at first. The couple had seemed relaxed enough on

Christmas Eve. Matt placed an affectionate arm around Amy several times over the evening. Amy gazed at him like a love-struck girl. But now that Irene thinks about it, Matt stared off into the distance a couple of times. Like a man with a lot on his mind. And Amy had an uncertain way about her.

With a groan, Irene pulls herself to her feet, wincing at her stiff knees and back. She'll pay later for weeding so long, but you have to make the most of cooler summer days when you have a garden. Removing her garden gloves, she wipes her clammy hands on her shorts and surveys the past hour's effort. Not bad. At the pace she's going she'll have the garden weeded by next winter. She wipes her forehead and then empties the bucket onto the compost heap. Even with temperatures in the mid-twenties, she's still covered in sweat.

As she walks to the house to get a cool drink, she's surprised to see Amy next to the verandah stairs.

'Hi, Irene,' Amy says. She looks thin and sad.

'Amy,' Irene says, returning the smile. 'I was thinking about you.'

'Were you?' Amy gestures towards the garden. 'Do you need some help?'

'Thanks, but I've done my bit for the day. The back's feeling a bit stiff.' At Amy's look of concern, she tuts. 'Phht. Don't worry about that, dear, it's only because I've been bending over in the garden for an hour. I'm not getting any younger, you know. Now, can I invite you in for a cool drink? I was just about to make myself an iced tea.' She starts walking up the stairs, assuming Amy will follow. Irene knows when someone needs to talk.

'Where's Ashlee today?' Amy asks when they reach the kitchen. There's a *blink and you'll miss it* catch in her voice that makes Irene stop and turn, but Amy is looking at a drawing on the fridge.

'I dropped her off at her friend's a while ago. They're going to the pools.' Irene adds ice cubes to two tall glasses of homemade mint and lime iced tea. After topping them with a mint leaf and a slice of lime, she passes a glass to a distracted Amy, who's now gazing at the wall behind the dining table as if she's never seen it before. Hanging on the wall is a mosaic of mismatched wooden frames Irene found in the local op shop and spray-painted white.

Irene comes to stand beside Amy, taking in the family portraits. She never tires of looking at them, even says hello to them now and again. Not that she'd admit that to anyone. They'd think she was going batty in her old age.

'Shall we sit here or on the verandah?' Irene asks, turning to her friend. She is startled to see a tear trace its way down Amy's pale skin. 'What's wrong?'

Her gentle question unleashes a flood of words and tears. Irene pops a box of tissues on the table and listens to Amy's sob-muddled words, her iced tea forgotten. Her intuition was spot on about the Bennets.

'What do you want to happen?' she asks the younger woman, passing a tissue.

'I want Matt to come home. For things to go back to the way they were,' Amy bursts out.

'Of course. But what if they can't?'

'What do you mean?' Amy blows her nose.

'Well,' Irene chooses her words carefully. 'My sense is that Matt has been unhappy for a long time.'

'Has he said something to you?'

'No. But I can see it. It's like he's ... like he's been holding back. Too busy making sure *you're* okay to ... to look after his own needs.' Irene holds her breath, knowing that Amy might not like what she's saying. But she needs to hear it.

Amy gives her a sharp look, then swallows. 'That's sort of what he said. He said it wasn't all about me,' she says, her voice quiet, 'as if that's what I'd turned our relationship into.'

'Have you?' Irene is gentle.

'No!' Amy takes a moment to collect herself. 'If I have, I didn't mean to. I just ... it's just been so hard. Losing Pandora. It almost killed me. In one instant I went from being a mother and being pregnant to not being either. I wanted to die. I screamed at God, whoever, "Why did you let me live?".'

'Oh, love,' Irene says. 'You're still a mother. Your love for Pandora is always part of who you are.'

Amy sniffs. After a moment, she goes on, shredding her tissue in her lap. 'I know Matt blames me. He doesn't say it, but I feel it every day.'

It's not the first time Amy's said that. Irene wants to reassure her – *No, he doesn't* – but Sid was the same after Erin died. The memory of a long-ago argument flits in, words hurled in pain before Sid walked out the door to deal with his own demons. 'I think I know what you mean,' she offers.

Amy waves her hand and pieces of tissue float to the floor. 'I suppose all along I've been taking my guilt and pain out on Matt. Not intentionally, but …'

Her eyes drift back to the portraits and Irene finally asks the question that's been bothering her since Amy invited her to dinner months before. 'Why don't you have any photos of Pandora on display?'

'I can't. I can't bear to see them every day. It hurts too much.'

'So it's easier to pretend she doesn't exist?'

Amy's intake of breath slices the air. 'How can you say that? I cry for her every day, all the time.' Her face crumples again.

Irene waits. She knows Amy wants her to give her a break, to say, *It's okay. Of course, you're doing exactly the right thing. I'd do the same.* But it's not what Amy needs now. 'You know what I think?' The way Amy glowers reminds her of Ashlee when she's in a snit. 'I think you want the photos out of sight so you feel less guilt.'

'No!'

'And in turn, you're stopping Matt from grieving his way.' She pauses. 'How is that working for you?'

'It's not. It's not working at all. Because no matter what I do, I can't get away from the guilt.'

'Do you think it works for Matt?'

Amy's eyes widen as the implications of what Irene is saying hit home. 'No,' she admits, so quietly Irene almost misses it. 'He wants the photos up. So he can remember Pandora the way she was.'

'So he can grieve.'

MONIQUE MULLIGAN

'Yes,' Amy whispers. She drops her head onto the table, body heaving. Irene shifts her chair closer and puts an arm around Amy, absorbing her shudders as Irene remembers her own *aha* moment at this very spot.

'You're not the only one to think she can outrun guilt,' Irene says when Amy calms. 'I did it in a different way. When Erin was going through all her breakdowns, she had all my attention. And then when she died, it all went to Bonnie. There was nothing left for Sid. In the end, he left.'

'What? I thought—'

'He came back,' Irene says. 'And that's a story for another day. My point is that sometimes we can be so caught up in trying to deal with our own pain, whichever way we choose to do it, that we let down the other people we love.'

'But he – Sid – came back. I don't know if Matt will. He's got this job offer … he wants another baby … and I don't think I can do it. I wouldn't be a good enough mother.'

'Nonsense. Of course you will.'

'Why does everyone say that?'

'Because it's plain as the nose on your face, love. I've seen you with Ashlee. Goodness me, get that out of your head. At some point or another, every mother wonders if she's good enough. Every mother has guilt of some sort. But you have to stop asking if you're good enough, mother or not. Trust yourself.' Irene waits before going on. 'Look, if you really want to have another child with Matt, go for it. If you really don't want to, because *you* want a different life for yourself and not because you're feeling guilty, then make that choice.' She takes a breath. 'Either way, you need to talk to him. Not only talk, but listen. Let him pour his heart out. The only way you will move forward together is if you face this grief together.'

'But what if he doesn't want to? If he leaves?'

'You'll have to face that if it happens,' Irene says. 'What do you think you would do?'

'I don't know. Maybe stay here. I've got a life here. Or, maybe I'd

306

just, I don't know … sell up and move to the other side of the country!'

'Hmmm,' Irene says, pouring them fresh glasses of iced tea. She'll be running off to the loo any moment now. 'We talked about this before, remember? How it's natural to want to run when life gets tough. But remember this, wherever you go, there you are. Read that in a book once. Can't remember who said it.'

'Wherever you go, there you are.' Amy repeats the words. 'Gran said the same thing to me once or twice, but it's finally making sense.'

'It's one of those obvious statements, isn't it? Of course, physically, you are where you are. But emotionally, wherever you go, whatever you do, however you try to reinvent yourself, the essence of you will also be there. Your fears, joys, guilt, life experiences, everything that makes you *you* will come along for the ride. It may take a back seat, but that experience of being you is always with you.'

Amy pulls out another tissue and starts to twist that one between her fingers. 'What you're really saying is that even though I came to Blackwood for a new life, a simple life, all that is complicated about me has come along, too. And the same for Matt.'

'Yes. You can try to lock it away – some people successfully do for years – but inside the struggle to mask it is evidence that it's there. And eventually, it's going to come out. That's what's happening with Matt, I suspect.'

'How are we supposed to move on with so much holding us to the past?'

'You're looking at it wrong,' Irene says. 'Your past is part of you and it defines some aspects of who you are and what you do, but your present and future are also part of you. You can't change the past and how that is part of you, but you have some say in your future, and what you do with that part of you.'

'But that's what I've been doing, trying to build a future – buying the café, starting the supper club …'

'Yes, and you've achieved so much since you first came here. You've blossomed. But you're still trying to bury that other side of you. You're trying to bury it in Matt. And he doesn't want to do that anymore. He can't. And,' Irene reaches for Amy's hand again, 'if you keep forcing him to bury his pain to make it easier for you, I suspect it will end your marriage.'

Did she say the right things? Had she given Amy an ultimatum she had no right to give? Was it too late for them? As she replays her conversation, Irene hopes the Bennets will make things work – it's clear they love each other. But what if Amy is offended or hurt by Irene's words? She'd left in rather a hurry.

It's not my problem, Irene tells herself. It's up to Amy and Matt to sort out. All she's done is talk Amy through it, much in the same way she'd talked Bonnie and Erin through one thing or another. What happens next is up to Amy and Matt.

And what happens next in Irene's life is up to her. She opens a drawer on her desk and pulls out brochures the travel agent gave her last month. Undecided about a river cruise or a bus tour, she put them away and hasn't looked at them since. Too busy, she told herself. Procrastinating, more like. But last night, Bonnie saw an ad on Facebook about a tour called 'Highlights of European Spring' and when they checked it out online, Irene had almost swooned reading the tour description. It was a tantalising mix of tulip displays, flower markets and palace gardens in Amsterdam, Monet's Giverny and the Parc de Bagatelle in France, and the Chelsea Flower Show in the UK. It wasn't cheap, but even if she could never afford to go anywhere else, this was the trip Irene wanted to do.

Bonnie urged her to book immediately, but Irene had resisted. 'Do it, you've been going on about it for ages,' Bonnie had argued.

But Irene had said she wanted to think it over some more, and ignored Bonnie's exaggerated eye-roll. 'You let me do it in my time, love,' she'd said.

After dinner, Bonnie suggested they watch a movie called *A Little Chaos*, about two landscape artists who built a garden at Versailles. The love story (and Bonnie's obvious contrivance) had impressed

Irene less than the magnificence and scope of the gardens, but told her one thing: she had to see these gardens for herself.

So, what was stopping her now?

I'm scared to go by myself.

That was it. She'd always hoped Sid would travel with her one day and part of her feels disloyal, even now. And the other part feels plain old scared. She's imagined herself walking through exquisite gardens, breathing in the perfumes of nature. And then she imagines how she'll look to everyone else: a fuddy-duddy who asks questions that probably sound stupid, a backward country bumpkin, an unsophisticated and inexperienced old woman.

'Now, you jump right off that silly train of thought, Irene Knight,' she scolds herself out loud. After all, Una Mickle manages well enough on her own. If Una can do it, so can she. Shame Una had to cancel her cruise after Sharon's accident, though.

Irene flicks through the brochures once more and drops them into the bin. She opens the search engine on the computer and finds the website Bonnie saved. She reads over the tour itinerary once more, soaking in the descriptions of flowering cherries forming a canopy over blankets of hyacinths, roses and tulips; of walled gardens and orangeries; of grottoes and waterfalls and romantic lake gardens. And then she clicks on the online information form, types in her details and presses enter. It's time to do something for herself. By herself.

Next May, she'll be in Europe.

CHAPTER 51
AMY

Amy bolts up the steps and unlocks the back door with shaking hands. After seven months, she still hasn't let go of the lock-and-leave habit. The house is stifling after being closed up all day. Ignoring the suffocating pressure, not even pausing to switch on the air conditioner, Amy bursts into Matt's study. Irene's words drill into her: 'If you keep forcing him to bury his pain ... it will end your marriage.'

She's not sure what she's looking for. All she knows is that his study is the closest she can get to Matt right now. Her eyes flick around the room. It doesn't smell like him anymore. It smells like dust and stale memories. Sweat beads on her forehead and she opens the window. Heat streams in and she shoves it closed, wincing at the scrape of wood on wood. She swings around to switch on the ceiling fan. Her movements are clumsy, too fast for her mind to temper, and her elbow catches on something, which thuds to the ground. Amy reaches down to pick the object up. It's the wooden trinket box she gave Matt a few years ago. She turns it over in her hands, checking for breaks or dents, before placing it back on the shelf. A gleam catches her eye. There's a small key on the floor. It must have fallen out of the box.

Is this the key to his locked drawer?

In seconds, she's standing in front of the desk, pushing away thoughts that she's invading Matt's privacy. The key might not even fit, she thinks, as her trembling hand hovers near the lock, the key poised for action. In a short, sharp move she thrusts the key in, twists. Click. Amy closes her eyes briefly to steady herself, then slides the drawer open.

Reaching in, she pulls out two books: a day-to-a-page diary and the notebook she's seen Matt writing in, the one she suspected was a journal. A business card falls from the diary onto her lap. Amy reads the card, frowning at the unfamiliar name: Jon Barker. More precisely, Jon Barker, Psychologist. The counsellor Matt wanted her to see – Amy still hasn't made an appointment – was called Maureen, so who is this? She scans the diary, her mouth drying as she sees a repeated entry on intermittent pages: Jon – Skype.

And then it hits her.

Matt's been talking to a psychologist for months and she had no idea. The appointments date back to the beginning of the year, before they moved to Blackwood. Why hadn't he told her? She thought he was coping; she was even jealous of his ability to move on. She reaches for the notebook, wiping her eyes with her free hand, and opens it.

It's definitely a journal. Amy slams it shut, dropping it like a hot coal. It would be wrong to read it. But its existence compels her to open it, to enter this magnetic library of his mind. It will eat at her if she doesn't. But once she does, there's no looking back.

If you keep forcing him to bury his pain … it will end your marriage.

Irene's warning rings like tinnitus in the dead of night. She swats the words away, but they have a tenacious grip on her future and tease her hands into action. Her eyes flow over Matt's neat writing, shoving her conscience aside as his words reach into her soul. Pages and pages of words; dark, disturbing, laced with pain. Dreams, nightmares, thoughts recorded with such exquisite detail she might have been dreaming them herself. Matt's capacity to evoke images astounds her. He writes like he's born to it.

Amy sucks in his words until there are no more. The dated entries stop abruptly only days before Matt left.

We are walking up a gravelly path, our feet slipping, sliding on loose stones. I tell you to be careful, to watch your step, to plan your moves. You laugh and carry on the way you were.

I am carrying a backpack, loaded with items. You're wearing layer upon layer of clothing, like Heidi when she went up the mountain to meet her grandfather in that book you love so much. The more we walk, and the hotter it gets, the more items you offload into my backpack.

You skip ahead, leaving me with the weight of our baggage, but my feet drag. I call out, 'I can't carry it all, can you help?' But you march onwards and upwards, oblivious, and then turn a corner. I can no longer see you. I'm on my own.

The landscape is suddenly barren, the sky dark and threatening. As I trudge upwards, fog settles its weight around me. I can't see. My feet slip and I'm down on my knees, scrambling. Wind whips around me, its eerie song reaching into my bones.

I can't go any further. There is no one to share my load.

I can't go on like this.

I can't.

Hairs bristle Amy's arms as the implications of Matt's pain-seared words sink in. It was difficult enough that Matt left. What if he'd done something worse? What if—

No. Do not *think it.*

Thank God he had talked to a counsellor. If he hadn't— *Stop!*

Her mind reels with hurt and shock. Matt has never shared his pain with her, not like this. She doesn't know him at all. He's shared the secret parts of his soul with a stranger, with a book, because she didn't give him the chance, assumed he was the strong one. Did she place him in that role to make it easier for herself? Force him to be the foundation that stops her crumbling completely?

Matt was right. She has made Pandora's death all about her. The realisation crushes Amy, and she slumps deep into his chair. All along she's told herself he was just better at dealing with it. Better at grief. At loss. At losing his daughter. She'd even resented him for it. Paid lip service to marriage when, really, she's been largely absent from it for years. And now her husband has been sucked dry emotionally, drained of all he could offer. *She's* done that to him.

If you keep forcing him to bury his pain ... it will end your marriage.

Amy's heart twists. The only way Matt could stop carrying all their baggage was to drop the load and walk away. Away from their marriage. Away from her. How is she supposed to fix this? What if it's too late for them? But it can't be. Their lives, their history, are bound together.

'It can't be too late.' Her voice is ethereal in the echoing house. 'It can't be.'

She cannot let herself believe it's impossible to remedy the sorry state her marriage is in, but no matter how hard she tries Amy can't come up with a solution. Where would she start? How could she even begin to undo the damage she's done?

The room shadows as the sun goes behind a cloud. Amy makes no attempt to move. Her stomach grumbles, but she's not hungry. Her face is tight, her eyes sore from rubbing, her emotional wellspring dry. She ignores the reproachful pile of tissues on the floor. Matt's words have temporarily numbed her, have disabled her capacity to act on the cries of her heart. Darkness has her in its grip.

Amy's eyes land on the walnut cabinet filled with spirits. She walked away last time she heard its siren call. Now, she has an urge to let darkness consume her. But it's just another way of running.

Amy forces her eyes away, down to the journal clenched in her hands. If she opens that drinks cabinet, she'll be repeating history. Making the same mistakes her mother made. She's not her mother. She doesn't have to perpetuate the cycle. What if she simply learnt to live with her life as it is now? What if she welcomed darkness as a friend, not an enemy, and allowed growth to emerge? These thoughts emerge from her darkness, a glimmer of light and strength, in a day that has rocked her to the core.

Dropping the journal on the desk, Amy heads outdoors, into the golden late afternoon light. Balmy air brushes her skin. Silvereyes and honeyeaters twitter and flitter, in and out of fruit trees and the near-empty birdbath. Out here is life. Out here, hope lives on.

'I'm sorry,' she says to the wilted herb and vegetable plots. Dragging the hose over, she waters the parched plants. Fills the birdbath.

'I'm sorry,' she speaks into the light, warm wind, willing the words to fly to her absent husband. 'Is it too late?'

Amy sinks into her rocking chair. Fumbling in her pocket for her mobile phone, she tries to concoct a text message to Matt. Something meaningful. Simple. Something he'll get straight away. She deletes the first few efforts – nothing sounds right – and finally settles on two words: *Come home.*

CHAPTER 52
AMY

Half an hour later, the sun is lower still and Matt hasn't responded. Pacing around the garden, then the house, Amy checks her phone every few minutes. Is it on silent? Is the volume too low? Once again, she has that jittery sensation of desperately waiting for The Call. Irritation flares now. She's no teenager. She's Matt's wife. Why is he ignoring her? It takes every ounce of willpower she has to walk away from the phone and the arguments in her head. Time to find something else to fill in the empty hours.

A wave of dizziness stops her in her tracks. Amy leans against a wall and waits for the unsteadiness to pass. When did she last eat? Breakfast? Making her way to the kitchen, she takes a handful of grapes from the fridge. Pours a glass of juice and sits at the table. The grapes are crisp and sweet, and she finishes them quickly. Her stomach grumbles anew. Amy opens the fridge again and looks blankly at the shelves before pulling out an avocado and a tomato. Working quickly, she cuts the avocado in half, scoops out the flesh, and mashes it in a bowl with lemon juice and minced garlic. Toasts a slice of two-day-old sourdough. She spreads the avocado mix on the bread and adds thick slices of tomato from her garden. A sprinkle of sea salt, a twist of pepper, and *voila!* She bites down, allowing the tastes to mingle, and closes her eyes. Why does it feel like she's only just figured out how soothing food can be? She's a chef. She *knows* this.

Perhaps cooking will distract her. Should she bake some biscuits for the café? Make that chocolate-raspberry buttercream layer cake her dad told her about? After checking the pantry, she realises that won't work. The pantry is overdue for a top-up. Tomorrow, perhaps.

Amy turns her attention to the kitchen. She's been neglecting it lately. When was the last time she wiped down the cupboards? Cleaned the fridge? Or the oven, for that matter? She settles for washing the dishes and wiping down the cupboards and bench. Opens the windows and front and back doors to let the hot air vent out. It's cooling quickly tonight.

Laundry is her next task. She chucks a load in, collects towels from the bathroom and kitchen ready for the next load, and moves on to dusting. Cleaning the house from top to bottom is one thing she *can* control. She dusts every surface she can reach and then some. And then she drags the vacuum cleaner behind her, moving furniture and lifting rugs, until finally she's done everything except change the sheets.

Still no message.

Throwing her phone on the bed, she opens the linen closet, reaches in for fresh sheets, and pauses. Matt wrote about a box full of Pandora's belongings hidden in the linen cupboard.

Amy remembers the argument they had when they moved in. She told him to get rid of it. He practically dared her to. She couldn't do it. Shoved the box high in this cupboard when Matt was out and pretended it didn't exist. Amy drags a chair to the linen cupboard, and fumbles around the dark recesses up high. She can feel boxes, but which is the right one? Marching back to the kitchen she finds a torch, then takes up her position scanning the labels on the dusty boxes. She sees it, labelled in Matt's writing: Pandora's Box.

Amy grips the cardboard and slides it forward. She hesitates. For three years, Pandora has existed in her mind as a translucent apparition. A memory boxed away. But you can't do that when you lose someone you love. They are tied to you in a knot that cannot be undone.

What was the last thing she'd said to Pandora before she lost her for good? Had she barked at her for some misdemeanour? She can't remember. What she does remember is calling her name over and over in a car somewhere in the German countryside. Calling but hearing only the ticking of an engine.

And then shouts. Sirens. Nothing.

Amy almost shoves the box back in the cupboard. All she has to do is close the door and walk away. She's so close, her hand resting on the box, and it only needs a little push, but then Irene's warning sounds from somewhere in her mind.

Amy stiffens. If she doesn't stop hiding, she'll lose everything. Stop denying her daughter's existence. Stop flinching when someone says her perfect, precious name, for fear pain will lash her like a whip. Her daughter existed. She lived. She was loved. Every time Amy tears up at a memory, all the panic attacks – that was Pandora crying to be remembered. *Remember me. Talk about me. Hold on to me.*

She can no longer ignore the call. There's more at stake than her resistance to pain. Lifting down the box, she tears packing tape away and lifts the flaps.

And there she is: Pandora.

Her little girl in a box filled with photo albums. Baby clothes. The christening dress passed down from Gran. Moo-Moo, Pandora's favourite stuffed toy. A small, silver keepsake box holding her first tooth. A baby book meticulously filled in with heights and weights. Scribbly drawings.

Amy sifts through the items slowly, tenderly, as if seeing each one for the first time. She smells the tiny clothes and remembers Pandora wearing them. She strokes each photograph of her daughter, imagining the glossy paper materialising into soft baby skin. And she cries heavy tears of longing, of loss. Her nose is stuffy from dust and tears, but she stays where she is, buried in her daughter's belongings. Buried in memories.

'I miss you, Panda-Bear,' she whispers.

CHAPTER 53
AMY

S unlight filters into the bedroom, stirring Amy from the deepest
sleep she's had in months. She stretches. Amy doesn't remember
coming to bed, or removing her shorts and putting them on the
armchair. All she remembers is opening Pandora's box. She sits up
suddenly. Did she leave everything piled on the floor?

A sharp, clanging noise startles her. Amy tilts her head sideways.
It's coming from the kitchen. Has Irene let herself in? Bonnie? Sliding
out of bed, Amy pulls on her discarded shorts. The smell of bacon
wafts into the room when she creaks open the bedroom door. On
tiptoes, she follows her nose to the kitchen, gasping when she sees
who is at the stove, oblivious to her presence.

Amy stares at her husband, unable to believe that he's really here.
Hot tears spring to her eyes and she wipes them away, sniffing. Matt
turns. His expression is inscrutable, and then tenderness washes over
his face. With a flick of the wrist, he switches off the burner and
strides to her, three big steps, before folding her into his arms. Amy
hears his quickened heartbeat, mirroring her own.

'You came back,' she whispers.

'I did.'

'I read your journal.'

'I know.'

'I opened Pandora's box.'

'I know.' Matt gestures to the table, where the box is packed once more, but open. Hopeful. 'I'm making breakfast,' he says. 'Mushrooms, tomatoes, poached eggs, baked beans, bacon, toasted sourdough. Hungry?'

At Amy's nod, he kisses her forehead. His two-day growth brushes her skin and she shivers. 'Good,' he says, pulling away and moving back to the stove. He flicks the burner back on. 'Something tells me you haven't been eating well. You're light as a feather. Noticed when I carried you to bed last night. We'll need to fix that.' He heads back to the stove, calling over his shoulder. 'This'll take about ten minutes. Why don't you have a quick shower and meet me back here?'

In the shower, lukewarm water sluices her body. She imagines the water stripping away something, exfoliating a layer of protection and revealing a new, vulnerable Amy underneath. She towel-dries her hair, rubs moisturiser onto her face and body, and returns to the kitchen, dressed in a clean tank top and boxer shorts. Damp hair hangs over her shoulders, dripping down her back in cool trickles.

Matt's set the table. Orange juice in tall glasses. A lone daisy sits in a makeshift vase. Amy hovers at the door, unsure. What does this mean?

'Just in time,' he says. He carries the plates over. The food smells delicious. He's even added garlic and chopped herbs to the mushrooms, the way she does. Is this a dream? She pinches her bare leg under the table.

It's not a dream. He's really here.

'This looks delicious.' It's all she can think of to fill in the gaps of uncertainty. Silence can be companionable, but it can also be fraught with tension. And an expectant tension is unmistakable in this room. Picking up her fork, she starts to eat. Buttery and fragrant with herbs, the mushrooms pop in her mouth. The poached eggs are perfect: liquid gold dribbles over crunchy toast. 'I didn't know I had all this food in the fridge.'

'You didn't.' Matt layers mushroom, bacon and egg onto a slice of toast. 'I went down to Blackwood Fresh this morning.'

'Already? What time is it?' Even as she asks, Amy's head swivels to the clock. 'Ten o'clock? Really? I'm supposed to be at—'

'I called in sick for you. You were dead to the world. Didn't even move when I carried you to bed, or took off your shorts.'

'But when did you get here?'

'Last night.' He chews on toast. 'I didn't see your message for a couple of hours. I was playing cards with Frank and his mates. They have a poker night every month. Lucky I didn't drink. I was designated driver. Had to drop Frank off and then I came straight here.'

Amy processes this. 'Where … where did you sleep?'

'In our bed.' He meets her eyes. 'By the time I finished tidying up here, I got into bed without really thinking.'

She wishes she'd known he was there. 'Thank you for coming.'

'Eat,' he says. 'You can thank me later.'

Amy helps Matt clean up, ignoring his protests. They load the dishwasher, easing back into intimate routines they know by heart. But Amy can't ignore the unsettling undercurrent. Is this the calm before the storm? Her skin tingles and chest aches from the relentless tattoo of her heart.

'Coffee?' Matt closes the dishwasher and turns to face her.

He's acting like it's just another lazy weekend morning. A lie-in and breakfast. The what-are-we-going-to-do-today discussion. 'Sure,' she says, even though she doesn't want coffee, not at all.

Matt squints at her. 'Good. I need another one to keep my eyes open. Didn't sleep well.' He focuses on the coffee machine, shoulders bunched tight. From Amy's vantage point, it appears he's taking deep breaths.

He's just as nervous as me, she thinks. *We're feeling our way around each other like we've woken up together for the first time.*

'I'll wait in the lounge room.' She needs space to psych her up for whatever's coming.

'Yep. Be there in a tick.'

In the lounge room, she stands between her armchair and the two-seater sofa, wishing she had a cardigan. Not because it's cold, but because pulling it around her reminds her of Gran's embrace whenever Amy was uncertain. Where should she sit? On her chair? Should they sit side by side on the sofa? Would that be weird? Does it matter?

Matt decides for her. He places the tray with two steaming flat whites on the coffee table, lowers himself onto the two-seater and pats the cushion next to him. He picks up his cup, takes a hesitant sip. Like Amy, he hasn't relaxed into the sofa. Amy moves to pick up her cup, then pulls her hand back. She can't drink it. There's too much to say.

'Matt,' she bursts out. He looks up. 'I know about the counsellor. About everything you've been holding onto for me. I'm sorry. So deeply sorry for everything.'

She swallows and he opens his mouth.

'No. Let me just get it out. I've been so completely, utterly self-absorbed for so long. I haven't let you grieve for Pandora, not the way you needed. And I'm so, so sorry for that.' She plunges on. 'Boxing away what happened ... it was the only way I knew how to deal with it. I couldn't bear the pain of not being a mother anymore. Of having that part of who I am – was – taken away. It's like ...' she swallows again to keep the rising sob at bay, 'it's like the only way I could stop myself from joining her, from ending it, was to block her from my mind as much as possible. But it didn't work. No matter what I did, she was always there. And so was the guilt.'

'I know, Aims, I know.' He puts his cup on the tray. Moves closer. Squeezes her hand.

'You're always so good to me.' Her voice is laced with tears. 'I'm sorry I made this all about me. I'm sorry I didn't think about how you were coping. God, if I'd known ... your journals, those dreams ... I had no idea you were struggling so much. You always seemed to get on with things. I didn't know. I didn't *know*.'

Her thoughts are tumbleweeds, blowing every which way. Is she making sense? 'And, honestly, maybe I didn't *want* to know. And for that, I am *so* sorry. I only hope you can forgive me.'

Matt exhales. Amy watches him as he twists his wedding ring –

he's still wearing it, thank God. His jaw works and his Adam's apple bobs up and down. She waits for him to speak, fighting the urge to fill the silence with more words.

He clears his throat and faces her. His eyes hold hers for what feels like hours. 'For what it's worth,' he finally says, 'I'm glad you read my journal. If it's helped you to … to understand how hard it's been for me, then that's a good thing. And, you're right. I have been struggling. For a really long time. All of a sudden, I stopped being a father. One day I was a dad … then I wasn't.' Amy's unable to stop the sob that escapes at his admission and he takes her hands. 'I know, in a way, I still am, but I'm also not.'

After a moment, he continues. 'It just … it all came to a head, you know? I couldn't … can't keep on going the same way, pretending what happened *didn't* happen. I wish it didn't, I wish it with every piece of me, but it did. But I don't want to box Pandora away either. I can't do that anymore. I won't.'

Tears trickle down his face. She reaches up and wipes them away, tracing her finger down the stubble. 'I'm sorry,' she whispers and reaches for him.

He crumples in her arms. 'I'm sorry too.'

'It's hard,' Amy says much later. They've moved back to the kitchen. Amy's written a shopping list. Matt's brought his suitcase inside. It's in the hallway just outside the kitchen door, as if waiting for permission to enter. 'I know we moved here to start again, away from the city, away from … from people who know us and pity us, who look at us and feel sorry for us, and don't know what to say. And yet, I'm scared to move on. I don't want to forget, but I don't want to wake every day remembering either. I'm scared of the memories, but I'm scared of forgetting, too. And I'm shit-scared of being a mother again. Of stuffing it up. Of letting you down.'

He opens his mouth to say something but she shakes her head. Instead, he comes to her and holds her tightly. Amy thinks she'll never get tired of being held by him. They have months to catch up on.

Years. 'The thing is, I'm *never* going to get over this. Never. What happened will happen *every* day for the rest of my life,' she taps her heart and head, 'in here and here. What happened is part of me. And I know I have to learn to live with it but sometimes ... sometimes I don't want to.'

Her gaze burns into him. He returns the look with equal fire.

'Sometimes I don't want to either,' he admits. Minutes pass as they absorb this. 'It happened to me too, Aims. It's part of me now, in everything I do. It's there every time I wake.' A fat tear trickles down his face.

She squeezes his arm. 'Me too.'

He folds her hand into his, rubbing his fingers over hers. 'I didn't want us to come here to forget, to *move on*.' A bitter laugh escapes as he considers his next words. 'Moving on is overrated. It's a nice phrase said by people who mean well but don't really get it.' He pauses again. Amy bites the inside of her lip to keep from interrupting. 'I wanted to come here so we could rebuild our lives. To find ways to *live* with our grief and heal – not forget – but *live*. Together.'

Matt takes her head in his hands, drawing her drowning eyes to his. 'It's not a crime if we continue living. Living life – *that* is how we will heal in time. Whether another child is part of that, we'll find out.' His eyes dig deep and, slowly, she nods. 'All I want, all I've wanted for so long, is for you to live it, here, with me.'

Amy's heard this before, so many times. Not just from Matt. From counsellors, friends, well-meaning strangers. She knows all about Elisabeth Kübler-Ross's grief theory. It used to piss her off, especially when people tried to tell her which stage they thought she was in. Now, a smile creeps onto her face. Maybe the theory wasn't that far off the mark after all.

'Matt? Am I understanding you right? Can we move on from this, from the past few months?'

'I'd like to give it a try.' He gestures towards the hall. 'Shall I unpack?'

'Yes!' He moves away and she grabs his arm. 'Matt? About another baby? I'd like to try for that too.'

CHAPTER 54
EIGHT WEEKS LATER

AMY

'It looks fantastic,' Matt whispers in Amy's ear.

'You think?'

'Aims, you've been fussing about with the table for ages. Trust me.' He lowers two bags of ice to the ground.

Amy sweeps a critical glance over the long table they've set up on the verandah. She's filled jam jars with flowers – gerberas, roses, dwarf sunflowers – whatever she's been able to get her hands on. She's re-used the makeshift hessian table runner from the French-themed Around the World Supper Club night and added her gold-rimmed white dinner set to complete the simple, but summery effect. Battery-operated twinkle lights have been looped around alternate jars in readiness for evening.

'Hmm. Will you bring out the cocktail cabinet?'

'I'll need your help.'

Once the cabinet is in place, Matt strings up fairy lights under the verandah and Amy writes up the menu for the first Around the World Supper Club gathering of the year. They're meeting at the house because Bonnie couldn't get a sitter for Ashlee and, at Matt's request, they've gone for a Greek theme. Greece is where he and Amy first met; she literally fell into his arms after tripping on uneven flooring in a taverna.

'She fell for me the minute she saw me,' Matt liked to tell people.

Remembering that long-ago day, Amy smiles. She's never told him that he's right: she tripped on purpose. She'd liked the look of him, even with his nerdy glasses. Likes the look of him even more now.

Leaving Matt to it, Amy heads back to the kitchen. Peeling prawns under cold water, she reflects on how far she and Matt have come in the past eight weeks. Matt turned down the London job and got promoted when his boss relocated to Sydney; Amy went down to a four-day week at the café. Since then, they've been finding their way forward together. Amy has committed to weekly chats with Maureen for now, while Matt's kept up his Skype sessions with Jon. She and Matt are communicating better than they have in years.

The oven preheats while Amy prepares a traditional Greek salad. At the bench, her eyes drift to the photo collage on the opposite wall. With Irene's help, she's framed a collection of Pandora moments, and mounted them on the wall in a heart shape. When Matt first saw the completed collage, he'd frozen in place for a long moment, before turning tear-filled eyes to Amy's. She'd known then it was the right thing to do. Just as she'd known it was right to order a memorial plaque for their garden, identical to the one in Germany. Her father helped arrange it. The plaque had arrived in time for Matt's birthday the week earlier and they'd placed it in the garden under a rose bush.

Amy heads to the shower. Her body is coated with dried perspiration, and she desperately needs to freshen up. She'd thought it would be cooler in Blackwood by now, but summer's hold shows no sign of letting go. She lingers under the shower's cool waterfall massage, turning off the tap with reluctance. Naked, she steps into the bedroom at the same time as Matt walks in, his T-shirt half over his head.

His face lights up. 'Well, I came in at the right time, didn't I?'

'Or the wrong time, depending on which way you look at it,' she quips, pulling on lacy briefs. 'You could have joined me in the shower.'

Their banter flows easily once more. It's as if their desire for each other has been turned on – and up a notch – since the night they stripped their hearts bare.

'Damn. Don't suppose we've got time …'

'No can do, hon.' Amy flicks her fingers over his exposed nipples, smiling at his intake of breath and the way his eyes darken. 'But hold that thought.'

'I'd rather hold you. But I suppose the thought will have to do.'

He disappears into the shower, whistling. After stepping into her floral halter-neck dress, and twisting her hair into a loose topknot, Amy sits on the edge of the bed and removes a box from her top drawer. She's itching to open it, but can't. Not yet.

'You've got two minutes, hon,' she calls, as a car pulls up outside.

Frank has taken the Greek theme to heart. When he walks into the kitchen, Amy bursts out laughing. He's wearing a shirt that's open a few buttons, displaying the most hirsute chest Amy's ever seen. He's even added a thick gold necklace.

'I told him not to,' June says. 'But he insisted.'

'Found the necklace at the op shop. Bargain. Reckon I might wear shirts unbuttoned like this more often. Natural air conditioning. Those Greeks were onto something.'

June rolls her eyes to Amy. 'You see what I have to put up with?'

'I'll ignore that.' Frank hands two bottles of Tsantali retsina to Amy. 'Found some Greek wine, too. *Not* from the op shop. In one of the big grog shops in Bunbury. Hope it's okay.' He looks around. 'Where's the menu?'

'Outside on the verandah,' Matt says, coming into the room. He's wearing his nerdy glasses, a white T-shirt and jeans that fit snugly around his butt, just like the first time Amy saw him. He meets Amy's eye and winks before turning back to Frank. 'Want a coldie? Bring those bottles with you, mate. There's ice outside.'

'That smells good.' June almost swoons when Amy opens the oven door. 'What is that?'

'*Spanakopita*. A filo pie with chopped spinach, feta and dill.' Amy tilts the baking dish. 'It's almost done. It slides a bit in the dish when it's cooked. About fifteen minutes more, I think.' She adjusts the timer and wipes her hands on a tea towel.

'Sounds wonderful. Speaking of wonderful, I wanted to tell you something before—'

June's cut off when Ashlee barrels in, wearing an Elsa dress and carrying her *Frozen 2* DVD.

'Mummy said I could watch *Frozen 2* after I eat my dinner. Can I eat my dinner now? I'm busting hungry.'

'Patience, Ash.' Amy didn't even see Bonnie and Irene enter. Bonnie bends down to her daughter. 'Remember what I was saying about patience.'

'Ye-es, Mum. You told me a million times.' For a nearly five-year-old, Ashlee sometimes sounds ten years older. 'Can I have a biscuit?' She points at the wooden platter on the bench, piled with bread sticks, wedges of cheese, plump feta-filled olives, stuffed peppers and a bowl of taramasalata dip. Without waiting for an answer, Ashlee grabs a handful of bread sticks and runs outside.

'She's such a great kid,' Amy tells Bonnie.

Grinning, Bonnie pops an olive in her mouth. 'She is. You know,' she swallows her mouthful, 'you had a lot to do with me leaving that FIFO job.'

'I did?' Amy can't think why. She passes the platter to June, who takes it outside. 'How?'

'Remember that day I was moaning about work and asked what to do? You said, "If it were me, I would make every moment with my daughter count." That's what I decided to do. Aw, look at you, all sooky.' Bonnie embraces Amy for a long moment and then disappears out the back.

After wiping her eyes, Amy reaches into the fridge for platters of souvlaki and falafel.

'How have things been?' Irene says from behind her.

Amy jumps. She'd forgotten Irene was in the room. 'Really good, Irene. The counselling's doing us both good. It's still hard, talking about Pandora sometimes, but we're taking it a day at a time.'

'You still look a little tired. But stronger in yourself. And there's colour in your cheeks.' Irene looks Amy up and down. 'And—'

'You can say it. I've put on a little weight.' Amy laughs. 'You remind me of Gran so much. She was always telling me to put some meat on my bones.'

Irene grins. 'She was right. And you're glowing. I love that dress.'

'I was wearing one like it when I first met Matt.'

Fairy lights sway in the gentle breeze that follows the sun's slow goodnight kiss. Music dances a quiet ballet under the flowing conversation. Wine glasses clink as the friends toast the unknown future. Matt barbecues souvlaki and falafel. In the distance, Irene's chooks gabble in response to a mournful honk from Henry.

Matt leans in close to Amy. 'You look gorgeous.'

'You don't look so bad yourself.' On impulse, she pinches his bum.

'Oi. Save that for later,' Frank calls out.

Matt ignores him and kisses Amy anyway. Handing over the tongs, he leaves her to sauté the prawns on the barbecue wok, and joins Frank and June in the garden. Frank says something to Matt – the words are lost over the sizzle of the prawns – and she smiles as Frank pulls Matt in for a quick man hug. Three pats on the back and it's done. Amy pours the chilli-spiked tomato sauce over the prawns, simmers it and then tips the *saganaki* into a serving dish. She adds chopped parsley and a generous squeeze of lemon, listening as Irene tells Nick and Devi about her travel plans. Bonnie's inside settling Ashlee in front of the television. Flossie has wandered over from next door and is perched on the railing.

At last, they take their seats around the long table, murmuring appreciation at the feast in front of them. A loaded meze platter with, Amy tells them, feta-stuffed peppers, dolmades, haloumi, taramasalata, tzatziki, hummus, Greek-style mushrooms cooked in balsamic vinegar and port, plump olives, marinated eggplant and chunks of Turkish bread. Pork souvlaki with mint yoghurt dressing. Chicken souvlaki with lemon, chilli, and oregano. Prawn *saganaki* topped with crumbled feta next to wedges of warm *spanakopita*. Greek salad bursting with colour. *Keftedes* swimming in a spiced tomato sauce next to a pot of rice pilaf. Falafel with wedges of lemon. A spicy bouquet of cinnamon, oregano and chilli mixes with the summer smells of cut grass, citronella and mint.

'Blimey!' Frank pulls out a chair for a red-faced June. They'd been sprung kissing in the garden. 'This looks bloody good,' he says, stealing a prawn. The chilli sauce makes him cough and, spluttering, he gestures to the menu. 'So, we're eating meatballs, rissoles and kebabs? Why doesn't it just say so instead of all these fancy names?'

Amy watches as they take their first bites, listening to their murmurs and sighs. She'll never tire of watching people enjoy food. Only when everyone is eating does she fill her own plate. She bites into the souvlaki, savouring the minty yoghurt tang. Sips her mineral water. Memories of Greece, of meeting Matt, lurk at the edges of her mind, before the present draws her back.

'What's in this cocktail?' Bonnie is asking.

'It's a Santorini Sunrise,' Matt tells her. 'Grapefruit-infused vodka mixed with honey, mint leaves, Campari, pink grapefruit juice.' He makes Bonnie another one. 'Amy, you want one?'

'I'm good with this,' she says, indicating her water, ignoring his raised eyebrows.

'Didn't know rissoles were Greek,' Frank says after a while, helping himself to two falafel patties. Nick snorts.

'They're falafel. Chickpea patties,' Amy says with a smile. 'They're Middle Eastern really, but I thought they'd go down well as a meat alternative.'

'Meat alternative? Just the whaddyacallit, chickpea things?' Frank prods the patties suspiciously, before nibbling a corner. 'Not bad,' he admits.

Matt tells Nick and Devi how he and Amy met in Greece, hamming up the part where Amy fell into his arms.

'You guys should totally go back to Greece,' Bonnie says. 'You could renew your vows or something.'

'As a matter of fact, we are. That is, if my lovely wife agrees.' Amy looks at Matt in surprise. He takes her hand. 'Amy and I are going to Germany for a couple of weeks in May. I thought we'd spend a week on the Greek islands after that. What do you reckon? Santorini with me?'

'Are you kidding? Yes!'

'Speaking of lovely wives,' Frank speaks up. He pulls June to him, who blushes. 'I've asked this wonderful woman to marry me and she said yes.'

'We're getting married in April,' June says, holding her hand up to show off the ring she's kept hidden.

'You cheeky monkey,' Irene says. 'You never said!' She pulls herself out of her chair and embraces her friend.

'I've been dying to tell you for weeks,' June confesses, addressing them all, 'but Frank, well, he wanted to wait until tonight.'

Matt proposes a toast to the happy couple. As he fills champagne flutes and passes them around, Amy observes the way Frank looks at June. His face is soft, eyes tender. A man in love. Amy thinks back to the first Around the World Supper Club, when June asked Frank to dance. Did Frank and June fall in love at that moment? She likes to think so. Frank catches her watching and winks. Funny. She never thought she'd be celebrating his engagement when she first met him. She charges her glass. 'To Frank and June.'

'To Frank and June,' her friends echo.

Someone turns up the music. Frank and June drift down the verandah and dance, swaying slowly, their bodies close. A sleepy Ashlee appears and clambers onto her mother's lap, thumb in her mouth, eyes fluttering in an effort not to miss out on the fun. Matt scrapes down the barbecue. Nick and Devi join him, drinks in hand. Their faces are wine-soft, their voices animated, but Amy can't hear what they're talking about. Laughter peppers their conversation. Piglet has joined the party and is sniffing around the table for scraps. Irene's talking softly to Bonnie. Looking around at her friends is all the confirmation Amy needs that she's in the right place. There'll be no more running, no more hiding. Just life, with all the good and bad.

Gathering the plates in a pile, Amy heads for the kitchen and starts stacking the dishwasher. Irene brings in serving dishes and packs away leftovers.

'How do you feel about going back to Germany? You must be looking forward to seeing your dad,' Irene says.

Amy thinks before answering, wanting to speak her truth. 'Part excited, part nervous. I want to see my dad. But … I'm worried I'll be crushed by memories. And yet it's something I have to do.'

Irene listens without comment and Amy's overcome with appreciation for this woman who always listens but never seems to judge. 'Thank you, Irene. For being you. For being here.'

'No thanks necessary. That's what friends are for.'

Matt walks in and looks from Amy to Irene. 'Is everything okay?'

'It's more than okay,' Amy says, going to him. 'We're just having a heart-to-heart.'

He searches her eyes. Nods. 'Okay. So … coffee time? Dessert?'

Moments later, Frank has them in fits of laughter. 'Galactic-boo-ree—' Frank tries out the unfamiliar word amid laughter. He pokes at the generous serve of dessert on his plate. 'You got me this time, Amy. What is this galactic thing?'

'*Galaktoboureko*,' Amy sounds out, smiling. 'It's a traditional Greek custard pie. You'll love it. Trust me. Watch.' She bites through the butter-crisp filo pastry and into the creamy, orange zest-infused custard. The sweet syrup lingers on her tongue.

Frank forks up a mouthful of the dessert and breaks into a huge grin. 'Bloody good, Amy.' Frank scrapes his plate clean and gives Amy a hopeful look. 'Seconds?'

'Frank!'

'More of me to love,' he booms, kissing his embarrassed wife-to-be on the lips.

'Oi, save that for later,' Matt calls out.

Amy leans back in her seat and soaks up love and friendship. These people, these shared experiences, are more than she expected when she moved to Blackwood. She'd gone along with Matt's hopes for a fresh start, never believing they'd achieve anything more than a different location. The only hope she'd had was that the pain would be left behind.

How wrong she'd been. How much had changed. For her. For Matt. For both of them. Their lives had changed location and direction, but they were still living. They'd stopped running. They'd moved to Blackwood to escape memories that haunted them – and sometimes still did – but they'd learnt that these memories could never be left behind. Memories are part of the fabric that weaves your Self together and they stay with you wherever you go.

Excusing herself, Amy goes to her bedroom. *It's time.* She carries the box from her bedside drawer to the bathroom. Locks the door. Paces for precisely three minutes, an eternity.

Amy opens her eyes and breathes hope into a new life.

RECIPES

AMY'S LENTIL SOUP

Serves 6 | Prep 15 mins | Cook time 35 mins

Ingredients
- 1½ cups split red lentils
- ½ cup chopped yellow onion
- ½ cup chopped celery
- ½ cup chopped carrot
- 2 garlic cloves, minced
- 1 tbsp olive oil
- 4 cups chicken (or vegetable) stock, preferably homemade
- 2 cups water
- 2 bay leaves
- 1 lemon, juiced
- 2½ tsp salt
- ½ tsp freshly ground black pepper
- ¾ tsp cumin powder
- ½ tsp turmeric

• A wedge of preserved lemon in a bouquet garni bag (or reusable teabag) – optional

Method

1. Rinse and soak the lentils for 15–20 minutes. Drain and set aside.

2. Heat the oil in a large pot over low–medium heat.

3. Cook the onions, celery, and carrots for 7–10 minutes over low heat until the onions are slightly translucent. You don't want to brown them.

4. Add minced garlic and cook for 30 seconds, then add in the bay leaves, cumin powder, turmeric, drained lentils, stock, preserved lemon (if using), and water. Cook for 15–20 minutes, or until the lentils have softened.

5. Remove the bay leaves and preserved lemon.

6. Blend the soup to your preferred consistency (it will be a thin soup).

7. Season with the lemon juice, salt, and pepper.

8. Serve with crusty bread, and chopped mint or parsley (or both) to garnish.

Amy's notes: *Even better the next day + preserved lemon adds depth.*

CLÉMENCE'S CAKE

From *A Little Bite of Happiness* by V.P. Colombo (p. 154). Used with permission.

Serves 6 | Prep 15 mins | Cook time 30 mins

Ingredients
- 220g dark chocolate, at least 58 per cent cocoa
- 140g caster sugar
- 150g butter
- 4 large eggs
- Pinch of salt
- 50g flour (optional for a gluten-free version)

Method
1. Preheat oven to 150°C. Generously grease a round cake pan.
2. Heat the butter in a small saucepan.
3. Melt the chocolate in a bowl over a saucepan of simmering water (make sure the water does not touch the bowl).
4. Pour the butter over the caster sugar and whisk until the mixture becomes whitish. Add the silky chocolate and mix.
5. Separate the eggs. Mix the yolks into the batter, setting aside the whites. If using flour, sprinkle over the batter and mix, making sure there are no lumps.
6. Beat the whites and a pinch of salt until they look like snow. Delicately fold the whites into the batter in three batches.
7. Pour batter into the prepared cake pan and bake for 25–30 minutes. Check regularly.

8. Once the cake is done, let it cool on a rack for a few minutes and prepare a plate and a cake stand. Place the plate over the cake and carefully flip it upside down so the cake slides onto the plate (you may want to lightly run a knife around the edge first). Then, holding the cake stand with one hand and the plate in the other, flip the cake right way up onto the stand.

ACKNOWLEDGEMENTS

To the fabulous team at Pilyara Press – you demonstrate sisterhood at its best. Thank you for inviting me into your circle. My editors Sydney Wayland Smith and Kathryn Ledson – for keen insight and guidance. Proofreader Desney King, for her eagle eye, and publisher Jennifer Scoullar, for patience with my many questions.

Thanks to Teena Raffa-Mulligan, Lily Malone and Louise Allen for reading early versions and providing insightful feedback. To my kindred spirit Maureen Eppen, my critique buddy when I started this writing caper – you've always been in my corner. Double act Jenn J McLeod and Jeannette McAnderson for critiquing the first few chapters at a memorable writers retreat. Beta reader Claire Louisa Holderness, who bumped my manuscript to the top of her pile.

To the Lollygaggers for 'You got this' encouragement all the way, and Kim Kelly, for listening that time I was in the depths of despair. To my family and friends, thanks for your belief in me (and for encouraging me to talk about something different once in a while). And to Boogle, for keeping my lap warm – any typos may or may not be her contribution.

Mostly, I want to thank my husband Aaron, for putting up with endless conversations and questions about The Book over countless

ACKNOWLEDGEMENTS

cups of coffee and during walks that were supposed to be about exercise and stress relief. Despite his aversion to pink, he sat in a pink floral Queen Anne armchair whenever I asked 'Have you got a minute', and never once sighed on the outside. Okay, maybe once or twice. And he read the manuscript multiple times, even though he prefers books about trees, weather and French grammar. Wherever my writing journey goes, I want him by my side.

ABOUT THE AUTHOR

A former journalist and news editor, Monique Mulligan juggles creative writing with a part-time job and freelance editing. When she's not working you will usually find her a) writing b) reading c) cooking or d) taking photos for her cat's Instagram page. When she's socialising, she's usually behind a camera or in a corner hanging out with other introverts and making mental notes for stories. Monique is also a keen amateur photographer who loves taking close-up shots of flowers, and a passionate but messy cook, who believes love is the best ingredient in food. Her husband, adult children and cat agree.

Monique has had three children's picture books published, and short fiction in various anthologies. *Wherever You Go* is her debut novel.

Visit Monique's website for *Wherever You Go* Book Club Notes, recipes and menus, or to sign up for Monique's e-newsletter.

If you have enjoyed this book and have a moment or two, please leave an online rating or review. Reviews are of great help to authors.

www.moniquemulligan.com

Lightning Source UK Ltd.
Milton Keynes UK
UKHW012209081220
374848UK00001B/139